Hi Annie

Thank you for  in my book. I hope you enjoy it. If you do maybe you could leave a review on Amazon books.

Take care

Love

Kevin Tranter

A Penguin Rolling Down a Hill

KEVIN TRANTER

authorHOUSE

AuthorHouse™ UK
1663 Liberty Drive
Bloomington, IN 47403 USA
www.authorhouse.co.uk
Phone: 0800.197.4150

Published by AuthorHouse 11/28/2016

ISBN: 978-1-5246-3770-5 (sc)
ISBN: 978-1-5246-3771-2 (hc)
ISBN: 978-1-5246-3769-9 (e)

Part 1

Summoned

Chapter 1

Everywhere was white. Yet to refer to it simply as 'white' would be doing it an injustice. It was whiter than the whitest thing you can think of. It was as if a brighter, more brilliant white had been discovered, a blinding white that hung in every direction and as far as the eye could see.

Into this whiteness, a young girl suddenly appeared.

Her arrival was totally unexpected. Only moments earlier, she had been in her own bedroom in her own bed, and now she found herself in this strange white place.

Incredibly, she was still in her own bed.

Her bed? Here? How?

Amidst all this strangeness and confusion, she sensed she was wearing the blue V-neck jumper over the white round-neck T-shirt she had planned to wear for school. *But it's not easy to be attentive when you're so bewildered and dizzy and all you can do is squint because your eyes haven't become accustomed to all that whiteness.*

Gradually the young girl composed herself. Slowly, she focused.

It was then that she first saw the two giants.

"What happened?" she asked as she lowered herself off her bed and moved closer to the very tall men. "Where am I?"

"Look," growled the slightly smaller giant. He stood twelve feet tall in his red, pointy shoes, which curved up at the toes in a kind of hook. In the four yards between his extraordinary footwear and the crimson, padded turban upon his head, he wore a deep purplish-red gown of fine woollen cloth that was pleated and belted and hung in neat folds just above his ankles. "We've got better things to do than stand here all dream span waiting for you, you know."

"Were you expecting me?" She was puzzled. "Please, would one of you like to tell me what's going on? Who are you? What is this place?"

"You ask a lot of questions for someone so short." Flagellum raised his voice slightly and regarded her with his beady eyes. "By my reckoning, that's five questions you've asked already." He held up a huge hand. "What happened? Where am I? Were you expecting me? What's going on? Who are you? What is this place?" He counted them off on his fingers as he said them.

"That was six," she replied, somewhat confused.

"What?"

"That was six questions," she informed the cantankerous giant. "Not five. You used up," she hesitated before saying it, "all *six* fingers of your left hand?"

"Yes, but you miss the point." Flagellum frowned a giant frown. "The point is, we've got better things to do than stand here all dream span answering your pointless questions."

"No, we haven't got better things to do, Flagellum," the other giant said. This giant was dressed in a long green woollen tunic that was belted at the waist and neatly embroidered around the hem. "We are here to help. To meet and greet."

"Meet and greet?" Flagellum gave Zygote a scornful look accompanied by a slight raising of one corner of his thin upper lip. "Poppycock!"

"It's not poppycock, Flagellum." Zygote tried to remain patient. "We are the guardians of the White Room, as well you know."

"White Room?" Flagellum scoffed. "I've never heard it called that before."

"Of course it's the White Room." Zygote gestured with his arm in a wide arc. "What else could you possibly call this place other than the 'White Room'?"

The young girl surveyed her surroundings closely for the first time. It was very white; there was no getting away from that. But was it a room? If it was a room, it was impossible to see where the flooring ended, the walls started, or even if a ceiling began. It was a whiteness seemingly without beginning or end.

"The Room with Two Doors," declared Flagellum suddenly.

"What?" Zygote groaned.

"This place," he continued. "I call it the 'Room with Two Doors'. Where you get this White Room nonsense from, I don't know."

"You call it the Room with Two Doors, do you?" Zygote summoned up an ounce of patience from somewhere. "Despite the fact there is only one door."

"Two doors."

"One door."

The young girl barged in on their quarrel. "Look! I've got to get back," she pleaded. "My mum will be bringing a cup of coffee up to my room very shortly, and she'll be worried when she finds I'm not there ... not to mention *astonished* to find my bed gone."

"Two doors!"

Her three teddy bears sat, unmoved, at the foot of her bed.

"I think there must be some sort of mistake," she whispered to herself. "I shouldn't be here."

Lorraine was sensible. If you could rate sensibleness on a one-to-a-hundred scale, she would score somewhere in the region of ninety-five or ninety-six. Now, for a sixteen-year-old lower sixth student, that is sensible. It's also one of the reasons why she was chosen.

"One door!"

Of course, she had no idea yet she had been chosen for anything. Her mum would be beside herself with worry if she knew her daughter had been singled out to embark on an unearthly adventure in a peculiar land. She was sensible and had common sense, but "unearthly adventures in peculiar lands" might be a bit too much for one so young.

Lorraine didn't know what was happening or why. Had she been studying too much? Worrying about the exams, maybe? All that revising late into the night, perhaps? Not getting a good eight hours' sleep? Her mum had warned her about all of it. Had she crammed so much information into her head that it was now all spilling out? There must be some reason why she was imagining all this.

In the corner of her eye, something moved. In an area somewhere behind the giants, a portion of white fluttered for a moment. It was a door. The white door, barely discernible against the milky backdrop, just hung there, unsupported, giving the impression it was floating. It rippled like a curtain blowing in the breeze.

She looked up at the giants and noticed they weren't arguing anymore. Instead, they were leaning forward slightly and looking down at her as if they were seeing her for the very first time. It took her a few moments to realise they weren't looking down at her at all; they were looking past her. She turned.

At the side of her bed, there was now one of those student sleeper bunk beds. It was the type of bed that would usually have a sofa underneath, opens out into a single bed, and would probably have a work desk and chair too. But only the mattress and the tubular metal frame had made the journey here.

The occupant of the bed removed his blue-rimmed glasses and rubbed his eyes. He had a head of tightly curled ginger hair. Lorraine estimated he was about her age, maybe a little older.

"Hello," Lorraine called out to him hesitantly.

Chapter 2

Vile jumped up suddenly, propelling the black leather swivel chair across the room with such force that it collided with a solid oak Welsh dresser and knocked a porcelain teapot off a shelf, breaking its spout.

There were over thirty closed-circuit television monitors lined up along the opposite wall. Each one of those monitors was divided into a multi-screen of sixteen different images. With a few deft touches of the keypad, he selected the image that had caught his attention and reproduced it, full screen, on a spot monitor below. Vile was a tad concerned with what he saw.

"Terrence!"

Grabbing the joystick, he zoomed in so close he could count the freckles on the face of the ginger-haired youth. He watched with displeasure as the brat climbed off a bed. With distaste, Vile followed him with a pan and a tilt of the joystick. He saw that there were two of them – and that one was of the *female* variety. Vile was a touch perturbed with what was going on here.

"Terrence!"

Vile was splendiferous in his black and gold pinstriped jacket that was fully lined with red satin and cuffed trousers with red braces. He fidgeted from one shiny two-toned shoe to the other as Terrence squirmed into the control room. Terrence was every bit as slovenly and shabby as Vile was dazzling and resplendent. He wore a black, moth-eaten blazer (that was too tight), faded and threadbare black trousers (that were too short), and grubby white trainers (that were too out of fashion).

"You called, your offensiveness?" Terrence asked.

"Take a look at these snotty-nosed kids here." Vile didn't take his eyes off the screen for a moment. "What do you make of them?"

Terrence followed Vile's gaze to the spot monitor. He saw two uninteresting-looking teenagers. They were so insignificant he didn't make anything of them.

"Well?" Vile pushed for an answer.

"W – well ..." Terrence stuttered nervously. He knew if he didn't come up with a good answer, Vile would most probably hurt him. He took a closer look. "Well, they're ugly."

"Apart from that!" Vile snapped.

Terrence grimaced. They were ugly; he was right about that. Unfortunately, it just wasn't the answer Vile was looking for. Terrence ran his hands anxiously through his unkempt, mousy hair. "Let me see." He examined the youngsters even more closely.

Vile's considerable nose and ample chin were virtually touching the screen. "Don't you get a funny feeling when you look at them?" he persisted.

"A funny feeling, your evilness?" He didn't. "Should I?"

"Yes, Terrence, you should." For the first time, Vile turned away from the screen and looked menacingly at Terrence. "I rather think you should."

Terrence instinctively took a step backwards. "A funny feeling? Oh yes." He still didn't. "Now that you come to mention it, your disgustingness, I do." He forced a far-from-convincing laugh. "It is funny, isn't it?"

Vile positioned his voluminous nose and his substantial chin less than an inch from Terrence's clammy face. "On second thoughts, funny is not the right word at all." As Terrence backed away and Vile advanced across the room, the proximity of their noses remained unchanged. "Let me think of a better word."

Terrence tripped backwards and fell into the black leather swivel chair.

"Now that you have this feeling, Terrence, what word do you suggest we use to describe it?" Vile stood over the chair dangerously.

Terrence could feel the perspiration trickling down the back of his neck. "What word?" He knew he had to come up with a word for a feeling he didn't have, and very quickly, or Vile would injure him in some way.

"I'm waiting, Terrence," said Vile impatiently.

"Is it –" He closed his eyes and blurted out the first word that came into his head. "Hilarious?"

"Hilarious!" Vile reacted angrily. He grabbed hold of the swivel chair and gave it an almighty spin. Terrence held on to the black leather armrests for dear life as he rotated half a dozen times or more. When the chair eventually came to a halt, Vile poked him in the eye for good measure.

"Thank you, your appallingness," gasped Terrence. "You're so wicked and nasty."

Vile was too preoccupied to listen to compliments. There were more pressing matters to consider. He studied the pesky kids again. He had a feeling about them that he couldn't quite put his finger on. It wasn't funny, and it most certainly wasn't hilarious. But whatever the feeling was, it worried him. The fact that it worried him, worried him even more. He was Vile, and Vile just doesn't do worried. "These kids are a threat," he concluded.

Terrence stood up out of the black leather swivel chair, shakily. He was not quite able to believe his ears.

"A threat? To whom?"

"To me, to you, and to all things wicked and nasty."

"Those kids, your obnoxiousness?"

"Yes! Those kids!"

"But they're puny."

"Physique doesn't come into it, Terrence. They're a threat without a doubt. It took me many eras to get this place off Mr Good, and I'm not going to surrender it now. I don't want to go back to the old place. I like it here. I've got a feeling that Mr Good is at the bottom of all this, and that's why he's summoned these two brats here. I'm sure of it." All these worries were swarming around inside Vile's paranoid mind.

"So you'll kill them?" Terrence asked matter-of-factly.

"Kill them?" Vile put aside his musings. "What do you take me for?"

"But you're Vile," said Terrence. "You're so wicked and nasty, I've known you seriously injure a man just for –" He paused momentarily to recall a worthy example. "Just for breathing!"

Despite feeling uneasy, Vile managed an evil grin. "Yes, I can be quite spiteful, it's true."

"Too right, your wretchedness," encouraged Terrence. "So, if you're not going to kill them, then …"

"I shall make friends with them."

"What!" Terrence almost choked. "Friends? But if they're a threat?"

Vile took hold of the joystick and zoomed in on the interlopers as if to confirm his thinking. "They are only a threat in the wrong hands."

"You mean …"

"Exactly. Mr Good is hatching a plan," Vile said with certainty.

"A plan? But surely he can't believe he'll succeed." Terrence glanced at the intruders on the monitor screen. "With kids? When we've got guards with incredible biceps?"

Vile pondered this. "With their muscles and my brains it is a formidable combination, I must agree." He continued to ponder, more to himself than to Terrence. "Maybe I am worrying over nothing." He brooded as he twiddled with the end of his wide white kipper tie, abstractedly. "Yes, but then again it's better to be safe than sorry. I want to stay here because it has central heating."

"And wall-to-wall carpeting," Terrence added.

Vile stared at Terrence for a long moment. "I was talking to myself," he said in a slow and menacing manner. "Don't listen to me when I'm thinking out loud. Do I make myself clear?"

"Crystal clear, your dirtiness." Terrence gulped.

"We've got to nip this plan in the bud," Vile went on. "I want you to go out there and waylay these juveniles. I want you to pretend to be Mr Good. Okay?" He grinned as a fiendishly clever counter-plan was taking shape. "Okay, Terrence?"

Terrence was staring blankly at nothing in particular.

"I said, okay, Terrence?" Vile repeated more loudly this time, enhanced with a bang of a fist on the desk.

Terrence jumped.

"Are you listening to me?" Vile shouted.

"No!" Terrence responded vehemently. "I promise!"

"What?" Vile was nonplussed. "Did you just say you weren't listening to me?"

"You told me not to listen when you were thinking out loud, your dreadfulness."

Vile knew that simple relaxation techniques, such as breathing deeply from your diaphragm and visualising a relaxing experience from either your memory or your imagination, could help calm down angry feelings.

He knew slowly repeating a calm word or phrase, such as 'relax' or 'take it easy', could help too. He also knew that nonstrenuous, slow, yoga-like exercises could relax your muscles and make you feel much calmer. Vile knew it, but he didn't give a toss about any of that claptrap.

"You halfwit!" From the Welsh dresser Vile picked up a cup and threw it, followed swiftly by the matching saucer. Both struck Terrence smack on the side of the head. "Who needs deep breathing and relaxing imagery when you've got crockery?"

Terrence groaned and rubbed the flat region at the side of his forehead.

"Now Terrence, unless you want the rest of the porcelain tea set thrown in your direction, I suggest you listen." From his repertoire of glares Vile chose a cold, unsympathetic one.

"I'm listening, your unsympatheticness," Terrence replied. "I'm listening."

"Now, if these two punks were to think Mr Good is an imbecile, an idiot, a person whose mental acumen is well below par, far too foolish to be bothered with, they might not be so keen to be a part of his plan. Am I right, Terrence?"

"Too right, your repulsiveness."

Vile drew back his thin lips to reveal two rows of yellow teeth. It was a grin. "Meanwhile, I'll have a couple of muscular guards on hand." He located the black leather swivel chair, pushed it back to his spacious walnut desk, and sat. "I'll have them under lock and key and out of harm's way in no time."

Terrence took a filthy rag from his blazer pocket and wiped away a thin line of blood that had made its way from in front of his ear down to his cheekbone.

Vile's grin ended abruptly. "Are you still here?"

"No! I mean yes. I mean, I'm on my way." He bowed as he backed away towards the door. "I'll have them here in a brace of shakes. You can count on it."

Vile waited until Terrence opened the door. "And Terrence –" He waited until Terrence turned to face him. "Remember, act daft."

Terrence nodded. "I'll be barmy, sir. You can rely on me. Totally barmy."

"That shouldn't be too difficult," Vile said under his breath.

When Terrence had gone and Vile was alone, all the uncertainties returned.

"That Mr Good-for-nothing is up to something. Why has he called these two brats here?" he pondered.

He looked at the two brats on the screen again.

The ginger-haired one was wiping the lenses of his blue-rimmed glasses clean with a soft, lint-free cloth.

Chapter 3

Melvin was slowly becoming accustomed to the glare. "What happened?" With his clean lenses he had a clearer view of the giants now. "Where the dickens am I?"

Zygote produced a parchment from the folds of his green tunic and examined the written text on a sheet of goatskin. "Welcome," he began. "You have been summoned to a mysterious and fascinating world of dreams where the rules of reality do not apply."

Melvin had surprised himself with how quickly he had come to terms with this seriously weird situation. It's not every day you enter a mysterious and fascinating world of dreams, especially one where the rules of reality do not apply. Even though all this was beyond what is ordinary, he had, somehow, managed to take it all in his stride.

That was one of the reasons why he was chosen.

"World of dreams? Rules of reality?" Flagellum scoffed. "You're making this up."

"Summoned?" interrupted Lorraine. "Did you say summoned?"

Zygote nodded. "You have been summoned by a Dream Ambassador, of course."

Melvin tried to figure out when all this strangeness had started. Was it something to do with the dream? He had woken from a strange dream about a hill with a steep, grassy slope. He remembered flame-coloured trees and low shrubs too, but was there something else? Something important? A message? A sign? He tried to grasp at the memory, but it faded. Then it was gone.

"A Dream Ambassador?" Lorraine was intrigued now.

"Don't listen to Zygote," said Flagellum with a laugh. "He's a compulsive fibber."

"I tell the truth!"

The two argumentative giants were experiencing a difference of opinion.

"You tell big whoppers!"

"Only Dream Ambassadors can summon folk from the physical world, as well you know, Flagellum."

"Poppycock!"

Zygote sighed. "Summoning from the physical world doesn't happen often. Maybe six times –" Zygote cast his mind back as far as the beginning of time. "In the last seven or eight eras, I guess."

Suddenly, Flagellum, with his beady eyes, swooped out of the white mist and regarded Melvin and Lorraine closely. "Isn't it about time you two made a decision?"

"Decision?" asked Lorraine.

"What decision?" wondered Melvin.

"Which door to go through, of course." Flagellum moved his giant head closer still. "We've got better things to do than stand here all dream span waiting for you to make a decision, you know."

"Which door to go through?" Lorraine was puzzled.

"If you don't choose very soon you'll be marooned here, in this room with two doors, for eternity." His grin unveiled a full set of enormous, crooked teeth. "Which I think falls on a Monday next time."

Zygote sighed. "There are no decisions to be made here, Flagellum, on account of there being only one door."

"Two doors."

"One door."

"Look," Lorraine muscled in on their disagreement. "Will one of you please tell us what is going on? Who has brought us here?"

"And why?" added Melvin.

The two giants stopped in mid-feud.

"More questions?" Flagellum exhaled a long, deep breath.

Zygote ignored Flagellum and took no notice of his long, deep breath. In fact, he turned his back on him and gave Melvin and Lorraine his full attention. "To answer your questions adequately I need to tell you what has been happening around here just lately."

Actually, to answer their questions with complete satisfaction Zygote would have had to tell them the entire history of the mysterious and fascinating world of dreams, from the Big Bang to the present dream span, inclusive. But, that's a very long tale indeed, so he decided on a sort of abridged version.

"Out there in Limbo," he began, "up near the Zenith Territory, lies the Palace of Somnium." He went on to tell them that ever since the beginning of time, this had been the residence of the Dream Ambassador, Mr Good. The Palace of Somnium was where all the nice, pleasant, happy dreams were conceived, the ones with the beautiful colours and the pretty flowers. He informed them that Vile, another Dream Ambassador who specialised in nightmares, did all his scary stuff down in the Nether Regions in a dark and gloomy place called Torment Towers. All that was until recently. But with the advent of 3D computer-animated dreams up at the palace and the development of the Digital Dreamscaper, Vile suddenly found himself lagging behind somewhat in the technology Dream Stakes. And he didn't like it.

Zygote noticed that Melvin and Lorraine were staring blankly when he mentioned the Digital Dreamscaper. So, he explained that the Digital Dreamscaper was a gun-shaped object which, when you pulled the trigger, created a Dreamspace. It instantly arranged the scenery on the Dream Stage, a setting as elaborate or as simple as you wished. He pointed out that Vile didn't have any of these luxuries at Torment Towers, and he was determined to do something about it.

One dream span not so very long ago, Vile did do something about it. "He packed up his belongings," revealed Zygote, "and with his sidekick, Terrence, his niece, and his army of muscular guards, he marched across Limbo and kicked Mr Good's butt out."

Melvin and Lorraine listened in a state of wonder.

"You've always had this romantic streak, haven't you, Zygote?" said Flagellum.

"Are you saying it was Mr Good who summoned us?" asked Melvin.

Zygote shook his head and shrugged. "I couldn't possibly say."

"What has happened to Mr Good?" Lorraine was concerned.

"Banished into Limbo, as far as we can gather," answered Zygote.

"Limbo?" Lorraine asked. "Where is Limbo?"

"Limbo, in all its magnitude –" He turned and pointed to an area barely perceptible to the eye. "Is through the door."

"Yes, but which door?" interrupted Flagellum with a roguish grin. "One door is for those born under fire and water signs and the other for those born under earth and air signs." His roguish grin widened. "They are, in fact, astrological doors."

Zygote wrinkled his brow in annoyance. "Our visitors are not interested in your astrological twaddle, Flagellum." For confirmation he looked at Melvin and Lorraine.

Melvin and Lorraine, in turn, looked at each other.

"We need to find the way back to our bedrooms," suggested Lorraine.

Melvin, who, incidentally, was not the slightest bit interested in Flagellum's astrological twaddle, pondered this for a moment. "The way to our bedrooms must be through the floating door," he concluded.

Lorraine was surprised at Melvin's certainty.

"If Mr Good has summoned us from our bedrooms, then he must know the way back," Melvin figured. "So, if Mr Good knows the way back, then we need to find him. Fortunately, we know he has been banished into Limbo, and, apparently, Limbo is …"

"Through the floating door." Lorraine smiled.

Melvin and Lorraine sensed it was time to go through the floating door into Limbo. Remarkably, the floating door sensed it was time too; it edged forward and began to expand and contract rhythmically.

Zygote cleared his throat, held up the parchment, and examined the written text. "Warning," he read." You are about to enter the corridors of Limbo."

The door moved through the whiteness towards Melvin and Lorraine in a smooth, effortless manner, like a submarine gliding through the water.

"Be careful," Zygote continued. "The corridors of Limbo are like a puzzle to be solved. Limbo has twists and turns and blind alleys. It has dead ends, and it has cul-de-sacs. You will meander back and forth, and you will turn 180 degrees a lot. Each time you shift your direction, you will also shift your awareness from the right side of the brain to the left. This can induce altered states of consciousness."

As the floating door approached them, it released wisps of white mist, like transparent chiffon, into the air.

"Beware," Zygote proceeded after a pause for dramatic effect. "It will require a logical, sequential, and analytical mind to be able to find the correct path."

Melvin and Lorraine both had logical, sequential, and analytical minds.

That was one of the reasons why they were chosen.

It soon became evident that Melvin and Lorraine were not going to go through the floating door at all. It was going to go through them. They stood, transfixed yet calm, as the door opened wide and swallowed them whole.

Although the giants had disappeared from view, their voices could still be heard. "States of consciousness? Analytical minds?" said one of them. "I've never heard such poppycock."

"Shut up," said the other one.

"And you have the cheek to say astrology is twaddle."

"But astrology *is* twaddle!"

Beyond the door, Melvin and Lorraine were finding out how it felt to float freely in a weightless condition inside a big, fluffy, white cloud.

Chapter 4

It wasn't the first time Terrence had been out in the corridors of Limbo on his own, but it was the first time he had been out in the corridors of Limbo with a Digital Dreamscaper in his possession. The possibilities for mischief were endless. He had always fancied himself as a bit of an outlaw, a gun slinger: the fastest, deadliest man with a six-gun you ever saw. Before he could stop himself, he was setting the coordinates for the Wild West.

The Digital Dreamscaper works by a cocking mechanism. It's activated by a lever on the top, which pulls back on a rubber diaphragm at the base of the concave funnel at the front. As Terrence pulled the trigger, the rubber diaphragm snapped forward and pushed out a blast of chainsaw-shaped air that cut a giant hole in the wall and created a Dreamspace.

The next thing he knew, he was wearing a cowboy hat and standing on a hot, dusty street in a small, hot, dusty Wild West town where lawlessness and gun-slinging were rife. It was a town with no local law enforcement, where the military had no jurisdiction. It was a town where buffalo hunters, railroad workers, drifters and soldiers scrap and fight – a town where men die with their boots on.

He raised the Digital Dreamscaper to his lips and blew away imaginary smoke. He kicked open the swinging doors of the saloon. As he did so, the music came to a screeching halt. The joint was full to the rafters with convicts, bandits, gunmen, cutthroats, and muggers, and they all turned as one to look at the stranger in their midst. Satisfied that the scruffy little man before them posed no threat, they returned to their own little quarrels and squabbles, and the music resumed. The bar was polished to a splendid shine, and encircling its base was a gleaming brass foot rail with a row of spittoons spaced along the floor. Terrence ordered a whisky without saying please and grabbed it from the bartender without saying thank you, a rudeness that met with the approval of a bunch of lawbreakers who were sitting close by. They called him over to join them. Terrence soon discovered that one was a hoodlum, one was a ruffian, and the other was a thug.

Terrence couldn't have wished for better company.

The alcohol flowed, and gradually their tongues loosened. It turned out that the three of them were plotting to ambush a stagecoach later that night. The hoodlum and the ruffian were keen for Terrence to be a part of their planned robbery. The extra gun would be handy, they said. But the thug wasn't so sure. Trust issues were raised, as were their voices. This alerted a band of desperadoes at the next table who, coincidentally, were in the advanced stages of a plan to bushwhack the very same stagecoach. They didn't like what they were overhearing. One of the desperadoes stood up and put a recommendation forward to Terrence and his new buddies for their acceptance. He proposed that if anyone were going to do any holding up of stagecoaches around here, it was going to be them because … well, because they had been planning it since last Tuesday. His fellow desperadoes were impressed with his reasoning. They sat back and waited for a formal contest of argumentation to take place, where the two opposing sides defend and attack the given proposition: a discussion where reasons are advanced for and against the proposal.

The thug, however, preferred to let his fists do the talking. The desperado didn't see the punch coming. When the desperado landed, it was on the top of a table occupied by a cutthroat and a bandit, knocking their drinks all over their starched jeans.

All hell broke loose. The disagreement spread like wildfire across the alehouse. Tables were sent flying, tops of heads were hit by chairs, eyes were blackened, and noses were bloodied. The proprietor of the establishment tried, in vain, to restore order. Amidst all the bedlam he appealed to their better nature. Unfortunately, none of his patrons had one.

Suddenly, a shadow darkened the doorway at Terrence's back. The shadow belonged to Scarface, the leader of the most notorious gang of outlaws the Wild West has ever known. Half a dozen of his unshaven, notorious gang of outlaws stood menacingly at his shoulder. The room fell silent. Scarface waited until he was sure he had everyone's undivided attention. He growled as he informed the assembled crowd, in his southern drawl, that it would, in fact, be his gang who would be relieving the passengers on the stagecoach, later that night, of their valuables and little trinkets. His eyes narrowed and carefully surveyed the faces in the room, looking for any signs of defiance. He went on to notify them in a gruff and surly manner that if, in the unlikely event there was anyone who had a problem with that, now might be a good time to mention it.

Nobody moved – apart from Terrence. He wasn't scared of Scarface. It wasn't that Terrence was particularly brave or completely stupid. It's just that he knew this was a Dreamspace. A sequence of events passing through a sleeping person's mind somewhere, and no harm could befall him. Besides, he was used to dealing with Vile on a dream span to dream span basis, and compared to Vile, this Scarface was a pussycat. He stood up and faced him. Terrence advised Scarface that he did have a problem with that, actually, and asked, did Scarface have a problem with him having a problem with it? Terrence didn't wait for an answer; instead, he got straight to the point. He explained to the stunned outlaw that his own gang would be the ones lying in wait, later that night, to attack the stagecoach from a concealed position and without warning. He turned to his right to formally introduce his gang members. Surprisingly, the hoodlum, the ruffian, and the thug weren't there. He looked quickly to his left and was somewhat taken aback; they weren't there either. He promptly spun round in case they were lurking behind him somewhere, but they were nowhere to be seen. Self-consciously, he slowly turned back to face the smirking Scarface.

Their eyes met. Scarface's offensive, self-satisfied smile continued, and his gun hand twitched. Time stood still. Whilst time was standing still, a few of the bystanders escaped to the safety of the street. Terrence took the opportunity to admire the steer horns, spurs, and saddles that adorned the walls. The proprietor and the bartender dived for cover behind the long, panelled bar. Time stood still some more – or at least it seemed to move in slow motion.

Chapter 5

Melvin and Lorraine continued to float freely in a weightless condition for ages, but they just didn't seem to be getting anywhere. Unfortunately, there was a malfunction with the gravitational pull in the local area. Melvin and Lorraine were a little frustrated; they were keen to get on with things and find Mr Good, which would, ultimately, lead them back home to their bedrooms. But they remained philosophical. They shrugged and even managed a smile. *These things happen,* they thought. They would just have to hang around for a while.

"I'm Loz by the way," she said as she attempted a back flip. "That's short for Lorraine."

"Hi. I'm Melvin," he replied as he completed a forward one and a half flip with a twist, wearing his maroon school blazer, black trousers, and smart black leather shoes. "That's long for Mel."

They shook hands and did a forward roll together. Gradually, the effects of gravity began to return, and they were lowered steadily, a little at a time, to the ground.

The view that greeted them when they landed was not one they could have expected even in their wildest dreams. They found themselves standing on the banks of the Jamuna River. The Taj Mahal, opposite, seemed to glow in the light of the full moon. In the east the seven wonders of the ancient world were lined up all in a row. To the west, Mount Kilimanjaro looked magnificent silhouetted against the purple sky. Behind them, and only a few yards away, were, literally, hundreds of entrances cut into the side of a grassy knoll. There were passageways twisting and turning and disappearing into the distance, corridors with steps going up, and openings with ramps going down. They were decorated in every colour you could possibly imagine – and every shade of every colour, too. There were passages with turnstiles and passages with stable doors, corridors with audio door entry-controlled systems and corridors with cattle grids, openings with wrought-iron gates and openings with moats, and a cave guarded by a dragon.

"A dragon!" said Lorraine, alarmed.

The dragon was green with a darker green underbelly. Its long, powerful tail thrashed to and fro as if it were trying to swat some unseen flying insect. Its handsome, elongated head featured large, bulging eyes, the widest mouth, the sharpest, pointiest teeth, and, to top it all, a right pair of snorting nostrils. He was as tall as a double-decker bus and twice as long and was just about the scariest monster imaginable. All of which only goes to show that looks can be deceptive, because this dragon was the most charming of beasts.

"Frightfully pleased to make your acquaintance," the dragon greeted them as he trotted down the gentle incline to the riverside. For a creature so big, he was surprisingly light on his feet.

"But, you're a ... d ..." Melvin stammered.

"We've never met a ... d ..." Lorraine stuttered.

The dragon wondered why they were staring at him with a combination of respect, fear, and wonder. When he glanced at his reflection in the river, he realised why. "Sorry, I sometimes forget how frightfully big and terrifying I must look. Please forgive me." He held up a hoof. "The name's Derek."

Melvin and Lorraine introduced themselves too and, self-consciously, gave his hoof a high five.

"Would I be right in thinking you've never met a dragon before?" he asked. "I can assure you, there's no need to be frightened of little ol' me, or rather big ol' me. I wouldn't hurt a fly." He gave his tail an almighty swish.

"Well, a fly maybe," he admitted with a twinkle in his eye. "And I can be a bit of a fire hazard, at times, too." To demonstrate, he threw his head back and released a ball of fire that shot across the landscape, hitting an innocent juniper bush that was minding its own business somewhere up near the Hanging Gardens of Babylon.

"But apart from that," he told them, "I'm almost completely harmless."

"That's impressive," said Melvin as he watched the smoke rising up from the burning bush in the distance.

"That's some view you've got here," commented Lorraine as they strolled back up the slope towards the entrances.

Derek nodded in agreement. "I've always said that the dial on the Digital Dreamscaper must have been set to 'over the top' when this Dreamspace was created."

As it happens, there isn't an 'over the top' setting on a Digital Dreamscaper, but Derek didn't know that. It wasn't the only thing he didn't know. He didn't know the answer to Melvin's next question either.

"Do you know where we can find Mr Good?"

Derek considered the question with thoroughness and care as he paused outside the dark cave he called home. "Mr Good, you say?" He gestured for Melvin and Lorraine to sit. They chose a deck chair each.

"Let me see." Derek stooped and lay full length on the patio in the shade of the grassy knoll. "I do believe he lives in a frightfully splendid residence. The Palace of ..." He faltered.

"Somnium?" suggested Lorraine.

"That's the place!" His memory was jogged. "That's where you'll find him."

Lorraine shook her head. "No, we won't." She told Derek the latest news: that Vile had been angry about something or other, so angry that one morning he got out of bed on the wrong side and marched over to the Palace of Somnium with rebellion and revolution on his mind.

"To overthrow goodness and replace it with evilness, I guess," guessed Melvin.

Lorraine nodded. "That's right."

Derek loved gossip as much as the next dragon, so he listened attentively to their every word as the sun slowly set in the east, beyond the Lighthouse of Alexandria.

"Mr Good has been banished into Limbo," continued Lorraine.

"Wherever that is," added Melvin.

Derek lifted his long, green head off his two front hooves. "Limbo? Did you say Limbo?" He was delighted because he knew the answer to this one. "Strictly speaking," he told them as he sat up, "you're in Limbo now."

Due west, another sun began its climb up the morning sky, high above the Mediterranean Sea.

"We are?" asked Melvin as he looked around, bemused. "This doesn't look like a corridor to me."

"Or a passageway, for that matter," concurred Lorraine.

"You're right, it isn't." Derek laughed. "This is just an old, abandoned Dreamspace. But what a Digital Dreamscaper does is slice clean through those corridors or passageways, like a knife through butter, and then forces the Dreamspace into the gap." He paused for this information to sink in. "The corridors and passageways of Limbo you seek are here." He nodded towards the myriad of coloured entrances nearby.

"So this is Limbo," said Lorraine as they stood and followed the direction of Derek's nod. "At last."

"At last," agreed Melvin. "Now all we need to do is find Mr Good." He peered into one of the openings, half expecting to see him leaning against one of the walls and waving.

"Easier said than done, I'm afraid," Derek said as he jumped nimbly to his feet and joined them at the foot of the hillock. "Half of these openings are mazes, half of them are labyrinths, and the other half you could well and truly lose your way in." He had that twinkle in his eye again. "It's a frightfully difficult decision, I know, but you must make one."

The entrances were too numerous to be counted. "How the dickens are we going to choose the right one?" Melvin looked at Lorraine for support.

There was an idea brewing in Lorraine's mind. "What's your favourite colour, Melvin?"

Melvin was a little taken aback by this. "My favourite colour? Well, it's blue. But why do you ask?"

"I thought so." She didn't know why she thought so, but she smiled without taking her eyes off the multitude of entrances. "Mine too."

Melvin and Lorraine shared the same favourite colour.

That was one of the reasons why they were chosen.

"Okay," said Melvin doubtfully. "So, you're thinking, because blue is our favourite colour, we are bound to find Mr Good if we choose a blue entrance?"

"Melvin, blue isn't just my favourite colour. It's also my lucky colour, too."

"But by my reckoning there are over twenty different shades of blue here, Loz," counted Melvin quickly. "Ranging from azure to ultramarine. Which one do we go for?"

"Moe," she replied almost immediately.

"Moe?" asked Melvin baffled. "I must admit, that's not a shade of blue I am aware of."

"Catch a tiger by the toe, if he hollers let him go …" Lorraine gestured in the general direction of the indigo-coloured corridor.

"Eenie." She swiftly followed this with a wave of her hand at the navy blue passageway.

"Meenie," she continued with a point of her finger at the lavender opening.

"Minie." She stood at the threshold of the royal blue entrance.

"Moe!" she announced with a definiteness and a sureness.

"But Loz." Melvin was surprised how definite and sure Lorraine was. "Do you remember what the giant told us? How it would require a logical, sequential, and analytical mind to be able to find the correct path?"

"You can't get more logical, sequential, or analytical than eenie meenie miney moe, Melvin."

"That's right," joined in Derek. "As methods of choosing go, eenie, meenie, miney moe is frightfully underrated."

Seeing he was outnumbered, Melvin resigned himself to the fact they were going to choose the royal blue path. Lorraine gave Derek's long neck a huge hug and, eager to make a start, skipped off into the unknown. Melvin said his good-byes to Derek and thanked him for all his help before following Lorraine into the royal blueness.

"If you ever get into any trouble or if you ever need any help," Derek called after them, "just call me, and I'll be there immediately."

Far to the north of the Dreamspace, the Empire State Building launched, like a rocket, into the sky and set off on an orbit of the planet.

Chapter 6

Each man went for his pistol. The sound of the gunshot that followed reverberated around the room as Scarface fell to the ground. Terrence stared, in awe, at his Digital Dreamscaper, then at Scarface lying prone on the floor, and then in wonderment at his Digital Dreamscaper again. The notorious gang of outlaws stared in disbelief at Terrence, then at Scarface lying prone on the floor, and then furiously at Terrence again.

Someone had shot Scarface, but somehow, Terrence didn't think it was him. This could mean only one thing. There was someone, almost certainly someone with evil tendencies, sitting in a black leather swivel chair right now, watching this dream sequence unfold on a monitor screen. This evil individual had, more than likely, activated the influence button: a button that, when pressed, can alter the course of Dream Destiny. It could only be Vile. Terrence experienced a sudden, overpowering feeling of terror. Vile had sent him on a simple errand to waylay a couple of pesky kids, but it had completely slipped his mind. He should be in Limbo now, acting dafter than a brush yet more cunning than a fox. But instead here he was in this one-horse town pretending to be Billy the Kid.

The first to congratulate Terrence, as the whole place erupted, were the hoodlum, the ruffian, and the thug. They were closely followed, in the middle of all the violence and flying furniture, by the convicts, some bandits, a couple of gunmen, several cutthroats, and a mugger, who formed a protective barrier in front of their new hero. Although they were cornered and were forced to fight at close quarters, they outnumbered the gang and so managed to drive them backwards until the fighting spilled outdoors. An angry mob of notorious outlaws swelled on the street, clamouring for Terrence's blood.

Inside the saloon, with the help of the proprietor, the delinquents managed to smuggle Terrence out through a rear door to safety. In the heat of the midday sun his followers gathered around him. They were prepared to hang on to his every word. The consensus of opinion, amongst his admirers, was that they should form one big gang with Terrence as their leader. Terrence was flattered, but his obsession with outlawing and gun slinging and all things Wild West had diminished somewhat. A cowboy life was not for him, he decided. Without saying a word, Terrence walked briskly away.

Besides, he had important business to attend to and was running late – very late. The kind of late that could seriously damage his health.

He walked quickly out of town without once looking back. His disciples followed him to an old shack situated on a triangular piece of land on the edge of town. From this crudely built cabin, one road went directly north. Another ran parallel with the railroad track in a north-westerly direction. There in the distance across the prairie were the entrances: each one a different colour, every colour you could possibly imagine and every shade of every colour too.

To the hoodlum, the ruffian, the thug, and the others, the strange, varicoloured entrances appeared as a flickering image through the heat waves in the air. They stood and watched, with mouths agape, as Terrence crossed the flat, treeless, grassy plain towards whatever was shimmering out there on the horizon.

Meanwhile, the notorious gang of outlaws had been given a tipoff that Terrence was out near the railroad track. They hurriedly mounted their horses in front of the livery barn, fired a parting salute from their six-shooters, and rode out of town to the north. They galloped past the run-down wooden shack and onwards across the grassland towards Terrence.

As he approached the entrances to Limbo, Terrence couldn't for the life of him remember which corridor he had been in when he fired the Digital Dreamscaper and created this accursed place. As he walked alongside the vast array of openings, frantically hoping for inspiration, he heard the unmistakable sound of hooves galloping on prairie. Instinctively, he went for his Digital Dreamscaper and dived for cover. Unfortunately, he chose to dive for cover inside a pink passageway that afforded him no cover at all.

The six notorious, now leaderless, still unshaven, and very angry gang of outlaws pulled hard on their reins, forcing their mounts to rear up and stop abruptly, just a stone's throw away. They had 'shoot now and ask questions later' expressions on their faces as they sat atop their unsettled horses. A divergence of opinion broke out as some of the outlaws suggested the colourful corridors and passageways before them were indeed real, while others suspected they were merely an optical effect caused by the reflection of light rays on a layer of heated air of varying density. Eventually, they agreed to disagree on that one. However, they did agree, unanimously, that the scum of the earth that shot Scarface was going to bite the dust before sundown. So, without further ado, they removed their guns from their holsters and took aim.

The instruction manual that accompanies a Digital Dreamscaper strongly recommends you seal a Dreamspace immediately after use, in the same corridor where you created it. In practice this was not always adhered to, hence the great many abandoned ones up and down the length and breadth of Limbo. Terrence never usually bothered, even though it was just a simple matter of reversing the settings on the control panel. On this occasion he thought it might be a good idea.

By this time the outlaws had pulled their triggers, and the bullets were almost halfway along their journey from gun to intended target: Terrence's head. The outlaws were happy with the state of play at this point. The projected forecast was that five of the bullets would be making contact with the head region, with just one bullet veering slightly to the left and expected to hit him in the right upper arm or possibly the shoulder area.

With deft, nimble fingers, Terrence quickly and skilfully inverted the coordinates and with little or no delay fired the Digital Dreamscaper into the air. It fired a powerful, arrow-shaped puff of air that instantaneously popped the Dreamspace like a balloon. An almost imperceptible space of time later, the two ends of the passageway met and merged in a continuous, seamless, shocking pinkness.

#

Someone, somewhere in the physical world, woke up in a cold sweat with five bullets literally inches from their head.

Chapter 7

"How far have we walked?" asked Lorraine as the royal blue corridor continued its downward incline and very gradual curve to the right.

This wasn't easy for Melvin to calculate without a watch. His watch had stopped at 07:32:07, the moment he had left his own world. But this problem did remind him of an experiment they did at school in year ten. They used a calculator, a piece of paper, a pencil, and a stopwatch. They worked on the assumption his stride was three feet long, which is the average stride a person takes. He started his stopwatch and counted how many strides he took in one minute. He remembered that he took one hundred and five steps in that time. He divided that number by thirty, with his calculator, and wrote down the result on the piece of paper, with his pencil. This was an estimate of his walking speed in miles per hour.

"About three and a half miles," replied Melvin. He figured they had been walking for about one hour.

"I thought this was supposed to be a maze," sighed Lorraine. "I thought that giant said Limbo has twists and turns and blind alleys and dead ends and cul-de-sacs and such like."

"Yes, Loz, but remember what Derek said."

Lorraine tried to remember what the friendly dragon had said about mazes, but she couldn't recall anything that had a bearing on the matter at hand.

"He said that Limbo was half maze and half labyrinth."

Lorraine shrugged. "Mazes. Labyrinths. What's the difference?"

"This is a labyrinth," said Melvin.

"How can you tell?"

"Labyrinths are different from mazes, Loz. Labyrinths are unicursal. There are no tricks to them, you see – no blind alleys or dead ends or cul-de-sacs." Melvin continued being knowledgeable on the subject. "Labyrinths have one well-defined path that leads us to the centre and back out again."

Lorraine considered this information. "So if we follow this corridor to the centre of the labyrinth, maybe we'll find Mr Good there."

"Possibly," agreed Melvin.

Lorraine was partly right. Mr Good had been waiting for them at the centre of the royal blue labyrinth but had become increasingly impatient and worried too. In fact, he had been worried enough to leave the centre and meet them halfway. Little did they know that Mr Good was just a few minutes away and heading in their direction.

They couldn't possibly know, either, that Vile had been frantically scanning the numerous closed-circuit television monitors in a systematic pattern across Limbo. So it was no surprise when he finally located them.

Vile had the technology to alter the course of Dream Destiny, to insert intersecting paths, and to change things from labyrinth to maze mode with just the touch of the Influence button on his keypad. And that is just what he was about to do.

They continued to walk in silence for a while, hardly noticing that the gentle downhill slope that had been evident for nearly four miles had finally levelled out.

"Did you have a dream, Loz?" asked Melvin eventually. "Just before we arrived here? About a hill with a steep, grassy slope, flame-coloured trees, and low shrubs?"

Lorraine tried to recall the moments leading up to her arrival here. She had been lying in bed listening to her mum preparing breakfast downstairs, waiting for her to bring a cup of coffee up as she did every morning. But what had woken her? Yes, it was a dream that woke her. She remembered fragments of it now. She turned to Melvin and nodded. "There was a placard."

"A placard?" whispered Melvin. "A paperboard sign on a heavy length of wood. Yes, I remember it too. It was carried aloft along a narrow stretch of lowland between the hills."

"In the tangerine sunshine."

"As far as a small stream that ran along the bottom of the valley."

The fact that they had both had the same dream stunned them into silence for a long moment.

"What do you make of all this, Melvin?" asked Lorraine finally. "What's happening to us? It's all very odd, isn't it?"

Melvin smiled. "It's seriously weird, Loz."

"Look!" It was Lorraine who noticed it first.

Up ahead, there was a door. She quickened her pace immediately, leaving Melvin, who was unprepared and unable to react quickly, a little way behind.

The door stood out because it was black. After nearly four miles of nothing but royal blue, it was no surprise it stood out.

"Hello," called out Lorraine, hesitantly, when she reached the half-open door. Just inside the door she could just make out metal, track-like grooves on the floor.

"Hello," repeated Melvin when he finally arrived.

They listened and waited, but no reply was forthcoming. Cautiously, Melvin opened the door a little wider and looked in. He saw that it was quite a small room, and there was nobody there. The two side walls and the far wall had laminated panels over mirrored stainless steel. The floor was covered in white marble, and there was a satin stainless steel handrail along the back wall. In the corner on a small square table was a mahogany and maple chessboard complete with hand-painted resin chess pieces.

"I don't believe it," exclaimed Melvin. Putting aside his caution, he quickly entered the room.

Curious to know what had excited Melvin so much, Lorraine followed him inside. But as soon as she did so, the black door slammed shut behind her.

"This is amazing." Melvin saw that the white pieces had been developed to effective squares, the king was protected, and a strong pawn structure had been created.

Lorraine frantically tried to reopen the door.

"This is incredible," Melvin cried out vehemently. He studied the board closely. "I played my dad last night in the conservatory, and believe it or not, this is the exact position we left it before I went up to bed." He puzzled over this for a brief amount of time.

"For pity's sake!" Lorraine made a noise very similar to a shriek. "You might not believe it, Melvin, but there are more important things to worry about here!" She was virtually swinging on the door handle, but it was hopeless. "We're trapped!"

"Trapped?" Melvin suddenly took an interest in his surroundings again. "Did you say trapped?"

With a soft swishing sound, another stainless-steel wall appeared from nowhere and glided along the tracks, like a train, towards Lorraine. Just in time, she let go of the handle and fell to the white marble floor at Melvin's feet. The wall, or maybe it was a door, had no intention of stopping.

"Please press a button for the required floor," said a friendly, soothing female voice.

"What's happening?" Melvin wondered as he helped to pull Lorraine to her feet. "What button?"

They quickly scanned the enclosed space in search of one.

"Please press a button for the required floor," said the friendly, soothing female voice again.

Sure enough, behind them on the wall they found an integrated operating panel. At the centre of this panel was a pink button.

"Please press a button for the required floor," said the friendly, soothing female voice once more.

They hesitated.

"Will one of you two brats just press the damn button!"

Melvin and Lorraine were horrified. It wasn't the friendly, soothing female voice this time. In contrast, this voice was unfriendly and severe. This voice was impatient. This voice had an evil edge to it. This voice was a male voice, and he sure sounded angry.

Not wishing to incur the wrath of the voice again, Lorraine hurriedly pressed the pink button.

The response was surprising.

"Going up."

Even before the friendly, soothing female voice had finished, the room elevated, gently at first and then with a sudden whoosh, in a decidedly upward direction. With white knuckles they hung on to the satin stainless-steel handrail for dear life. It took a few moments for them to realise they were in some sort of elevator. It took a few moments more for their stomachs to catch up. They tried to scream, but the forces pummelling their bodies strangled them into silence. Within seconds they were travelling at somewhere approaching the speed of sound.

Then the elevator accelerated. The pink button on the operating panel suddenly illuminated and pulsated rhythmically.

A few moments later, without warning, the elevator slowed so abruptly, it was as if a parachute had been deployed to slow its motion by creating drag. It crawled the last few feet before it stopped with a clunk.

"Door opening."

"Pink," was how Lorraine summed up the scene that confronted them as the door opened. Just the one word was sufficient, although Melvin used two.

"Very pink!"

Despite having legs like jelly, Lorraine staggered out of the elevator into the pinkness. Melvin paused, momentarily, for one final peek at the chess board. He missed his dad. When would he see him again? He was somewhat weak at the knees too as he followed Lorraine out.

"Door closing."

They were surprised to see, standing just a few yards away, a slovenly and shabby little man.

"You can relax secure in the knowledge that a job will be well done, your yuckiness," said the slovenly and shabby little man.

Terrence recognised the pesky kids immediately. He thought, if anything, they were actually peskier in real life.

"I shall act dafter than a fox yet more cunning than a brush," he said, looking up at seemingly nothing and talking to seemingly himself.

Chapter 8

"We've never seen the stars, have we?" Zygote asked all of a sudden. Flagellum looked at his fellow giant, wearily, and shrugged his shoulders. "So?"

"And we've never set foot in the physical world either, have we?"

"Excuse me," sighed Flagellum, "but your point is?"

A succession of large, fluffy, white bodies of very fine water droplets drifted by as if carried along by currents of air.

"Tell me, Flagellum," continued Zygote. "How can the pattern of light from stars we have never seen, which twinkle billions of miles above the physical world, where we have never been, possibly influence the nature of individuals here in the white room?"

Flagellum squirmed. "It just does, that's all."

All the fluffy whiteness, from all four corners of the white room, unified and descended slowly on the floating door, overflowing and enclosing it completely.

"No, it doesn't," insisted Zygote. "It's twaddle."

"Will you stop saying astrology is twaddle."

"But it is."

"It isn't …"

It was the unmistakable sound of someone in flip-flops climbing up a flight of stone steps that made the giants cut short their disagreement. As they turned to face the floating door, they saw the large mass of fluffiness divide into two smaller groups. The two smaller collections of shapeless white particles lined up on either side of the door, as if they were forming a guard of honour to welcome a distinguished visitor. Meanwhile, the echo of each flip and each flop, caused by the reflection of sound waves off a dank cellar wall, steadily increased in intensity until it seemed to reach a peak of loudness.

Then a pause.

The guardians of the white room were well used to visitors. Ever since the opening epoch all those eras ago, they had averaged a visitor once every blue moon, so it could never be said they were inexperienced in such matters. Meeting and greeting was their game. Yet neither of the giants could ever remember a visitor arriving by the back way. Well, not in recent times anyway. After all, the floating door was an exit, not an entrance. Everyone knew that.

As they looked on and waited, in anticipation, they heard what sounded like a bit of a shuffle, followed by a couple of hesitant steps. Then there was another pause.

Finally, the door revolved, and into the white room stepped a figure silhouetted against the whiteness. The figure lifted a foot and set it down again a little closer to the giants. This was followed by a similar manoeuvre, of equal distance, with the other foot.

The visitor was walking.

"There you are!" said the stranger as he approached. He wore a hood to cover his head and a calf-length brown tunic confined at the waist by a belt of white cord. "I was beginning to think I would never find you." Somehow, he managed to speak clearly through a bird's nest of a silver beard. "It's been many epochs since I was in this neck of the woods: quite a passage of time indeed, I can tell you." The clouds lifted and formed a protective curve around him. "And it was quite a lot further than I remembered, too. But not to worry, I'm here now. All is well. Now then, chums, long time no see. How are you both?"

The flabbergasted giants stared at the newcomer with their mouths agape and their expressions set somewhere between puzzlement and bewilderment.

"Who are you?" Flagellum managed to ask despite his stunned condition.

"Come, come, gentlemen, I know it's been several eras since we last met." He slowly removed his hood to fully reveal his identity. "But surely you remember me?"

Flagellum shook his head. "No."

They saw that the man before them had a mop of unruly, unkempt silver hair. His blue eyes, though, sparkled with kindness. "Does the Dream Ambassador for Tranquil Dreams ring a bell?"

Flagellum shook his head. "No."

"You mean?" Zygote's state of mental numbness was, at last, beginning to thaw. "Mr Good? You are Mr Good?"

"Exactly precise and precisely exact, chums," said the dream ambassador, beaming.

"Delighted to meet you again, Mr Good," said Zygote enthusiastically. He leaned forward to shake his hand. This was not easy because Zygote was well over twice as tall as Mr Good. He managed it, though, by bending his long legs and performing a sort of curtsy.

"The pleasure is all mine," replied Mr Good. "I remember you two, of course. You are Zygote."

Zygote nodded excitedly.

"And you are Flagellum. Am I right?"

Flagellum shook his head. "No."

"Will you stop saying no and shaking your head, Flagellum?" Zygote gave Flagellum a baleful look before turning his attention back to the distinguished visitor. "Yes, Mr Good, you're right."

"But for the life of me I can't remember which one of you it is that tells the ... porky pies." He smiled.

Flagellum pointed one of the six long, bony fingers of his right hand in the direction of Zygote. "It's him."

Zygote was outraged. "It's him! He's the storyteller."

"It's not me, it's you, Flagellum," said Flagellum.

"I'm Zygote," replied Zygote. "You're Flagellum."

"I'm Zygote," insisted Flagellum.

"Sorry about this, Mr Good." Zygote sighed. "But do you see what I have to put up with?"

Mr Good threw his head back and let go a loud, unrestrained burst of laughter. "Now chums, it really doesn't matter," he assured them. "It really doesn't matter at all."

The fluffy curls of white recoiled, momentarily, at Mr Good's sudden expression of merriment before settling again in an arc around him.

"It matters to me, Mr Good. Flagellum has no idea how to behave. It's the same every time we have a visitor."

"Look, let me tell you why I'm here, chums," said Mr Good as he walked in between the two giants, closely followed by the overprotective clouds. "I do realise you're a bit cut off from things out here, so I don't know if you've heard."

"A bit cut off from things?" Flagellum silently mouthed the words. He could hardly believe the audacity of the man.

"You see," continued Mr Good, "just recently there's been a bit of unrest out there in Dream Land. Tempers have been somewhat frayed, to say the least. It's nothing to worry your heads over. It's just that ..."

"Vile has kicked you out of the Palace. We know," interrupted Flagellum with a smirk.

"Flagellum!" shrieked Zygote with a flush of embarrassment on his face. "Be quiet!" He put his finger to his lips in an effort to shush his fellow giant. "I apologise, Mr Good, for my friend's lack of tact." He looked down on the dream ambassador. "And for the smirk."

"Not to worry, Zygote old chum," said Mr Good with a smile. "Flagellum is indeed correct. Although I wouldn't go as far as saying kicked. It was more like tricked – tricked out of my home."

Zygote gave him a concerned look. "Yes, Mr Good, we did hear something." He shook his head sympathetically. "And we've been very worried."

"There really is no need to worry, Zygote," said Mr Good cheerfully. "And no need, either, for the concerned look or the sympathetic shake of the head. No need to worry at all," he added. "Because I have a plan."

"A plan," marvelled Zygote. "Did you hear that, Flagellum? Mr Good has a plan."

"Yippee," responded Flagellum with little or no interest, followed by a yawn.

"I have summoned three visitors from the physical world," he announced as he placed his hand inside a pocket in his brown tunic and pulled out a satin and woven striped cotton handkerchief.

"Brilliant," said Zygote. "Three visitors? That's a really good plan. Isn't it, Flagellum?"

Flagellum sighed. "It's rubbish."

Wrapped inside the handkerchief was a scrap of paper. "I have their names written down." He read aloud the scribbled words. "Melvin, Lorraine, and ..." Mr Good stopped suddenly, looked up from the scrap of paper, and cried out.

Zygote was unsure if Mr Good's cry was in pain, fright, or surprise. He soon concluded it was the latter because a third bed had suddenly appeared from nowhere and was parked alongside the other two.

Sitting on a single adjustable bed with beech effect surround and wooden legs was an old man.

"And Arthur," said Mr Good happily.

Chapter 9

"What runs but never walks?"

Melvin and Lorraine were anxious to know the whereabouts of Mr Good. They wanted to know if this odd character could help them. They wanted to know if he could point them in the right direction. What they didn't want to know was what ran but never walked.

"Water," said Terrence as he sat down cross-legged on the ground.

"Actually, we were wondering," began Melvin, "if you could help us?"

"What are the most unsociable things in the world?"

"We're looking for Mr Good," continued Melvin.

"Milestones. Because you never see two together."

"Have you seen him?" asked Lorraine.

"By any chance?" added Melvin hopefully.

"What do you give a nervous elephant? Trunkuillizers. What books should be kept on the top shelf? Tall stories. What kind of doctor has a quick temper? A –"

"A doctor with no patients," interrupted Lorraine.

Terrence looked at Lorraine with an expression of open-mouthed astonishment. "Oh, so you've heard that one before, have you?"

"That's an old joke," Lorraine informed him.

Terrence jumped to his feet and produced a small beanbag from his pocket. Someone had chalked a white hopscotch pattern on the pink floor. There were eight squares, drawn rather hurriedly and a little haphazardly and numbered one to eight.

"Look. I can see you're busy ..." Melvin persisted.

Terrence leaned forward and dropped the beanbag into square one.

"But is there any chance you could point us ..."

He hopped over square one to square two and on to square three.

"In the general direction of Mr Good?"

Squares four and five were side by side, and so he landed with one foot in each square. "Why did the duck cross the road?"

Lorraine sighed. "I don't know. Why did the duck cross the road?"

"Because he saw a quack in the pavement." He looked at Lorraine. "That's not an old joke, is it? You haven't heard that one before, have you?"

"I must admit," groaned Lorraine, "I haven't heard that one before."

"Look! Whoever you are!" Melvin continued to persist, just a tad impatiently now. "We're in a bit of a hurry. We'd love to stop and chat, only maybe some other time. You see, at the moment, we are looking for Mr Good."

"It's very important," added Lorraine.

He hopped on to square six before landing with his left foot in square seven and his right in the eighth square. "How do you communicate with a fish?"

"I suppose you could drop it a line," Lorraine responded immediately.

Terrence's face twisted into a strained expression of disgust.

"Do you, or do you not, know where we can find Mr Good?" pleaded Melvin.

His face slowly untwisted and returned to its normal blankness. "Mr Good?" he answered after a short pause.

"Yes!" Melvin looked at Lorraine hopefully. "Mr Good. You've seen him?"

Terrence stared thoughtfully into the pink distance. "Have you tried the Palace?" he said after another pause.

He obviously wasn't up to date with the latest news, but at least there was some hope of a sensible conversation taking place now. "I've some bad news," Lorraine told him. "I'm afraid Mr Good has been banished from the Palace."

"When is a palace like a fish?" Terrence cut in.

Melvin frowned. "Look, we can't stand around all day listening to your fishy riddles. We've got school in the morning."

"When is a school like a fish?" said Terrence as he began to hop back. He stopped in square two to pick up the beanbag.

Melvin scowled this time.

Terrence offered the beanbag to Lorraine. "Would you like to play?"

"This is hardly the time to be playing hopscotch," she told him.

"When is a game of hopscotch like a fish?"

"For goodness sake," Melvin signalled his disapproval with an angry stare. "We're wasting our time here, Loz." He walked across the chalked squares. "Let's go. He's driving me up the wall."

Terrence watched Melvin walk away. For the first time there was the merest hint of a smile on his face. "When is a wall like a fish?"

"When it is scaled," replied Lorraine as she followed Melvin along the passageway.

His smile disappeared. "How did you know that? I only made that one up this morning."

Melvin walked to the door of the elevator. But it wasn't there. He looked around, confused. There was a long pink wall where the elevator was. He shrugged and walked on. All he wanted to do was get away from the guy and his riddles. He climbed up three little pink steps, closely followed by Lorraine, and turned left at a pink T-junction.

Terrence stood expressionless for a long time after they had disappeared from view.

Suddenly, he seemed to remember where he was, why he was there, and what he was supposed to say. He quickly cleared his throat.

"Pesky kids! Oh pesky kids!" He yelled after them. "I'm Mr Good, by the way!"

Although he shouted loudly, Melvin and Lorraine were long gone and way out of earshot.

"Rats!" he said to himself.

He looked up at the dome camera with trepidation.

"How did I do, your nastiness?"

#

The two external openings of Vile's considerable nose were flaring; his eyes were open wide and bulging, and the thin line of his mouth was misshapen and distorted.

"I'll kill him!"

His face was the colour of beetroot, and there was steam coming out of his ears.

"No, on second thoughts, I won't kill him. I'll dunk him in a vat full of soggy semolina. That's worse."

It was fair to say that Vile was angry – furious, even.

"It's my fault. I should never have sent a boy to do a man's job," he growled as he paced up and down in front of the bank of monitor screens like an unfed, caged lion. He stroked his whiskers pensively, beginning at the middle of his upper lip. His whiskers were very long and pulled to the side, slightly curled, and pointed upwards at the ends. With a preoccupied frown, he walked around the spacious walnut desk, sat in the black leather swivel chair, and meditated in silence for a while.

"I'm not to blame," he concluded. "Is it my fault Terrence is an idiot? An imbecile? Of course it isn't." He was pleased he had come to a definite decision on this one.

His positivity was fleeting, though.

You did trust an imbecile to carry out your plan.

"Yes, but," he argued, "my plan required someone to act daft. Who better to act daft than an imbecile? It was brilliant." He grinned. "It was a master stroke." His grin widened.

It was a failure.

Something was inside his head and talking to him.

You were irresponsible. You were negligent. You were a disgrace. Call yourself a dream ambassador?

"Silence!" Vile jumped to his feet. "I'm not listening to you."

Mr Good is up to something. But what? You don't know. It took you many eras to get this place off Mr Good. You don't want to surrender it now.

"I said I'm not listening!" He covered his ears with the palms of his hands.

Mr Good has a plan. He's coming back.

"Look. Who are you? What are you? What you doing inside my head?" Something had taken residence in there. Something had been tickling the inside of his mind. He tried to recall when he had first noticed it. It was on the journey from Torment Towers, he realised. Somehow, somewhere along the way something strange had happened. But he didn't know what, how, or why. There was a gap in his memory.

That's why he's called these two smart kids here. Mr Good has a plan. He has a plan. You're a beaten man, Vile.

The carpet tiles were square and alternated between dark and light blue. "Beaten man, eh? We'll see about that," he said defiantly as he marched up and down the large room. "I have a plan too."

Sure you do.

He found himself at the keypad. He jabbed the multi-screen button repeatedly. With each jab, sixteen different images rotated on his chosen monitor until the screen was a mass of pink. He proceeded to hit the multi-screen button in sequence until he found the two images he wanted. One of them he put up full screen and the other on the spot monitor below.

"If I seal both ends of this pink passageway, then those so-called smart kids won't be going anywhere until I say so." He grinned as he skilfully pressed a few more buttons: Insert Command to add a new corridor, Colour Mode to select turquoise, and finally Aroma Control. From an extensive list of odours, he chose freshly cut grass.

All that was left for him to do was hit the Influence button.

"See, I do have a plan."

He waited, half expecting a sarcastic comment. He waited a little longer, but nothing happened. All was silent inside his head.

He withdrew his thin lips and showed his teeth.

It was an evil smile.

"Then I will throw them in a cell and let them rot." The smile broadened. "Forever," he decided. "Or possibly longer."

Chapter 10

"What's the point of a maze with no entrances or exits?" groaned Melvin. They had reached yet another dead-end. He hit the offending pink wall with his fist in frustration. "It's as pointless as ..." He paused to consider a suitable analogy.

The object of the exercise was to find a way through the elaborately twisted paths to reach a specific goal. They knew there would be dead ends and cul-de-sacs; they expected trick corners and blind alleys too, so that was no surprise. It was a maze, after all. They challenge the choice-making part of ourselves; Melvin had told Lorraine this more than once during the last couple of tiresome hours.

"As pointless as general studies?" suggested Lorraine.

The maze offered a choice of paths, and they had explored each and every one of them, but each one ended up like this one: in disappointment.

"General studies?" Melvin looked at Lorraine curiously.

"It's compulsory for every pupil to take general studies," explained Lorraine. "This is a waste of time because all the best universities specify that they do not take points from general studies into consideration."

"Yes, you're right, Loz. General studies are pointless," agreed Melvin. "But, you see, schools get money for every pupil they enter into the exam."

Lorraine nodded. "That's why we are made to take it."

Together they moved, a little despondently, away from the dead end. The corridor elbowed sharply to the left and then dipped appreciably for forty or fifty paces before levelling out again as it approached the juncture of two pink passageways.

"There must be a way out." Melvin breathed deeply and heavily. "There must be."

They paused to consider their options. The right fork meandered away into the distance. But they knew there was no point going that way. That way continued to meander, like a river winding through the hills, for a while, only to eventually reach an irritating full stop.

"We'll go this way," decided Melvin. The left fork at least had more possibilities. They knew, because they had just come that way, that about a mile ahead was a T-junction. A right turn would take them back to the hopscotch squares where they started. Turning left, however, would take them in the opposite direction.

Side by side they walked on, retracing their steps back towards the T-junction and the main passageway.

"How about this one?" It was Melvin who broke the silence a hundred yards or so along the way. "As pointless as," he said with a smile, "spending your last penny on a purse."

Lorraine smiled too, albeit a little sadly.

"What's up?" asked Melvin.

"I've been thinking about the hopscotch man."

Melvin nodded. "What an oddball he was." He shook his head in despair as he recalled the hopscotch man, his fishy riddles, and their total failure to achieve any amusement or laughter. "Seriously weird!"

"I felt a bit sorry for him, actually," admitted Lorraine.

The main passageway ahead had frequent sharp turns in alternating directions. At intervals, less significant, narrower paths branched off and twisted away out of view. All of these less significant, narrower paths sooner or later terminated in annoying dead ends. Meanwhile, the pink passageway pressed on in a zigzag manner. Eventually, after an incalculable number of zigs and an inestimable amount of zags, the passageway passed the hopscotch squares again from the other direction.

"You felt sorry for him?" Melvin was rendered utterly perplexed. "For the hopscotch man? What the dickens for, Loz?"

"I don't know," said Lorraine with a touch of uncertainty. "I sensed a sadness in his eyes, that's all." She shrugged.

"I would like to cheer him up," she sighed. "But he's gone."

Melvin stopped dead in his tracks. His head jolted back, and his jaw dropped.

Lorraine stopped a couple of paces ahead and turned. "Are you all right?" It looked as though he had been hit by a heavy punch.

He stared at Lorraine with bulging eyes. "What did you say?" he asked.

"I said, are you all right?"

"No. Not that. The hopscotch man. What did you say about the hopscotch man?"

"I said," she tried to recall what she had said about the hopscotch man that could have caused Melvin such concern. "All I said was, I would like to cheer him up."

"After that," he persisted. "What did you say after that?"

"After that? What did I say after that? I can't remember what I said after that." She desperately tried to. "I said he's gone. I only said he's gone."

Melvin nodded. "Yes," he smiled. "That's what I thought you said." He continued to nod and smile for a long moment.

"I don't understand." She looked at Melvin, waiting and hoping for an explanation.

"Don't you see, Loz?" began Melvin. "If the hopscotch man has gone then, obviously, there must be a way out of here." He began to walk again, this time with renewed vigour and enthusiasm. "There has to be a way out of this place. It makes sense."

"Makes sense?" She watched him walk away vigorously and enthusiastically.

"For pity's sake, Melvin, nothing has made any sense since we arrived here," she shouted after him. "We've met a couple of giants and a talking dragon, and we entered this pink maze in an elevator, if you remember, which promptly disappeared moments later."

She stood with her hands on her hips and watched Melvin pass out of sight around a sweeping turn ahead. "Melvin? Wait for me." She was just about to set off in hot pursuit when a brief, passing odour carried in the air distracted her. She drew air through her nose in short, audible inhalations.

"Melvin!" she called out, but not nearly loud enough. "I can smell something." She sniffed. "I know that aroma." She inhaled through her nose once more. "It smells like ..."

Chapter 11

"Arthur!" repeated Mr Good excitedly. "How wonderfully delightful and delightfully wonderful to see you."

Wearing a plum, long-sleeved, woven pyjama set and sitting up on his medically approved bed was a frail, elderly man. He was so physically weak and delicate-looking that for a moment it was touch and go whether he'd survive Mr Good's enthusiastic handshake.

"What happened?" The elderly man trembled. His face had an unnatural, sickly pallor. "Where am I?"

"That's what they all say." Flagellum grinned.

As if by magic, Zygote produced the goatskin parchment from the folds of his green tunic and addressed the visitor. "Welcome," he began. "You have been summoned to this mysterious and fascinating world of dreams, where ..."

Mr Good held up his hand and halted Zygote in full flow. "I'm sorry, old chum, but there really is no time for all that."

Standing by the bed, Mr Good held Arthur's arm and helped him to his feet. Still dazzled by the whiteness, Arthur stood jellylike and somewhat stunned in front of the two giants. He had a large, red, bulbous nose and a turned-up chin that made his head, when viewed in profile, look half-moon-shaped.

"No time? But, Mr Good, you must allow me to inform the visitor about the rules of reality," appealed Zygote. "And how they do not apply."

"Unfortunately, I can't wait a jiffy longer. I have a plan to execute, and Arthur and I have a long journey ahead."

"A long journey?" Arthur's wan face suddenly flushed. "At my time of life and with my ailments?"

Arthur had a list of ailments as long as a giant's arm. Apart from the arthritis, rheumatism, and lumbago, there was the asthma, the diabetes, the hiatus hernia, and a couple of swollen ankles, not forgetting the circulation disorders, the dodgy ticker, the high blood pressure, and a few neck and shoulder conditions. So, a long journey could prove tricky.

"I've had some strange dreams just lately," wheezed Arthur, "but this one just about takes the biscuit." He coughed. "I'm almost sorry I'll be waking up shortly," he added despite a shortness of breath and a tightness in his chest.

"I'm afraid this is no dream," replied Mr Good with as much sensitivity as he could muster. "I have borrowed you from the physical world. But it will only be for a short time. I have a plan, old chum, and you are an important part of it."

"A plan?" Arthur gasped. There was a hoarse whistling sound as the air squeezed through his narrow airways.

Flagellum exaggerated a short intake of breath. "A plan to oust the most evil guy in Dream Land." He grinned. "It could turn nasty."

"Long journeys? Plans? Evil guys?" Arthur looked at the man with the uncombed silver hair, the silver tousled beard, and the deep blue eyes that sparkled with kindness and wondered if he knew what he was doing.

"Not to worry, young Arthur," Mr Good assured him. "You will be perfectly safe." He put his arm around Arthur's shoulder protectively and turned him gently to face the giants.

Arthur remained unconvinced. "Even so," he grumbled under his breath. "I think I'm a bit long in the tooth for all this."

The brilliant white mass of watery vapour surrounding the dream ambassador stirred. The two ends of the white arc slowly began to lengthen, widen, and distend and gradually blended into a whole, encircling Mr Good and Arthur.

"My other two visitors," Mr Good said as he looked up through the white mist at the other two beds, "Did they make their way to the centre of the royal blue labyrinth?"

"Unfortunately," Zygote sighed. "We have no control. When a visitor sets foot through the floating door, they are the little white marble, and Limbo is the spinning roulette wheel. Where they land is down to pure chance."

"White marbles? Spinning roulette wheels?" interrupted Flagellum. "I've never heard such nonsense."

"They could end up in the Zenith Territory," continued Zygote, ignoring his fellow giant. "Or down in the Nether Regions. Or even in some old forsaken or deserted dream space somewhere. It's pot luck."

"It's poppycock!" responded Flagellum with a contemptuous facial expression.

"So you see, Mr Good." Zygote looked and saw that Mr Good didn't see. He didn't see because the whiteness was overwhelming him, overflowing, and enclosing him.

"Help!" Arthur let out a prolonged, sharp, shrill cry. He was drowning in a sea of cotton wool.

"Are you sure this isn't a dream?" he managed to ask before they were both submerged completely in the foamy white fog.

All was quiet.

#

Flagellum and Zygote had been the guardians of the white room for a very long time. When the dinosaurs were roaming the physical world they were, even then, guarding the floating door to Limbo. In the beginning, they were told that two other giants would be taking over at some stage, giving them a chance to take a break, to maybe grab a coffee or something. They were still waiting.

It had been a long shift. They didn't know how many millennia had passed, but they did know it was a heck of a long time to be on your feet. They had no system or method for measuring the passage of time. All they knew was, there was an awful lot of it, and it had to be filled.

They filled their time with arguments. From the outset the two giants discovered they disagreed on almost every matter. They bickered about most things and argued vehemently about everything else, especially astrology. Flagellum was forever coming up with new subjects for them to squabble over.

"Indian elephants," Flagellum suddenly announced.

The natural world? Now this was a topic they hadn't disputed before.

"Excuse me?" replied Zygote.

"Indian elephants have larger ears than African elephants."

"They don't."

"They do."

"No, they don't, Flagellum. And you know it."

"I don't know it."

"You do."

"I don't."

And so on. This was how they chose to fill their time as they waited, and waited, and waited for the other two giants to arrive.

#

When the thick rolling layer of whiteness lifted, Mr Good and Arthur were gone, and the floating door to Limbo was ajar.

Chapter 12

"Freshly cut grass!" she gasped in between deep breaths.

Lorraine had been chasing Melvin for the best part of a quarter of a mile. She eventually found him waiting for her at the T-junction. Except it wasn't a T-junction any longer; it was a crossroads.

"You're right," agreed Melvin. "It is. It is the scent of freshly cut grass."

Opposite them, a corridor jutted out and away from the main pink passageway. It was a new corridor. It hadn't been there the last time they passed this way.

"This corridor wasn't here the last time we passed this way," confirmed Melvin.

"I did tell you that nothing made sense around here, Melvin."

"There's no way we could have missed it," said Melvin thoughtfully. "It sticks out like a sore thumb."

"A turquoise sore thumb, anyway." Lorraine recognised the colour: a shade of blue tinged with green. Her mother had a headscarf in the exact same shade.

Melvin tentatively took a few paces along the turquoise corridor. He raised his nose and sniffed the air. "It does appear that the smell is coming from this way, Loz."

She stood and watched him from the safety of the main passageway. "So what we going to do?" she asked. She was a little worried and unsure about this new corridor.

As far as Melvin was concerned, it wasn't a difficult decision. They had exhausted every possibility the pink maze had to offer. They had been walking around in circles for a couple of hours now and were still no closer to finding their way out.

"Tell me, Loz. What does freshly cut grass suggest to you?"

She gave the question a momentary thought and raised her shoulders. "A garden and a lawnmower?" she replied doubtfully.

"No, Loz. Well, yes. Actually, it does suggest that. It does specifically suggest that. Of course it does," he agreed. "But I was thinking more generally. I was thinking more along the lines of ... the outdoors."

Lorraine was blessed with something called female intuition. She wasn't one hundred per cent sure about this turquoise corridor, but she realised that Melvin knew more about mazes and labyrinths than she did, so she was prepared to let him make the decisions.

"Outdoors, to me, means a way out of this maze," continued Melvin. He sensed that Lorraine had her doubts about the corridor. "Maybe we'll find Mr Good waiting for us at the other end."

"With a pair of edging shears and a watering can, no doubt," Lorraine answered with just a hint of sarcasm.

"Maybe so," said Melvin with a smile. "Or perhaps a hoe and a pair of hedge clippers."

Lorraine couldn't help but smile too. Melvin beckoned her with an inviting wave of his arm.

She sighed and took a reluctant step into the turquoise corridor, followed by a cautious one.

"Or a garden fork and a half-moon sod cutter." He grinned.

"A what?" exclaimed Lorraine as she reached his side.

"A half-moon sod cutter. It's a tool for cutting turf," explained Melvin. "It creates a neat edge along paths, walls, and even around trees."

Together they set off along the turquoise way.

"Do you really think Mr Good will have a half-moon sod cutter?" laughed Lorraine.

Incidentally, Mr Good did have an extensive collection of garden implements hanging up neatly in his potting shed back at the Palace. Vile, of course, has the benefit of them now, but he doesn't use them. Well, he doesn't use them for their intended purpose, anyway.

The turquoise way undulated like an ocean wave: up and down, up and down, and then two ups and two downs followed by three ups and only two downs, and so on. Despite the rising and falling, the corridor turned out to be a direct, straight path. Initially, Lorraine was wary of the corridor that had suddenly appeared from nowhere, but as they journeyed on up and down the direct, straight path, she relaxed. Their conversation moved on and away from the subject of gardening tools.

They went on to talk about themselves, discussing their plans for the future and school. Lorraine revealed she wanted to be a journalist. She was studying English literature, history, sociology, and French in lower sixth.

Melvin was studying maths, biology, and chemistry and had set his heart on being a doctor or a vet one day. He had dropped physics at the end of his first year.

Towards the end of the turquoise corridor, Lorraine returned to her pet topic.

"He held an assembly saying that we must turn up to general studies, or else our names would be reported to the headmistress."

Melvin nodded. "Our head of sixth form tells us exactly the same thing almost every week."

"Most students, including myself and all of my friends, never bother to attend the lesson," she continued.

"At our school, even the teacher doesn't bother turning up most of the time," added Melvin.

Lorraine smiled. "And when I did turn up one time, having never been to one of the lessons before, the teacher asked me to leave."

"Really?" laughed Melvin. "Because she hadn't seen you there before?"

"Exactly." Lorraine laughed too. "She said I wasn't in this class."

A gentle wind blew towards them through the corridor.

"And yet, despite never going to a general studies lesson, I still managed to get one hundred per cent in the politics paper."

"It's a joke," sighed Melvin, shaking his head. His next step was his last in the turquoise corridor.

The breeze sent a ripple through Lorraine's cornrow braids as she set foot outside.

The end of the direct, straight turquoise path caught them unawares. The Dreamspace, too, was an unexpected development. They found themselves on a stretch of open, grass-covered land. Before them were sweeping lawns, small woods, culverts, and areas covered by huge, ancient oak trees. It was dawn.

"That's the grandest house I think I've ever seen." Lorraine stood in awed silence.

They stared in wonder through an avenue of elm trees at a magnificent palace of white marble shimmering in the morning mist.

"A house?" Melvin moved closer to get a better look. The morning grass was wet with dew. He had never seen a house before with a central dome that reached seventy metres into the sky, flanked by four slightly smaller subsidiary domed chambers. "More like a palace," he decided.

Lorraine nodded without once taking her eyes off the large and stately residence. "I wonder who lives there."

"I do," said a voice.

Melvin and Lorraine nearly jumped out of their skin. Startled, they turned to see the owner of the voice step out from behind a nearby bush. He moved a step closer.

"And you pesky kids are trespassing."

Chapter 13

The grand entrance hall was large and square and floored with pink and white marble. On the walls hung rich old tapestries and rare paintings with a row of marble columns and pointed arches, surmounted by intricate carvings in the stone leading to the staircase.

A freestanding graceful staircase, with a balustrade of solid oak, rose to the first floor. On the landing, where the stairs divided into two, a monumental stained-glass window depicted a scene from dream folklore: a brave dream hero, by the name of George, slaying a nasty, fiery dream dragon.

On the first floor was a spacious drawing room, carpeted, curtained, panelled, and finished in mauve, with a balcony overlooking the grand entrance hall. Panels of mirrors filled spaces not occupied by doors. The furniture was white, with caned seats and backs covered with tapestried cushions.

Sitting at occasional tables was a large gathering of dream actors and dream actresses relaxing after a long and busy dream span. Demons and devils were conversing in an easy and familiar manner as vampires and zombies talked lightly and casually. A hoodlum, a ruffian, and a thug, standing next to two large, empty decorative pots with caned sides that once displayed plants or pretty flowers, were in the middle of a deep and meaningful discussion with a dream character with an antisocial personality disorder armed with a machete and a lunatic armed with a half-moon sod cutter.

Four ghosts entered the room through a gap in a great curtain that hung across the room at the far end. They found an empty table near the top of the staircase.

"Come, come, Larry. You can tell me. I am your best friend," said Harry as he removed his mask and placed it under the table.

"I thought I was your best friend." Barry put himself between the two disputing dream actors and squeezed himself into the chair next to Larry, forcing Harry to sit opposite.

"You?" Harry retorted. He undid the zip at the front of his ghost costume. "What foolishness. We've been close for eras."

"Well, excuse me. I've known him since dream nursery," insisted Barry. "We sat next to each other. I'm his best friend."

"Then let's ask him, shall we?" Harry stared at Larry. "Which one of us is your best friend? Just to settle the argument."

"Well." Larry faltered. He was very tall and ungracefully thin. He was no giant but a seven-footer for sure.

"It's me, isn't it? Tell him it's me," pleaded Barry.

"It's me. I'm his best friend. Tell him, Larry," begged Harry.

"Look, when you get to our age you don't have best friends," said Larry tactfully. "I mean, 'best friend' is a bit dream primary schoolish, don't you think?"

It was Garry, the fourth dream actor, who came to Larry's rescue. "Can I just say something at this point?" he squeaked. Garry was the quiet and timid one.

"Yes? What is it?" the other three dream actors chorused impatiently.

"Are those children down there?" He looked through the balusters that supported the solid oak rail and pointed at the grand entrance hall below.

The hand-crafted, solid mahogany arched door was open. Vile was down there with five muscular guards and two children, Melvin and Lorraine.

#

It had been a frightening and painful ordeal for them. Lorraine knew there was something amiss about the turquoise corridor, but she couldn't put her finger on what it was. But the smell of freshly cut grass had lured Melvin in. It was a trap. They found themselves walking in the grounds of the Palace of Somnium, and lying in wait behind a bush was Vile.

They didn't know it was someone vile at first. Rude, maybe. Obnoxious, possibly. But not vile. Not at first.

They were desperate to find Mr Good and keen for any news of his whereabouts, and the rude and obnoxious guy was surprisingly willing to help. For some reason, Lorraine's female intuition didn't kick in. He told them he'd met the Dream Ambassador for Tranquil Dreams quite recently and only a short distance away; he had been playing hopscotch and talking in riddles.

Melvin and Lorraine were stunned. Could the hopscotch man really be Mr Good? The news made Lorraine even more determined to find him and to cheer him up. So she gratefully accepted Vile's offer to show them exactly where Mr Good had last been seen.

Behind a thicket of small trees were the entrances of every colour you could possibly imagine and every shade of every colour too. From the selection of colours and shades Vile chose the magenta one. Well, to cut a fairly long story a little shorter, they were ushered inside the magenta entrance. The Dreamspace disappeared. Vile laughed an evil laugh, and five muscular guards appeared from nowhere.

They were grabbed by an average of two and a half guards each. The guards wore iron helmets. Over the top of their tunics they had cloaks, and their kilts were made of strips of leather plated with metal. On their feet they wore strong leather sandals with leather straps

Vile laughed another annoying evil laugh as the guards pushed, shoved, and dragged them screaming through the maze. Within a matter of minutes they reached a large wooden door. Vile kicked it open, and the guards threw Melvin and Lorraine unceremoniously to the pink and white marble floor.

If they hadn't known who this rude and obnoxious man was before, they certainly had an inkling now.

"Vile?" asked Melvin apprehensively as he pulled himself to his feet, replaced his glasses, and began to tuck his shirt back inside his black school trousers. "Are you the evil Vile?"

"Indeed I am." Vile grinned proudly. "Look, just because I'm evil doesn't mean I'm all bad. My mother loves me." He considered this for a moment. "Well, that's not strictly true. Let's just say she sort of tolerates me."

"What do you want with us?" asked Lorraine, rubbing a couple of sore knees.

"Want with you?" Vile, under normal circumstances, wouldn't want anything to do with a couple of insignificant pesky kids. But this was different. He had a feeling about these two. "Let's just say you'll be staying here for a while."

"We're not stopping here," announced Lorraine boldly.

"Obviously, when I say a while I really mean forever." His grin was incessant, but then it wavered.

"What did you say?" He looked closely at Lorraine.

"I said, we're not stopping," she repeated. "We're going to find Mr Good."

Vile had heard enough. "Guards!" he shouted. He always shouted at the guards, not because they were deaf but because he thought it helped them understand more.

"Excuse me, Vile," interrupted Melvin. "Loz has got a bee in her bonnet over this," he explained. "She just wants to find Mr Good and cheer him up."

Vile gave Melvin and Lorraine one of his angry stares. "Guards!" he shouted again. This time he chose one of the guards, jabbed at his chest, and pointed to the door. The guard, surprisingly, responded immediately, closing the door with a thud and assuming a guarding stance in front of it.

"See? You're not going anywhere," he told her.

"Vile," sighed Lorraine. She refused to give way to fear or be intimidated by an angry stare. "I really must insist. Mr Good is possibly the only one who can help –"

Before she could finish, two of the guards grabbed her, lifted her off the ground, and set off up the staircase. The remaining two dealt with Melvin in a similar fashion.

"Surely you don't want to leave now," Vile called after them. His face assumed an expression of mild amusement. "Not with opening night so close."

"Opening night?" asked Melvin and Lorraine together with their legs kicking thin air.

He nodded and laughed softly. "Opening night of my new nightmare, of course." He stood on the landing under the large stained-glass window.

"My most fearful, gruesome, hideously horrid nightmare yet is just five dream spans away," he added with great pleasure. "It will hit the unsuspecting population of the physical world like a thunderbolt from something blue."

"You mean everyone is going to have the same nightmare?" asked Lorraine.

"Everyone? Everywhere?" queried Melvin.

"Everyone." Vile smiled with just a slight raising of one corner of his upper lip. "Everywhere."

The four guards reached the top of the staircase and, without hesitation, dropped Melvin and Lorraine in a pile on the carpeted floor of the drawing room.

Vile marched off mumbling something about a large brass key, leaving the guards to keep watch on the pesky kids. The guards stood at the top of the staircase and stared blankly at nothing in particular.

Chapter 14

"Tell me again." Arthur stopped to catch his breath. "Where are we going?"

"To the centre of the royal blue labyrinth," replied Mr Good with a patient smile.

Arthur suffered from many conditions that made walking difficult. If the arthritis didn't stop him then the asthma would, or the swollen ankles. He couldn't walk for more than twenty paces without stopping for a rest.

"I've been staying there," explained Mr Good kindly and for the forty-seventh time. "With my old chum Mugwump."

Arthur leaned wearily against the royal blue wall, for support, and waited for Mr Good to explain.

"Mugwump is a wizard," he began ... and ended. That was it. Mugwump was a wizard. That summed it up perfectly. "What more needs to be said?" He smiled cheerfully.

"A wizard?" Arthur winced. It was a twinge of arthritis. "Forgive my ignorance, but what do wizards do?" He had never met one. Yesterday he was driving his mobility scooter around the shopping centre. Today, he was in another world having a conversation with a dream ambassador about wizards. He could feel his blood pressure rising.

"What do wizards do? Well." Mr Good ran his fingers, thoughtfully, like a comb through his knotted silver beard. "Mugwump does wizardy things, of course, like magic and spells and stuff. Sometimes, he waves a golden wand around a bit." Mr Good recalled him doing that on several occasions. "Oh, and he also says 'salmon' a lot."

Arthur expelled air from his lungs in a sudden and noisy cough. "He says what?"

"Mugwump has an involuntary but natural impulse to utter the word 'salmon," explained Mr Good. "A lot," he added. "He is often called 'The wizard who says salmon a lot', for short."

"For short?" Arthur gasped. "But surely it takes longer to say 'The wizard who says salmon a lot' than it does to say 'Mugwump'?"

"It depends how quick you say it," Mr Good concluded after a moment's consideration.

Arthur shook his head and sighed. "I'll never get used to this place." He took a deep, wheezy breath and set off again along the royal blue corridor.

Nineteen and a half strides later he had to stop again for a breather.

Despite his cheerful exterior, Mr Good was becoming concerned. The royal blue corridor was a very long, snakelike passage that coiled and spiralled for a very long way until it eventually reached the centre. At this rate it could take them an epoch or more to get there. It was an epoch he couldn't afford to waste. As each grain of hypothetical sand trickled through an equally hypothetical hourglass, his concerns grew. It was on occasions like this that he really could do with some help.

"I wish Mugwump were here," he muttered quietly to himself.

"Oh? Why?" asked Arthur in between short, laboured breaths. There was obviously nothing wrong with his hearing.

"He can see portals," replied Mr Good, deeply absorbed in thought. He really needed to have his plan up and running. He had summoned three visitors from the physical world and had hoped to have them all together by this time.

"What's a portal?" panted Arthur.

Portals were hidden openings.

"Invisible gateways" was how Mr Good chose to describe them.

Arthur was fascinated. He had never seen anything invisible before. "Will you show me one?" he asked.

"I wish I could." Mr Good smiled. He looked at Arthur with his deep blue eyes that sparkled with kindness and told him exactly why he couldn't. "Because they are invisible," he began, "only black-robed wizards can see portals. Chaps like us can't see them, unless we are lucky enough to be in possession of a hand-held Dream Navigation Device with built-in Portal Locater, of course."

Unfortunately, Mr Good's hand-held Dream Navigation Device with built-in Portal Locater was back at the palace in a drawer.

Mr Good went on to explain how a portal allows one to journey between labyrinths, to move from maze to maze across Limbo fairly quickly. "Portals can be useful," he concluded.

The dream ambassador gently took hold of Arthur's arm and encouraged him to stand up, away from the security of the wall. Slowly but surely they set off again along the royal blue way.

"Are we in a hurry?" Arthur asked after a while. He was oblivious to the enormity of the situation.

Mr Good nodded. So far he had shielded Arthur from the seriousness of it all. He told him there had been a bit of unrest out there in Dream Land. He had only mentioned Vile in passing, telling him he was a little unpleasant. He thought it best not to mention how depraved, loathsome, and spiteful he was. "I wish we were a little further along, that's all," he told him. "A little nearer the centre, perhaps."

"I'm holding you back," Arthur suddenly realised.

"Not to worry," Mr Good assured him. "All is well. If my plan is delayed a little, then so be it."

"A plan?" It wasn't the first time Mr Good had mentioned a plan. It made Arthur nervous. "Why have I been picked?" he wondered. "I'm an old man."

Arthur removed his arm from Mr Good's gentle grip and halted. He was fatigued to the point of exhaustion.

"I chose you, old chum, for a reason. A very important reason." Mr Good gave Arthur a serious look. "Without you the plan will fail. If the plan fails, the consequences for the physical world will be catastrophic."

He waited a moment for the momentousness of what he was saying to sink in. "You are a vital part of my plan," he added.

Arthur's dodgy ticker missed a couple of beats.

Chapter 15

Lorraine sat up, a little dazed. Melvin climbed, gingerly, to his feet. He took Lorraine's hand and pulled her up too.

It was Melvin who looked up first. What he saw temporarily deprived him of the power of speech. With his mouth wide open he nudged Lorraine in the ribs with his elbow. But she had seen them too by now. Together they stared in horror at Dracula, Frankenstein, and a handful of werewolves, who were sitting at a nearby table chatting in hushed tones.

"Ahoy there!" someone shouted. It was a ghost.

Four ghosts were sitting at a nearby table. The tallest one was waving its arms around frantically, desperately trying to attract the attention of someone. Melvin and Lorraine wondered whom the ghost could possibly be trying to call. They looked behind themselves and were surprised and visibly shaken to see there was no one there. It was at this moment they realised who the ghost was attempting to attract.

It was them.

"My friend Garry here," the ghost said as he beckoned them over, "was just saying that you two children look remarkably like two children, or something similar."

Melvin and Lorraine looked at each other with apprehension as they slowly approached their table. "We're teenagers, actually," Melvin replied nervously.

"Sixth-form students," added Lorraine.

"Well call me a taxi!" exclaimed Larry.

"So, tell me, two children – I mean, two teenagers," said Harry with a smile. He was a short and stocky ghost. "Why are you here?"

Melvin shrugged. "To be honest, we don't really know."

"Visitors from the physical world, I shouldn't wonder," concluded Barry. He was much taller than Harry but less stocky, though not nearly as tall as Larry – or as thin.

"Well, that is peculiar," said Harry. "That hasn't happened in a while, has it?"

"You mean it's happened before?" asked Lorraine, suddenly filled with wonder.

"It's happened six times in the last seven or eight eras," Barry told her.

"It's a freak happening," explained Larry. "The membrane between the physical world and Dream Land is usually strong enough to keep them from slipping into each other."

"Membrane?" Harry looked at Larry in a questioning kind of way. "What membrane?"

"It's all very technical," said Larry. He knew because he'd read a book on the subject. "Negative dimensions. The altering of conscious frequencies and such like."

"Is it? I didn't know that," admitted Harry. "That's all very interesting, Larry."

"That's all very interesting, Larry," mocked Barry.

Harry frowned. "You just don't like the fact that I am Larry's best friend, do you?"

"I am Larry's best friend!" Barry retorted.

It was Larry who frowned this time. He had to act quickly to steer the course of the conversation away from the issue of best friends. He stood up and leaned towards the two teenagers. "Please forgive us. We haven't introduced ourselves. I'm Larry."

"I'm Harry."

"I'm Barry."

"And he's Garry," they cried in unison.

Garry looked up shyly and gave the two teenagers a timid little wave.

"Although for some reason Vile calls us all Norman," added Larry, a little puzzled.

"Very pleased to meet you all. I'm Melvin, and this is Loz. That's short for Lorraine."

The guard who had been left alone guarding the door in the entrance hall below suddenly appeared at the top of the staircase. He wasn't happy about being left alone downstairs. He exchanged a succession of angry grunts with the four guards who had been left to watch over Melvin and Lorraine. The guards communicated with deep, guttural sounds or grunts similar to those of a hog. Yet, unbelievably, it was a language, a system they used for communication with, somewhat surprisingly, a set of grammatical rules. To the untrained ear, though, it was almost impossible to distinguish one grunt from another.

"So, what are you doing here?" asked Lorraine, ignoring the fracas developing between the guards. "You don't look evil. You all seem friendly enough."

"We are dream actors," revealed Larry. "We were Mr Good's dream actors."

"But since Vile took over it's been, well, it's been a nightmare," Harry pointed out.

"Nightmares are all we do now," continued Barry. "We hate it."

Lorraine was horrified. "Have you tried to escape?"

"Of course."

"Really?"

"Well, no. Not really."

"We've nowhere to escape to," sighed Harry.

"And besides, we have no idea where Mr Good is," bemoaned Larry. "We're sure he hasn't gone to Torment Towers. Mr Good is allergic to uncleanliness of any kind. He …"

Larry was interrupted by the volume of the guard's grunts and the violent pushing and shoving that was taking place at the top of the staircase. The lonely guard suggested it might be a good idea if they took it in turns to be the one in the entrance hall. But the other guards weren't interested and told him so with some very loud, pig-like noises. The guard responded by placing his thumb on his nose and waving four fingers at them. Placing your thumb on your nose and waving four fingers is an extremely offensive gesture in muscular guard circles. Two of the guards took umbrage and decided to chase him. They chased him in and out of the tables and across the drawing room before crashing through the great curtain at the far end of the room, almost pulling it off its heavy-duty curved track.

Meanwhile, the remaining two guards stood unmoved, impassive and emotionless.

"We've seen him. We've seen Mr Good," announced Lorraine after all the excitement had died down. "We met him on our way here."

Four jaws dropped so far they almost hit the table top. They had waited so long for news of Mr Good. To say they were excited and emotionally stirred was an understatement. They had a hundred and one questions they wanted to ask. And they wanted to ask them all at once.

"You did?"

"Where?"

"How is he?"

They asked three. The other ninety-eight could maybe wait until later.

"He wasn't too good, I'm afraid," replied Lorraine. "We think he's depressed."

Melvin told them about the hopscotch squares and the riddles.

"Oh dear," said Harry sadly. "All this distress must have affected him more than we thought it would."

"If only there was some way we could help him," sighed Barry.

"Oh, but there is," Lorraine whispered lest the guards could hear her. "Melvin and I are going to leave here, find him, and cheer him up."

The dream actors took sharp intakes of breath and shook their heads. They proceeded to tell her that, in their opinion, escape was impossible.

"Surely not." Lorraine was determined. "The door to Limbo is only down there. What is to stop us just walking down the staircase now and leaving?"

They all gave this some thought.

"The muscular guards?" suggested Larry.

The other dream actors nodded in agreement. It was true. Those muscular guards were big.

"Vile?" It was Harry who offered this for consideration.

The actors were in accord on this one. Vile would most certainly stop the children from leaving.

"The door's locked," said Barry.

This one was greeted with more nods of agreement around the table. Even if you could outwit the guards or outrun Vile, you still had the locked door to contend with. And it was a formidable door. Barry reckoned it was made of mahogany or some other metal.

"No," Larry suddenly remembered. "The door isn't locked," he declared, interrupting the nodding heads. "Vile doesn't bother to lock the door. He knows we're all too scared to escape."

Barry was taken aback by this revelation. Harry was too. Even Garry, who never missed a thing, didn't know that Vile never locked the front door.

"See?" Lorraine turned to Melvin. "We can do this."

"Okay, Loz," said Melvin, nodding. "But not now. Let's wait until it's a bit safer. Vile could be watching us right now." He looked around nervously. "He's probably expecting us to escape."

Lorraine agreed. It might be a good idea to hang around for a while just to gain Vile's trust. She leaned towards the dream actors and spoke softly. "How would you all like to escape with us?"

It was Barry who answered first. He told her he would have escaped before if he had known the door wasn't locked.

Harry was of the same opinion. He claimed it was only the locked door that had stopped him in the past.

"So," ventured Melvin. "Now that you know the door isn't locked, does this mean you will be escaping with us?" He examined them closely, one by one, with a searching look.

"Of course."

"Yes."

"Definitely."

The dream actors replied excitedly. They replied excitedly because, well, because they were excited. They were going to escape! They were going to find Mr Good!

"Excellent. That's really good news," said Lorraine with a smile. "Mr Good will be so pleased to see you. We'll go in an hour or so."

The buzz of excitement around the table ceased immediately.

"An hour or so?" queried Larry.

"You mean, an hour or so from now?" asked Harry.

"Yes. An hour or so from now," confirmed Lorraine.

"Is there a problem?" asked Melvin, a little puzzled.

A problem? Harry knew he had to hurriedly and swiftly come up with one. "I've just remembered I've got a headache," he hurriedly and swiftly remembered.

"Oh dear, I've got my piano lesson later," recalled Barry. "Then later still, I might have a headache too."

"So, if you could make it another time. Like another epoch perhaps," Larry begged.

"Or maybe the following era," suggested Harry.

"For pity's sake!" Lorraine stared in disbelief at the four dream actors.

In the corner of his eye, Melvin noticed several dream actors around the room were looking his way. When he looked, they quickly turned away and resumed their private whisperings. "Would any of you like to escape?" he called out to the gathering of beasts, phantoms, and bogeymen sitting around the drawing room.

"Can I just say something at this point?" It was Garry, the quiet and timid one.

Larry, Harry, and Barry rounded on him impatiently.

"Yes."

"What is it?"

"Chatterbox!"

"Are you willing to escape with us?" asked Lorraine hopefully.

"I just wanted to inform you that Vile is heading this way, holding a large brass key."

Vile entered the room through one of the mirrored panels along the wall and was now striding across the room, purposefully. The large brass key he was carrying was as big as his forearm. His purposefulness waned a touch, though, when he spotted the pesky kids in conversation with some of his dream actors.

"I hope you're not thinking about escaping," he said, regarding the pesky kids suspiciously. "Because if you are, you can forget it right now!"

"Escape? Us? Of course not," Lorraine lied.

"Where would we go?" added Melvin.

"Exactly," said Vile with a grin. "Where would you go? There is nowhere to go, is there?" He brought the large brass key down hard on the top of Larry's skull. "Is there, Norman? You like it here, don't you?"

Larry sat up rigid in his chair. He tried to answer, but the blow rendered his voice box temporarily out of order. He braced himself for the inevitable follow-up smack around the head. When it came, it caught him just above the temple.

"Don't you?" Vile demanded a reply.

A spasm of pain twisted his face for a moment. "Yes!" Larry somehow responded. "Yes. I like it here!"

Satisfied, Vile turned to the pesky kids. "This is the key to your room," he told them. "Of course, when I say room I really mean cell. My guards will show you the way."

Melvin and Lorraine looked at each other in dismay. So much for hanging around and gaining Vile's trust. How could they do that while locked up in a cell somewhere?

"Guards!" Vile shouted. "Take these pesky kids down to the –" He paused in mid-sentence. Vile prided himself on his observational skills, and when he looked at the guards he instinctively knew something wasn't quite right. He did a quick head count.

"I could have sworn there were more than two of them." He brooded on this quietly to himself. He checked again in case he had miscounted, but he hadn't. There were definitely only two guards stood there. He decided he didn't have time to dwell on that right now; he had a plan to thwart. Besides, two muscular guards were more than enough to despatch a couple of pesky kids down to the cell. "Guards!" he shouted again.

"Ugh?" the guards grunted. An accurate translation of the grunt would be difficult, but it's possible their response went something along the lines of *'Hello, oh evil one, how can we be of assistance to you at this time?'*

"Key! Pesky kids! Cell!" barked Vile with a brusqueness. He thrust the large brass key into their possession and motioned for them to push and shove the pesky ones out of the room. The guards were good at pushing and shoving. They had certificates.

To prove it, one of the guards grabbed Melvin by the scruff of his neck and squeezed it painfully before giving him an almighty shove across the carpet. The other guard pulled Lorraine's cornrow ponytail and pushed her headlong through the curtain.

Vile assumed a facial expression indicating pleasure as he witnessed the unnecessary and unwarranted assault on the pesky kids. At last they were locked up and out of harm's way. Mr Good's plan was in tatters. He had won.

His elation was short-lived, however.

There's sure to be a Plan B.

"A Plan B?" His smug glow of self-congratulation slowly dissolved.

Or maybe Mr Good wanted you to capture the pesky kids. Maybe it's all part of his plan. Maybe it's a trap and you've walked right into it.

"A trap?" he loosened his wide white kipper tie and gulped nervously. "Surely not?"

#

The mahogany door creaked open a few inches. A face, framed by uncombed, drab, pale brown hair, peeped inside. A pair of scruffy white trainers then tiptoed across the pink and white marble floor. The figure froze at the foot of the staircase. He was hoping his entrance would pass unnoticed. He was hoping to slip into the Palace and up to his room unobserved. Most of all, he was hoping to avoid Vile.

"Terrence!"

He was out of luck.

Chapter 16

"They're larger!"

"They're smaller!"

"Larger!"

"Smaller!"

"Once and for all, Flagellum, an African elephant has larger ears than an Indian elephant."

The two giants were still persisting with their natural world dispute.

"That's poppycock and you know it!"

"The African elephant also has a bigger trunk," continued Zygote. "It has longer tusks and is twice the weight of its Indian counterpart."

"I've never heard such nonsense," retorted Flagellum. "The Indian elephant is altogether bigger."

Large chunks of whiteness, like massive cloud cubes, passed by just as a Scandinavian pine bed with brushed metal and a whitewashed finish gradually materialised alongside the other three.

"Don't be ridiculous, Flagellum."

A boy sat up. "Excuse me," he said, interrupting the giants in full flow. He was a thickset lad with wavy brown hair and dimples.

"I don't believe this," exclaimed Flagellum. "We don't see a soul for seven epochs, and then suddenly it's Piccadilly Circus around here!"

Keith climbed off his bed and approached the giants cautiously. "Am I really here?" he mused. "So soon?" He was wearing a smart beige shirt with a red and blue diagonal neckerchief and navy blue activity trousers.

Zygote recognised the lad's uniform as that of a Boy Scout.

"I thought I'd have a little more time to get used to the idea," he went on, musing quietly to himself as he lifted a plum and grey travel suitcase off the bed and rested it on the ground.

"Now," announced Flagellum. "This is the moment when you say, what happened and where am I?" He exposed his enormous, crooked teeth in a sickly grin. "So, let's get that out of the way."

"Yes, that's what they all say." Zygote smiled with his hand poised and ready to reveal the goatskin parchment again.

The two giants towered above the youngster and waited.

"No need," said the Boy Scout. "I know exactly where I am." He gave the white room a cursory glance. "It's just that I didn't think I'd be here so soon. Gosh and double gosh! I'm a bag of nerves. I said to myself: myself, you won't be nervous when it happens. But now it's happened, look at me." He held out his hand. It was shaking like a very shaky leaf.

"You knew you were coming?" Zygote was intrigued. He stared at the suitcase. It was a classic square shape with two front pockets. "That's odd. He's even had time to pack a bag." He tried to recall the last time a visitor arrived in the white room and didn't say 'What happened' or 'Where am I'. Then he remembered. It was never.

"So, what do you want?" asked Flagellum abruptly. "What is your business here in the room with two doors?"

"Room with two doors?" Keith stared, confused, at the giant wearing the crimson padded turban. "But this is the white room. I'm sure of it." He recognised the whiteness. It was like a huge glob of whipped cream. "I've been here before."

Flagellum looked at Zygote, and Zygote looked at Flagellum. "You've been here before?" they shrieked in unison. Zygote was stunned, and Flagellum was flabbergasted.

"Well, that's not strictly true. I haven't actually been here, as such. Not physically," he struggled to explain. "But I don't think it was a dream. Yet it must've been a dream," he decided. He tried desperately to make some sense of it. "It seemed so real."

"Tell me, in this dream that seemed so real," probed Zygote, "was it Mr Good who spoke to you?"

Why was this giant so interested? What business was it of his anyway? "All I will say to you is we chatted for a while."

"You chatted for a while!" scoffed Flagellum, who had never heard such nonsense.

"But what we chatted about I can't tell you," he said defiantly.

A scout is to be trusted. It's the first rule of the scout law.

"I'm sworn to secrecy," he continued. "My lips are sealed, Mr Flagellum."

Did he say 'Mr Flagellum'? The giant regarded the Boy Scout with his beady eyes for a long moment before turning to Zygote. "He knows your name."

Zygote sighed. "He said Mr Flagellum, actually. He was talking to you."

"He was looking at me, yes," he admitted. "But he was talking to you. You're Mr Flagellum."

"I'm not. I'm Zy..."

"Look," Keith interrupted the giants. "I know both your names, actually." He activated the push-button retractable trolley system, pulled the suitcase forward, and headed tentatively through the mist towards the floating door. "I was told all about you."

"You were?" Zygote asked. He was curious to know what Mr Good had said. Surely it was Mr Good he had chatted to. Mr Good was doing all the summoning around here just lately.

Flagellum was annoyed. He liked to dominate visitors. He liked to taunt them and insult them and be sarcastic. Most of all, he liked to bully them and force them to choose which door to go through. But this one knew too much. He'd been having cosy chats with Mr Good.

"Untrustworthy,' was one word mentioned." A mischievous smile crossed Keith's lips.

This time Flagellum was stunned, and it was Zygote who was the flabbergasted one. "Untrustworthy?"

It had happened this morning, in the early hours, just as the day was dawning. He had just woken from a series of strange dreams. Or had he woken? Maybe he had still been sleeping. As he lay in his bed he felt a calmness overcome him. This was quickly followed by a voice. The voice didn't really say that Flagellum and Zygote were untrustworthy; he made that bit up. Keith was teasing them.

"I was told to be wary of everyone. So, if you don't mind, wary is what I'll be. I'm to tell no one, not a soul, not a living thing, what's in my suitcase. Not a …"

Keith stopped himself before he said too much. "That's the trouble. I always talk a lot when I'm nervous. Gosh and double gosh! My heart's beating nineteen to the dozen. I'd better go before I tell you all about the plan. Oops, there I go again."

"Don't worry," said Zygote with a laugh. "We know about it. We don't know the precise details, of course. But I promise you, we are on Mr Good's team."

Flagellum was bored with all this nonsense. He wanted to hurry things up a bit. He looked Keith directly in the eye. "Look, we've got better things to do than stand here all dream span waiting for you to choose which door to go through, you know." It isn't easy to look at someone directly in the eye when you're over twelve feet tall, but he somehow managed it by spreading his long legs wide and bending forward like a giraffe eating from the lower branches of an acacia tree.

"Begging your pardon, Mr Flagellum, but I happen to know that it doesn't matter a jot which door I go through because, well, because there is only one door, isn't there?"

Flagellum stood up straight again. His forehead wrinkled, and his eyebrows lowered. It was a frown.

"I suppose the royal blue corridor is through this door, is it?" Keith reached out and touched the white door. His hand disappeared through it. He panicked and withdrew his hand rapidly as if he had burned his fingers on something hot. He reached out again. This time the door swung open invitingly. He smiled and turned to the two giants. "Maybe I'll see you around." He waved and planted one foot through the exit.

"Mr Good told us all about you too, you know," Flagellum called after him.

Keith hesitated. "Oh?" *They seem very sure it was Mr Good that summoned me. Maybe it was.* He wasn't sure. No names had been mentioned. He half turned and regarded Flagellum warily. "Did he? Did he say I was loyal?" he asked. "And did he say I was friendly and considerate?"

He hoped so. After all, those were the second and third rules of the scout law.

"No." Flagellum grinned. "He said you were a twit!"

Keith sighed and shook his head in despair.

"No he didn't, Flagellum."

"Yes he did."

The two giants didn't see Keith or the suitcase slip away, and they didn't hear the floating door close gently behind him, either. They were too busy disagreeing.

"No he didn't."

"Yes he did, Flagellum."

"No he didn't ... and stop calling me Flagellum."

Chapter 17

They were thrown headlong through the curtain and found themselves in a sort of enclosed antechamber. This opened out immediately into a library crammed full of books, manuscripts, and plants. They were pushed and they were shoved across this room and on through a doorway that, in turn, led to a magnificent lounge finished in a cool shade of blue. The room was thronged with choice pieces of furniture and spineless yucca, evergreen indoor house plants.

The next room they were pushed through was curtained and richly decked with vases, lamps, paintings, and more plants. Each room the two guards pushed and shoved them through appeared finer and grander than the one before it.

Eventually, through a vaulted corridor, they reached the great central hall. Passages and palatial rooms spread out from this vast hexagonal hall in six different directions. It was not only the central room of the palace but also the most important. For here, directly ahead, were Vile's private quarters: a sumptuous apartment, several stories in height and built into the huge domed ceiling.

At the end of the vaulted corridor the two guards took a sharp left. Hidden behind a huge houseplant, an evergreen perennial with large, handsome basal leaves, was a small, narrow stairway panelled in oak. The first guard gripped the heavily carved railing tightly and carefully descended. Melvin and Lorraine were encouraged to follow him by the guard carrying the large brass key, who brought up the rear. Bronze lamps hung at irregular intervals from the low ceiling, but, unfortunately, they threw out little or no light. Despite her sensible shoes, Lorraine stumbled a couple of times in the dimness.

They guessed they had reached the bottom of the stairway when, after a minute or so, they felt a cold, uneven stone floor under their feet. They were in some kind of undercroft, and a little way ahead it was just possible to make out the vague outline of a large door in the semidarkness. The clang of the large brass key striking the metal door resonated through the gloom. A chink of light shone from the keyhole. Fortunately, it cast just enough glow for Melvin to see the guard struggling with the key. The guard, whose fingers were like sausages, was having difficulty locating it in the lock. Melvin reached out and guided the key into the hole for him. The guard swatted Melvin away with the back of his hand, pushed the key home, and turned it, all in one quick movement.

The large metal door opened towards them. A streak of light flowed forth suddenly and in great volume through the gap, like water gushing from a hydrant. Melvin and Lorraine shielded their eyes from the glare as they were pushed and shoved one final time into the cell. Before they had a chance to react, the door shut behind them with a metallic thump.

The cell was small and damp. It was illuminated by a dazzling, purplish-red light that shone through the bars of the little window situated high up on the far wall. Behind the door was a pump and a storage tank with three thick, black iron pipes coming out of it that disappeared through the wall in three different directions. Four oak beams spanned the length of the room from the door to the window. Below the window there was a wooden bench. On the bench was a cardboard box. It contained broken porcelain cups, saucers, side plates, and a teapot with its spout missing.

Lorraine listened to the guard's leather sandals on the stone floor and waited to hear them climbing up the oak stairway before beating the metal door with her fists in frustration.

The door moved! Just a touch, but there was movement without a doubt.

Melvin heard Lorraine's audible gasp. He watched as she placed the palms of her hands flat against the door, and with her fingers outstretched she persuaded it to move some more. Remarkably, he saw it open, first by millimetres, then centimetres, and finally wide enough to put her head through.

There wasn't time to dwell on why the big brass key was still in the unlocked door. There wasn't time, either, to consider the reasons why the guards hadn't secured the door before they left. There just wasn't time to ponder these matters. They had to move quickly.

So they did. They moved quickly across the stone floor of the undercroft and up the oak stairway, fully expecting, at any moment, to come face to face with the two guards. By now they would have realised they had forgotten the key and remembered they hadn't even locked the door and would surely be heading back down the stairs. They stopped under the faint light of a bronze lamp and listened. All was quiet, which was encouraging. Melvin reached out and grasped Lorraine's hand tightly, and together they ran. Two steps at a time they ran. All the way to the top without stopping they ran.

From behind the giant aspidistra, they took the opportunity to catch their breath and observe the comings and goings of the strange dream folk who inhabit the central areas of the palace. Men in dark blue overalls wearing tool belts and tall, slender ladies with pale faces and bright red lipstick were buzzing to and fro and in and out of the enormous six-sided hall like a swarm of bees in a hive. Dream actors, too, dressed in scary costumes passed by, but even scarier than that were the two guards striding purposefully across the parquet floor in their direction.

Melvin and Lorraine cowered behind a cluster of large leaves as the guards stomped past. Hardly daring to move a muscle, they watched the guards disappear down the oak stairway. Melvin reasoned it would take the guards quite a while to reach the empty cell and, due to the steepness of the stairs, even longer to return to the summit. They had a good few minutes' start, but they needed to make every second of it count. Hurriedly, they slipped away from the great central hall along the vaulted corridor and into the first of the impressive rooms. It was a room of rich furnishings, lamps, easy chairs, tables, and, of course, plants. The room was dominated by the fireplace. The facing of the fireplace was green and blue glass mosaic with touches of purple. Above it was a portrait, specially painted to harmonize with the colours of the mantel, of another brave dream hero: a king by the name of Arthur wielding a magical dream sword.

But fireplaces and paintings were of no interest at all to the two teenagers at this point. They were more interested in putting as much distance as possible between themselves and the two guards. They set about achieving this by moving swiftly from room to room. They deliberately avoided the time-worn trail in the carpet, now showing the effects of countless eras of use, deciding instead to keep to an area away from the middle where it was safer. This proved fortunate; on a couple of occasions their rapid progress was held up by the sound of approaching footsteps. On each of these occasions, though, they managed to hide behind one of the many examples of native flora or a conveniently placed vase until the danger had passed. Finally, their escape to freedom brought them back to the library, the enclosed anteroom, and, at last, the great curtain.

#

A head of tightly curled ginger hair appeared through the gap in the curtain. Two eyes surveyed the room, aided by a pair of blue-rimmed glasses that rested firmly on the bridge of his freckled nose. He saw that the spacious lounge was now virtually empty apart from seven or eight dream actors who had pushed two tables together and were talking quietly amongst themselves on the right-hand side of the room.

A moment later another head emerged. This one had cornrow braids. "Is the coast clear?" she asked. Her ebony face was reddened from exertion.

The first head nodded. "It appears our luck is holding out," he replied.

"You're right," Lorraine agreed. "We've been lucky so far." She observed the spacious drawing room. The last time she had seen this room it was filled to the brim with bizarre characters: dream actors dressed as monsters, muscular guards, and of course Vile himself. Now, apart from a few dream actors, it was quiet. The atmosphere was calm, peaceful, even tranquil.

At the far end of the room, below the tiered chandelier, was the top of the graceful staircase. "Let's go," said Melvin as he pulled back the curtain.

Lorraine was worried. If she was surprised that the dream actors hadn't heard the screech of the curtain as it travelled along the heavy duty curved track or puzzled that they hadn't reacted when Melvin banged his knee on one of the white caned seats, then she was amazed that they weren't disturbed by the thump-thump of her heartbeat, a sound so deafening to her that it seemed to fill the room.

Yet they were able to creep across the carpet as silently as snowfall in the night. The dream actors were leaning forward over the tables in a huddle, as if they were discussing some top-secret business, so Melvin and

Lorraine were able to pass by unnoticed. They tiptoed down the stairs and irresistibly on until they reached the bottom step. The light from the chandelier, high above the staircase, struggled to penetrate the poorly lit grand entrance hall below.

"There it is," Lorraine whispered. She peered through the gloom towards the solid reddish brown door as the columns and arches cast eerie shadows across the pink and white marble floor. "I hope after all this it isn't locked," she added.

"Only one way to find out." Melvin smiled nervously.

So without further delay they took a step in the direction of the mahogany exit. Before they could take a second step a light flickered. Then another one blinked on, closely followed by another. In no time at all the grand entrance hall was bathed in vivid fluorescent light.

Someone coughed. They spun round. On the landing where the stairs divided into two stood a familiar figure.

"Going somewhere?" said the familiar figure with a familiar voice.

Melvin and Lorraine stood like statues, paralysed by fear, as Vile descended the staircase slowly towards them.

Chapter 18

What is the well-dressed wizard about town wearing this season? Mugwump stepped out of the portal sporting a designer ankle-length black robe with large gold stars. The sleeves had a touch of ermine at the wrists, and the hem was decorated with a series of looped stitches of golden thread. He had accessorised the outfit with a rope-tie fastened at the waist with a bright metallic yellow brooch. His black hat tapered to a very sharp point high above his head, and to complete the impressive ensemble he wore a pair of topaz slippers.

He did a quick twirl on an imaginary catwalk as Mr Good materialised out of thin air too. "How fortuitously marvellous and marvellously fortuitous to bump into you, old chum." Mr Good beamed.

"Salmon," said Mugwump with a grin. He had a round, jolly face with rosy red cheeks. Tufts of curly hair the colour of straw peeked out from under his pointy hat.

Arthur was the next to appear. "Where are we?" he asked, looking around inquisitively.

"At the centre of the royal blue labyrinth, of course," said Mr Good happily.

"My dear fellow," said the wizard with a bow. "Welcome to my residence."

Arthur was too exhausted to acknowledge the greeting. Instead, he collapsed in a heap on the sofa. It was a chocolate-brown sofa with cream, rust, and white stripes and shiny chrome highlight strips on the arms. A rainbow of brown, orange, tan, and yellow wallpaper adorned the walls of the labyrinth's final turn. Although Mugwump wore the latest wizardy fashions by top dream designers, his residence was well and truly stuck in a 1970s time warp.

I chose you for a reason, a very important reason. Without you the plan will fail. If the plan fails, the consequences for the physical world will be catastrophic. You are a vital part of my plan.

Mr Good's words were still reverberating inside Arthur's head as he closed his eyes.

Mugwump took the opportunity to examine the old man's features. "Interesting," he remarked as he leaned closer. "Very interesting."

Mr Good hoped that his selection had met with Mugwump's approval. "The likeness is incredible, don't you think?" he asked.

The wizard didn't reply immediately. He stood up and moved quickly over to a teak sideboard situated against the wall behind the sofa. It had a section of four graduated drawers. The top drawer had removable dividers for cutlery, the second drawer was where he stored his odds and ends, and the third drawer was for his bits and pieces. The bottom drawer was where he hid his golden wand.

The wand felt ice cold in his grasp. He knew as he waved it around a bit, his own body heat would flow through it. He stood over Arthur, and after a ritual recitation of a few magic words under his breath, the wand began to sizzle like a red-hot poker.

Arthur was still resting his eyes when a few random hairs began to appear at the centre of his upper lip. In both directions, the whiskers began to grow at an alarming rate across the width of his face. In a matter of seconds he had a long, impressive moustache, slightly curled and pointed upwards at the ends.

From the bits and pieces drawer Mugwump hurriedly removed a magnifying glass. He used it to inspect Arthur's face carefully and critically.

"Well?" Mr Good pressed the wizard for an answer as he sat on one of the matching cream armchairs and waited.

"Uncanny," Mugwump whispered as he continued his detailed inspection of Arthur's countenance. "You have chosen well, Mr Good."

The Dream Ambassador for Tranquil Dreams breathed a huge sigh of relief.

"I'm beginning to think this salmon of yours ... I mean, plan of yours might just work."

"Plan!" The first thing that Arthur saw was an enormous eye looking at him through a convex lens just inches away from his own rather large nose.

"What are you staring at?" he demanded. He wanted to sit bolt upright, but his lumbago prevented it. "Will one of you please tell me what is going on here?"

Mugwump took a step backwards and placed the heavy brass and shell magnifying glass back in its protective pouch.

"Not to worry," said Mr Good kindly as he sat down next to Arthur on the sofa. "All will be revealed when the others arrive."

"Others?"

Mr Good left Arthur to ponder on who the others might be. He placed the palm of his hand on the small of the wizard's back and steered him a safe distance away. "I need your help, old chum," he said with a soft, hushed tone. "The plan isn't going ... to plan."

Mr Good glanced over his shoulder. Arthur was watching them, but he was too far away to hear what he was about to tell Mugwump. He was about to tell Mugwump that he had only found one visitor when he had summoned three.

Mugwump smiled. "You've lost two visitors?"

Mugwump listened as Mr Good explained. He heard how Mr Good had become increasingly impatient waiting here at the centre of the royal blue labyrinth and how he decided to leave to meet the visitors halfway. But he didn't meet the visitors halfway, or even three-quarters of the way; in fact, he didn't meet any of them anywhere at all, apart from Arthur, of course, whom he met in the white room.

Arthur thought he heard his name mentioned. Mr Good gave him a smile and a little wave.

"The white room? That's quite a journey without a handheld Dream Navigation Device complete with a built-in Portal Locater," said Mugwump, amazed. The wizard finally appreciated the seriousness of the situation. Two visitors were lost somewhere in Limbo. He contemplated Mr Good's predicament for a long moment as he sat on one of the six chairs around the teak dining table.

Mr Good sighed. "I have left messages for them to meet me at the centre of the royal blue labyrinth during all their recent dreams," he replied. "In the part of the mind just below the level of conscious perception."

"Then they should be here. They should be here already." Mugwump didn't know much about the transmitting of messages to the subconscious

83

of folk in the physical world. It wasn't really his area of expertise. But he knew enough to know that the part of the mind just below the level of conscious perception was a good spot. "It doesn't make sense," he concluded.

"It doesn't make sense at all," Mr Good agreed. "It's most peculiar."

Peculiar? The word triggered a lever in the area of Mugwump's brain that stored his short-term memory. It released a spring that, in turn, precipitated a series of reactions. "That reminds me," he announced excitedly as he stood up and fumbled in the pocket of his black robe. "There are other peculiar things afoot out there in Limbo, Mr Good."

"Oh?" asked Mr Good curiously. "What sort of peculiar things?"

"Well, someone has chalked hopscotch squares on the floor of the pink passageway." From his pocket he produced a soft, white, powdery limestone stick. "And here is the salmon."

Mr Good took the chalk stick and held it between his thumb and forefinger before placing it flat on the palm of his other hand. He examined it closely.

"That's not all," continued the wizard. From deep inside another pocket he removed a small bean bag. "I found this too."

As Mr Good stared at the two unusual objects he felt a steadily escalating sense of foreboding. It was a sense of impending misfortune that he couldn't shake off. "Tell me, old chum," he asked as the foreboding increased a little bit more. "Can you recall anything remotely similar ever happening before?"

Mugwump gave it a little thought and shook his head slowly. "I once found a water pistol in the magnolia maze down in the Nether Regions," he remembered. "That must have been five eras ago now. But hopscotch?" There were no matches for hopscotch anywhere in his long-term memory database. "Never!"

Could it be? Could Vile be at the bottom of all this peculiarity? Mr Good was beginning to believe it was probable as his sense of foreboding scaled new heights. "I need your help," he reiterated after a worry-filled pause. Behind his silver beard there was no hiding the concern and the apprehension on his face. Yet despite all this, his deep blue eyes still sparkled with kindness. "I need you to go out there into Limbo, old chum, and find the visitors."

As a fully paid-up member of the good guy club, Mugwump was more than willing to nip out and round up the two visitors. He was eager to see Mr Good's plan up and running. He was determined to see Vile sent back to Torment Towers where he belonged, with the rest of his entourage. He dreaded to think what nightmares the unsuspecting folk in the physical world were about to suffer. He wanted so much to see Mr Good return to the Palace of Somnium and resume the pleasant, happy dreams with the beautiful colours and the pretty flowers before it was too late. Besides, it would be nice to have his residence to himself again. "Leave it to me," he replied. "I'm on my way."

Arthur watched as the wizard disappeared through a row of colourful beads hanging in an invisible doorway.

Chapter 19

"Ouch! Get off!"

"Let go! You're hurting!"

Vile maintained a secure grasp of their earlobes. "You're not escaping, are you?" he said with a grin. "Not after what I said."

"Escaping?" laughed Melvin nervously. "No, of course not. We were …"

"Just popping out," explained Lorraine despite the acute physical discomfort she was experiencing.

"Popping out?" Vile had never heard such impudence. He gave the soft, fleshy, pendulous lower part of her ear a painful twist.

She winced. "For pity's sake! That hurt!"

"Nobody pops out!"

"Well, let me put it this way. We …"

Lorraine interrupted Melvin again. "We're going to find Mr Good."

"Loz!"

"Well, it's true."

"Yes, but –" Melvin attempted to mollify the angry Vile by speaking gently. "All we intended to do was leave, find Mr Good, cheer him up, and come back before anyone had missed us."

Vile eyed Melvin suspiciously for a long moment. "Come off it."

"We were!" Melvin insisted. "We are! We are going to come back. Afterwards. Honestly. We do like it here. Don't we, Loz?"

Lorraine glowered. "I don't want to spend another minute in this rotten place!"

"Loz!" Melvin groaned. She wasn't really helping with his efforts as a peacemaker.

"We're leaving!" announced Lorraine as she forced her ear away from Vile's grip. Immediately, she grabbed Melvin's arm and managed to pull him clear too. In doing so, she lost her balance, and they both fell backwards on to the ground. Lorraine hit her head hard on the pink and white marble floor. Melvin was unhurt. Fortunately, Lorraine had cushioned his fall.

Vile stood over them menacingly. "I've been quite reasonable for quite long enough with you pesky kids," he growled.

"Reasonable?" Lorraine scoffed. She sat up, rubbing the back of her head. "You had us thrown in a cell!" she pointed out.

"Yes, I did," admitted Vile with a smirk. "But I had you thrown in the most luxurious cell."

"Luxurious cell?" It was Melvin who scoffed this time.

"The one with tea-making facilities," explained Vile.

"Do you mean that old teapot?" This was Melvin's second scoff. "It had a broken spout."

"Look!" Vile was annoyed. There was too much scoffing going on for his liking. "What did you expect? A five-star hotel?"

Melvin wanted to tell him that he didn't really expect a five-star hotel, and Lorraine wanted to say that they hadn't done anything wrong, so she didn't expect to be held prisoner at all, actually. They wanted him to know that they weren't here, in his world, by choice, and they wanted to explain to him that there must be some sort of mistake and they just wanted to go home. They wanted to mention all those things, but they couldn't because Vile was kicking their shins and shouting at them to stand up.

With a little help from each other they climbed to their feet slowly.

"Now that we've established that I have been reasonable," Vile addressed them calmly, "I think you'll find, from now on, I'll tend to be a touch more unreasonable."

He sniggered. "I'm going to teach you pesky kids a lesson. I'm going to …" His voice suddenly trailed off as if he were lost in a state of unpleasant dreamy thought.

His unpleasant dreamy thoughts were clearly troubling him greatly. Melvin and Lorraine spent an anxious few moments watching Vile's face contort and twist.

"How did you escape?" he asked after a lengthy pause. "That cell is impregnable. Not even my guards with all their brawn could force their way through that metal door in a hurry."

He prodded Melvin's chest with a bony finger. "Look at you! Specky four eyes! You're puny!" Vile moved closer and stared him in the eyes. "Tell me how you did it," he demanded.

"It wasn't locked." It was Lorraine who answered.

Vile shifted his focus from Melvin to the girl. "What? What did you say?"

"It wasn't locked," she repeated. "Physique didn't really play a part." She smiled. "Because the guards didn't lock the door."

The guards didn't lock the door? He recited the words several times in his head before he could fully comprehend their meaning. The guards didn't lock the door! Vile was incensed. He was infuriated. His anger was not so much with the guards; he already knew they were imbeciles. He would punish them later, of course, by dipping them in a vat of cold porridge or something. For now he was more annoyed with Lorraine's smarty-pants smile. He looked at her with contempt. "I'm going to wipe that grin off your face."

But before he could do any wiping of grins off faces he was interrupted by a most unexpected source.

"Can I just say something at this point?"

Vile turned and looked up in surprise.

Garry stood at the top of the staircase. With his right hand the dream actor held on to the solid oak rail. In his left hand he held a large cream envelope. "Can I just say something at this point?" he asked again.

"What are you doing here, Norman?" Vile frowned. "Shouldn't you be doing something mind-numbingly uninteresting, like knitting, or whatever it is you do between dream spans."

"I was just wondering ... if I could just say something at this point?"

Vile sighed. "Yes, yes. Get on with it, man!"

"I understand," Garry began nervously, "those two children will be seeing ..." He hesitated. "Do you think they would give him this?" He held out the cream envelope.

"Give who? What?" Vile was confused and getting angrier by the second.

"It's a get-well-soon card," explained Garry. "I believe he hasn't been feeling too well. I was hoping the children could give it to him. To Mr Good."

Vile was livid. "They will not be leaving. No one, I repeat no one, leaves!"

"Yes, but –"

"But nothing!" snapped Vile. "Look, when I've finished being wicked and nasty with these pesky kids, I'm going to injure you in some way, quite possibly fatally. Do I make myself clear?"

Garry stood small and mouse-like on the staircase and nodded timidly.

"But for now, shut up and run along." Vile waved him away and shook his head in despair. "A get-well-soon card! What rot!" he muttered to himself as he turned back to face Melvin and Lorraine, ready to resume his wicked and nasty ways.

But Melvin and Lorraine were gone. And the hand-crafted, solid mahogany arched door was ajar.

#

On the other side of the door the pink and white marble flooring continued along a narrow passageway for about twenty paces. Vile reached the corridors of Limbo in a maniacal frenzy.

"Of all the sneaky, dirty rotten tricks!" he screamed as he reached a junction where a cyan, a magenta and a yellow corridor came together. He stopped to consider his options. He wasn't particularly fond of any of the colours; they were too bright and cheerful for his liking. He made a mental note to have all the corridors in the general vicinity of the palace painted black or something darker.

He chose the magenta corridor and immediately set off in hot pursuit. Well, it was more of a lukewarm pursuit, actually, but it was the fastest he could go. He wasn't sure, of course, if the pesky kids had passed this way or not, but he desperately hoped so. It had taken him many eras to get the palace off Mr Good, and he wasn't going to give it up now without a fight.

"They must not escape!" he screamed over and over again as he ran blindly through the maze. He took left turns and he took right turns, but the passages tended to coil around and run back into each other, and so he spent all his time going round in circles instead of bumping into dead ends as in other mazes. Each time he shifted his direction he also shifted his awareness from the right side of his brain to the left side. This made him dizzy.

He stumbled on gamely, but in the end it was a sudden sharp pain in his side that stopped him. He fell back against the magenta wall, breathing rapidly in short, laboured gasps, and bent over double in distress and exhaustion.

"Now," he managed to say in a low-pitched, rasping voice, "I'm angry!"

#

"Excuse me?" Garry exited tentatively through the mahogany door. "Hello."

He listened but heard nothing apart from his own voice reflecting off the walls of the corridors ahead.

"Is there anybody there?" he called out weakly as he proceeded nervously along the narrow passageway. "Can I just say something at this point?"

He was faced with the same three choices: cyan, magenta, or yellow. Actually, he had a fourth option: turning back. He looked around. The comfort and familiarity of the palace was tempting. He took a deep breath and resisted the temptation.

"This is my chance," he whispered, "to follow my dream."

He was about to enter the unknown, to embark on a journey to find Lord Riddle.

"I will," he decided. "I'm going to do it."

He took a step along the yellow corridor. He took another. Then he hesitated. "Maybe."

Chapter 20

Peggy Sue walked on to the dream stage to a ripple of applause and a few wolf whistles. They were surprised to see she was a vivacious and attractive girl with long, golden curls and a dazzling smile.

"Hello guys," she began. "I'd like to thank you all for giving up your free time to be here."

She wasn't aware that the assembled audience didn't really have a choice. Vile had sent them all a dream-mail explaining in no uncertain terms that if they didn't turn up they would be immersed in a vat full of a nasty, unpleasant sticky substance.

"Can everyone hear me?" she called out. The interior of the auditorium was overwhelming, with its predominant colours of cream and claret and its impressive ornate ceiling plasterwork. There was some nodding of heads in the stalls to confirm that they could.

"Can you all hear me up there in the cheap seats?" That was her little joke directed towards those sitting high up in the grand circle. Actually, nobody had paid to be here.

"Good. Right. As you know," she continued, "opening night of my uncle's new nightmare is just four dream spans away now."

They all knew, of course. They knew the nightmare would take the form of virtual reality. The illusion would be so complete as to be immersive and rendered in three dimensions, which would completely surround the dream person. There wasn't a dream actor who didn't shudder at the thought of it. There wasn't a dream actor, either, who didn't wonder how this kind, considerate, and friendly girl could possibly be Vile's niece.

"I understand the 3D computer dream animation team have almost completed their artwork."

91

The dream actors also knew that the poor dream person would be able to experience and even interact with the artwork as if they were inside it.

"And you have all learned your lines and practised your scary faces." Her mouth curled into a smile. "So, that just leaves the big song and dance routine at the end."

An audible groan swept around the auditorium. They were actors, thespians. The prospect of singing and dancing didn't fill them with glee.

"I've been asked to choreograph the grand finale," she added.

Actually, she hadn't been asked. She had been told. Vile thought he was punishing her, but little did he know she loved music. She loved singing, and she loved dancing. She wanted to be a dance teacher or a voice coach. They were ambitions she didn't know she had, until recently. Until recently she had been a wild, sometimes boisterous girl who played rough games and enjoyed boyish things like wrestling, sword fighting, and climbing trees in abandoned Dreamspaces. But since her arrival at the palace she had changed. Something happened on that journey from Torment Towers with her uncle, Terrence, and the guards. Yet, for the life of her, she couldn't remember what it was. There was a gap in her memory.

Peggy Sue laughed. "What's this?" She cupped her ear with the palm of her hand. "Is that the sound of discontent I hear?"

The groans subsided, but the dissatisfaction in the audience was tangible.

"Look, guys. I promise it won't hurt." Her smile was incessant. "You never know, you may even enjoy it."

The dream actors sighed. It was a collective sigh of resignation. They had allowed themselves to be captivated by a warm and friendly smile.

"Obviously, this stage isn't anyway near big enough for all you guys," she told them. "But, nearer the time, once the coordinates for the Digital Dreamscaper have been set and a suitable corridor out there in Limbo has been selected, we should have the actual haunted house dream stage to rehearse on." She could hardly contain her excitement.

The dream actors, though, were completely and utterly underwhelmed.

"Meanwhile, what I want to do, guys, is see you all, in turn, in your groups, so we can run through a few things." From a pouch in her beautiful poppy-printed cotton dress she removed a couple of sheets of lavender notepaper.

"Firstly," she read, "can I have the werewolves?"

From somewhere up in the dress circle the werewolves made themselves known.

"Hi guys, can you make your way down to the stage please? Also, can I have –" She consulted her notes. "Can I have the ghosts?"

With her hand she shielded her eyes from the spotlight and peered out into the arena. "Where are the ghosts?" she asked. "Has anyone seen the ghosts?"

Nobody had.

#

"Maybe he's gone on ahead," suggested Harry.

"Yes," agreed Barry. "To make sure we get decent seats."

Larry wasn't so sure. "This is so unlike Garry," he reasoned. "He's far too shy and self-conscious to go into the theatre on his own."

They had found the very, very old book that he always read open and face down on his chair, but there was no sign at all of the quiet and timid dream actor. They searched high and low for him, but by this time they were running dangerously late. With the threat of Vile's dream-mail hanging over them, they hurriedly set off for the meeting.

As they entered the great central hall they met Terrence.

"Nice costumes," Terrence sniggered. "Don't tell me. Ghouls, right?"

"Ghosts!" The dream actors responded as one.

"Ghouls, ghosts. What's the difference?" said Terrence as he joined them on their brisk walk across the parquet floor. "Look, have you heard about the dwarf who got onto the basketball team?"

"No," Larry said, shaking his head. "I don't think so." He tried to recall if he had read an article about it in the *Dream Times*.

"He lied about his height." Terrence grinned.

Larry didn't.

"I don't think we have," said Barry. "Please tell us about it."

"I just have," Terrence whined. "That was it. He lied about his height. Get it?"

Barry didn't.

Terrence was undeterred. "What's the difference between an African elephant and an Indian elephant?"

The avenue they chose to leave the great central hall by had marble columns along the walls supporting a deep-coffered ceiling. The crimson flock wallpaper on a deep pink background complemented the red carpet.

"Hasn't one got larger ears or something?" asked Harry.

"Three thousand miles." Terrence grinned. "Get it?"

Harry didn't.

"Knock knock." Terrence didn't expect them to roll around on the floor laughing at his jokes, but a polite smile wasn't too much to ask for, surely. "Knock knock," he persisted.

The three dream actors looked at each other and shrugged.

"Now, you are supposed to say, 'who's there'."

Larry was puzzled. "Who's where?"

Terrence was struggling to keep pace with them. "At the door," he said. "I've just knocked the door." His little legs had to work overtime to keep up. "Knock knock."

The three dream actors looked at each other and shrugged once more.

"What door?" asked Barry, confused.

"It's an imaginary door," Terrence explained. "I've just knocked an imaginary door. Now you say to me, 'who's there'!"

Harry thought about this for a moment. "Why should we ask who's there? You've just told us it's you!"

Terrence frowned. "Yes, but I'm on the other side of the imaginary door, you see. So, you don't know who I am, and you don't know my name. Okay?"

"We do," said Harry confidently. "You're Terrence."

"Yes, I know. But –" He was gradually losing the will to live. "For the duration of this joke, I'm not. I've got another name. Understand?"

They didn't.

"Look." He sighed. "It's quite simple. When I say 'knock knock', just reply, 'who's there?' Will you do that?" The avenue of marble columns opened out into a large carpeted piazza before continuing on its way at a right angle. "Will you?"

The gentle sound of splashing water from the water feature at the centre of the deserted open space was intended to have a cool, calming effect. However, it wasn't working for Terrence. "Will one of you just say 'who's there?'" he pleaded. He was neither cool nor calm.

In the corner of the piazza between two columns was the impressive glass façade of the Dream Theatre. Terrence raced ahead of the dream actors and stood at the entrance, barring their way.

They were running very late. They couldn't afford any hold ups. So, Larry said it. "Who's there?" he said.

"Matthew!" responded Terrence, quicker than a flash.

The three dream actors looked at each other and shrugged yet again.

"Matthew!" he repeated, louder this time and with just a touch of desperation.

"What do you want, Matthew?" asked Barry hesitantly.

"What!" Terrence was becoming increasingly exasperated with each passing moment. "I don't want anything!"

"So, if you don't want anything," yelled Harry, "why are you knocking the door?"

The dream actors had had enough of this. They pushed their way forcibly past Terrence, and in doing so they knocked him flying to the ground. Two glass doors glided from each direction on an overhead track, sliding past each other.

Terrence sat in the doorway and watched their rapid, nimble feet make their way quickly across the foyer. "Aren't you just a teeny, weeny bit interested to know what my other name is?" he shouted after them. "Obviously, the knock knock joke was a bit complicated for you. Okay, try this one. What's blue and has yellow wheels?"

The dream actors disappeared through a curtained door that led to the rear stalls area.

"Oh, forget it!" he mumbled to himself. "I've got more important things to do than waste my time talking to those bozos."

He stood up and brushed himself down.

"Very important things, actually," he whispered. "I need to talk to Peg."

#

The auditorium held two gold-painted box seats situated at the edges of the dress circle to the left and right of the stage. It was in the box to the right of the stage that Terrence suddenly appeared. He saw the love of his life, and his heart leapt.

"Peg," he called out.

She was just running through a new dance move with a couple of werewolves. She stopped in mid-step and looked up in the direction of the voice. In contrast, her heart sank.

"Terry." She tried to smile but couldn't quite manage it.

"We need to talk, Peg."

"This really isn't the time or the place, Terry."

"It never is the right time or the right place, just lately," he sulked.

Peggy Sue didn't appreciate her private life being acted out on such a public stage. "Not here!" She glared at him with a face like thunder. "Not now!"

Terrence knew it was pointless to argue with her when she wore that thunder face. So instead he retreated to the back of the box and sat in moody silence for a while.

Chapter 21

Lorraine was doubled up with her hands on her knees breathing rapidly in short gasps. They had run nonstop through three mazes and two labyrinths until they physically couldn't run a step farther.

"I think we're safe now," said Melvin, looking back along the dark, greenish-blue corridor as if he didn't quite believe his own words.

"I'm so pleased we got away from that place," panted Lorraine. "That dream actor …"

"Garry."

"Yes, Garry." Lorraine nodded. "He came along at just the right moment. As if …"

"As if he was helping us."

Lorraine contemplated this for a moment. "What do you think Vile will do to him?"

"I dread to think." Melvin shuddered.

#

Keith didn't really know what to hope for when he left the white room, but he was half expecting someone to be waiting to meet him when he landed. Failing that, maybe he would find a big arrow with the words 'this way' written on it. Unfortunately, he had been left alone to get on with it. He wasn't an expert on shades of blue by any means, but even he knew that the corridor he found himself on wasn't the royal blue labyrinth. It was more of a deep bluish green colour.

So he started walking. Walking along a labyrinth is not difficult, unless you accidentally get turned around halfway through and make your way back to the beginning again. And that is exactly what Keith managed to do – twice. Without knowing it, he had walked and walked for miles and not really reached anywhere. And in all those hours he hadn't met a soul ... until now.

Up ahead, with their backs to him, he came upon two suspicious-looking characters.

#

"It was a brigantine merchant ship just entering the Bay of Gibraltar, and when they went aboard they discovered that Captain Briggs, his entire crew, and all the passengers had mysteriously disappeared. There were no signs of a struggle or anything. Everything was neat and tidy. There were just no people."

"That's the oddest story, Melvin."

"A similar thing happened at a lighthouse on Flannan Isle in 1900," continued Melvin. "Three lighthouse keepers disappeared in the same mysterious circumstances. It was seriously weird."

"Do you think that all those missing people from the *Mary Celeste* and the lighthouse came here?" Lorraine marvelled. "To Dream Land?"

"Who can say?" Melvin shrugged. "But those Dream Actors implied that slipping from there to here didn't happen too often. Six times in the last seven or eight eras, they told us."

Lorraine nodded. "Whatever that means." She smiled.

#

Keith chose to interrupt the plotting and the scheming of the suspicious characters with a gentle, well-timed cough. Judging by their startled expressions, it had the desired effect. He instantly followed up the cough with a question. "And who might you be?" he asked as he approached them.

It took a few seconds for the shock of a Boy Scout, pulling a suitcase, creeping up behind them to subside.

"Who are you?" was Melvin's response.

"I asked first," said Keith.

Melvin had to concede he was right. "Well, I'm Melvin, and this is Lorraine. That's short for Loz." He faltered. "Or something like that."

Keith wasn't really interested in their names; they were most probably aliases anyway. He didn't trust them. His second question was ready and waiting to be asked. "Why are you sneaking around?"

"Sneaking around?" cried Lorraine. "We're not sneaking around. You are!"

"I'm not!" replied Keith.

"So, who are you?" Melvin asked again.

"If you must know," he said with a sigh, "my name is Keith, and I have been summoned."

Lorraine's jaw dropped. "By Mr Good?"

"So, if you could point me in the direction of the royal blue labyrinth, I'll be on my way." A smile dimpled his face.

"Is that where Mr Good is?" asked Lorraine excitedly. "At the royal blue labyrinth?"

"My lips are sealed." He pulled an imaginary zip across his mouth.

"You see, we think we've been summoned by Mr Good too," she told him. "We've met him, and he seemed awfully sad, and –"

"Look!" Keith interjected. "The royal blue labyrinth." He pointed in a hopeful manner along the corridor. "This way, is it?"

"We want to cheer him up, you see," Lorraine persisted.

"We need his help to return to our bedrooms," added Melvin.

"If I tell you any more you'll probably rush off and tell nightmare guy everything." Keith gave them his leeriest stare. "And the plan will be ruined."

"Plan?"

"What plan?" If Melvin's curiosity hadn't been aroused before, it certainly was now.

"Gosh and double gosh!" Keith frowned. "I didn't mean to mention the plan. But now that I have, forget that I ever brought it up."

"Mr Good has a plan." Lorraine smiled.

"A plan to oust Vile and return to the palace, I shouldn't wonder." Melvin smiled too.

Keith eyed them suspiciously. "You both seem very interested. I just knew you were in cahoots with the nightmare guy."

"We're not!" Melvin protested. "Vile had us thrown in a cell."

"And he twisted my ear." Lorraine turned her head and presented a red, tender lobe as evidence.

Keith was far from convinced. With his back pressed up against the wall, he edged closer by moving sideways with short, sliding steps. He had to admit it was very smart of the nightmare guy to send two of his cronies to pose as schoolchildren and pretend to be friendly in an effort to lure him into his dubious clutches.

"I just thought," said Melvin as he watched Keith gradually shuffle nearer, "seeing as we're all searching for Mr Good, maybe we could walk together."

"Together!" Keith almost choked. "Not likely!" He had been forewarned to be wary of everyone and not to trust a soul, so he wasn't about to be fooled. "If it's all the same with you, I'll find my own way." He moved carefully along the corridor, maintaining continuous contact with the wall.

Melvin stood aside to allow Keith and his plum and grey suitcase to pass by.

Keith counted ten strides before he even considered stopping. Just to be on the safe side, he took three more and turned. "The first time I saw you two," he called to them, "I just knew you were untrustworthy sorts."

Melvin and Lorraine watched Keith backpedal a couple of paces, turn on his heels, walk briskly away, and disappear around the curve of the Prussian blue corridor.

"And I thought I had an honest face." Melvin smiled.

"Obviously not." Lorraine grinned as they set off too, but in the opposite direction.

Chapter 22

Vile's anger continued unabated.

He grabbed the joystick like it was Terrence's neck. He panned left and right, tilted up and down, and zoomed in and out, but the pesky kids were nowhere to be seen. He yanked the joystick clean out of its socket and hurled it across the room.

"Where's Terrence?" He paced back and forth a bit, diagonally, like a bishop on a giant chess board, stepping only on the dark blue carpet tiles. "Where the heck is he?"

Something inside his head was enjoying this.

Outwitted by a couple of schoolchildren. I told you they were smart. Mr Good is coming home. Pack your bags, loser!

He decided he'd had enough of pacing. He needed to sit. It had suddenly become very warm under his collar. He slumped into the black leather swivel chair and loosened his tie. "Where is that lazy, good-for-nothing layabout?"

"You called, your filthiness?"

With all the teasing, taunting, and provoking going on in his head he hadn't heard the door open. "Terrence." He grinned. "There you are, at last." He slipped effortlessly into sarcasm mode. "Nice of you to saunter over. Met some old friends on the way, did you? Got chatting, is that it?" He stood up and stepped from behind his spacious walnut desk.

"I came as quickly as I could, your surliness."

"I haven't interrupted anything, have I?" Vile approached him slowly. "You weren't doing anything of importance, were you?"

Terrence shook his head and wondered where all this was leading.

"I haven't called you at an inconvenient time, then? You weren't feeding the cat or anything vital like that, I hope?"

"No, your ghastliness. Not at all. Nothing that you could call vital. Actually, I've been watching Peg."

Vile's eyes narrowed.

"The rehearsals at the Dream Theatre," he explained.

Of course: Opening night, with the big song and dance routine at the end. With everything that was going on here he had almost forgotten about the grand finale. Those pesky kids were distracting him. They were threatening to ruin everything.

"Is there something wrong, sir?" asked Terrence as Vile disappeared behind his back.

"Something wrong?" he replied from somewhere behind him.

Terrence stood like a guard on sentry duty, his eyes fixed straight ahead, as Vile reappeared on the other side and began pacing to and fro.

"I do believe there is something wrong, but for the life of me I can't think what it is." He pondered as he paced to. "The washing-up's done, and the plants have been watered." He paced fro. "The windows are clean, and my shirts are ironed." To. "Three people have escaped, and the cat's fed." Fro.

"What?" Terrence gasped as he made eye contact with Vile for the first time. It was a gape, a prolonged, open-mouthed one. "What did you say?"

Vile stopped in mid-fro and returned Terrence's gape with a hard, piercing stare. "The palace cat," he repeated, "has been fed."

Terrence let out a long, deep breath. "For a moment there I thought you said that three people had escaped."

"I did!" Vile took a step or two closer "Three people have escaped, you halfwit!" He placed his considerable nose and his ample chin less than an inch from Terrence's moist face. "Now give me one good reason why I shouldn't kill you."

"What? Kill me?" Terrence gulped. "Why?"

Vile considered those questions carefully and at length as he circled him once more, slowly this time and without saying a word. "Terrence," he said as he came back into view. "Do you remember going out earlier to lure two kids here for me?" He sat on the edge of his desk, folded his arms, and waited.

"You mean the ones you had the feeling about? The pesky ones?"

"Exactly. The pesky ones. You do remember."

"I heard you had them thrown in the cell, your rottenness."

"Well." He paused. "They've escaped."

Only one question popped into Terrence's head at this point as he stood there in a state of discomfort, and it wasn't how did the pesky kids escape. The question on his lips was how this could possibly be his fault. "What have I done?" he asked.

"You're the reason they've escaped," replied Vile with a dark scowl.

"Me? But I don't see ..."

"Did you or did you not act daft?"

"Yes, of course," said Terrence. "A total loony. You would have been proud of me."

Vile banged his fist on the desk, sending drawing pins and paper clips scurrying for cover. "Proud of you? I couldn't possibly be proud of you! You simpleton! You're a constant embarrassment to me. You're an imbecile, do you know that?"

Another question popped into his head now. How was he going to get out of this alive? "Yes, your revoltingness." Terrence nodded nervously. "I am aware of that."

Vile stood and moved around to the front of his desk. "The object of the exercise was to act a touch eccentric, a little erratic perhaps, a wee odd maybe, slightly peculiar even. Just enough to make them think that the Dream Ambassador for Tranquil Dreams would be best left alone. So, therefore, they would have settled here, quite happily and out of harm's way. Agreed?"

"Well, yes, of course." He trembled. "But ..."

"But what do you do?" He sat in his black leather swivel chair again and rested his elbows on the armrests. "An over-the-top, no-holds-barred, twenty-four-carat, crazy, loony performance with knobs on! And what happens? Well, they feel sorry for you, don't they. So they escape to try and find you, don't they. To try and cheer you up, can you believe? Of course they think it's Mr Good they're looking for. I shudder to think what will happen if they find the real one. It could be the end for us. Do you understand?"

Terrence lowered and raised his head quickly to show that he did.

Vile sat forward and looked him up and down. "I want those pesky kids back."

Terrence took a step back towards the door like a convicted criminal at the gallows who had been pardoned by the governor. "I'm on my way, your depravedness."

"Take three guards with you. The ones with the biggest muscles would be a fine idea," Vile advised. "And when you find them, no acting daft this time. Use force. Now off you go, you blockhead."

Terrence hesitated in the doorway.

"Yes, what is it?" Vile barked.

Something occurred to him. Vile had spared his life, and now perhaps he could push his luck a little. He wondered if this might be the moment to ask him for Peggy Sue's hand in marriage. A quick glance at the expression on Vile's face, however, told him it probably wasn't a good time. Something else occurred to him. "Three? Did you say three people had escaped?"

Vile grimaced. "I did indeed, Terrence. One of those dream actors has escaped, too. One of those Normans. Can you believe it? With the opening night of my new nightmare four dream spans away, I'm an actor short. What am I going to do?"

Terrence shrugged.

"I'll tell you, shall I?" He pointed a long, thin index finger at Terrence. "You are going to take his place."

"Me?" Terrence's face turned ashen. "But I'm not an actor."

"He only had one line. Even you should be able to manage that. All you have to say is: 'Can I just say something at this point?' See? Piece of cake. Try it."

"Can ... I ... just ... say ... something ... at ... this ... point," repeated Terrence blandly.

"Pathetic," groaned Vile. "But it will have to do. Now go before I change my mind about killing you."

He watched as Terrence reached for the doorknob. "You need to find those pesky kids before Mr Good does. Do I make myself clear?"

"Crystal," Terrence replied as he pulled the door open. "You can rely on me, your deceitfulness. I ..."

"Oh, just go, will you!"

Terrence backed out apologetically and closed the door gently behind him, leaving Vile alone with whatever it was that was making itself comfortable inside his head.

What will you do if Mr Good finds the pesky kids first?

"That would be unbearable."

What if he finds them before you do?

"I don't even want to think about that."

But what will you do if he does?

"I said I don't want to think about it."

Perhaps you should start packing your bags.

"Oh, shut up!"

He took a long deep breath and let it out slowly. "Talking to myself? Out loud?" He stood up in a daze, walked round his desk, trod on the joystick, kicked it as far as he could, made a mental note to call maintenance, and decided it might be best if he had a lie down in a darkened room somewhere.

Chapter 23

Melvin and Lorraine swept round a corner, fully expecting to come face to face with yet another dead end. They had left the palace by the cyan maze. Then it was cobalt blue, and that was a maze too. They circumnavigated a couple of labyrinths – cerulean blue and monestial blue – before solving the ultramarine maze. Prussian blue was proving a tougher nut to crack, though, with its trick corners and its blind alleys. Since their encounter with Keith, the untrusting Boy Scout, their progress had been halted by a succession of cul-de-sacs.

What they saw, when they turned this particular corner, surprised them. The Prussian blue maze came to a sudden halt, but it wasn't a dead end this time. Someone, at some time, had passed this way and used a Digital Dreamscaper here. The Dreamspace it created, however, was not as picturesque as the other two they'd visited previously.

They walked out into the bright sunlight onto a large paved area: an enormous patio that stretched maybe two hundred paces to the foot of a tall building. It was not a skyscraper but a tower block that reached up towards the clouds, all windows and concrete. Two more identical high-rise structures stood away to their left and right. Turning round they saw three others behind them.

Running between these very tall buildings were rows of three-storey maisonettes, like long, triple-decker trains, spreading out in different directions, interconnected by concourses, deck access landings, and footbridges. These walkways in the sky gave the impression that one could orbit this urban sprawl without one's feet ever touching the ground.

"The place is deserted," whispered Lorraine. Indeed, the only signs of life were the weeds, two or three feet tall in places, that had somehow pushed their way through the slabs around them.

"An abandoned Dreamspace," replied Melvin, remembering how Derek, the friendly dragon, had described them. When was that? he wondered. Yesterday? Last week? Longer? So much had happened to them that the passing of time was difficult to gauge.

"Hello!" Lorraine shouted at the top of her voice.

Hello ... ello ... lo.

Her voice echoed off the walls.

"Is there anybody there?"

There anybody there ... anybody there ... there.

They laughed. A moment of light relief arose in the middle of a concrete jungle.

Melvin was keen to hear his own voice rebound back too. "Can you help us?" he bellowed.

You help us ... us ... s.

"We're looking for Mr Good!"

Looking for Mr Good ... for Mr Good ... ood.

"Have you seen him?"

Seen him ... him ... m.

"He's not here!"

Not here ... here ... ere.

"Not here?" Melvin was confused. The echo of his own voice had answered his question. How could that be? They both spun round and scanned the windows and the doors of the maisonettes nearby.

It was Lorraine who spotted the figure leaning against a wall on a second-floor landing. "Hello!" she called out.

Hello ... ello ... lo.

"Who are you?" added Melvin.

Are you ... you ... ou.

Five minutes later they were able to continue the conversation without shouting. The stranger made his way along the landing down a stone stairwell to join them on the paved area. "The name's Elvis," he answered.

"Elvis?" asked Lorraine with a smile. "Really?"

He was tall and very strong across the shoulders. He wore a blue, three-quarter-length drape jacket with black velour trim around the collar, lapels, pockets, and cuffs. His suede shoes were a matching blue. "Well no, not really," he admitted. "Although y'can call me Elvis if y'like."

"You can call me Melvin," said Melvin as he offered him his hand.

He shook it. "I'm Vince, really," he told them. From a pocket he took a comb and opened it up with a flick action. "You can call me Vince."

"Hi Vince," said Lorraine. "I'm Loz."

He ran the comb through his thick, black, wavy hair, paying particular attention to the curl of hair brought forward over his forehead. "So, you're lookin' for y'actual Mr Good, eh?" he asked as the sun beat down. He sat on the bottom step in the shade of the stairwell.

Melvin nodded and Lorraine sighed as they sat down too either side of him.

"We need his help to get back," Melvin told him. "To our bedrooms. To our own world."

"But first, we need to cheer him up," Lorraine reminded Melvin.

Vince slipped the comb back into the inside pocket of his jacket and looked at them closely. "I can always tell the new ones," he said with a grin. "Rushin' around and dashin' about, like there's never goin' to be another dream span."

"New ones?" asked Melvin.

Vince didn't answer straight away. Vince never did. His expression was seriously thoughtful now. "I'm from the physical world too," he said finally.

"Really?" gasped Melvin. "How long have you been here?"

Vince delayed his response. "It was 1960, and some mates and me had this big party to celebrate y'actual Elvis comin' out the army."

If the news that Vince was from the physical world astonished them, then his latest revelation struck them dumb.

Nine...teen...six... ty? The flabbergasted pair stared at each other and mouthed the words soundlessly.

Vince shrugged. "The party went on long into the night," he recalled. "I crashed out on the floor, and when I woke up I was in this white place with a couple of bickerin' giants." He paused as he cast his mind back to that time when he was new here himself.

"Nineteen," gasped Melvin as he gradually found his voice again, "sixty?"

Vince nodded. "So, when you've lived in these Dreamspaces and corridors for as long as I have," he explained, "you stop rushin' around and dashin' about, and you kind of learn to be patient."

Can you imagine being stuck in this place for all those years? Lorraine could not. The year 1960 was before her parents were born, for pity's sake! She didn't want to learn to be patient. She was worried. She wanted to go home.

"Are you looking for Mr Good, Vince?" asked Melvin.

Vince rested his hands on the knees of his slim-fitting drainpipe trousers. "Am I looking for Mr Good?" He thought about it for a moment and then shrugged. "I suppose you could say I am."

I suppose you could say I am? Lorraine repeated Vince's words in her head. This guy had been away from his family and friends for all this time, and all he could say was, *I suppose you could say I am.* She had never met anyone so laid-back.

Vince sighed. "It's only recently that I've had the urge to find him," he told them. "Yet I don't know why I want to. It's as if someone's callin' me." He held the top of his head with both hands as if it hurt. "In my head. All the time. Callin' me."

"Really?" asked Lorraine. This was more like it, she thought. "You believe Mr Good is trying to contact you?"

Vince shook his head slowly. "Maybe. Maybe not. Maybe someone else," he replied.

"Oh," said Lorraine, a touch disappointed. "Who?"

He stood up and rubbed his long sideburns, thoughtfully, with the tips of his fingers as he stared across the large paved area. "Think it's the wizard who says 'salmon' a lot. Maybe."

#

They were being watched.

The watcher quietly made his way along at ground level. Then he lifted up his super-tough, yet lightweight, polyester suitcase up a flight of stone steps so he could spy on them through a gap in the hardwood

109

slats. On the opposite side of the paved area, sitting on the bottom step in the shade of a stairwell, the two suspicious characters he had been following were conspiring with a third, taller untrustworthy sort. He was frustrated because he couldn't hear their plotting and their scheming and was wondering if there was some way he could move a little closer when the taller man stood up. He saw him scratch the thick growth of hair down one side of his face and stare off into the distance.

The Boy Scout followed the direction of his gaze across the sunlit concourse to the tallest tower block. Enclosed firmly in a surrounding mass around its base were the entrances: each one a different colour, in every colour you could possibly imagine and every shade of every colour too.

Keith saw something move. Something black was silhouetted against deep, purplish red. Was it something or someone? He strained his eyes to see. It was someone, definitely. Someone wearing a black robe with gold stars and matching pointed hat emerged from the shadows and was striding confidently across the paved area towards the others. They stepped out into the sunshine to meet him, and the newcomer greeted them all with a hug, like old friends.

From his vantage point, Keith watched the meeting of the untrustworthy sorts unfold. He noticed the one with the round face and the pointy hat was doing most of the talking as the others were listening intently. Again, he considered making his way along the balcony, across the footbridge, up the ramp, and back along the walkway on the other side. From there he could slip down to the stairwell's half landing. From there, maybe he could hear what was being said. Before he could do so, though, the meeting ended. The four conspirators were making their way back towards the corridors and passageways.

Keith hurriedly left the platform between the flight of stairs, ascended to the deck access landing that runs parallel with the paved area, and ran quickly down a short, concave slope and through a maze of rabbit-run walkways to within touching distance of the entrances. He carefully positioned himself between his suitcase and a brick pillar as the untrustworthy sorts fellowship arrived at the brink of Limbo.

He could hear their voices now and catch a snatch of dialogue. They were plotting, obviously.

Royal blue ... portal ... centre of ... the wizard who ... labyrinth ... says salmon ... a lot ...

Fragmented conversation. They were scheming for sure.

The suspicious character in the ankle-length robe held the hand of the girl in the blue V-neck jumper and the boy in the maroon school blazer as they swept through the crimson doorway. The taller man nonchalantly removed a comb from inside his blue-draped jacket before following on behind.

After a moment Keith stepped out from behind the upright post. "Gosh and double gosh," he whispered to himself. "The wizard who says 'salmon' a lot? I've heard of fish repeating on you, but that's ridiculous." He shook his head in disbelief and followed them all into the crimson maze.

Chapter 24

"Knock knock."

By sheer coincidence, Terrence was walking along the crimson maze too.

"Knock knock," he repeated as he glanced over his shoulder at the three muscular guards of his choice, who were marching three abreast behind him.

Their expressions were blank, and their eyes stared fixedly ahead.

"Look, it's quite simple," he persisted. "I say 'knock knock', and you say 'who's there'. Then I say 'Matthew', and you reply 'Matthew who'. And I say …" He looked round again, hoping for just a flicker of interest. "And I say … Matthew lace is undone!" He grinned.

Their expressions remained expressionless.

His grin turned to a grimace in an instant. "Matthew. It sounds like 'my shoe' with a lisp. My shoelace is undone. Get it?"

They clearly didn't, and they marched on in silence.

"Try this one," said Terrence finally with a hint of desperation. "This one made Vile chuckle when I told him it earlier," he fibbed. "What's blue and has yellow wheels?" He turned to face them, which meant he had to run backwards as fast as he could. "What … is … blue … and … has … yellow … wheels?" he repeated. For each of the guard's long strides, Terrence's little legs were having to take three small ones.

"It's the sky." He looked deep into their eyes, hoping for signs of intelligent life, but his findings were inconclusive. "I lied about the wheels," he added and studied their faces for any developments in the smile department. He saw nothing.

"Oh, forget it." He frowned as he turned to face the front again. "Let's find those pesky kids, shall we?"

The passageway took a sharp turn to the left, followed immediately by an even sharper right.

#

It was Arthur, reclining on the chocolate-brown sofa, whom Mugwump saw first. He stepped through the portal holding Lorraine's left hand in his right and Melvin's right hand with his left.

"Arthur, my dear fellow." He beamed. "May I introduce Melvin, Lorraine –" He loosened his grip on their hands and did a half turn. "And Vince."

These are the others, thought Arthur. *The ones Mr Good mentioned earlier.* He nodded weakly.

"They have been salmoned too."

"Summoned," Melvin corrected Mugwump.

"Sorry. I mean summoned." He flushed. "Not salmoned. Well, not yet, anyway."

"Where's Mr Good?" asked Lorraine as she looked about the room. She saw lava lamps, macramé plant hangers, and bright plastic accessories but not a Dream Ambassador for Tranquil Dreams.

"Keith!" yelled Arthur suddenly, sitting up straight despite the backache affecting his lumbar region.

All heads turned as one. Standing behind Vince was a startled Boy Scout pulling a suitcase.

"Grandpa?" What was his grandpa doing here? The last person he would ever expect to be a member of the untrustworthy sorts fellowship was his own grandpa. But was it his grandpa? He was sporting the longest moustache he had ever seen in his life.

"Your face!" gasped Keith. "What happened?"

Arthur was puzzled and examined his features with his fingers. He was shocked to feel very long whiskers, pulled to the side, slightly curled and pointed upwards at the ends. "I don't know," was his stunned reply.

Vince held his comb in mid-air and stared into the distance. "It's y'actual Mr Good," he cried.

All heads turned as one again but this time in the opposite direction. Standing at the penultimate curve of the labyrinth, with a towel draped around his shoulders, was the Dream Ambassador for Tranquil Dreams.

"Mr G – Good?" stuttered Melvin.

"B – but?" stammered Lorraine.

"Melvin, Lorraine, Vince!" Mr Good faltered. "And a Boy Scout?" He stood on the bright orange carpet. "How pleasantly tremendous and tremendously pleasant to see you all." He smiled broadly. "At last."

His deep blue eyes sparkled with kindness.

Part 2

The Plan

Chapter 25

"Time is different here," Mr Good said with a smile. "Whereas the Palace of Somnium has been under Vile's control for nearly six of your weeks, the effects on Earth have so far been minimal and won't become serious for a little while yet."

Melvin and Lorraine were sitting either side of Arthur on the sofa.

Mr Good continued. "Dream Land is an octave higher, a completely different frequency, if you like, to the physical world. It's all very complicated. It can be explained, but only by a very long formula using a lot of x's and some y's." He rubbed his silver beard as he struggled to recall some more information lurking deep in his memory. "And a z too, if I remember correctly."

Melvin was fascinated. Lorraine was thinking, *If this is Mr Good, then who was the man playing hopscotch?*

The matching cream armchairs were occupied by Keith, who had one hand resting on his suitcase and was watching everyone warily, and Vince, who was watching no one. He was asleep.

"Do people sleep here?" asked Arthur. "Because I haven't had my afternoon nap." With his two hands he was idly twisting both ends of his newly discovered moustache.

Keith looked up in surprise. "You always have your afternoon nap, Grandpa."

It was Mugwump who offered an explanation. "Vince isn't actually asleep in the strict sense of the word. When you live an eternal existence, life can be a little tedious at times." The wizard was sitting at the teak dining table. "So, he's sort of developed a knack of switching his brain off."

Everyone looked curiously at Vince. His eyes were closed, and he breathed in with a snort and out with a high-pitched whistle.

"You see," the wizard continued, "in the physical world, when a dream person falls asleep his or her conscious or unconscious frequencies link to the most accessible signal in Dream Land. That is usually the Palace of Somnium but sometimes, unfortunately, Torment Towers."

Melvin, Lorraine, and Keith shifted uneasily in their seats as Vince continued to breathe in and out noisily.

Mr Good was impatient to continue. There was a negative amount of time to squander, and he still had a lot of explaining to do. He stood in the middle of the centre of the royal blue labyrinth, commanding everyone's attention, and watched his visitors closely for a moment. "We have to remove Vile from the Palace of Somnium," he began. "If we don't, in three or four dream spans' time, everyone, everywhere, every night will be having nightmares." He paused to allow his audience the chance to fully appreciate the gravity of the situation. "The consequences for the physical world will be catastrophic. We have to stop him, and we must hurry."

"We?" gasped Lorraine.

"Why us?" asked Melvin.

"Why me?" queried Arthur. "I'm an old man."

Mr Good ignored their questions and concerns. "I have chosen you all for a specific reason. I kept a file on everyone living in the physical world, including their likes, dislikes, hopes, and fears, in a filing cabinet back at the palace."

"Everyone?" Melvin tried to imagine how big that filing cabinet must be.

"From those records, I needed to find someone sensible. I wanted someone with a rating in the mid to high nineties for sensibleness, someone with a logical, sequential, and analytical mind for solving the problems the mazes and labyrinths of Limbo pose, and someone with a natural inclination to choose blue." He paused and turned his attention to the occupants of the chocolate brown sofa, smiling. "I chose Melvin and Lorraine because they tick all of those boxes."

Melvin and Lorraine wriggled self-consciously on either side of Arthur.

"Vince," he continued, "I have chosen you because –"

"Mr Good," Arthur interrupted the dream ambassador in mid-sentence. "But Vince is still asleep."

Mugwump looked up. "My dear fellow, there's no need for concern." Between his fingers he held up a short, slender tube of wood, containing a core of graphite, for everyone to see. "The minutes of this meeting are being downloaded into his subconscious as we speak. So he won't miss a salmon."

"Thank you again, old chum," said Mr Good as he turned his attention back to Vince. "I have chosen you for your knowledge of Limbo. You have been here almost an epoch now, moving from abandoned Dreamspace to abandoned Dreamspace, so you must know those corridors like the back of your hand."

One of Vince's eyes twitched. His head was flipped to the side and resting on his shoulder, and his mouth was drooped and ever so slightly open. Then his other eye twitched.

"Also, you're a big, strong lad," added Mr Good. "Invaluable if things cut up a bit rough."

"Cut up a bit rough?" Arthur gulped. He was beginning to fret now.

Mr Good took a long, deep breath. "Arthur," he said when he eventually exhaled. "You are a vital part of my plan."

Arthur frowned. *A vital part of Mr Good's plan? At my time of life? With my ailments?* The groovy mix of brown, orange, tan, and yellow wallpaper was giving him a headache. What kind of a plan was this? Why was he wearing this ridiculous moustache? He didn't know the answer to any of these questions, but he figured he was just about to find out.

"To explain why Arthur's role in the plan is so vital I will hand you over to our resident wizard, Mugwump." Mr Good took control of the pencil and replaced his old chum at the teak dining table.

Mugwump thanked him very salmon and quickly opened two cupboard doors in the teak sideboard. Inside was a double-sized fixed shelf and a dropped-flap door, which, when opened, revealed a single adjustable shelf. Contained within were dozens of bottles of all shapes and sizes and colours, each filled with all manner of different medicines and potions. He carefully chose a glass bottle half full of a thick yellow liquid. It had a narrow neck and a chiselled, clear glass stopper. Then from the bottom drawer he removed his golden wand.

He asked Arthur to stand. Taking hold of his wrist, he helped him up out of his seat as Melvin and Lorraine gently pushed him until he was in a vertical position. Mugwump faced Arthur and looked deep into his eyes. Suddenly, and most unexpectedly, the wizard began to sing.

The words of the song were unfamiliar, seldom-used words; they were powerful, magical spell words. With a range higher than a bass but lower than a tenor, the haunting melody of the wizard's song was having a strange effect on Arthur's clothing.

It was the slippers that changed first. Arthur's maroon slippers with the soft velour uppers slowly but surely transformed into a pair of shiny, two-toned shoes. His plum, long-sleeved, woven pyjama set, in the blink of an eye, became a black and gold pinstriped jacket with matching cuffed trousers.

As he sang he waved his golden wand around a bit. Arthur's grey hair gradually darkened and thickened until it was jet black and very shiny.

The wizard's song ended as suddenly as it had begun. For a long time nobody spoke, moved, or did anything apart from stare at Arthur in stunned silence.

"Seriously weird," uttered Melvin eventually.

"Arthur, you're the spitting image ..." Lorraine's words trailed off.

"Grandpa?" cried Keith. "Gosh and double gosh! What's happening?"

Vince stirred. His back arched in a long stretch, and his eyes opened with a pop. They slowly focused and looked Arthur up and down. "The likeness is uncanny," he said with a yawn.

Mr Good put down his pencil and pushed the large sheet of lined paper towards the centre of the teak dining table. "Vince," he said as he crossed the room and stood at Mugwump's side. "I wasn't aware you had ever met Vile."

Vince shook his head. "Never have," he said with a shrug. "But that's exactly how I imagined y'actual Vile would look."

"Vile?" gasped Arthur. His dodgy ticker dodged a couple of ticks. "Are you trying to say I look like him?"

Mugwump nodded. "You're a dead ringer, Arthur."

"You're a vital part of my plan," Mr Good reminded him.

"But I'm an old man." He could feel his ankles starting to swell. "I'm sick."

Mr Good was well aware of Arthur's medical history. He knew he had a list of ailments as long as a giant's arm. "Not to worry." He smiled and turned to the wizard at his side. "Mugwump can help you."

Mugwump carefully separated the clear stopper from the glass bottle and poured a measure of the thick yellow liquid into a white plastic spoon. "This medicine temporarily cures ninety-nine per cent of all known ailments," he said as he offered it to Arthur.

Arthur regarded the contents of the spoon with suspicion. "What about the other one per cent?" he asked. "I'm sure to suffer from those too."

"Try it and see what happens," said Mugwump with a smile.

Arthur did. His face contorted and bent out of shape, and his body shook uncontrollably. It tasted horrible, like a cross between cod liver oil and bitter lemon. He retched. Somehow he managed to swallow three spoonfuls before Mr Good and Mugwump took hold of an elbow each and lowered the old man down into his seat.

Mr Good resumed his position in the middle of the centre of the royal blue labyrinth, and with his deep blue eyes that sparkled with kindness he observed his visitors one by one: Vince, Lorraine, Arthur, and Melvin. His gaze settled on Keith for the shortest of moments, and a look of puzzlement crossed his face.

Keith held his breath and closed his eyes. It was his turn to find out why he had been chosen. Mr Good had deliberately left him until last because he was obviously more important than the others. Melvin and Lorraine had been chosen because they were sensible. So what? Vince knew his way around. Big deal! Of course his grandpa was a vital part of the plan, admittedly. He looked like the nightmare guy or someone with a silly moustache. But Keith was the only one who had been asked to bring a suitcase, with specific instructions not to reveal its contents to anyone. After holding his breath for an uncomfortably long time, he half opened one eye and looked. He was disappointed to see Mr Good was now in a hurried discussion with the wizard.

"You will all need a keyword," Mr Good announced, turning back to the others.

Melvin leaned forward in the chocolate-brown sofa. "What's a keyword, Mr Good?"

"A sort of password. Everyone who travels the corridors of Limbo should have one during these troubled times."

"It helps you to get about unaided. Allows you to negotiate turnstiles and audio-door entry-controlled salmons and the like," explained Mugwump.

"Quickly," said Mr Good. "All of you, tell me the first word that comes into your head. Now!" He pointed. "Lorraine?"

Lorraine shrugged. "Penguin?"

"Rolling," spluttered Arthur.

"Downhill," gasped Melvin.

The three of them looked at each other in bewilderment and then burst out laughing. Where had those words come from?

Mr Good was astonished. "A penguin rolling downhill," he whispered. "It's an image. They have an image in their subconscious."

Mugwump nodded. He was equally astounded.

"But how did it get there?" Mr Good wondered and brooded.

Mugwump looked at Mr Good closely. "It wasn't you?"

Mr Good shook his head slowly. "I left them a message in their mind, just below the level of conscious perception. It was not an image. I can't do images."

"So," Mugwump sighed, "it was Vile."

Mr Good considered this for a long moment. Then he shook his head again. "I don't think so, old chum. Not really his style. A touch too subtle. And besides, penguins are cute. Vile doesn't do cute."

"Well, if it's not you and it's not Vile, then ..." Mugwump stumbled on his words when he realised what it was he was about to suggest.

Mr Good smiled, knowingly.

The alternative was absurd, too far-fetched. It was quite fantastical.

Keith was feeling a little left out. Why didn't he have an image in his subconscious?

Mr Good quickly regained his composure, stood again in the middle of the centre of the royal blue labyrinth, and took a deep breath. "Now, all of you, remember your keyword. Lorraine, yours is 'penguin'. Arthur, 'rolling'. And Melvin, yours is 'downhill'. It may help you along the way. Do you all understand?"

They all nodded, apart from Keith. Mugwump, still a little dazed, sat at the teak dining table.

"So, what's the plan, Mr Good?" asked Lorraine.

"My plan – or rather, the first part of it –" He paused. "Is to take possession of something called a Digital Dreamscaper."

"We've heard of that," said Melvin. "The giants in the white room told us."

"It's a gun-shaped object which, when you pull the trigger, creates a Dreamspace," recalled Lorraine.

"Instantly arranging the scenery on the Dream Stage," added Melvin.

Mr Good smiled to himself. They remembered things. It was one of the reasons why they were chosen.

"That's right, and without it Vile's plans could be scuppered."

"I see," said Lorraine. "So, where is it? This Digital Dreamscaper?" she asked.

Mr Good looked at Melvin and Lorraine gravely. "As we speak three muscular guards and Terrence are marching along the crimson maze in search of you."

"In search of us?" Melvin shuddered.

"Three muscular guards?" Lorraine shivered.

"And Terrence." Melvin was about to shudder once more when he stopped himself. "Who's Terrence?"

"Terrence is an idiot. He is also Vile's left-hand salmon, his sidekick, and his accomplice." Mugwump held up a stick of chalk and a small beanbag. "Terrence is the gentleman you met earlier."

Melvin and Lorraine looked at each other blankly.

"Indulging in a game of hopscotch, I believe," added Mr Good.

Lorraine's jaw dropped.

"The hopscotch man!" exclaimed Melvin.

Mr Good nodded. "And a thoroughly rotten egg he is too. He is the one in possession of the Digital Dreamscaper."

Lorraine's mind was elsewhere. "But, he seemed so sad," she reflected.

"No," said Melvin firmly. "Before you say it, Loz, we are not going to cheer him up. We are staying well away from the crimson maze. We are not going anywhere near those muscular guards. Is that not right, Mr Good?"

"On the contrary." Mr Good's smile was warm, and it was friendly. "I want them to capture you."

Chapter 26

Barry waited in the enclosed antechamber, scanning the faces of the dream actors as they filed past. He was searching for his best friend, Larry. During rehearsals for the big song and dance routine at the end, the ghosts had been divided into different groups. Afterwards, he had seen Larry mingling with a party of ugly, mischievous goblins and an ogre at the bottom of the red-carpeted stairs. But by the time he had fought his way through the crowd, to the far side of the foyer, Larry was gone. Barry guessed he had made his own way to the drawing room.

As he stood on the tips of his toes, hoping to catch a glimpse of the lean, gaunt frame of his best friend making his way through the library, he felt a poke in the ribs. He looked down to see a short, chubby dream actor grinning up at him. It was Harry.

"Have you heard?" Harry was excited.

Barry had heard. The grapevine was buzzing with the news. "I presume you are talking about Garry?"

Harry nodded. "Garry! Our Garry! He was so quiet, so innocuous, so, so ..."

Together they stepped through the curtain and managed to find an empty table, in the middle of the spacious room, with just two chairs.

Dream actors nudged dream actors. Heads turned. "It's the ghosts," voices whispered. They regarded them with fear mingled with reverence.

"So boring?" suggested Barry as they sat opposite each other.

"Exactly."

"Can I just say something at this point?" Barry was mocking Garry's high-pitched, squeaky voice.

They laughed.

"I truly believe in Lord Riddle," mimicked Harry.

They laughed again.

"Over here!" waved Barry.

Larry was standing by the great curtain. He was amongst the final few dream actors to reach the drawing room.

"Have you heard?" he said as he joined them. Judging by their expressions Larry guessed they had. "But, have you heard what our quiet, our innocuous, our ..."

"Boring?" Harry and Barry prompted Larry together.

"Exactly." Their best friend nodded. "Do you know what our Garry did?" Larry borrowed a caned seat, with a missing cushion, from a nearby table and sat between Harry and Barry.

"Yes," replied Barry. "I heard, on the grapevine of course, that he helped those child persons escape by kicking Vile on the shins and –"

"No," Harry cut in. "As you know, I don't listen to tittle tattle, hearsay, or gossip of any kind, but rumour has it that –"

"And then," Barry continued, "he jumped on Vile's back and wrapped his arms around his neck and his legs around his waist, just long enough for the teenagers to make good their escape."

Harry shook his head. "That isn't what happened at all. The rumour is that Vile was just about to capture the two children and give them a good ticking off when Garry appeared holding a long rope with a running noose at one end."

Barry scoffed. There was no mention of long ropes or running nooses on the grapevine.

"Then he lassoed him," said Harry as he mimed Garry's heroic act. Holding up his arm and keeping it perfectly still, he rotated his hand at the wrist in a circular motion. "He pulled the rope, and the loop tightened around Vile's neck."

Larry smiled as he listened to both versions of events. "Now, that isn't what I heard."

Harry frowned. "So, what rumour have you been listening to?"

"What have you heard on the grapevine?" asked Barry.

"I've heard nothing on the grapevine or listened to any rumours," replied Larry. "My information comes from a very reliable source." He leaned closer. "It appears that Garry distracted Vile by holding out a … wait for it …"

Harry and Barry leaned closer too as they waited patiently for it.

"A get-well-soon card."

"What!"

"A get-well-soon card?"

Larry nodded. "It seems Garry asked Vile if the two youngsters could pass the card on to Mr Good."

Harry looked at Barry with doubt clouding his features. "What foolishness."

"It does seem a little far-fetched, Larry," Barry agreed.

Larry shrugged. "If you think that's far-fetched, then you won't believe it when I tell you where our Garry has gone."

With her long, golden curls and dazzling smile, Peggy Sue's presence suddenly lit up the room. "Hello, guys!" she cried out in her loudest voice. "I'd just wanted to thank you all for putting so much effort in earlier." The dream actors at the back stretched their necks, craning for a better view of Vile's niece.

But Harry and Barry were more interested in what Larry had to say. He leaned closer still. "He's gone to find Lord Riddle," he whispered.

Harry's eyes rolled around in their sockets, and Barry laughed.

"My unrevealed source of confidential information told me so," insisted Larry.

"I know some of you weren't keen to begin with." The first practice session for the big song and dance routine at the end had gone better than Peggy Sue expected. "But I think you all enjoyed it. Am I right, guys?" A few reluctant nods and some begrudging yeses followed.

"Lord Riddle? The fictional third dream ambassador who lives in the fabled Land of Nod?" jeered Harry.

"It's only a story," added Barry. "A story told to amuse children – or, more likely, to frighten them. But he doesn't really exist."

"You know that. I know that. But for some inexplicable reason, Garry doesn't."

"I promise I'll make dancers of you all yet." Peggy Sue laughed.

Harry tutted. "Garry has always had this obsession with Lord Riddle. He refused to subscribe to the notion that it was all just make-believe."

Barry nodded. "And now he's gone on a wild goose chase," he sighed, "to find a fictional character."

"All alone out there in Limbo." Harry shook his head in disbelief. "Our Garry."

Quiet? Innocuous? Boring?

The three Dream Actors looked at each other wide-eyed and wondered how they could have been so wrong.

Chapter 27

Terrence only had one line to learn.

"Can I ... just say ... something at ... this point? Can I just ... say something ... at this point?" Can I just say ... something at this ... point?"

He was having trouble with it.

"Can ... I just say ... something at ... this point?"

Each time he repeated it he changed either the stress, the pitch, the loudness, or the tone of his voice. He was trying to make the line sound as frightening as possible.

"Can I just ... say ... something at ... this point?"

The three muscular guards followed closely behind with their faces blank.

"It was Vile who first spotted my acting potential," said Terrence as he swivelled his head and looked up at their blank faces. "He said I was a natural. Thinks I have wonderful voice projection and enunciation." He shrugged. "Whatever that means."

The metal plates on the guard's leather skirts made a light, sharp ringing sound as they marched along the crimson maze.

"He has created a role in his new nightmare especially for me." They reached a T-junction, and without hesitation Terrence took a left turn. "I play a ghost. Well, more of a poltergeist, really. A poltergeist is similar to a ghost," he informed them. "Except it makes noises, bangs around a bit, and knocks ornaments off shelves a lot."

He paused momentarily at a crimson crossroads, wondering if he should go right or left, before continuing directly ahead. "I'm going to scare those foolish folk in the physical world something rotten." He grinned. "Can I just say something ... at this point?"

The guard's blank expressions, for the first time, began to show signs of weariness around the eyes.

Terrence walked on in silence. He took one right and two left turns before he spoke again.

"Vile thinks I'm great, you know."

Terrence didn't look back, but if he had he would have seen the guards staring at him in disbelief.

"A little earlier he said to me, 'You're a credit to all things wicked and nasty, Terrence, and I don't know what I'd do without you, my son.'"

The guards nudged each other and assumed a facial expression indicating mild amusement.

"Well, Vile didn't actually say 'my son'," he admitted. "But, he used that tone of voice. You know, the tone of voice a father uses when he's talking to the son he loves."

This caused one of the guards to develop a giggle, which of course started the other two off.

"'I trust you implicitly to bring those pesky kids back,' he said. 'You can rely on me, your noxiousness,' I told him." Terrence took a right. "I was going to say, 'you can rely on me, Dad,' but I thought no, that will only embarrass him."

They bit down hard on their bottom lips in a desperate attempt to suppress their titters.

"Mind you, when Peg and I are married he will call me 'son'. After all, I will be his son-in-law. Yes, I know strictly speaking he's Peg's uncle, but he is her guardian, so you can be sure he'll want me to start calling him 'Dad'."

This was all too much for the three guards. A vocal expulsion of air from their lungs resulted in a loud burst of laughter.

Terrence looked round in surprise. He saw the three muscular guards following closely behind. With difficulty they had reverted back to their blank expressions. Were they laughing at him? He stared at them for a long moment. Then he shrugged and took a left turn this time. It was a short corridor. Ahead, maybe forty or fifty paces away, was yet another T-junction.

The guards nearly bumped into Terrence's back. He had stopped only five strides into the short corridor, his attention sharply focused on something. "I can hear voices." He tilted his head and listened intently. "Can you hear voices?" he asked.

The guards said nothing in reply and gave no indication they even understood him.

"Definitely voices," Terrence whispered. "It's those pesky kids for sure – and quite close, too," he surmised as he looked along the short crimson way. "Maybe just around that next corner."

The guards' spirits lifted at the prospect of some pushing and shoving.

"Come on, let's capture them," cried Terrence as he set off, more quickly now and with more purpose than before. "Follow me, you bozos."

"Ugh!" The guard in the middle took exception to being referred to as a bozo. He placed his thumb on his nose and waved four fingers at the back of Terrence's head.

#

Vince was looking about him as he walked as if seeking something he had lost. Melvin and Lorraine followed him curiously.

Arthur was dancing. "I haven't felt this frisky since –" He faltered. "Come to think of it, I don't think I have ever felt this frisky." He performed a little jig and a pirouette. "That medicine the salmon guy gave me is amazing," he declared. "Wish I could get some on prescription." He jogged back along the corridor. "By the way, where is the salmon guy?" he asked as he turned again and ran ahead of them this time.

"He's waiting for us at the entrance to the portal, of course," replied Lorraine.

"It's all part of Mr Good's plan," Melvin told him. "Remember?"

Arthur didn't remember.

Vince halted. He stared at the crimson floor and rubbed his chin thoughtfully. "This is y'actual spot," he decided.

"Are you sure?" asked Melvin.

Vince nodded.

Melvin wondered how he could possibly know. This spot didn't look any different to any other spot.

"Spot?" Arthur stopped shadow boxing and looked down at the place on the ground that Vince was staring at so thoughtfully. "What spot?"

"The spot where Terrence and the muscular guards will capture us," said Lorraine.

"Capture us!" shrieked Arthur.

"Didn't you listen to anything Mr Good told us?" sighed Melvin.

"Mr Who?" Arthur shrugged.

Lorraine told him that at any moment now Terrence and the guards would be sweeping around the bend ahead. Arthur hopped around Vince on his left leg. She explained that he must hide around the corner they had just passed. She turned and pointed back along the corridor.

Arthur changed to his right leg, followed the direction of her finger, and nodded.

"Once the guards have grabbed us, manhandled us, and dragged us past the corner where you will be waiting," he emphasised, "you will step out."

"Of course, they will believe you to be Vile," said Lorraine. "You will order the guards away and lure Terrence back along the corridor to the portal and the waiting Mugwump. Once through the portal, Terrence will be captured. His Digital Dreamscaper will be confiscated, and the first part of Mr Good's plan will be successfully completed."

"Any questions?" asked Melvin.

Arthur bunny-hopped forwards, backwards, and finally three hops sideways. Then he stopped. "Plan?" He looked puzzled. "What plan?"

Melvin and Lorraine groaned.

Vince looked up. He knew Terrence and the guards were approaching. He could hear them. But what he didn't understand was why Arthur wasn't hiding around the next corner already. What would Terrence think if he saw Vile hopping around like a bunny rabbit? He might be a little suspicious, and the first part of Mr Good's plan could be compromised. It was not his nature to be impulsive, but on this occasion Vince knew he had to act quickly. He pulled his sleeves up, moved the black velour trim around the cuffs of his blue drape jacket from his wrist to just below the elbow, and then gently but firmly took hold of Arthur's neck by the scruff.

"Old timer," he growled.

"Let me go!" choked Arthur. "You're strangling me!"

Vince released Arthur's neck and manoeuvred him round by the shoulders. "May I suggest you do less jumpin' and hoppin' and more hidin' around corners?" he advised as he pushed him in the direction of the turn in question.

"Okay, teddy boy." Arthur grimaced. "Keep your hair on." For a long moment he stood halfway between Vince and the corner, rubbing the nape of his neck.

"Now!" insisted Melvin.

"Yes," Lorraine agreed. "Now might be a good idea."

Time was of the essence. She could hear the beat now. The steady rhythm of leather sandals on Limbo's floor was getting louder and nearer.

"This corner, you say?" asked Arthur.

Three heads nodded.

"And you want me to hide round it?"

Three heads nodded again but with a touch more impatience this time.

Arthur felt another strong, swelling, wavelike surge of energy rush through his body. He had an uncontrollable urge to run and jump and perform acrobatics. "Now?" he asked. He asked but didn't wait to see if their heads were nodding in confirmation this time. Instead, he turned and skipped away. Then he cartwheeled, with his arms and legs spread like spokes, around the turn in the maze.

#

"Well!" Terrence walked towards them with an arrogant air, grinning. "Well, if it isn't the pesky kids."

Melvin and Lorraine turned and looked at Terrence with feigned surprise. "The hopscotch man!"

The last time Terrence saw them, he had acted daft. Too daft, apparently. This time he wasn't going to let Vile down. This time he was going to use force. "So, we meet again." His triumphant grin was incessant.

The three guards quickly surrounded them.

"I am Vile's number two," he informed them. He stood with his head held high and chest thrown out. "I am his left-hand man, his buddy."

He cast a quick glance at the guards, and his eyes narrowed as he did so. He watched, waiting for a very slight upturning of the lips at the corners or maybe a barely noticeable twinkle of amusement in the eyes. Satisfied that their blank expressions had not altered, he continued. "I am, in fact, Vile's trusty sidekick, Terrence."

He held out his hand. Nobody made a move to shake it.

Vince looked the guards up and down. "And what are their names?" he asked.

"Their names!" scoffed Terrence as if it were the most ridiculous question he had ever been asked. "They don't have names. They're guards!"

He regarded Vince for the first time. "Who are you?" he demanded.

Vince's first impression of Terrence was one of disappointment. To be Vile's assistant, someone who was second-in-command of Torment Towers and all scary dreams, it wasn't unrealistic to expect a more impressive figure. Yet this guy was short, scruffy, unwashed, and had a face that resembled a sewer rat. "The name's Elvis," he replied. "But you can call me V –"

"Elvis, is it?" This was an unexpected bonus. Vile would be ever so pleased when he returned to the palace with an extra pesky person in tow. "Well, Elvis, any friend of the pesky kids is no friend of mine." Terrence smirked.

Mugwump at the portal entrance and Mr Good at the centre of the royal blue labyrinth would be waiting anxiously for their return, so Melvin was keen for the capturing to begin now. "Well, it was nice meeting you," Melvin said with a smile and a wave as he set off. "Let's go, Loz. Come on, Vince." Two of the guards, though, closed ranks, forming an impregnable muscular wall that stopped Melvin in his tracks.

"Going somewhere, ginger?" Terrence laughed loudly.

Melvin beat his fists against their pectorals.

"There's no escape," sighed Lorraine. "We've been captured."

The other guard came from behind Melvin and lifted him clear off the ground by the collar of his blazer.

"My guards practice the ancient art of pushing and shoving," Terrence informed them. When he clicked his fingers, the guard gave them a demonstration. Melvin landed on his knees several yards away. "Guards! Push and shove them all the way back to the palace," he barked.

With his left hand the guard dealt with Lorraine in a similar fashion. His shove sent her flying, and she tripped over Melvin's feet, crash landing face down on the floor.

"You'll be back in the cold and damp cell before you know it." Terrence grinned.

Vince was a big lad, very strong across the shoulders, so it would take two guards to handle him. They grabbed an arm each, but he resisted their close attention and tried to wriggle free.

"Watch my feet. These are y'actual blue suede shoes," he warned them. But they ignored him and pushed him towards Melvin and Lorraine, who were slowly climbing to their feet.

"I know a shortcut," announced Terrence, pointing along the corridor.

Lorraine was relieved. How clever of Mr Good to know that Terrence would know a short cut that would take them along the corridor past the corner where Arthur was hiding. It was a good plan, she decided.

A very good plan, thought Melvin. It would be sweet to see that triumphant grin wiped off Terrence's face soon.

A shove and a couple of pushes later they reached the turning.

Where was Arthur? The corridor ahead was Arthur-less, completely and utterly Arthur-less. Melvin and Lorraine looked at each other in shock and in horror.

"For pity's sake," Lorraine gasped out the words.

"Where the –" A large, flat hand suddenly hit Melvin in the back, between the shoulder blades, like a battering ram – "dickens is he?"

Vince was dumbfounded too. Where was the old-timer? He was flummoxed by the old-timer-less-ness of the scene before him.

The guards pushed and shoved their prey mercilessly along the crimson maze back towards the Palace of Somnium. And Terrence laughed to see such fun.

Chapter 28

"Why have I been chosen?"

In the space between the chocolate-brown sofa and the teak sideboard, Mr Good stood with his bare feet a little wider than shoulder width apart and his knees slightly bent.

"Why am I here?" Keith tried again, tapping the suitcase with his fingers.

Mr Good held his right arm parallel with the ground across the front of his tunic. "Sorry, old chum." He bent his left arm up and used his left forearm to ease his right arm closer to his chest. "Did you say something?"

"Melvin and Lorraine are here because they are smart or sensible. Vince is a guide and knows his way around, and Grandpa looks like Vile." He sat forward in the cream armchair. "So, why me?" He tried to draw Mr Good's attention to the suitcase by moving it a couple of inches.

Mr Good could feel the stretch in his shoulder and looked at Keith with his face contorted sharply. "Why you?"

"Yes." Keith nodded. "Why me?" He assumed it was something important, too important for the others to know about. Now they were alone, away from prying eyes and ears, he was sure Mr Good was about to reveal his role in the great plan.

"It's because –" Mr Good took a long, deep-sounding breath. "You're a Boy Scout, I think."

"You think?"

He repeated the stretching exercise again with the other arm. "I was excited when I discovered your grandpa, someone identical to Vile in every detail. They have such a close similarity, like twins derived from a single egg." He grimaced again as he felt his shoulder muscles stretch once more. "The truth is, I don't recall summoning you at all. You weren't on my list."

"List?"

"I have a list of those I summoned somewhere. I'm not very good with technology and summoning and stuff like that." With one arm holding the back of the sofa he performed a couple of knee bends. "Between you and me, I've never actually done it before."

"But I spoke to you." Was it this really this morning? It seems so long ago now. "I was awake, or I was dreaming I was awake."

Mr Good slipped his feet into his flip-flops, sat on the arm of the sofa, and listened.

"You told me to meet you here at the centre of the royal blue labyrinth. You told me there was a plan, and you told me not to trust anyone."

"Good advice," said Mr Good.

"You also told me to climb up into my loft, crawl along to the very end, lift up the fibreglass matting, and carefully pack everything I found there into a suitcase."

"Did I?" Mr Good was puzzled. "Why would I do that?"

Keith shrugged. "Something to do with the plan. Something important, I presumed." He shook his head slowly. "But obviously not."

If Mr Good didn't summon me, then who did? He mused.

Mr Good smiled. "Not to worry." His eyes were blue, and they sparkled with kindness. "You're a Boy Scout. I'm sure you will come in jolly useful."

Keith ran a hand through his wavy brown hair. "Gosh and double gosh." He sighed.

"All is well, old chum," Mr Good assured him. "Meanwhile, you could treat this as your explorer belt expedition."

The look of surprise on the Boy Scout's face produced a small natural hollow in both cheeks. "Explorer belt expedition?" he repeated the words.

"Why not?" Mr Good stood up and nodded enthusiastically. "It requires participants to undertake a ten-day expedition in a foreign country. Am I right, young Keith?"

Before Keith could respond, Mr Good continued. "What could be more foreign than this?" He spread his arms wide. "Dream Land."

"Yes, but ..." Keith faltered. There had to be a but, though he couldn't think of one at first. "But ..."

"Working in a small team? Devoting some time to travelling around? Exploring and meeting local people? It's perfect," he enthused.

"But one has to undertake a major project." Keith just knew there was a but.

Mr Good laughed because he knew Keith was going to say that. He had his response ready and waiting. "Projects don't come more major than saving the world, old chum."

"But." Another but? "My explorer belt expedition is already planned, Mr Good. I'm off to France in July."

The Dream Ambassador for Tranquil Dreams looked at the Boy Scout gravely. "Remember, when four dream spans have passed us by, everyone, everywhere in your world will have nightmares every night. There will be no explorer belt expedition in July. You will be too tired. Your coach driver will be too tired and have puffy eyes. The captain of the ferry across the channel will be too tired and be in a grumpy mood. Everyone, everywhere, even those living in France, will be too tired. Lack of sleep will lead to anxiety and depression right across the physical world. Do you understand what I'm telling you, young Keith?" He waited until he was sure Keith fully understood the significance of what he was saying.

Keith nodded slowly. "But do you have the authority to award an explorer belt?"

Mr Good shrugged. "I could pull a few strings and send a message to your local scout network co-ordinator. It shouldn't be a problem, old chum."

Keith was unsure.

"Bad things are going to happen unless you and I and the others do something about it quickly."

"Do something? How can I do something?" He loosened his neckerchief a touch. "Your plan is already in motion. Any minute now the others will return with Terrence in tow, and we still don't know why I'm here."

"Terrence in tow?" Mr Good suddenly grinned. "That's it!"

"That's what?"

"I knew you would come in jolly useful. That's it," he exclaimed as he sat on the sofa adjacent to a now-puzzled Keith. "How foolishly silly and sillily foolish of me not to see it."

Keith watched and waited as Mr Good shook his head several times and berated himself for his foolishness and silliness. "So, are you going to enlighten me?"

"It's obvious." Mr Good chuckled. "What are Boy Scouts good at?"

"I don't know." Keith shrugged. "Climbing? Hill walking? Hiking?"

"All good guesses," admitted Mr Good. "But not correct."

"Pitching a tent?"

Mr Good shook his head. "Do you give up?" He smiled.

Keith knew that the list of things a Boy Scout was good at was a very long list indeed, so he agreed to give up to save time.

"Boy Scouts are good at –" Mr Good teased him with a little pause. "Tying knots."

"Tying knots?"

"Terrence is a slippery customer, old chum, so we will need to tie him up to that chair." Mr Good pointed vaguely to one of possibly six chairs that were randomly positioned around the teak dining table. "With Terrence tied up we can continue with the second part of my plan with confidence."

Tying knots had never been Keith's strong point. He did, for his creative challenge badge, demonstrate some decorative knotting in front of an audience. But would a couple of decorative knots be strong enough to hold a slippery customer like Terrence? He doubted it, but how could he tell Mr Good this?

"I've seen some slender cord or thick thread, somewhere, that would be ideal for binding," said Mr Good as he rummaged through the third drawer of the teak sideboard. "Here it is." He found the ball of string just as something else caught his eye. What he saw was red and made of plastic.

Keith wasn't expecting Mr Good to toss something in his direction, but his reactions were excellent, and he caught the red plastic object cleanly.

It's a water pistol," said Mr Good when he saw the confusion on Keith's face. "I believe Mugwump found it in a magnolia maze down in the Nether Regions about five eras ago."

Keith looked at it and then at Mr Good, hoping for an explanation.

"It's a toy gun that shoots a stream of liquid."

"I know what it is." Keith frowned. "I just don't know why I'm holding it."

Finding the toy gun amongst Mugwump's bits and pieces had given Mr Good another idea. He smiled kindly and took a deep breath. "You could be a part of my plan after all, old chum," he began.

"You want me to point this water pistol at Terrence?" yelped Keith.

"With a gun pointing at his head, I'm thinking, he may actually think twice about attempting to disentangle himself," Mr Good explained.

Keith fell silent and stared at the water pistol in his hands. It was vivid red and so obviously plastic he doubted very much if anyone would believe it was a real gun. He was a bag of nerves, and he trembled at the thought of what lay ahead.

"But there is nothing we can do until our friends return." Mr Good sighed as he kicked off his flip-flops and sat on the bright orange carpet with both legs set straight out in front.

Keith glanced up. "How long have they been gone now?" he asked curiously.

Mr Good bent his left leg and placed the sole of his foot alongside the knee of his right leg. "About twenty," he replied.

"Twenty? Twenty what? Is that minutes? Hours? Days? Inches?"

Mr Good nodded. "All of those," he replied.

"Time is different here," he reminded Keith as he allowed his left leg to lie relaxed on the ground. "Time flies, I believe, is an expression often used in your world."

Keith shrugged.

"Unfortunately, time here doesn't fly. Time here isn't blessed with a feather-covered appendage." He bent forward, remembering to keep his back straight. "Time here moves mostly crabwise."

The Boy Scout sighed and shook his head slowly. "I'll never get used to this place."

Mr Good winced as he felt the stretch in the hamstring of his right leg.

Chapter 29

Arthur ran. Or rather his legs ran. His legs were in control, and he had no choice in the matter. His black-cuffed trousers moved along the deep, purplish-red corridors at a terrific speed. Meanwhile, his brain was sending signals, frantic electrochemical impulses, to his lower limbs in a desperate effort to make them stop, or at least slow down a bit. Either the messages weren't getting through or, more worryingly, the legs were deliberately ignoring the brain's polite request. Yesterday, because of the stiffness in his knee joints, he had difficulty standing, and his ankles were so swollen he could barely walk. Today his legs were galloping at such a rapid pace that the two-toned shoes on his feet only touched the ground every third or fourth stride. Crimson gave way, eventually, to magenta, and still Arthur ran.

#

The oak stairway wasn't wide enough to go two abreast, so they descended into the gloom in single file with a guard at the front, another bringing up the rear, and one in the middle somewhere.

Terrence leaned forward and whispered in the pesky girl's ear. "What's the noisiest game in the world?" he asked her.

The brass candle lantern, held aloft by the guard at Terrence's back, sent giant, spooky shadows ahead of them down the stairway.

"Tennis," replied Lorraine immediately. "Because you can't play without a racket."

Terrence grimaced. "What did the balloon say to the pin?"

"Hi there, buster."

Melvin smiled. He couldn't see the look on Terrence's face, but he guessed he was peeved.

"You're beginning to annoy me now," he growled. "You think you're really smart, don't you?"

"No, I don't," responded Lorraine as she gripped the carved handrail tightly and negotiated the last few oak steps with care. "Really, I don't."

The guard in front stepped off the bottom step and set foot on the cold, uneven stone floor of the undercroft. Vince came next, sniffing the musty, stale air, followed closely by the second guard. Vince offered no resistance as his two arms were clutched by a muscular guard each. Melvin, Lorraine, and then Terrence soon joined them in the dark underground chamber. The third guard, with the lantern raised, positioned himself at the foot of the stairs.

In the dim artificial light, Melvin could see the large brass key still located in the lock. The metal door itself was open no more than a finger breadth.

The two guards pushed and shoved Vince forward as Terrence slowly pulled open the door.

"Here is your room." Terrence grinned. "Make yourself at home."

Vince's eyes dazzled in the glare of the magenta light as the door opened wider. The guards threw him forcefully to the floor of the cell, and from there he looked up at Terrence squint eyed.

Melvin and Lorraine guessed it was now their turn to be grabbed forcefully and propelled unceremoniously into the cell. They landed on Vince, bounced off him, hit a side wall, and then tripped over a cardboard box, spilling the broken cups and saucers onto the floor and smashing them into even smaller pieces.

Terrence nodded his approval. *Credit where credit's due,* he thought. The guards certainly know how to push and shove and propel a victim unceremoniously. "May I suggest you all make yourselves comfortable?" he said when the commotion was over. "Because you may be here for some time."

When she regained her balance Lorraine looked around the cell at the pump, the storage tank, the pipes, the oak beams, the bench, and the window. It was familiar to her, of course. After all, they were here only … she struggled to recall. Two days ago? Two weeks ago? The past was a little blurred around the edges. Well, Mr Good did say that time was different here.

"Thank you," replied Melvin. "We will call if we need anything."

Terrence stood in the doorway and regarded Melvin closely. "You can call if you like, but I won't come. Nobody will come. Nobody will ever come. Ever." He grinned as he took a step back, closing the door slowly behind him. "In fact, Vile mentioned something about throwing away the key." He poked his head inside the cell before the door shut completely. "Into a bottomless pit, I believe." He laughed an evil laugh.

The metal door shut with a clang, and the large brass key turned in the lock. On reflection, his laugh perhaps lacked the resonance, the sharp, vibrating, nasal tone, of Vile's celebrated evil laugh, but it was quite a nasty laugh nonetheless.

"This is your home now," he shouted. "Forever!" His quite nasty laugh echoed off the walls of the underground chamber.

Melvin, Lorraine, and Vince listened to the guards' leather sandals ascending the oak stairway, gradually decreasing in volume. Eventually, Terrence's laugh faded into the distance too.

"Forever?" gulped Melvin.

Vince sat down on the wooden bench under the window. "You both must learn to be patient."

"Patient?" Lorraine stared at him in surprise. "But forever is a long time, Vince."

From an inside pocket Vince took a comb and opened it up with a flick action. "It will soon pass."

Lorraine sighed.

#

"One ... two ... three ..."

Go or stay? Walk to the end of the long crimson corridor and poke his head around the corner to see if Melvin, Lorraine, and the others were there? Or remain unseen inside this hidden opening?

The wizard mused. "Six ... salmon ... eight ..."

Of course, popping back through the portal and discussing his next move with Mr Good was an option.

"Eleven ... twelve ... thirteen ..."

But risky. What if Melvin, Lorraine, and Vince showed up while he was away? They would pass by the invisible gateway without knowing it was even there and head off towards the redder mazes and labyrinths and the Nether Regions, getting lost forever.

"Sixteen ... seventeen ... eighteen ..."

Mr Good's plan was for Mugwump to take Terrence by surprise, as he passed by, and bundle him through the portal.

But where were they? Had something gone wrong?

"Twenty-one ... twenty-two ... twenty-three ..."

He decided to count to thirty and then, if there was still no sign of them, make a decision. Go or stay?

"Twenty-seven ... twenty-eight ... twenty-nine ..."

#

"Mr Good trusted us, and we've let him down." Lorraine sat on the wooden bench opposite the metal door.

Although he had forever to do so, Vince was acquainting himself with his new surroundings. He circled the square room a couple of times, tapped the walls with his knuckles here and there, and replaced the broken crockery back in the cardboard box. "Nobody can go blamin' me," he said as he stood on the bench and looked out through the window. "It was the old-timer's fault."

Melvin was contemplating the prospect of spending time without end here in this strange world, locked away for everlasting time in this cold and damp cell. For eternity. Forever. He shook his head sadly and thought of his parents. They must be beside themselves with worry. He thought of the questions they would be asking. Had he run away? Why had he run away? Where was he? Why had he dismantled his large student sleeper bunk bed and taken that too?

"Melvin?"

Their questions would never have answers.

"What do you think, Melvin?"

It was Lorraine calling his name twice that roused Melvin from his reverie. "Think?" he blinked rapidly. "Think about what?"

"Do you think Mr Good regrets choosing us now?" She looked at him quizzically. "After all, we have messed up his plan."

The magenta light from the corridor that Vince looked out on illuminated the cell so brightly. "It was the old-timer's fault," he repeated without taking his eyes off the tiny portion of Limbo below.

Lorraine chose to ignore Vince. Instead she probed Melvin further. "Will Mr Good be angry with us?"

"No, of course not. Mr Good will not be angry with us." Melvin put on his bravest face. "Mr Good will be fine. Everything will work out, Loz. Don't worry. Good always triumphs over evil."

Vince pushed his face as far as he possibly could between the iron bars in an effort to see a little bit more corridor. "Maybe so in y'actual physical world," he told them. "But here it's different."

It was Melvin's turn to ignore Vince. "Mr Good will know what to do. He'll guess something has gone wrong when we don't return as planned. You'll see."

Lorraine was worried. "I don't see that there's much he can do about it now. His plan has failed."

"On the contrary." Melvin smiled. "He'll probably put Plan B into operation immediately."

"Plan B?"

"All good plans worth their salt have a Plan B, Loz. Everyone knows that."

Lorraine didn't. "Do they?"

Vince wasn't aware that all good plans worth their salt had a Plan B either. But right now he was more interested in the view from the window.

"Of course. It's a substitute plan for use in the event of the original plan going wrong."

"Mr Good never mentioned anything about a Plan B."

"No he didn't, because he was hoping …"

"Plan B?" Lorraine stood and paced up and down. "Plan B? Why didn't he use Plan B in the first place?"

"Well –" began Melvin.

"I'll tell you why, shall I?" She stopped pacing and stood with her back against the metal door. "Because it's not as good as Plan A, that's why!

And what happened to that ingenious little scheme?" She looked directly at Melvin. "It failed. Thanks to us."

Vince's body stiffened. "Old-timer!" he called out, standing as rigid as the iron bars he gripped so tightly.

"And before you say another word, Vince." Lorraine anticipated his response. "It wasn't the old-timer's fault. We can't blame Arthur. Mr Good relied on us as a team, and the team let him down."

Vince shook his head. "It's not that." He saw something through the window. "It's the old-timer." His words came out in gasps. "I've just seen y'actual old-timer."

"What?"

In an instant Melvin was standing on the wooden bench.

"Arthur?"

Lorraine too had eased Vince aside and was peering through the bars at a small, empty section of magenta maze.

"Where?"

Vince positioned himself behind them, looking through the window over their heads. "He was there," he insisted. "I saw him."

They were on the verge of disbelieving him when Arthur suddenly appeared, staring up at them and jogging on the spot.

"Arthur?"

Was it Arthur? Or was it Vile? It was impossible to distinguish between them.

"How can we be sure?" whispered Lorraine.

"I have an idea," said Melvin. "Mr Good did say it may help us along the way."

Melvin watched the person, who was probably Arthur but by the same token could possibly be Vile, and saw he was slowing down. His run was a gentle jog now. "Your keyword?" Melvin asked him hesitantly. "What is it?"

Arthur looked up. The effects of the medicine were gradually wearing off, and recollections of Mr Good and the plan were trickling back into his memory bank drop by drop, leaving a vague memory and an image resting somewhere in his subconscious. "Rolling," he replied. "And your keywords, if I'm not mistaken, are 'penguin' and 'downhill'."

"Arthur!" Lorraine smiled. "It is you."

"What the dickens happened to you?" demanded Melvin. "You were supposed to be waiting around that corner."

"I'm sorry, children, It was the medicine. I got confused." His upturned face looked at them reproachfully. "I must have gone round two corners by mistake."

Melvin sighed.

"Then I had an uncontrollable urge to run."

"Listen, Arthur," said Melvin. "You need to keep running. You need to find Mugwump and tell him we've been captured and thrown in a cell."

Arthur jogged in a wide circle and momentarily disappeared from their limited view.

Lorraine waited for him to reappear. "Mr Good needs to know the plan has failed."

"Find Mr Good? Find the salmon guy? That's easy for you to say. Which way do I go? It's like a maze out here!"

With his elbows, Vince nudged himself in between Melvin and Lorraine. He positioned his face in the middle of their two heads and looked out. "It's that way ... ish," he told Arthur, pointing in the direction that Arthur had just come from. He advised him to take two left turns and a right turn. He should keep taking two left turns and a right turn until the purplish red corridor met the deep purplish red corridor. Then the sequence must be reversed. Two right turns, one left turn, two right turns, and one left until ...

The key turned in the lock, and the metal door opened slowly.

Chapter 30

Vile sat comfortably on his black leather swivel chair. He leaned forward and hit a few buttons on the keypad. On a spot monitor he watched, with interest, as Terrence and three guards pushed and shoved the pesky prisoners across the great central hall. He changed the image and waited for them to reach the front security door area of his private quarters. Full screen on another monitor, he followed them across the ground floor of his sumptuous apartment.

A few moments later there came the anticipated knock on his door. He ignored it.

#

The high ceiling was supported by a dozen huge hammer beams.

"What is green then red, green then red?" asked Terrence as he waited at the door at the end of the wide hallway.

Lavish tapestries and paintings decorated the walls on both sides.

"I don't know." Lorraine shrugged. "What is green then red, green then red?"

The gold carpet under their feet had a nap longer and softer than velvet.

"I'm not telling you."

Lorraine sighed.

"It will give you something to think about, something to pass the time." Terrence grinned. "During the endless, lonely epochs that lie ahead."

He gave the door another knock and listened.

#

Vile needed to assume a particular attitude: a feeling of superiority. To that end he experimented with a number of different poses. He tried sitting forward nonchalantly, tried casually resting his elbows on the black leather armrests, and tried clasping both hands together behind his head with a look of cool indifference. He wanted to create a sense of overbearing self-importance and an arrogant contempt for the weak.

Finally, he leaned the chair back, stretched his legs out on the spacious walnut desk, and bid them enter.

"The pesky kids!" he beamed after the door had opened and Melvin, Lorraine, and Vince were pushed and shoved inside. "Nice of you to drop in."

The three guards stood like guards in front of the door, and Terrence hovered in the background.

Melvin quickly regained his composure. "We told you we'd be back."

"We were on our way back, actually," fibbed Lorraine. "When those gorillas of yours seized us."

"Of course you were." Vile smiled derisively. "Of course you were, but I thought I'd send them out to meet you, just in case. We didn't want you getting lost, now did we?"

Vile uncrossed his ankles, swung his legs off the desk, and stood up.

"That was very considerate of you," admitted Melvin reluctantly.

"Yes, I agree." Vile approached them, and as he did so he switched his attention to Vince. "What have we here?"

He didn't blink an eyelid as Vile looked him up and down. "The name's Vince," said Vince.

"Vince, eh?" said Vile thoughtfully as he circled him. "I'm the evil Vile."

Vince nodded. "I've heard about you," he replied when Vile eventually reappeared.

"Have you now. What have you heard? Nothing good, I hope." He grinned.

Before Vince could respond Vile stamped on his foot, accidentally on purpose, as he passed him by on his way to address the guards. Vince didn't flinch.

"Guards! I want you to stay there by that door." He spoke slowly, clearly, and distinctly. "I may need you in a little while to help with the tor … ture." He carefully enunciated both syllables.

"Torture?" exclaimed Melvin from somewhere in the centre of the room.

"So stay there!" Vile watched the guards closely, hoping for a flicker of intelligence. "Understand?"

Two of the guards looked at each other in a puzzled way. "Ugh?" grunted one to the other.

"Look, it's quite simple." Vile frowned. "I want you to stay there. Don't move, be quiet, and pay attention. Get it?"

"Ugh!" nodded the third guard. He was possibly the more intelligent of the three.

"You do understand." Vile grinned. "Excellent." He turned, congratulating himself on his communication skills, to face the pesky kids and Vince.

Three guards exited the room in single file. Vile spun round in time to see the rear of the third guard disappearing through the door and out into the hallway.

"Come back, you bozos," yelled Terrence as he hurriedly chased after them.

"I don't believe it," groaned Vile. Overcome with surprise and bewilderment, he stood in the doorway and watched Terrence pursue the guards across the golden carpet and past the lavish tapestries and paintings. "That's just typical!" He uttered a long, deep sigh. "I'm surrounded by fools."

"Vile?" Lorraine broached the subject hesitantly. "You mentioned torture just now."

"You can't get the staff these days," he grumbled as he closed the door a little, leaving it only slightly ajar. "That's the trouble." For a moment he appeared distracted.

"You look like a smart lad. You have a good build, too – very strong across the shoulders, I notice," he said, eyeing Vince once more. "There could be a future for you here as a guard."

He stood directly in front of Vince and pushed his face close. "I'm looking for someone with initiative, drive, ambition, and a willingness to succeed. Could be just up your street. What do you think?"

The pungent onion aroma of Vile's breath made Vince's eyes fill up and overflow with drops of watery fluid.

"Excellent promotion prospects too," continued Vile. "In fact, there could be a vacancy as my left-hand man very shortly. The man in the position at the moment is totally unsuitable."

The man in the position at the moment squeezed through the open door into the room with just one muscular guard in tow.

"There you are, Terrence," Vile turned. "I was just saying what a useless, hopeless, worthless little twit you are,"

"Thank you, your odiousness."

Vince wiped his wet cheeks with the back of his hand. "What's all this about torture, Vile?" he asked.

"Torture." Vile grinned as he rounded his desk and sat on his black leather chair. "Torture is one of my favourite words beginning with the letter T."

"Would I be right in assuming," asked Melvin tentatively, "that we will be the recipients of this torture?"

Vile shrugged. "If I don't get satisfactory answers to the questions I'm about to ask you, then yes." He leaned forward. "Persuasive methods will be used."

"Persuasive methods?" said Lorraine with a gulp. "What sort of persuasive methods?"

"Well, it won't be very pleasant, if I know Vile," opined Terrence.

"Questions?" Melvin wondered. "What questions are you going to ask us?"

"Well, it won't be Trivial Pursuits, if I know Vile," opined Terrence again.

Vile looked at Terrence for a long moment, dangerously, with a fixed gaze. "Shut up, you halfwit."

"Sorry, your foulness."

"Questions like –" Vile swivelled his chair one revolution as he gave it some thought. "Why are you pesky kids here? What is that Mr Good up to? That sort of thing."

"Up to?" Melvin made a face of mock surprise. "Is Mr Good up to something, then?"

Vile slammed his open hand down hard, angrily, on the reddish brown desktop. The loud, explosive, resounding slap of skin on walnut made everyone jump, apart from the muscular guard and Vince.

"Don't give me that, kid," Vile snarled. "I know he's up to something, and I know that you know. So don't try to hoodwink me, and don't try to fob me off by pleading ignorance. You've chosen the wrong one for that. There's something brewing out there deep in the corridors of Limbo. Some scheme is being hatched. I want to know what it is, and I want to know right now!"

He jumped up, sending the black leather swivel chair careening across the room.

"Honestly, Vile, we don't know anything," said Lorraine in an effort to placate him. "Mr Good didn't say much to us. We only saw him briefly, as a matter of fact. Actually, I don't think it was Mr Good who brought us here at all. Well, if it was he didn't say so."

"Rubbish, of course he did. Who else could have brought you here? Lord Riddle?" Vile sneered.

Terrence laughed. "A fictional dream ambassador? Is he summoning folk from the physical world now? Whatever next, your cantankerousness?"

Vile ignored Terrence and resumed his interest in Vince. "You know more than you're letting on, I wager. What do you have to say for yourself? What's going on?"

Vince shot Lorraine a nervous glance and then Melvin a worried one. "You can torture me if you like," he said defiantly. "But I won't be tellin' you Mr Good's plan."

"Vince!" snapped Melvin.

Vile arched a brow. "So, there is a plan?" Across his mouth, the beginnings of an evil grin was already forming.

"For pity's sake, Vince," frowned Lorraine.

Vince stood red-faced, flushed with embarrassment. "Sorry, it just slipped out," he mumbled as he bowed his head apologetically. "I promise I won't say another word."

"We'll see about that," growled Vile as he moved in for the kill.

He was joined at his side by Terrence. "Let me cut the teddy boy's tongue out, your horridness," said Terrence with his unpleasant tinny voice. "He'll soon talk."

Vile was just about to admonish him for being such a dunderhead when he stopped himself. "Teddy boy?" He looked at Terrence curiously. "Did you say teddy boy?"

"Yes, that's what he is." Terrence nodded eagerly. "He's a teddy boy, and he likes that rocking and rolling music. Pathetic, isn't it?"

"Rocking and rolling music?" Vile mused, regarding Vince with a glassy stare. "I heard that niece of mine humming 'Heartbreak Rock' earlier. Or was it 'Jailhouse Hotel'? Either way, it's given me an idea."

Melvin, Lorraine, and Vince stood in uneasy silence in the centre of the room. The threat of torture hung dangerously in the air. Was this Vile's new idea? Did it involve persuasive methods too?

"A devilishly cunning idea." He paused in mid-muse to bark instructions at Terrence. "Tell the guard to take the pesky kids back to the cell. But be sure to leave the teddy boy here, and tell Peggy Sue I want to see her immediately."

His evil grin, in its rudimentary stage earlier, was now fully established. A broad smile exhibited two rows of yellow teeth. "I'm simply too clever for my own evil," he decided.

Chapter 31

Arthur paused momentarily at a T-junction at the very end of the magenta maze. He noticed the corridor ahead was a deeper, purpler, redder one. He took a left turn.

He wondered why Melvin, Lorraine, and Vince had disappeared so suddenly. One moment they were there, up in the window talking to him, and the next ...

He made a left turn again. They were gone. He had stayed and waited alone in the silence for a while, hoping they would reappear, but ...

Right turn this time.

They never did. Eventually, he shrugged, moved slowly away, and began his quest to find the salmon guy.

He made a left turn. He was moving at a speed somewhere between a gentle jog and a brisk walk now.

What was it Vince said? Take two left turns and a right turn? To keep taking two left turns and a right turn. Two left turns and a right turn. He repeated this over and over inside his head and took another left.

Until the purplish red corridor meets the deep purplish red corridor. He took a right.

Then the sequence must be reversed. He stopped dead in his tracks. Reversed?

Blood drained from his face, turning it unpleasantly pale.

#

Vince was alone. Ahead of him, lined up along one wall, were nearly three dozen glass screens. Each one of these transparent windows was

153

divided into sixteen different views of Limbo. Vince recognised many of them from his travels. Daring, now, to sit on the black leather swivel chair, he leaned across the spacious walnut desk and regarded the keypad with fascination. It was part of the desk, made of the same reddish brown wood and raised several inches above the surface.

Across the middle of it were three rows of black keys, some with numbers on and some with letters. It was similar to a typewriter, he thought, except there were other keys too with coloured dots on them: either red, blue, or green. Above those keys was a small, rectangular Perspex panel and above that a short, vertical lever with a black half-ball-shaped handle on top.

Down the left side were two columns of nine grey buttons. The buttons had unusual wording on them that made no sense to Vince at all, like Zonal Switch, Insert Command, Relay Monitor, Aroma Control, Select Preset, and other equally strange words.

In the bottom right-hand corner of the keypad was a big white button, and on it was a large black capital letter I.

He listened. The door was almost completely pushed to, and all was quiet in the passageway behind it. Hesitantly, Vince applied pressure to a random key somewhere across the middle of the keypad. Nothing noticeably happened.

He pressed another key, but again nothing of significance occurred.

The next key he tried was the one with the red dot on it. The moment Vince touched it, the Perspex panel lit, and the words Red Mode flashed up.

Encouraged by this, he chose the first of the grey buttons down the left side. Immediately, between ten and fifteen glass screens along the wall, the ones featuring red corridors in all their various shades altered from sixteen separate images to eight. The next button down divided the screens again, but into quarters this time. Realising the grey buttons made things happen, he moved his finger down the column and hit the next one marked Spot Monitor.

There were three spot monitors along the wall, one serving each of the three primary colours. A spot monitor allowed the operator to pick out an image from the multitude of images and reproduce it full screen on a separate one below. With the keypad in Red Mode, Vince hit the button marked Spot Monitor repeatedly and watched, spellbound, as different parts of Limbo, the red parts, appeared on just one of the glass screens.

Then, after thirty or forty hits, he saw something that forced him to take a sudden, short intake of breath. "The old-timer!" Vince gasped as he stood up and walked over and closer to the image. "Old-timer," he called out in a loud whisper as he rapped the glass screen with his knuckles.

Arthur didn't react, of course. He was leaning against a wall, exhausted, his face particularly pallid.

For a moment he doubted himself, but only for a moment. "Old-timer?" It had to be Arthur. Well, he was sure it wasn't Vile. How could it be? Vile had only just left the room, and the crimson maze was miles away.

Vince glanced across at the door. It still hadn't opened. Vile still hadn't returned. But any moment soon he could do. What if he saw Arthur dressed up as Vile? Vince figured that could interfere with the progress of Mr Good's plan somewhat. He knew what he had to do. He knew he had to change the image on that glass screen to another view of Limbo, to any view of Limbo. It mattered not which one as long as it didn't have Arthur in it.

He reached over the back of the desk. With the keypad the wrong way round and the strange words upside down, his fingers fumbled for the grey buttons. One clumsy finger landed in the narrow space between two buttons, activating both together. He looked around anxiously to see what effect hitting two buttons together at the same time had. He was horrified to see Arthur had turned to a stone statue, his face contorted with the surprise of it all.

Vince wasn't to know it was the image on the glass screen that had frozen and not Arthur himself. The twisted expression on his face wasn't surprise; it was pain. His arthritis was giving him gyp.

Vince scooted round to the front of the desk to face the keypad from a more favourable angle. Frantically, he pressed all eighteen of the grey buttons in turn.

Not a lot changed. Arthur remained in full view, still motionless, his expression still hideous and misshapen like a gargoyle on a church roof.

Using both hands and every available finger, Vince jabbed the letters, numbers, and coloured dots across the middle of the keypad in no particular pattern, desperately hoping each key he hit would be the one to make the old-timer disappear.

But Arthur didn't disappear. Vigorously, Vince grabbed the vertical lever with the domed top. He pushed it up, pulled it down, guided it left, and steered it to the right, but without success: Arthur continued to stare back at him with unseeing eyes.

Vince heard a noise outside. Out in the passageway was the sound of footsteps. At any moment now the door would open, and …

He panicked and instinctively pressed the big white button in the bottom right-hand corner of the keypad, the one emblazoned with the large black capital letter I. The beeping sound it made was short, sharp, and high-pitched, and it startled him. It made Arthur jump too.

#

"Thirty."

Go or stay? It was decision time for Mugwump. Would he walk to the end of the long crimson corridor and poke his head around the corner to see if Melvin, Lorraine, and the others were there? Or remain unseen inside this hidden opening?

Mugwump mused some more. After he had mused for a short while, two things took him by surprise. For a start he was surprised, when he looked up, to see he wasn't standing in a portal at all. The second surprise was leaning against a wall a few feet away: a figure wearing a black and gold pinstriped jacket, fully lined with red satin, and matching cuffed trousers with red braces.

The wizard removed his pointy hat, rubbed his curly, pale yellow hair, and hurriedly gave the new situation some urgent consideration. There were only four explanations that he could see. Either someone in the control room at the Palace of Somnium had activated the Influence button on the keypad, which was highly improbable, or … He shook his head. The other three explanations were virtually impossible and involved some extremely old and antiquated dream magic.

Mugwump replaced his hat and gently coughed to announce his presence. Arthur jumped out of his skin for the second time in as many minutes.

"My dear fellow," said the wizard with a bow. "Forgive me if I startled you, but –" He faltered, allowing himself a second or two of thinking time.

Arthur identified the person before him as someone he had previously seen or known at some time, but he was struggling to put a name to the face. His facial expression was blank for a moment. "The salmon guy?" he gasped.

Mugwump nodded and chose his words carefully. "If I mentioned 'keyword' to you, tell me, what would be your response?"

"Well, it wouldn't be," Arthur wheezed like an old steam train, "'penguin' or 'downhill'. My response would be 'rolling'."

"Salmon!" beamed Mugwump as he moved closer. "Arthur, it is you." He placed a caring hand on the old man's shoulder. "What happened?"

"What happened?" He grimaced. "What happened? That medicine you gave me, the effects have worn off, that's what's happened," he replied asthmatically. "All my joints ache, most of my tendons are inflamed, I am suffering from chronic lower back pain, and I'm experiencing a backflow of acid into my esophagus.

"He flinched as he attempted to find a more comfortable leaning position up against the crimson wall. "But apart from that I'm fine," he added.

Mugwump smiled sympathetically. "When I asked you what happened, Arthur, I was actually enquiring about the plan. Melvin, Lorraine, and Vince? Where are they? What happened?"

Arthur grunted and mumbled something under his breath about his health being more important than a silly old plan, especially a plan that had failed so miserably. But nevertheless he told the wizard what happened. He described everything from the beginning, from the moment they heard Terrence and the muscular guards approaching. He told Mugwump how he hid around the corner but ended up going round two corners by mistake and about his urge to run and run and how he couldn't stop. He also mentioned his encounter with Melvin, Lorraine, and Vince. The wizard was particularly interested in this bit.

"High up they were, looking down on me from a window with iron bars."

Mugwump mused. "A window, you say?" He pondered. "With iron bars?"

He rubbed his chin and mulled this information over for a while. "I know this place," he finally decided. "The pump room. Not a pleasant salmon to spend too much time in. It's very small, cold, and damp too. If you stand on the wooden bench it affords a view of Limbo and the magenta maze, I believe."

"I see," said Arthur, even though he didn't see at all. "What does it all mean?"

"I strongly suspect it could mean that Melvin, Lorraine, and Vince have been captured by a fellow who bears a striking resemblance to yourself." Mugwump carefully placed a hand in the hollow under the upper part of Arthur's arm and manoeuvred him into an upright position that was almost, but not quite, vertical. "Therefore, we must go," he announced.

"Go?" Arthur was resigned to spending the rest of his days leaning against this crimson wall; he certainly wasn't expecting to ever move again. "Go where?"

"To the centre of the royal blue labyrinth, of course."

"But I can't." Arthur's legs had taken three or four reluctant steps by now. His upper body was still held tightly by the wizard's strong grip. "How can I face Mr Good again? He will be upset." The old man heaved a heavy sigh. "The plan has failed, and maybe he will think it's all my fault."

Mugwump laughed. "Mr Good will think no such thing, Arthur. Mr Good will be fine. And anyway, I dare say he'll put Plan B into operation."

"Plan B?"

"Mr Good will have a Plan B. You mark my words. And besides, my dear salmon, you need medicine."

Arthur nodded. He couldn't disagree with that. Although the medicine made him hyperactive and forgetful, it also made him pain-free for the first time in decades, and he liked that.

"However, I think maybe I should reduce the dosage next time," continued the wizard. "Three spoonfuls was possibly a couple of spoonfuls too many."

Twenty paces into their journey Arthur had to stop for a breather.

Mugwump looked along the corridor ahead with a worried expression on his round face. Opening night of Vile's new nightmare was imminent, and the nearest portal was still over one hundred strides away. He quickly calculated Arthur would be taking five more of these rest breaks before they even entered it. At this rate they wouldn't be reaching the centre of the royal blue labyrinth or meeting Mr Good again during the current dream span.

By then it could be too late.

Chapter 32

"Vile was ever so angry," whispered Barry.

The subject of Garry's escape from the Palace of Somnium was still the main talking point amongst the dream actors.

"Apparently, he turned the colour of a ripe tomato," revealed Harry. "Well, that's the rumour I overheard."

"Actually, I have it on good authority, namely this trusty witness of mine who was passing by at the time and saw our Garry and Vile together, that he was crimson. Almost purple." Larry leaned closer.

"Crimson?" gasped Barry.

"Almost purple?" gulped Harry.

"With steam coming out of his ears," added Larry for good measure.

Barry trembled. "I don't like the sound of this at all."

"Neither do I," agreed Harry. "He'll take it out on us, for sure."

While Barry and Harry were contemplating this, one of the mirrored panels along the wall opened, and Terrence stepped into the spacious drawing room.

"Oh no." Peggy Sue saw him first. She saw him before he saw her. She covered her face with the palm of her hand and half turned away as he scanned the room.

"Peg," he cried. "There you are."

Reluctantly and gradually she removed her hand. "Terry," she said, smiling falsely.

"How about a little kiss for your fiancé?" He puckered his lips, knocking tables occupied by dream actors out of the way, as he approached her.

"I'm very busy, Terry," she told him as she took a step back.

He stopped suddenly, as if he'd walked into a double-glazed patio door that he thought was open. "Busy?"

"Rehearsing," she told him. "The big song and dance routine at the end," she explained and took another little step backwards.

Terrence frowned. "But, Peg, we need to talk."

"There isn't time, Terry. Opening night is only three dream spans away."

"Arrangements have to be made, Peg."

"Yes," she conceded. "But not now." She looked around the room shyly. "Not here." Every dream actor was watching her now as she washed her dirty linen in public.

"Vile has been pestering me to name the day," Terrence persisted.

"Uncle?" She laughed. "He's not interested. He doesn't like weddings."

"But you're his niece." Terrence took a step closer. "And I am, sort of, his friend."

"Friend?" Peggy Sue scoffed. "Come off it, Terry. He hates you."

"He doesn't." Terrence considered this to be unjust. "I make him laugh. Only just now I said to him, 'what runs but never walks, Vile?' 'I don't know, Terrence,' said he. What is it that runs but never walks?' 'A nose,' said I, and he roared with laughter."

Peggy Sue stared at him for a long moment. "He roared with laughter? At that old joke? I find that very hard to believe, Terry."

Terrence sighed. "There was a time when you thought my riddles were amusing, Peg."

"That's not true, Terry," she replied indignantly. "I have never found you funny."

He tried to recall an example of something in the past he had said to provoke laughter or to cause amusement, but he couldn't. He realised, then, he had never told a joke until the journey here. Something happened on that journey from Torment Towers with Vile, Peggy Sue, and the guards. What had happened? Now he had thousands of riddles inside his head trying to get out. But why? He didn't know why. There was a gap in his memory.

However, Terrence was undeterred. "There was a time when you wouldn't have objected to a little kiss either," he said as he pulled his lips tightly together, pushed them outwards, and moved menacingly towards her.

Peggy Sue quickly took a step to one side, putting a table and four Dream Actors between them. "Terry, this isn't the time or the place."

"It never is the right time or the right place just lately, is it?" he replied as he chased her around the table. "What am I going to tell Vile?"

"Just tell my uncle we believe in long engagements," she cried as she dodged this way and that. "Very long engagements, perhaps an era or more."

Terrence stopped. "You'll be able to tell him yourself," he told her in between deep breaths. "He wants to see you."

"What? When?" she gasped.

"Immediately." He grinned. "That's what he said."

"Why didn't you say?" She glowered.

"I just have." Terrence made no move towards her as she slowly backed away.

She moved carefully, feeling her way between the tables and chairs and towards the panelled mirror. Beyond the mirror was a passageway that afforded a short-cut to her uncle's apartment.

"Peg," he called out meekly as she almost reached the exit. "What have I got to do? What would I have to give you to get a little kiss?"

She looked at him. With every pair of eyes in the room watching her, awaiting her reply, she slowly opened the mirrored door. There was a pause.

"Anaesthetic?" she suggested.

Chapter 33

Mr Good lay face down on the bright orange carpet in a prone position. Supported only by his forearms and toes, he slowly raised his body off the ground.

Keith had removed the suitcase and placed it behind the sofa, out of the way. He was now sitting in an armchair scribbling furiously in a notebook. To achieve the explorer belt he had to keep a diary of personal notes about the expedition. He paid the Dream Ambassador for Tranquil Dreams no attention whatsoever.

"I'm becoming worried, old chum," said Mr Good as he lifted his right arm up, straightened it, pointed it ahead, and held it in the air for a count of five.

Keith paused, chewed the end of his pencil for a moment, and then continued to write eagerly once more.

"They should be back by now," added Mr Good as he repeated the exercise with his left arm.

Keith was still taking no notice.

"They've been gone for nearly eight hours." He lifted his right leg off the ground and held it there, making sure to keep his back straight.

Keith hesitated. His pencil hovered above the notebook for just an instant. "Eight hours?" He looked up from his work for the first time with a perplexed expression. "I thought you said time was different here?"

"It is." Mr Good swivelled his head in Keith's direction and raised a silvery eyebrow. "When I say eight hours, old chum, what I really mean is eight revolutions of the Dream/Time Continuum, converted by hypothesis, supposition, and ... and ..."

"Sheer guesswork?" suggested Keith.

"Exactly," agreed Mr Good as he put his right leg down and elevated his left leg now. "Where you come from, young Keith, time moves forward directly. Things tend to occur in chronological order. Time is measured by days, months, and years. And just recently, I've noticed, they've begun to give each year a number." He sighed and returned his left leg to its starting position. "As I said, time is different here and not so simple, I'm afraid. We have eras and we have epochs, of course, but their duration isn't fixed. They fluctuate. An era generally takes longer to pass by than an epoch. But not always. It all depends what angle time is travelling at."

"Angle?" Keith was still perplexed.

Mr Good raised his left arm and right leg simultaneously. "As a rule, time moves at an angle somewhere between forty-five and 180 degrees," he explained. "To tell you precisely the current angular measurement I would need to be in possession of a Dream Protractor." The toes of his right foot pointed towards the teak sideboard behind the sofa. "I've looked in Mugwump's drawers and searched through his odds, ends, bits, and pieces, but I couldn't find one, which is no surprise really." He reversed the exercise. "Mugwump is not interested in the passage of time. Wizards are rarely concerned with such matters."

Keith didn't understand a word of it, but he wrote it all down in his notebook anyway.

Mr Good sat up, crossed his legs, and rested his hands in the lap of his brown tunic. "There is a strong possibility, old chum, that the first part of my plan has failed." He said this with a doleful look on his face.

Keith was upset to see Mr Good's face looking so doleful. "You don't know that it's failed yet, Mr Good," he said cheerily. "They could have been delayed for any number of reasons. Grandpa's not as quick on his feet these days. That's what it is. He'll be holding them up, you'll see."

Mr Good nodded sadly. "Perhaps you're right, young Keith."

"Let's give them two more hours," continued Keith. "Or rather two more revolutions of that Dream/Time Continuum thingy before we start admitting defeat."

Mr Good managed a smile. He sat in the armchair opposite and brooded in silence. "I'm homesick, old chum," he sighed eventually.

Keith wanted to say he was missing his home too but decided now would not be a good time. "The Palace of Somnium sounds amazing, Mr Good," he said.

"It is," agreed Mr Good. "It is amazing."

He brooded some more. "I miss my exercise bike particularly," he added after a short pause. "Not to mention my beautiful little writing desk. And I miss my porcelain tea set, of course."

Keith missed his family and friends, actually. He wondered how one could possibly miss a porcelain tea set more than one's loved ones.

"I have it on display in my office on a Welsh dresser. But it's not just any tea set," Mr Good was quick to clarify. "It's very old."

"How old is old?" Keith tried to look interested. He stifled a yawn as he doodled in the top right-hand corner of the next blank page in his notebook.

"Pre–Big Bang," replied Mr Good matter-of-factly.

"What?" Keith almost choked. "The Big Bang? Do you mean the tremendous explosion that started the expansion of the universe? That Big Bang?"

Mr Good nodded.

Now Keith was interested. "But that was about fifteen billion years ago."

"A few hundred eras indeed," agreed Mr Good. He leaned forward. "Let me tell you the tale of the Ancient Tea Set of Firmamentum."

Keith sat comfortably with his pencil poised.

"'Twas the eve of the Big Bang," Mr Good began. "Picture the scene, young Keith, if you can: no space, no time, no light, no dark. Nothing. Not a sausage, apart from a large chunk of matter and energy. It was on this large chunk of matter and energy where the three legendary Dream Ancestors met for afternoon tea and buttered scones. One of those shadowy figures spread out the picnic blanket and another placed the scones on side plates while a third poured tea from a pot."

Keith listened in awed silence.

Mr Good loosened the belt of white cord around his waist, retied it, and then continued: "Sitting there in the vast expanse of the heavens the Dream Ancestors talked and disagreed and argued and fell out and made up and talked some more until all the important decisions were made."

"Decisions?" asked Keith enthralled.

Mr Good shrugged. "The size and shape of things were more or less sorted at this point, but they had yet to agree on colours."

"Colours?"

"Which colours should be included in the rainbow? Which ones should be the primary colours? What colour would suit grass best – and the sky and bananas and penguins? And, perhaps more importantly, who should do the washing-up afterwards?"

Keith looked at Mr Good in astonishment. "So, are you saying the tea set they used all those billions of years ago, as they were making all those decisions, is the one that is now in your office on a Welsh dresser?"

"On two illuminated display shelves," Mr Good confirmed proudly.

Keith stared at Mr Good in disbelief. "What happened to the picnic blanket?" he wondered.

"Still missing, I'm afraid." Mr Good sighed. "Following the subsequent explosion all remnants of that afternoon tea party were lost, it was presumed forever. Then, remarkably, my tea set was discovered many eras later on a brigantine heading for the Strait of Gibraltar. But that's another story for another time."

He sat back in the armchair. "So, old chum, that's the tale of the Ancient Tea Set of Firmamentum," he concluded.

It was several long moments before Keith could speak again. "Gosh and double gosh!" Then he realised his pencil was still poised and he hadn't yet written a thing. Hurriedly, he found a blank page in his notebook. "The ... Ancient ... Tea Set ... of ..."

He looked up.

Mr Good was standing with his hands on his hips, his body leaning to the left as far as it could go.

"How are you spelling 'Firmamentum'?" asked the Boy Scout.

Chapter 34

The door to the control room at the very end of the wide hallway was open just a touch. Vile peered through the narrow gap. "Do you know exactly what you've got to do?" he whispered.

Peggy Sue was standing a yard or two behind him. She nodded. "You want to know the plan."

"Yes, the plan." He grinned. "I want to know the plan. I must know what it is."

"Uncle." Her golden hair was in pigtails now, and she pulled at one of the plaits nervously. "If I find out what the plan is, you'll be pleased, won't you?"

Vile turned his head slowly and looked her up and down suspiciously. She was wearing a lime green circular skirt with pink polka dots, matching scarf, and a white short-sleeved top. "Yes?" he replied warily.

"So, if I do find out what the plan is, I was wondering, or rather hoping, Uncle, that you could possibly do me a favour too?"

Vile looked at her with a face like a volcano about to erupt.

Peggy Sue knew that facial expression only too well. "Yes, I know you don't do favours as a rule, uncle," she quickly added before his anger was expelled like molten lava. "But ..."

"The answer is no," snapped Vile before she could continue.

Peggy Sue wrinkled her nose in frustration. "I haven't told you what it is yet."

"I know very well what it is. It's the big song and dance routine at the end, isn't it? You don't want to do it, do you? Too girlie for you? Am I right?"

"It's not that, Uncle," she assured him. "Actually I love singing and dancing."

"You do?" Vile was visibly disappointed. He had only told her to choreograph the grand finale because she was a tomboy and he thought she would hate it. "You play rough games and enjoy boyish things like wrestling, sword fighting, and climbing trees in abandoned Dreamspaces, not singing and dancing."

"I've changed," she told him. "I think, perhaps, I've grown up or something."

"Grown up?" Vile was seething inside. This niece of his had deceived him. She hadn't had the decency to inform him of the change, and she was going to pay dearly for that. Her participation in his new nightmare, especially any involvement with the big song and dance routine at the end, was over. That much was obvious. Of course, he wasn't going to tell her that just yet. He needed her to find out all about the plan first. He'll give her the bad news later.

"I've never asked you for a favour before, Uncle, and I'm only asking now because, well, because I'm desperate."

Vile's smile was charmingly evil. "A favour, you say?"

"I need your help, uncle," she began. "It's Terry. Terrence."

He grimaced at the mention of his name.

"He's got this idea in his head. I don't know how it got into his head, but it's in there."

"An idea in Terrence's head?" Vile laughed. "It's going to be lonely."

She shuddered convulsively. "He sort of thinks we're getting married."

"Married?" For a short while Vile just stared at her as if she'd told him a joke but had delivered the punch line in Latin. "Married?" he repeated. "To Terrence? That nincompoop?"

Peggy Sue nodded, abashed.

"Now I understand why you are so upset," he said. With his hand, as he said it, he concealed a sickly grin.

Peggy Sue was encouraged by Vile's sympathetic tone. "Can you remove the idea from his head, uncle?" she pleaded.

He looked away and peeped once more through the crack between the jamb and the door. "Tell you what I'll do. Find out about the plan, and let me know all the details. If you do —" His grin widened. "I'll arrange for Terrence to marry one of the guards."

Peggy Sue nodded appreciatively and thanked him.

"You'll need this," from down by his feet, on the gold carpet, he picked up a pink vinyl-covered case.

Holding both arms outstretched, palms up, she took its weight.

"Now scram," he bellowed and stood aside.

Taking a deep breath, she brushed past him and, using her shoulder, pushed open the door.

#

The comb that a few moments earlier was gliding effortlessly through his thick, black, wavy hair, suddenly stopped. For a second he was paralysed, unable to move a muscle, until his lower jaw slackened, dropped, and just hung there a matter of inches above his chest. He watched her in speechless amazement as she shut the door with the medium heel of her white patent peep-toe shoes and smiled. It was a dazzling white smile, and Vince was immediately captivated.

"Sit down Vince."

He looked down at his legs. He was surprised to find himself in an upright position on his feet.

"It is Vince, isn't it?" said Peggy Sue as she crossed the room towards him.

It felt like his tongue was tied down by tent pegs. All he could manage was a sort of open-mouthed nod.

"I'm Peggy Sue," she announced. "Just like in that song by Buddy Holly." She rested the pink vinyl case on the spacious walnut desk. "How you rocking?" she asked.

Vince couldn't believe she had asked him that question. 'How you rockin'?' How long has it been since anyone asked him that? Too long. His gang, his mates – what were their names now? He couldn't remember. It had been too long. 'How you rockin'?' they would ask. 'I'm rollin',' he would say. 'I'm rollin'.

"I'm rollin'," he somehow managed to reply.

She smiled.

Using his hands to feel for the leather armrests behind and below, Vince carefully guided himself backwards and down into Vile's swivel chair.

"I'm a dance teacher," she told him. "I teach folk to sing and dance, sort of part-time." She smiled and leaned forward. "Has anyone ever told you that you look like Elvis?"

He shook his head slowly and tried to speak. The word he wanted got stuck somewhere in his respiratory tract between his pharynx and trachea, enveloped in folds of mucous membrane. He coughed to release it from the stickiness. "No," his high-pitched reply shot out, and he spluttered. "No," he repeated, this time in a much lower key.

"Well, I think you do, Vince," she said as she sat on the edge of the desk.

Vince remembered girls like this — maybe not as pretty as this, but girls dressed like this — at the Queens Ballroom on a Saturday night during the physical world phase of his life. They rarely talked to him and certainly didn't smile at him. And never, not once, did any of them ever tell him he looked like Elvis.

"What do you want with me?" He cast a nervous glance at the door. "And where is Vile?"

"Don't worry about him," she replied reassuringly. "It's just me and you."

She leaned closer, so close she could hear his heart thumping wildly. "I just had to talk to you, Vince, about rocking and rolling music. I love rocking and rolling music too."

Vince swooned.

"Elvis's middle name," she continued. "I've been trying to remember, but do you think I can remember what it is?" She shook her head, and her pigtails danced. "It's gone right out of my mind."

Vince could feel his heart thumping, pounding as if it would burst. "It's Aaron," he told her.

"Aaron!" She laughed. "Of course!" She slapped her thigh like the principal boy in that pantomime about the boy who wouldn't grow up. "Aaron. How could I forget?"

And then she used that smile again. Vince had to look away, shyly, down at his feet. He noticed how big and cumbersome his blue suede shoes looked in comparison to her small white shoes with the cute polka-dot chiffon bows.

"I have other questions," she said. There was a seriousness to her tone now.

He looked up, and despite the smile he thought he saw concern on her face too. However, it didn't spoil her beauty. Vince thought she was beautiful in a large round eyes, long dark lashes, high cheekbones, small button nose, fuller lips, flawless skin kind of way. He hoped he would know the answers.

"Do you know when Eddie Cochran was born?" she asked.

Eddie Cochran? Now there was a name from the distant past, an epoch or more ago now. It sent his head spinning back in time to that ballroom and those Saturday nights. "October 2 1938," he replied.

"Can you recall Jerry Lee Lewis's first UK chart entry?"

Of course he could. These questions were easy. "'Whole Lotta Shakin' Goin' On.'"

She put her hand on the back of his and ran her index finger up over his wrist. "Mr Good's plan?" she asked sweetly.

If she had asked for the moon at this moment, he would have found a ladder, climbed up, and given it to her somehow. "Mr Good's plan?"

She nodded even more sweetly and fluttered those long, dark lashes.

He wanted to tell her, wanted to please her. "I can't." He sighed. "I can't tell you. My friends wouldn't be pleased."

If Peggy Sue was disappointed, she didn't show it. "You're very loyal," she said. "I like that." Without moving from her perch on the edge of the walnut desk she turned and pushed the pink vinyl case towards Vince.

He looked at the strange box, wondering what it could possibly be, and then up at Peggy Sue, hoping she would explain. Her large round eyes were encouraging him to lift the lid. Cautiously, he placed a hand either side of it and raised the cover to its full extent. Inside was a feature wooden panel, and in the middle of it sat a turntable and a record. The record was shiny black, with a pale purple label with gold lettering. He leaned forward, and his eyes almost protruded from their sockets.

"Love me –" He gulped. "Tender," he read.

Peggy Sue beamed. She knew her work here was almost done. Yet something inside her stirred. Something in the way Vince had read those words had emotionally moved her, strongly affected her, somehow. Amazingly, it had something to do with – no, it had everything to do with the gap in her memory. What had happened on that journey from Torment Towers with her uncle, Terry, and the guards? And how was this moment connected? But she had to put these strange thoughts to one side for now. The prospect of getting Terry off her back, once and for all, spurred her on. All she needed to do was find out about the plan.

Vince couldn't take his eyes off the record. "It's y'actual Elvis."

"Would you like to hear it?"

Vince would have gladly given up his blue suede shoes to hear Elvis again. "Hear it?" he gasped. "Y'actual 'Love Me Tender'?" He nodded his head eagerly.

Peggy Sue lifted the needle arm and moved it over the spinning turntable.

Vince watched, hypnotised, his attention fixated by the shiny black record as it spun round and round at forty-five revolutions per minute.

"Are you sure you want to hear it?" she teased as she lowered the needle arm to within millimetres of the record's rim.

He braced himself and gripped the leather armrests tightly. "Yes!" He was just about to hear Elvis sing again. "Yes!" he shouted. "I do!"

"You do?" she smiled. "And you will, Vince."

His heart was pounding again and his breath coming out in gasps.

"When you tell me Mr Good's plan."

Vince was confused, unsure what was happening. He was unable, at first, to grasp what Peggy Sue meant. Then she pulled the needle arm away and smiled at him expectantly. Then he understood. It was Elvis or the plan? He wanted to hear Elvis more than anything. But he couldn't let his friends down. No way. Never. That was out of the question. He stared at the record, at the image of a Jack Russell terrier listening to a wind-up gramophone on the pale purple label. It was 'Love Me Tender'. He sighed. Surely Mr Good, Melvin, and Lorraine would understand? After all, it was his favourite song, and he hadn't heard it in such ages. Peggy Sue was beautiful, and she was asking so nicely. What harm could it do?

"Are you ready, Vince?"

And bit by bit, Vince could feel his resistance slipping away.

He nodded. He was ready.

"Good," she said gently. "Now, nice and slow. From the beginning."

Chapter 35

Arthur was resting. It was his fifth rest break since Mugwump had found him almost one hundred paces back along the corridor. "I would've loved to have seen their faces when they went aboard the ship and discovered the entire crew and passengers had all inexplicably disappeared."

Mugwump was preoccupied. He stood as patiently as he possibly could, waiting for the old man to catch his breath again.

"What happened to them, Mugwump?" asked Arthur.

The wizard's attention was diverted, distracted by the portal only a few agonising paces ahead. "Sorry," he replied. "What did you say?"

"What happened to the crew, the passengers on the ship?"

"The *Mary Celeste* was a brigantine."

Arthur stared blankly. "What's a brig ..."

"A brigantine is a two-masted sailing vessel," Mugwump explained. "Square-rigged on the foremast."

Arthur frowned. These details were irrelevant. "What became of the crew and passengers?" he asked again. They were the only details he was interested in.

Mugwump shrugged. "They're here," he replied dismissively. "Somewhere."

Here? Somewhere? Arthur's bloodless face turned a whiter shade of pale. But before he could ask further questions, Mugwump took hold of his upper arm and walked him the final few steps down a gentle crimson slope to the portal.

"I've been thinking." Mugwump had a sort of faraway look in his eyes as they stood at the portal's entrance. "We can't go back."

Arthur, with blanched cheeks and a puzzled expression, looked up at the wizard. "We can't go back where?"

"To the centre of the royal blue labyrinth, to see Mr Good," replied Mugwump, completely absorbed in thought. "Not yet, anyway."

"But, what about Plan B? You said ..."

"Well, that's the whole salmon, or rather point," replied the wizard. "Melvin, Lorraine, and Vince are bound to be a vital cog in the wheel of this Plan B. So, Mr Good wouldn't be too pleased if we turned up without them, would he?"

It was a rhetorical question, so Arthur remained silent and pulled nervously at the ends of his very long whiskers.

"But fear not, I have an idea," Mugwump announced. "Though it's not an idea I came up with readily, I assure you, Arthur. It's dangerous, hazardous, and decidedly risky."

"It is?" Arthur gulped. Anything dangerous or hazardous and especially anything decidedly risky was not a good idea when your ticker was a bit on the dodgy side.

"It involves being captured," he continued. "Captured by muscular guards, probably, and taken into the Palace of Somnium."

"What? Captured?" Arthur made a convulsive effort to breathe. "But ..."

"There's nothing to worry about, Arthur," he assured him.

"Nothing to worry about?" Arthur thought this might be a good moment to remind Mugwump he was actually quite unwell and elderly. "In my condition?" he gasped. "I can't afford to be manhandled by a gang of muscular guards."

"You won't be," said Mugwump softly as he stared abstractedly into the hidden, invisible gateway. "I am the one who is going to be captured, not you."

"... at my time of life. At my age I should be seeking gentler pursuits like stamp collecting, or ..." He faltered and looked up at the wizard. "What did you say?"

Mugwump was still gazing intently and intensely into the darkness of the portal. Arthur glanced in the same direction as the wizard but saw only a crimson wall.

"This is something I am going to have to do on my own." The wizard sighed. "I'm sorry, Arthur, but I'm afraid you won't be coming along."

Arthur gaped, wide eyed and open mouthed. "I was afraid I would be," he replied in an undertone. Mugwump, with his own thoughts fully occupied, didn't hear the aside.

"You're the dead spit of Vile," the wizard reminded him. "You're very much the surprise salmon, I mean element, and still the ace up the sleeve of Mr Good's tunic, as it were." He smiled and laid a caring hand on Arthur's shoulder. "My dear fellow, if Vile saw you it would put the mockers on the whole plan."

He paused. "You do understand?"

Arthur nodded. "I'm prepared to do anything you say. If you ask me to cut up rough with a few muscular guards I, admittedly, wouldn't be over the moon about it, but I'd do it willingly."

Mugwump admired the old man's courage.

"So, what shall I do while you are being captured?" Arthur asked boldly. "Where will I go when you are being manhandled and taken into the Palace of Somnium?"

The wizard hadn't considered this. He was so wrapped up in his idea and all the dangers it entailed. With his fingers he unfastened his bright metallic yellow brooch, tightened the rope-tie around his waist, and gave the matter some thought. "There's only one thing for it," he decided. "You'll have to stay here."

"Stay here?" Arthur's dodgy ticker palpitated wildly. He checked out his surroundings. They were in the middle of a long stretch of crimson corridor. Looking back in the direction they had come from, he noticed for the first time that they had been walking down a gentle slope. Ahead, in the distance, there appeared to be a dead end, but he knew it was most probably a trick corner; the corridor would continue to the left or to the right on its mazy way. "Stay here all alone?" he wheezed.

Mugwump wondered what had happened to the old man's courage.

"What if the muscular guards come along?" Arthur asked nervously.

The wizard shook his head. "They won't," he said. "The guards will have no reason to pass by this way, I promise you, Arthur."

It was very unlikely the guards would pass by this way unless ... Mugwump didn't want to think about that. It was extremely unlikely, he decided. Unless … Vile saw Arthur on one of those monitor screens. But what were the chances of that happening?

Arthur was unconvinced. "I'm not so sure."

"Don't worry, Arthur. I'll be back here with Melvin, Lorraine, and Vince before you know it," he told him. "Meanwhile, you rest. Get your salmon back."

Mugwump smiled, helped the old man into a sitting position, and made sure he was comfortable. "Sorry, I mean strength."

Arthur was exhausted. He leaned his back against the wall, completely drained of energy, and rested his eyes for a moment.

Mugwump took a deep breath. "I'll be off, then," he whispered.

When Arthur opened his eyes the wizard was gone. He looked up and down the gentle slope of the crimson corridor. He was all alone.

"I'll just wait here then, shall I?" he called out, but not too loudly. He didn't want the muscular guards to hear him.

Chapter 36

Vile took steady, measured steps across the carpet tiles, completely lost in his own thoughts. "So, they've got a guy who looks like me, have they?" He paused at the solid oak Welsh dresser, with its scalloped front edges and flared cornice, and regarded the porcelain tea set, or what remained of it, with a lack of interest.

"Arthur somebody or other," he pondered. As he pondered he picked up a milk jug and examined it impassively. "So, that is what Mr Goody-Goody two shoes is up to is it?"

Sneaky.

"What do you want?" Vile frowned. "Leave me alone."

Mr Good's plan. Very sneaky.

"I can be sneaky too," insisted Vile. "Sneakier, even."

There was no reply from whatever it was inside his head, but somehow he sensed it was smirking.

He let the milk jug slip from his fingers. It hit the corner of the Welsh dresser and smashed into several pieces on the floor. Vile continued to pace up and down, but his pace was not so steady and less measured now. "This Arthur person is going to try and fool all of my men into thinking he's me."

Ordering your guards to do goody-goody things.

"My men won't know who is me and who is Arthur?" he fretted.

How will you know who is you and who is Arthur?

"You're right." Vile nodded. "It's confusing. I have to put a stop to this."

Maybe it's too late. Maybe he's already here. Here in the palace ...

Vile trembled at the very idea of it.

Maybe you are Arthur. It's possible.

He stopped pacing and considered this. "That's ludicrous," he decided. "I'm not Arthur."

Well, of course, you would say that.

"I'm Vile," he snapped. Finding himself by the Welsh dresser again, he pulled open one of the two oak drawers and hurriedly foraged through its contents. "I'm sure of it."

He found the carved wooden hand mirror he was searching for and studied his reflection carefully. He contorted his face into a grotesque sneer, twisting, bending, and straining his features as he ran through his catalogue of evil looks, grins, and wicked facial expressions.

"Well, I certainly look like Vile," he concluded.

You look like Arthur too.

Vile frowned and hit the base of the Welsh dresser angrily with the hand mirror, cracking the glass from side to side. He turned, unconcerned about the prospect of seven epochs' bad luck, and headed for the door. "I'm going to ask for a second opinion," he yelled.

#

Silently, a wizard wearing an ankle-length black robe with gold stars appeared at the point where the cyan, magenta, and yellow corridors converged. He paused. With his round face drawn taut and his rosy red cheeks stretched tight, he nervously placed a topaz slipper on the pink and white marble flooring and began to walk. He took slow, hesitant steps along the narrow passageway.

#

The possibility he might not be Vile but somebody called Arthur concerned Vile greatly. The door opened with a kick. It bounced back off the rubber-covered stop, struck him on the head, knocked him sideways, and shattered the glass in the mirrored panel.

Vile cursed.

Another seven epochs of bad luck.

"Superstitious mumbo-jumbo," growled Vile, rubbing his forehead. He looked up. He needed a second opinion, and he needed it fast. "You!"

The person in the wrong place at the wrong time was a tall, angular dream actor on his way out of the drawing room. The dream actors ahead of him and closer to the curtain quickly escaped through it.

"You!" he shouted once more.

Larry stopped and looked at Vile, desperately hoping he was shouting at someone else. "Me?" he mouthed and pointed to his chest.

"Yes, you." Vile stood with his hands on his hips. "Yes, you. Norman. Come here."

Larry glanced round quickly, hoping for a little support from his friends. The dream actors who were still seated on white caned seats at occasional tables looked away or looked down at their knees.

"Tell me," said Vile as Larry approached him reluctantly. "Who am I?"

He swallowed several times. It was a trick question. It had to be. "You're Vile, sir," he stammered.

Vile took a step nearer. "Take a closer look." He thrust his considerable nose and ample chin towards the dream actor.

Larry bowed slightly and stared self-consciously into the evil face of the Dream Ambassador for Nightmares.

"Well?" asked Vile impatiently.

"No doubt about it, sir." Larry swallowed. "You're definitely Vile."

"Could I be a look-alike? Someone who closely resembles another?"

Larry straightened. Why was Vile asking such ridiculous questions? Where was this leading? Would he get out of this alive?

"Could I be an imposter?"

The dream actor took a step back and shook his head nervously. "No one else could be so wicked and nasty, sir."

Vile said nothing but nodded his head thoughtfully for a long moment. "You're right," he said finally. "No one else could be so wicked and nasty."

He repeated the dream actor's words, seeming pleased. "It would appear, therefore, I'm not Arthur."

Who was Arthur? Larry wondered as he took another step backwards away from Vile, who he noticed was lost in thought.

"So, if I am Vile," continued Vile to himself, "then I had better start thinking of a devilishly clever counterplan."

Larry retreated slowly and carefully, one step at a time. When he thought the time was right, he turned and made a run for it, followed closely by the sound of sliding tables, scraping chairs, and the remaining dream actors as they disappeared through the great curtain too.

"This Arthur person is going to regret being so handsome." Vile grinned, unaware of the mass exodus around him.

However, his grin was interrupted by what sounded like a noisy disturbance. He spun round but was surprised to see only empty chairs and empty tables. The commotion was coming from the staircase, probably on the landing where the stairs divide into two, and heading his way. The first person to reach the top step was Terrence. Then came two muscular guards on either side of a figure wearing a black pointy hat.

"Look what I found, your unpleasantness, lurking around in the corridor outside," said Terrence when he saw Vile standing there in the middle of the spacious drawing room.

Vile could hardly believe his bulging eyes. "Well, if it isn't the man who says 'salmon' far too often for my liking." He exposed his yellow teeth in a broad, mirthless smile.

"Vile, my dear salmon," said Mugwump. He attempted a bow, but a bow is never easy when you are flanked and gripped tightly by two muscular guards.

"Don't 'my dear salmon' me," responded Vile menacingly.

"I've an idea," said Terrence, confident he was now in Vile's good books. "Every time he says 'salmon', shall I kick him in the shins, like this?" He swung his right foot, and the toe end of a grubby white trainer struck the wizard just below the knee.

"Ouch!"

The two guards released Mugwump to allow him the opportunity to hop around on one leg.

Vile glared. "Terrence!"

"Yes, your monstrousness?"

"Shut up!"

"Sorry, your grossness." Terrence saw the ferocity of Vile's glare and withdrew a safe distance.

"So, fish face." Vile took a step closer. "What were you doing sniffing around outside?"

"I wasn't sniffing," said Mugwump indignantly. "I just happened to be passing, that's all."

"Just happened to be passing?" Vile scoffed. "Don't make me laugh. This has got something to do with the plan, hasn't it?"

"Plan?" replied Mugwump without missing a beat.

Vile stood a matter of inches away from the wizard and looked him directly in the eye. "This plan of Mr Good's. It doesn't seem to be going too well, does it?" He smirked. "First the pesky kids are captured, and now his pet wizard is permanently detained."

The muscular guards stood close behind Mugwump like two burly central defenders marking the star striker. Vile slowly circled the three of them, clockwise.

"Now, pointy-head, the question is, what shall I do with you?" he said when he returned to face the wizard again.

"Something diabolical I should think," said Terrence with a grin, poking his head around the side of one of the guards.

Vile ignored him. Instead he watched Mugwump and waited to see what his reaction would be to his next question. "Tell me, where's the guy who looks like me?"

All the colour drained from Mugwump's rosy red cheeks.

"What's his name? Is it Arthur?"

Vile knew about Arthur. Mugwump suddenly felt quite ill.

"Judging by the way the blood has just flowed out of your face I'm guessing you're a little surprised I know that." Vile smiled in a self-satisfied, smug kind of way.

"Not at all," replied Mugwump, recovering quickly. "You were meant to."

"What?"

"It was part of Mr Good's plan," he bluffed, "for you to know that part of Mr Good's plan."

"Don't be ludicrous." Vile growled a guttural sound of anger. "What possible advantage could be gained by having me know about Arthur?"

Mugwump shrugged. "It's a very crafty plan. It's all based on fraudulence and circumvention."

"Circum ... what?"

"Vile, I can see I've wasted enough of your valuable time. Mr Good only sent me here to tell you about Arthur, and yet it seems you already know. It appears I've had a wasted salmon. I'd better be making tracks. Mr

Good is expecting me. I'll see myself out," Mugwump called out cheerily. He turned and walked straight into the waiting arms of the two guards.

"Not so fast, salmon features," cried Vile. "You're not going anywhere. You are permanently detained, remember?"

The first guard took Mugwump by the shoulders and turned him round to face Vile again. "What are you going to do with me?" the wizard asked.

Terrence suddenly jumped out from behind the second guard. "Something horrible, I shouldn't wonder." He sniggered. "Am I not right, your contemptuousness?"

Vile sighed. "Are you still here, Terrence?"

"Sorry, your miserableness."

"With opening night so close I'm sure you must have things you could be doing."

"Yes. I do. I've got lines to learn," he remembered. "Well, one line anyway," he added after an awkward silence.

"I'm on my way," he mumbled as he made his way self-consciously across the drawing room.

Vile watched him all the way, waiting for him to exit through the gap in the curtain before turning his attention back to the wizard. "I haven't decided what I'm going to do with you yet," he told him. "But, fair play to Terrence, I don't think he was far wrong when he suggested it would be something horrible," he grinned.

"You can do anything to me, Vile." Mugwump attempted to move away from the guards, but they each grabbed a handful of his gown and hauled him back. "Anything apart from the cell. You can torture me, torment me, or salmon me, but please don't throw me in the cell. Anything but that."

Vile stared, taken aback by Mugwump's sudden outburst. "I didn't realise the cell was so abominable." He had only been down to the cell once, on a brief visit to isolate the flow of Dream Power to two of the three thick, black iron pipes, but he remembered thinking at the time that it was a bit on the small side and quite damp.

"Vile, you just can't imagine how much I'd hate it," said Mugwump as little drops of saline fluid appeared between the surface of his eyeball and eyelid. "You see, I suffer terribly with claustrophobia."

Vile was confused. Lots of thoughts were running through his mind, mostly evil ones. "So, you wouldn't like it very much if I had you thrown in the cell, then?"

"I'd loathe it, Vile," he cried. Tears spilled from his eyes and wet his rosy red cheeks. "If there's an ounce of goodness in you, a salmon of kindness, you won't throw me in that cell." He dropped down to his knees. "I beg of you, please, please, please don't."

Vile gave the guards the nod. It was the signal they had been waiting for. Immediately, they lifted him up clear off the ground and threw him with all their might. He bounced off a wall, then the solid oak rail, and then another wall like a pinball.

"Oh, look." Vile pointed and laughed. "A pinball wizard."

The two guards proceeded to push and shove Mugwump across the room. All the time he was screaming and shouting and appealing earnestly for Vile to reconsider his decision.

"Claustrophobia, eh?" smiled Vile. "What a stroke of good fortune." He turned to face the mirrored panel. "I should break glass more often," he decided.

Chapter 37

"You did what?"
Three prisoners from the physical world were serving eternal life sentences, with not a hope of parole, in a cell that was a bit on the small side.

Vince took a deep breath, and the smell of damp filled his nostrils. "I couldn't help it," he spluttered. "She had an Elvis record, and she said if I told her the plan, I could listen to …"

"I don't believe it." Melvin shook his head in disbelief. "I just don't believe it."

Vince stood uncomfortably in the dazzling purplish-red spotlight. "I couldn't resist it," he said. "It was y'actual 'Love Me Tender'."

Melvin sighed a heavy sigh of resignation. "Well, that's Mr Good's plan gone for a burton. I hope you're satisfied, Vince?"

Vince frowned. He had hoped that Melvin would be sympathetic. He had hoped Melvin would understand that it was y'actual Elvis, his favourite song, and that he hadn't heard it for over an epoch. "Don't worry," he replied. "She promised she wouldn't tell anyone."

Melvin threw his head back and rolled his eyes. "And you believe her, I suppose?"

Believe her? Vince tried to grasp the meaning of Melvin's words. The possibility Peggy Sue might betray him had never, not once entered his head. He had trusted her implicitly. "Well, yes, I do believe her, actually."

Melvin was unconvinced. Why was this girl so interested in the plan? He leaned his back against the metal door. "Who is she, Vince?" he asked. "What is she doing here in the palace?"

Vince thought of her. He saw her lips, how they formed that beautiful smile; her golden pigtails, how they bounced when she shook her head; and her long dark lashes, how they fluttered when she told him he looked like Elvis. "Her name's Peggy Sue," he said wistfully. "She's a teacher, a dancin' and singin' teacher. But only part time."

"Part time?"

Melvin and Vince turned their heads.

"Did you say part time?" It was Lorraine who spoke.

"That's it," she exclaimed. She was sitting on the wooden bench below the window, leaning forward now, excitedly. "That's it."

"That's what?" asked Melvin.

"The riddle. Remember? The riddle that Terrence posed earlier." She smiled "What's green then red, green then red?"

Melvin frowned. "Is that all you can think about, Loz? Here we are locked up in a cell, and any chance we had of getting out of here and returning to our world has gone, thanks to Vince here." He sat down heavily beside her. "And all you're concerned about is a riddle?"

Lorraine sat back and sighed. Vince took a seat too, and all three of them sat in silence for a while.

Eventually, curiosity got the better of Melvin. "So, what is it?" On reflection he decided a little light relief might be just what was needed in the circumstances. "What is it that's green then red, green then red?"

Lorraine ran her hand through her cornrow braids, from the edges at the front of her hairline up to the crown. "A cucumber," she told him.

"A cucumber?" replied Melvin. A look of puzzlement settled on his face. "But a cucumber is green, Loz. It's always green. It's never red."

"Yes." Lorraine nodded. "That bit was confusing me too."

Melvin stared, hoping an explanation was about to follow.

"I couldn't work it out until Vince," she said, flashing him a smile, "mentioned part time, just now."

Vince returned her smile with a shy one. He wasn't sure what he had done or said that had pleased her so. His thoughts were elsewhere. He closed his eyes and thought of Peggy Sue. He recalled her lovely lime-green circular skirt, her delicate white shoes with the cute polka-dot chiffon bows, and how they had danced to the rhythm of his favourite song.

"Don't you see?" she said. "Can't you guess? A cucumber that works part time –" She paused to see if Melvin could guess. "As a tomato."

Melvin remained hopeful that the answer to the riddle would be forthcoming. He stared. He waited. Then he realised that was it. That was the punch line. A cucumber that works part time as a tomato? He sighed. *So much for light relief,* he thought.

It was Lorraine who heard it first. She stood up, walked over to the door, and listened.

Then Melvin heard it: a long, loud high-pitched cry. "No! Please! No!"

There were footfalls on the oak stairway. They got louder. They were descending closer.

"Please! Please don't do this!"

They heard the slap of leather sandals on stone and screaming. "Don't throw me in the cell!"

Then came the scratching of a brass key against the metal door and turning in the lock. "Help! Help me!"

Now Vince heard it too. It irked him because it had interrupted his warm Peggy Sue thoughts.

The door opened out, and a new prisoner was unceremoniously pushed and shoved inside. The two guards grunted, a satisfied, job-well-done sort of grunt, and slammed the door shut.

"Mugwump!" cried Lorraine.

Vince climbed slowly to his feet. "The wizard who says 'salmon' a lot!"

The unexpected guest quickly composed himself and rearranged his clothing. He pulled the hem of his black robe, which had ridden up above his knees, down to his ankles and straightened his pointy hat.

"What the dickens are you doing here?" asked Melvin, beaming.

A smile spread along the diameter of the wizard's round face.

"Salmon!" He bowed. "I'm here to rescue you."

He looked at them all in turn. "We're going to escape."

"Escape?" Melvin glanced at the large metal door. "But ..."

"I know what you're thinking," said Mugwump. He had recently attended a course, for advanced graduate wizards, to strengthen his ability to discern the thoughts of others without the normal means of communication – mind reading, in other words. He was keen, now, to put all he had learned on that course into practice. "Melvin, you're thinking, how do I propose to escape when the door is locked."

Melvin nodded. "Well, it did cross my mind."

"Let me put your mind at ease," continued Mugwump. "You see, in happier times when the palace was the abode of Mr Good, the place where all the nice, pleasant, happy dreams were conceived, the ones with the beautiful colours and the pretty flowers, this room we now find ourselves confined in was in fact ..."

Mugwump paused for effect.

The other three waited patiently for the duration of the pause.

"The pump room," he announced finally.

Melvin had noticed the pump and storage tank and the three thick, black iron pipes that disappeared through the walls in three different directions, so the news it was called a pump room was not the biggest surprise ever. "So?" he shrugged.

"So," Mugwump said, still smiling. "Who do you think needed to gain access to this room, at regular intervals, to inspect the many parts of the pump for signs of damage or improper functioning?"

Vince stared at the wizard and shook his head in a puzzled way. He couldn't even begin to guess who inspected the many parts of the pump for signs of damage or improper functioning during those happier times.

"Was it, by any chance, you?" asked Lorraine.

The wizard's smile widened. "Indeed it was."

"Congratulations, Mugwump," said Melvin wearily. "I'm sure you were very thorough. But how the dickens is that going to help us get out of here?"

From beneath his black robe Mugwump produced a large brass key. "This," he said, holding the key aloft, "is going to help us get out of here."

Without further explanation the large brass key found its place in the lock of the metal door. It took both hands to turn the key, and when he did so the door opened an inch or so.

Melvin moved towards the door excitedly, but Lorraine held back.

Mugwump turned. "Lorraine, you are thinking –" He looked deep into her eyes. "That there are several Neanderthals outside and salmon knows how many between here and the corridors of Limbo. Am I right?"

Lorraine nodded. "Big brutes they are."

"Big brutes they may be," agreed Mugwump. "But fear not, I have an idea."

"Unless there's a secret trap door close by, perhaps one that leads down to a long-forgotten, underground passageway or something, then I don't see how we can escape," said Lorraine with a sigh.

"Funny you should say that." Mugwump smiled.

"So, tell us, what's your idea?" asked Melvin.

Mugwump took a deep breath. "Well, basically, my idea is to open this door," he replied with one hand still holding the key in the lock. "And when I open this door ... we run."

"Run?"

"Run," confirmed the wizard. "For dear life."

Melvin looked at Lorraine, then at the door, and finally at Mugwump. "Is that your idea?"

"We'll never make it," decided Lorraine with a worried expression. "Not with all those muscular guards about."

"But, Lorraine, you said yourself, they are big brutes. They are Neanderthals. So, I'll wager they are ponderous, cumbrous, salmonous, and slow of thought."

"Maybe." She shrugged.

"So, if we are fleet of foot and with the element of surprise on our side, I think we can do it." He removed the key from the lock, and with the help of magic – or perhaps it was sleight of hand – it disappeared into the folds of his robe. "Besides, what's the worst that can happen?"

Lorraine gave this some thought. "We run, and the muscular guards catch us and squeeze our earlobes," she answered, wincing at the very thought.

"Then they push and shove us back to the cell," said Melvin, seeing Mugwump's point. "So, we'd be no worse off than we are now."

Mugwump nodded.

Lorraine nodded her head too, slowly and reluctantly.

"And who knows?" continued Melvin. "Mugwump may be right. Perhaps we can do it."

Lorraine sighed, not yet fully convinced. She turned. "What do you think, Vince?" she asked, half hoping he agreed with her and would say it was a ridiculous idea and it would end in tears, probably her tears.

Vince was running a comb through his thick, black, wavy hair. Before he could reply, Mugwump answered for him. "Vince, in fact, is thinking –" The wizard faltered. "About Peggy?" He looked at Vince, puzzled. "Who's Peggy?"

"Jo," said Melvin. "Peggy Jo. Vince has only gone and told her Mr Good's plan, can you believe?"

Vince slowly and deliberately replaced the comb inside the lining of his blue, three-quarter-length drape jacket. "Sue," he informed them. "Her name's Peggy Sue, actually, and she's the most wonderful ..."

"That explains it," said Mugwump, cutting in. "That explains how Vile knows about Arthur. It had been puzzling me."

Melvin frowned. "I wonder how Vile knows?" He looked daggers at Vince. "Who could possibly have told him? Not your Peggy, surely. She promised not to, didn't she, Vince?"

Vince didn't understand it, couldn't explain it, and thought there had to be some other explanation. "But –" Vince was flustered. "Peggy Sue wouldn't."

"No time for a post-mortem, Vince," said Mugwump. "Now that Vile knows, I'm afraid there can be no delay." Surprisingly, he wasn't angry. In fact, he smiled as he opened the metal door just enough to peep out. "It's imperative that Mr Good knows that Vile knows, sooner rather than later, as it were. Agreed?"

They all nodded, although Mugwump didn't see them.

He was still staring out into the darkness of the undercroft. "Now, I'll open this door, and when I say 'run', run as though your life depended on it. I'll lead the way, but stay close to me at all salmons – or rather at all times." He turned. "Any questions?"

They shook their heads in unison.

"Good." Mugwump smiled, satisfied.

He opened the door wider and poked his head out.

#

It was rush hour in the great central hall, or it seemed to be. Innumerable dream characters of all shapes, sizes, and genders were scurrying to and fro and here and there across the parquet floor like demented ants. Mugwump

189

reached the top of the oak stairway, but instead of running round the giant aspidistra that stood in his way, the wizard ran through it, knocking the huge houseplant to the floor. Melvin, Lorraine, and Vince hurdled the stricken evergreen perennial too. Then they took a sharp right and chased after Mugwump through the vaulted corridor, followed by four muscular guards.

On they ran through impressive rooms of rich furnishings and lamps, swerving in and out of easy chairs and tables at top speed and on through rooms richly decked with vases and plants. Vince tried to slow down the progress of their pursuers by knocking over some of the bigger vases and plants as he passed them.

It wasn't working. If anything, the six muscular guards were gaining ground.

In the magnificent blue lounge they met a group of dream actors making their way back from rehearsals. The dream actors stood aside to let them pass by and were amazed to see, at the front of the group, someone who resembled the wizard who says 'salmon' a lot. Obviously it couldn't be him. They decided, not unreasonably, that this must be a scene from Vile's new nightmare. They stepped out into the centre of the room and watched them disappear, in a blur, through an archway at the far end of the lounge.

Before they could take their next breath, however, the dream actors were mowed down and badly injured by the unstoppable force of eight muscular guards.

Breathing heavily, they entered the library. Mugwump, without hesitation, reached up for a specific book in the far corner of the room on a shelf just above head height. Hurriedly, he pulled the book, a book bound in brown leather with gold print down the spine, forward like a lever. Immediately, the ceiling-high bookcase opened with a groan and a creak. Melvin, Lorraine, and Vince quickly followed Mugwump into the darkness beyond. The bookcase began to close slowly, agonisingly slowly. But before it could shut completely, ten muscular guards grabbed it, pulled it, and squeezed through too.

It wasn't quite the long-forgotten underground passageway that Lorraine was expecting. It was short. Within three or four strides she left the cobwebby darkness behind her and found herself, in daylight, on a long, sweeping lawn that gradually fell away from the Palace of Somnium down towards an avenue of elm trees. Vince had overtaken her now, and she was quickly losing contact with Mugwump and Melvin. The sensible shoes that had been so sensible for school were proving to be totally inadequate for running down a sweeping lawn whilst being pursued by a dozen angry, muscular guards. They were very close behind her now, running with their arms outstretched and their hands, the size of meat dishes, reaching out to grab her.

Mugwump ran through the trees, and as he reached the final elm, he turned. He was soon joined by Melvin and then Vince. The three of them watched in horror as Lorraine slipped and fell on a patch of wet grass. Fourteen muscular guards, silhouetted against the white marble of the magnificent Palace of Somnium, surrounded her like a pack of baying dogs.

A moment later a scruffy little man with unkempt, mousy hair pushed his way through the scrum of muscular guards. He stood over Lorraine and laughed. Lorraine looked up at Terrence and began to cry.

Chapter 38

Mugwump slipped quietly away from the scene and disappeared behind a nearby bush. The way out of the Dreamspace was hidden behind a dense growth of small trees and bushes. There were many hundreds of exits stretching away into the distance, each one a different colour, in every colour you could possibly imagine and every shade of every colour too. The wizard stepped out from the cover of the undergrowth and shrubbery, just a short distance from a dark, blackish-purple corridor. He knew of a portal nearby, in this maze, that led directly to where he wanted to go. He hurriedly scampered up the grass bank towards it.

He hesitated momentarily at the threshold of Limbo. With a quick glance behind to satisfy himself he wasn't being followed, he ran inside the passageway and immediately and unexpectedly bounced off an invisible barrier.

He picked himself up, gingerly, off the seat of his black robe and reached out his hand. He felt something solid to the touch. He frowned. The way forward was barred by some kind of force field, he reasoned. He looked about him. There to his right, at shoulder height, was a wall-mounted stainless steel unit with a speech panel and a silver button.

He pressed it. Nothing happened at first, so he jabbed at the button again, repeatedly and impatiently. This caused an uncomfortably high-pitched whistling sound, like a jumbling of radio signals, to penetrate his eardrums.

When the noise eventually subsided, Mugwump heard a voice. "What do you want?" it said.

Mugwump leaned forward, his mouth close to the speech panel. "My dear fellow, I would very much like to enter this –" He stopped to consider its colour. "This dark, blackish-purple maze, please."

A pause.

"It's burgundy," came the reply.

"Oh, is it?" Mugwump shrugged. "Then I would very much like to enter this burgundy maze, if that's at all possible."

There was another pause.

"Why?"

It was a male voice – and very young, too. Mugwump guessed he was probably aged no more than half an epoch.

"Because I am on urgent Dream Business, that's why," said Mugwump sharply.

A longer pause.

"What's the keyword?" asked the youthful voice.

Mugwump frowned. "I don't need a keyword." He raised his voice a touch. "I'm a wizard."

The adolescent made a sound, and it may have been a laugh. "That's what they all say," he replied.

Mugwump was slightly irritated at this point. He had never been the type to use his wizardness to impress folk. He never went around blowing his own trumpet, rarely used his status within Dream Land to obtain special treatment, and had always considered himself to be a regular sort of guy, a normal dream person. But this was different. This was important. The kid needed to be told exactly who he was dealing with.

"I am a wizard," said Mugwump proudly. "A good one. A black-robed one, no less." He stood defiantly in front of the wall-mounted stainless steel unit, staring at the speech panel. "With gold stars," he added.

After an awkward silence the boy spoke again. "Pull the other one. It's got bells on."

Mugwump sighed.

"If you really were a wizard," the youngster continued, "a simple force field wouldn't stop you, would it? I mean, a little bit of basic dream magic and you'd be inside the corridor in a flash and on your way, surely?" There was an unmistakable hint of amusement in his voice. "Not too difficult at all, not for a black-robed wizard with gold stars, anyway."

"Well, I would normally," replied Mugwump. "But I –" He faltered, bashfully, and completed the sentence in a sort of mumble.

"What was that?" asked the boy. "I didn't quite catch that."

193

"I said —" His voice raised another notch. "I would normally, but I don't have my wand with me."

"What kind of wizard doesn't have his wand with him?" scoffed the male child.

"The kind of wizard who doesn't have enough pockets in his robe, that's what kind," shouted Mugwump, very irritated now. "Look, lad." He took a deep breath and attempted to compose himself. "Will you kindly let me through? I really am on urgent dream business. As for the keyword, perhaps you could give me a salmon, or rather a clue, because, well, because I don't know it, and there's no reason why I should."

"Of course you don't know it," replied the juvenile. "It's new. There are three new keywords, actually."

"Three new keywords?" Mugwump's eyes narrowed. "Who authorised this?"

"It was all arranged at dream ambassador level, not that it's any business of yours."

"Dream ambassador level?" Could it be? Mugwump considered the possibility for a moment. Then he shook his head. It was a long shot, but it was worth a go.

"My name is Melvin. Melvin the wizard and if I said —" He hesitated. "'Downhill', what would happen?"

What happened was a gasp followed by a loud hissing noise, like a gust of wind rushing through the trees. It was the sound of the force field evaporating. Mugwump took his opportunity to run.

"Was that a guess?" called out the boy.

But the wizard was gone. Down the slope of the burgundy maze he ran before disappearing around a sharp bend at the bottom.

"What's the hurry?" said the minor quietly to himself. "Anyone would think he only had three dream spans to save the physical world from a fate worse than death or something."

#

Arthur was listening. He heard everything, every scrape, every scratch, and every squeak. There were noises that reminded him of creaking floorboards or an unoiled hinge in the distance – or was it close by? He wasn't quite sure. He was scared.

One time he thought he heard the echo of a pin drop somewhere across the vast expanse of Limbo, which in his imagination became the unmistakable sound of marching feet. Obviously an army of muscular guards was heading his way. He was convinced of it.

He was sitting uncomfortably with his aching back against the crimson wall, his legs spread out in front of him, and his feet turned abnormally out. Another time he thought he heard a scream from a girl far away.

From his seated position he could hear the slightest movement and the tiniest vibration. But, surprisingly, he didn't hear Mugwump arrive. He was looking the other way when the wizard appeared suddenly, silently, out of thin air.

"My dear fellow."

"Mugwump, you made me j –" Arthur faltered. He saw the worry in the wizard's eyes, the perspiration on his brow, and his pointy hat askew, and he came to the obvious conclusion.

"Are you being chased?" He looked up and down the corridor nervously.

"No time to explain, Arthur," said Mugwump. "Suffice to say that Lorraine has been captured and probably Melvin and Vince too by now. But there's still a chance. It's not far."

"Not far?" wheezed Arthur. "You mean Vile is near?"

Mugwump shook his head. "No. Not Vile, Arthur. Just some muscular guards."

"Some muscular guards!" The old man gulped. "How many muscular guards? Two? Three?"

Mugwump shrugged. "Maybe four –"

"Four?" Arthur tried to stand, but the floor of the corridor was suddenly very similar to an ice rink, and his feet gave way.

"– teen," added Mugwump as he took Arthur's hands and, with difficulty, pulled him upright.

Arthur began to shuffle away as quickly as his swollen ankles would allow him.

"Arthur, where are you going?"

"Fourteen muscular guards, you said. I thought maybe I would go in the opposite direction."

Mugwump sighed. "But Arthur, you are our only chance. Our only hope. You are Vile."

"I'm not. I'm Arthur." He stopped but didn't turn. "I'm an old man," he added with tears in his eyes.

"But with that impressive moustache and wearing those dazzling and resplendent clothes, Arthur, you are Vile. Don't you see what a splendid opportunity this is? Against all the odds, Mr Good's plan could be back on track."

"Yes, but ..." Arthur hesitated. Then with his back still to the wizard he continued. "Looking like Vile is one thing, but acting like him ... I've never even met him. How does Vile act?"

"If you're arrogant, inconsiderate, bad-tempered, rude, wicked, nasty, and spiteful, that should cover it." Mugwump smiled. "In fact, just act like a complete and utter salmon."

"Salmon?"

"I mean a complete and utter tyrant. Not salmon."

"But these are traits that don't come naturally to me, Mugwump."

"Of course they don't, Arthur. You are a good man. But I will help you. I will be with you at all times. If you do as I say and if you say exactly what I tell you to say, everything will be fine. Trust me."

Arthur turned slowly. "Okay then," he reluctantly decided. "I'll do it. But just this once."

"How marvellous," said Mugwump with a grin. "Quickly, Arthur – or rather, quickly, Vile – let's make haste." He took hold of Arthur's arm, put a hand around his waist, and gently guided him back towards the portal.

A moment later they disappeared and the crimson corridor was empty again, silent again apart from the occasional scrape, scratch, squeak, and creaking floorboard somewhere in the distance.

#

"I've been thinking," said Arthur to the wizard. "About the crew and the passengers on that ship, or rather that brigantine."

It was the first time either of them had spoken since they stepped out of the portal, safely navigated the dark, blackish-purple maze, and entered the Dreamspace. The Dreamspace was dominated by a magnificent palace, its façade of white marble twinkling in the twilight.

With Arthur's left arm draped around his shoulders, Mugwump placed his feet carefully on the sodden grass and traversed down a stretch of open land towards the cover of the underbrush.

"What did you mean when you said they were here somewhere?"

As he held the old man tightly around the waist and stumbled through the foliage and down a leafy woodland path, Mugwump narrated the facts and particulars of a quite remarkable tale. He told him that three or maybe four eras ago now, on a Friday morning, Mr Good was watching, on a spot monitor, as an unremarkable sailing vessel by the name of the *Mary Celeste* entered the Bay of Gibraltar. He recalled how Mr Good was making a great deal of fuss and noise and remembered how he could hardly conceal his excitement. The farther the *Mary Celeste* sailed along the strait, the more excited he became and the more convinced he was that aboard this nondescript sailboat, as unlikely as it may seem, was the Ancient Tea Set of Firmamentum. The wizard quickly explained that the Ancient Tea Set of Firmamentum was a matching collection of cups and saucers, side plates, a cake plate, a milk jug, a sugar bowl, and a teapot that, legend has it, were used by the dream ancestors the very afternoon prior to the Big Bang. It was the stuff of folklore, a traditional story transmitted orally down the eras. There were many theories and even more opinions, but the Ancient Tea Set of Firmamentum had remained lost for such a long time that most thought it would never be found Yet, remarkably, here it was, apparently, on this ordinary two-masted brigantine that had made its way unnoticed across the Atlantic. Unfortunately, Mr Good is not very good with technology and stuff. So Mugwump, without further ado, began a frantic search for the latitude and the longitude coordinates that together would identify the exact position on the Earth's surface of the *Mary Celeste* and its precious cargo. His nimble fingers began touch typing the black keys across the middle of the keypad until, in the rectangular Perspex panel, a picture of the earth appeared with two circles wrapped around it, one passing through the poles and another perpendicular to the axis. Then, below the globe, green and flashing, were the sequence of numbers and symbols he had been waiting for. Urgently, he activated the Influence button and hoped for the best.

197

"What happened?" asked Arthur, spellbound.

Mugwump paused. "Good news and bad news," he replied as he adjusted his grip around Arthur's waist and guided him across a narrow wooden bridge that spanned a small, shallow brook. "The good news being that moments later the tea set arrived safe and sound and neatly stacked on Mr Good's spacious walnut desk."

"And the bad news?"

The wizard sighed. "The bad news was, the crew and the passengers arrived too."

"No!" Arthur's jaw dropped.

"Mr Good and I were surprised," Mugwump admitted, remembering the incident clearly, as if it had only happened the dream span before last. "But not nearly as surprised as Captain Briggs and his men."

Arthur tried to contemplate just how surprised those nineteenth-century sailors must have been. To be aboard a brigantine out at sea in calm conditions one moment and then suddenly to find themselves in this strange world of dreams the next must have been a little disconcerting. Despite a stiff neck, he managed to turn his head sideways to look at the wizard. "And after all this time they are still here? These men?"

"Shush!" Mugwump halted abruptly. With his free hand, the one that wasn't wrapped around Arthur's waist, he grabbed a branch along with a handful of damp leaves and widened the gap slightly between two bushes to the left of the beaten path. There in the fading light, just a few yards away in the shadow of a large elm tree, they saw a muscular guard carrying Lorraine, like a sack of potatoes, across his shoulder. Arthur's dodgy ticker missed several beats.

"Put me down, you brute!" Lorraine was screaming and beating the guard's back with her fists and grabbing at his tunic. "Put me down!"

From their hiding place Mugwump and Arthur could see Melvin and Vince too. They were surrounded by half a dozen guards. A little further to the left another group of guards stood alongside Terrence.

"Tell me," Terrence addressed the three prisoners. "What did one ear say to the other ear?"

Melvin groaned. "I don't know. What did one ear say to the other ear?"

"Between you and me we need a haircut." Terrence grinned.

"Look, what the dickens are you going to do with us?" Melvin was getting more and more exasperated. "Please do something. I'm sick and tired of these so-called jokes."

"Why is the invisible man such a poor liar?"

"Put me down!" demanded Lorraine. She slapped the back of the guard's iron helmet repeatedly as he paced up and down. "Pick on someone your own size!"

"Because you can see right through him," continued Terrence. "Get it?" he asked and waited, expectantly, for the laughter. Nobody found it the slightest bit funny, though – apart from Vince.

It started with a giggle. Then it became a chuckle. In no time at all it had developed into a deep, loud, hearty laugh. "That's funny," Vince howled. "Between you and me we need a haircut!" he shrieked uncontrollably. "That is funny!"

All eyes turned on Vince. Even the muscular guards stared at him with ridicule and disbelief.

"You liked that one, did you?" said Terrence, delighted. As far as he could remember, no one had ever laughed so heartily at one of his jokes before.

By now, Vince's laughter had subsided to a series of little titters.

"If you liked that one, Elvis, you'll love this one." Terrence stood in front of Vince. Inside his head were thousands of riddles on a conveyor belt all vying for attention. He chose one at random. "Tell me," he cleared his throat. "What are big, red, and eat rocks?"

Surprisingly, Vince knew what was big, red, and eats rocks. He had seen them and was just about to reply when Terrence was distracted by the muscular guards at his side. A low, continuous succession of murmurs and grunts passed through their ranks. He noticed that something had caught their attention. They were all looking down the glade towards the bushes. He turned.

Two unlikely figures stood at the edge of the open space. Mugwump was holding Arthur in such a way that it looked for all the world as though it was Arthur who had the wizard in a vice-like grip.

"Vile?" gasped Terrence.

Arthur stared stupidly at Terrence, unable to speak, his mouth open wide like a yawn as the darkness of night slowly descended over the palace grounds.

Chapter 39

"Escaped?" Vile was sitting at his spacious walnut desk in a state of violent mental agitation. "Escaped?" he repeated. He was frantic with anger and frustration, and he hit every key on the raised keypad with a sharp, resounding blow. Every view on every monitor screen along the wall was of a different empty corridor in Limbo. "Are you sure?"

"Positive, Uncle." Peggy Sue nodded. Vile had called for her, saying he had some bad news to impart. But, when she arrived she had bad news of her own. "Larry told me," she added.

"Who?"

"Larry. One of the dream actors, Uncle."

Vile scoffed. "Bunch of Normans, that lot."

"Yes, but Larry says his information comes from a very reliable source."

He looked away from the monitor screens for the first time and regarded Peggy Sue with interest. "What reliable source?"

Peggy Sue shrugged. "I don't know. But apparently, the source said that they escaped through a secret passageway behind a bookcase in the library."

Vile quickly hit a couple of black keys across the middle of the keypad and a grey button down the left-hand side. Immediately, on a spot monitor a view of the library appeared. He grabbed the joystick and panned around the room. At first everything was as it should be, exactly how Vile imagined a library to be: row upon row of shelves neatly stacked with dull and boring books. But as the camera reached the far corner he noticed something wasn't quite right. Peggy Sue watched as Vile zoomed in closer. At the point where two large bookcases should meet at a right angle, one stood ajar like a door.

"A secret passageway," whispered Peggy Sue.

For a moment Vile didn't speak. Then he turned to her with a frenzied look in his eye. "How dare they escape?" He sat up straight and gripped the black leather armrests tightly. "When I get my hands on that salmon wretch I'll beat him black and blue, so help me I will. Telling me he didn't want to be thrown in the cell when all along that's exactly what he wanted! He must have had a key!" He stood up angrily, launching the swivel chair on a collision course with the Welsh dresser. The impact dislodged a sugar bowl that, in turn, hit an open carved oak drawer on its way down and ended up broken in two pieces on the carpet tiles.

"My name's not Nice. It's not Pleasant or Friendly. It's Vile. Vile. And no one pulls the wool over my eyes! No one!" He marched purposefully across the room and threw open the door. "Terrence!" he shouted. He listened, fully expecting to hear the patter of Terrence's tiny feet running across the golden carpet. "Terrence!" he shouted again.

"He's not here," said Peggy Sue.

"Not here?" Vile turned. "What do you mean, he's not here?"

"I've been trying to tell you, Uncle. Terrence and umpteen muscular guards were last seen chasing Vince and his friends through the palace when they all –" She hesitated. "Disappeared through the secret passageway.

Vile slammed the door shut.

"In hot pursuit they were, Larry said."

"Terrence in hot pursuit?" he sneered. "With those little legs?"

She couldn't resist a smile.

"Damn and blast! Now what am I going to do?" He stared at nothing in particular and brooded.

"Uncle! Look!" It was Peggy Sue who spotted them on the spot monitor. "The guards!"

"Guards?" Vile stood in front of the monitors and stared at the screen in disbelief. There were several of his guards in the library. He counted fourteen of them, all milling around in between the plants and looking confused. "What are they doing there?" he wondered. "I didn't know they could read."

"Uncle, they must be the guards who left with Terry. Terrence."

"Of course!" Vile placed his considerable nose considerably closer to the spot monitor and searched for Terrence. "So where is he? There's no sign of him. Typical! And no sign of the pesky kids either – or the salmon cretin."

"Or Vince," she said with a sigh.

"What?"

"Nothing."

Vile sat on the corner of his spacious walnut desk and pondered his next move. "Right," he said after only a short ponder. "I am not Dream Ambassador for Nightmares for no reason. I am Dream Ambassador for Nightmares because – well, obviously it's mainly because I am so wicked and nasty. But also it's because I can make decisions quickly and under extreme pressure. Is that not right, niece?"

"That's right, Uncle."

Decisions? Under pressure? You? Don't make me laugh.

"Shut up!" snapped Vile.

"Sorry, Uncle."

"Not you," said Vile as he glanced up. "I wasn't talking to you."

Peggy Sue looked at her uncle and wondered why he was acting so strangely. She might have mentioned at this point that if he wasn't talking to her, the only other person in the room, then she would have no choice but to assume that he must indeed be talking to himself. Now, if this was the case, she would then be obliged to point out that talking to one's self was indeed the very first sign of madness. She might have said these things, but she didn't. She remained silent. She thought it was for the best.

Meanwhile, Vile had retrieved the swivel chair, returned it to the desk, and sat down. "Now," he said, leaning forward, "in the absence of Terrence I find myself short of a pursuer."

"Pursuer?"

"Pursuer, yes. Pursuer: one who pursues, follows, chases, seeks. Get it?"

Peggy Sue nodded urgently. "Got it," she said.

"I am in need of a volunteer to do a spot of pursuing. And you, niece, are that volunteer." He grinned.

"Me?" she exclaimed in surprise.

Vile nodded. "I want to know where that fish face is, and I want to know where the pesky kids are going."

"And Vince?"

"What?"

"Nothing."

She twirled the end of a plait of golden hair around a finger, bashfully.

Vile watched her, but only for a fraction of an instant, before continuing. "You are to go out there now into Limbo and pursue. When you locate them you will then infiltrate enemy lines and spy on them all," he informed her.

"But am I not needed here?" asked Peggy Sue, finding it hard to hide her excitement. Yet somehow she managed to conceal it from her uncle. "Surely you will need me for the big song and dance routine at the end?"

Vile remembered now why he had called his niece here. He vacated the black leather swivel chair effortlessly. "Take a seat," he told her. "I have bad news."

Peggy Sue was puzzled. She circled the spacious walnut desk cautiously, sat down, and waited for her uncle to speak.

Vile paused to savour the moment. He enjoyed moments like this. Giving someone bad news had always, in the past, given him a lot of pleasure.

He had already given this some thought and had decided to take his time with this. He was going to start by letting her know he only told her to choreograph the grand finale, in the first place, as a punishment for something or other. To follow, he would move on to some shouting, something along the lines of *You've grown up? You've changed? You like singing and dancing now? Without informing me?* That sort of thing. Then he would calm down a touch and stare at her menacingly, and with one of his sinister smiles he would ask her what she thought dream folk would think if they heard that Vile wasn't punishing people, wasn't torturing people, but instead was encouraging them to take time out to enjoy their little hobbies and interests. At this point he planned to bang his fist down hard on the desk and ask her what she thought this could do for his reputation? Finally would come the bad news, the best bit. He couldn't wait to see the look on her face when he told her that her participation in his new nightmare, especially any involvement with the big song and dance routine at the end, was over. These were all the things he wanted to tell her, but giving bad news was all about finding the right words. So, he paced up and down and cogitated a bit more.

"Are you all right, Uncle?" asked Peggy Sue as she watched her uncle pace up and down, cogitating.

Vile stopped, looked at her, and smiled. It was a sickly one. "You're sacked!" he said and didn't bother with an explanation after all. There wasn't time. "Get out of my chair, niece," he shouted. "Go into Limbo. Pursue and find out everything. And I want you back in time for opening night."

Peggy Sue stood up hurriedly, smoothed the creases in her lime-green circular skirt, and rushed across the room. She was so excited. The prospect of freedom and the possibility of seeing Vince again was thrilling. She made her way quickly towards the door before her uncle changed his mind or realised that her chances of finding anyone out there in that vast expanse of Limbo, especially in less than three dream spans, were slightly more unlikely than absolutely impossible.

She opened the door and looked back at her uncle for what she hoped would be the final time. Vile didn't see her go or notice the door shut behind her. He was preoccupied.

"At last I have the upper hand," he mumbled in a completely engrossed, absorbed kind of way.

Upper hand? Hardly. It's not looking good for you from where I'm standing.

Vile sighed. "Where exactly are you standing?" he asked. "I can't see you."

I'm inside your head.

He frowned. "Yes, but who are you? What are you?"

I'm a kiwi bird, a small, flightless bird belonging to the family Aptergidae and genus Apteryx.

Vile wrinkled his large nose in disdain at this madness. "Utter rot!" he said as he sat down again in his black leather swivel chair. "You're mad!"

I'm mad? You're the one talking to yourself. It's the first sign, they say. Mr Good's plan has got you rattled, I see.

"On the contrary," snarled Vile. "I'm Vile. And, if you rearrange the letters of vile you can make the word ..."

Live?

"Evil. And as everyone knows, evil always, I repeat always, triumphs over good. It's a well-known fact." He grinned a satisfied grin. "Yes, Mr Good is going to be very sorry he tangled with me."

He leaned back in his seat and listened. Somewhere in the distance, or rather somewhere in between his ears, he thought he heard the soft, partly suppressed laugh of a small bird with no tail and tiny two-inch wings.

Chapter 40

Keith held the water pistol in his right hand and pressed the small projecting lever that actuated the mechanism to discharge the liquid. Nothing happened.

Mr Good was standing with his feet apart, his knees slightly bent, and his hands resting on his hips.

Keith breathed a heavy sigh. "I'm hungry," he said.

Mr Good was bending slightly to one side and was just about to come back to a vertical position when he realised what Keith had said. "Are you sure, old chum?" he asked.

Keith nodded as he shook the water pistol furiously.

"But that's impossible," said Mr Good. "Time here moves sideways at such an angle that it never quite reaches lunchtime," he informed him. "We don't need to eat."

"Try telling that to my digestive system," replied Keith, patting his stomach. "Actually, I don't think it's used to all this inactivity. Well, it's had to cope with three meals a day for nearly seventeen years, so to tell you the truth I think it's bored."

He pointed the water pistol in the direction of the teak sideboard and fired. Nothing happened.

"And it's not just my digestive system either. I'm bored too," added Keith with a yawn.

Mr Good had never quite understood the concept of boredom. Obviously, he was aware that folk from the physical world suffered from it on occasion, but he had never really understood why. After all, they only lived for a couple of epochs, threescore years and ten on average, and a third of that was taken up with sleep. He had often wondered how they managed to get everything done in such a short space of time.

He abandoned his side bends and sat on the chocolate-brown sofa. "This boredom?" he asked as he leaned closer. "What's it like, young Keith?"

"What it like?" Keith shrugged. He tapped the water pistol gently against the shiny chrome highlight strips on the arm of the chair, raised it up, aimed at a lava lamp, and pulled the trigger. Nothing happened.

"Well, I guess it's a feeling of utter weariness and listlessness, accompanied by an overwhelming urge to twiddle one's thumbs."

"Fascinating," said Mr Good as he stood up tall, rested his hands on his hips, and bent slowly to the left. "You should try exercising, old chum." His deep blue eyes were sparkling with kindness. "It purifies the mind."

Keith grimaced. Exercising was not for him. "I did a press-up once," he recalled. "My arms were limp for a whole week." He stared down the barrel of the water pistol, examining it.

Mr Good remained silent and continued with his side bends.

Keith fired. A jet of water hit him flush in the eyeball.

Keith shot up out of the armchair. "Gosh and double gosh," he yelled and threw the water pistol down angrily.

"Oh dear," said Mr Good. "Are you all right?" he asked as he placed a hand on Keith's shoulder.

Keith took a long, deep breath, nodded, and tried to wipe himself with his red and blue diagonal neckerchief.

"I'll fetch you a towel to dry your face properly," said Mr Good. He quickly disappeared around the penultimate curve of the labyrinth.

Keith was miserable and homesick. As he stood there and waited, he thought of the Scout motto: Be prepared.

He wondered how anyone could be prepared for this.

#

They stepped through yet another portal. Terrence could see there was something not quite right with Vile, something odd. Why was he holding the salmon dude himself? Terrence had never ever seen Vile do this before. It was the muscular guards who always did the holding – and the pushing and shoving. But for some inexplicable reason he had sent the guards away, back to the Palace. Now they were seriously outnumbered. It was just Vile and Terrence against the salmon guy, the pesky kids, and Elvis. He looked at Elvis and watched him striding along the royal blue corridor in his ridiculously large shoes with the thick crepe-rubber soles. He was a big lad and very strong across the shoulders. If he had a brain he would undoubtedly be dangerous.

"What's happening, your reprehensibleness?" Terrence called out. "Where are we going?"

Everyone turned to look at Terrence, who was bringing up the rear. Up at the front Vile turned his head slowly. It was as if he was suffering from a very stiff neck or some sort of rare shoulder condition.

"Not far now, Terrence," said Arthur. "You idiot," he added, trying desperately to look arrogant, inconsiderate, bad-tempered, rude, wicked, nasty, and spiteful all at the same time and failing miserably.

Terrence noticed that Vile's voice was sort of asthmatic and his breathing laboured. He didn't look well at all.

"Are you quite all right, your unhealthiness?" he asked. "You seem a little under the weather."

Up ahead Arthur and Mugwump stopped and turned to face the wall. It was another portal.

Terrence was worried. This salmon person seemed to be making all the decisions, showing Vile the way to go. It was most probably a trick. He thought about warning Vile, telling him to be careful. They could be walking into some sort of ambush or something.

Inside the portal, it was very dark. Terrence knew it would only be dark for a few strides. At the same time the floor would be moving too, sometimes up and sometimes down like an escalator. Then before your eyes had become accustomed to the darkness it would suddenly be light again, and you'd be standing in another corridor of another colour, somewhere else in Limbo. But this portal was different. The darkness faded gradually, and instead of another corridor they ended up in a little alcove. Ahead of them Terrence saw a row of colourful beads hanging in an invisible doorway.

Chapter 41

"Astrology is twaddle."

"No, it isn't."

"Yes, it is."

"It isn't."

"It is," insisted the giant in the green woollen tunic. "There is scarcely a shred of scientific evidence in its favour, Flagellum."

"Horoscopes are quite often astonishingly uncanny, actually," persisted the slightly shorter giant. "Take my astrological prediction for this dream span, as an example."

Zygote frowned.

From a pocket in his deep, purplish-red gown, Flagellum produced the latest edition of the *Dream Times*. "It says here on page thirteen," he read aloud, "that approximately seventeen large men may set about me forcibly and violently in an unprovoked and frenzied attack." He poked his turbaned head from behind the folded sheets and grinned. "Isn't that amazing?"

Zygote stared at Flagellum for a long moment. "But you haven't been attacked by any large men."

"It's early yet."

"Total balderdash."

"It's all here in black and white, Flagellum," said Flagellum, waving the newspaper in Zygote's face and taunting him.

"I'm Zygote," Zygote reminded Flagellum as he snatched the newspaper from his grasp. "Let me see." In between the current dream news, the editorials, the feature articles, and the advertising, he soon found what he was looking for. He scanned the horoscopes hastily before looking up at his fellow giant. "What you have just read is the astrological forecast for Sagittarius."

Flagellum nodded. "Yes, Sagittarius, that's me."

"But I am Sagittarius."

"No, I'm Sagittarius."

"You're not," insisted Zygote. "You're Taurus."

"I'm not."

"You are."

"I'm not. I'm Sagittarius, the bull," said Flagellum.

"You're Taurus the bull, you stupid tall person." Zygote quickly searched the page for Taurus. "Where are we? Yes, here it is. The sun is travelling through your own sign and is in conjunction with your ruler Venus. So beware of a dubious or questionable character who may attempt to lure you away and involve you in evil goings-on." He paused thoughtfully. "Money matters are highlighted," he added.

"Interesting," said Flagellum.

"I've never heard anything so ridiculous," said Zygote. "You don't know any dubious or questionable characters."

"I may do."

"You don't."

"I could do."

"So, who do you know who's dubious or questionable?" asked Zygote.

"Well, there's …"

As Flagellum struggled for an answer a large mass of moving whiteness wandered aimlessly by.

#

A monitor was divided into a multi-screen of sixteen different images of the white room. Therefore, Vile was able to view Flagellum and Zygote from sixteen different angles. He chose a close-up shot of the two giants and reproduced it, full screen, on a spot monitor.

Stop. Rewind. Play.

"So, who do you know who's dubious or questionable?" asked Zygote.

"Well, there's …"

Stop. Rewind. Play.

"So, who do you know who's dubious or questionable?" asked Zygote. "Well, there's …"

Vile watched a large dollop of whiteness drift slowly by and stroked his long whiskers thoughtfully. "I don't know any dubious or questionable characters either," he muttered quietly to himself. "But then I'm not a Taurus, am I?"

With his feet he pushed the black leather swivel chair nearer to the desk. "I'm a Gemini." Spread out before him was the latest edition of the *Dream Times*. He opened the newspaper in the middle, turned over two or three pages, and leaned closer. His finger jumped from column to column and then followed the text down until he found it.

"Gemini, May 21 to June 21," he read. "Be wary of a rival who is plotting to take back something that is rightfully his." He paused briefly to allow himself a little smirk. "With your ruler Mercury in conjunction with the sun in the early part of this dream span, you are advised to seek assistance in this, your hour of need."

With his elbows on the desk Vile rested his ample chin in his hands. "Assistance?" he mused. "The pesky kids have escaped again, the salmon cretin is roaming free, Terrence has disappeared without a trace, and there's a guy strolling around, bold as you like, pretending to be me!" He stood up and paced up and down anxiously.

"I need all the assistance I can get," he decided. "It took me many eras to get this place off Mr Good. I'm not going to surrender it now."

He hovered for a moment in front of the spot monitor and considered the two giants. "I think I'll pay this Flagegote and Zygellum, or whatever their names are, a visit."

Then, at the Welsh dresser, from one of the two oak drawers, he took out a hand-held Dream Navigation Device with built-in Portal Locater.

"And this," he said with a grin, "should get me to the white room in no time."

211

Part 3

Plan B

Chapter 42

"Well done, everyone. Excellent. The first part of my plan has been a complete success," announced Mr Good proudly.

Mugwump looked down at his topaz slippers.

"Is there something wrong?" Mr Good noticed his old chum was looking a little ill at ease.

"Well —" The wizard faltered and looked up. "It's just that …"

"It's just that Vile knows," said Melvin, interrupting the wizard. "He's discovered there's an exact likeness of himself wandering around Limbo."

Mr Good's happy, smiling facial expression barely altered. However, his legs buckled slightly at the knees, forcing him to sit. He lowered himself down on to the arm of the sofa. "Vile knows about Arthur?" He gulped.

Mugwump nodded gloomily.

"Vile is also aware there's a plan," added Lorraine.

"How?" asked Mr Good shakily.

Lorraine, together with Melvin and Mugwump, told Mr Good everything that had happened.

When they had finished, Mr Good was silent for a long moment. Then he ran his fingers thoughtfully through his wild, unkempt silvery beard and stood up. "How unfortunately calamitous and calamitously unfortunate," he concluded.

Vince took a step forward. "I'm sorry, Mr Good. It was all my fault."

"Not at all." Mr Good waved an arm dismissively. "'Love Me Tender' is a jolly good song, young Vince. I'm sure I would've done the same."

"I'm the one to blame," wheezed Arthur. He was lying full length on the chocolate brown sofa in an effort to recover his health and strength following the long and tiring journey across Limbo. He raised his head slightly as Mugwump held a white plastic spoon of yellow liquid to his lips. "My forgetfulness was the reason they were all captured in the first place. I let the side down," he managed to add before his face twisted and warped out of shape and his head collapsed into a cushion.

"No one has been let down, Arthur," said Mr Good kindly.

"So, the first part of the plan has not been a complete salmon after all," sighed Mugwump as he replaced the clear stopper carefully back on the glass medicine bottle.

"On the contrary," said Mr Good with a smile. His deep blue eyes sparkled. "Remember, old chum, the sole purpose of the first part of my plan was to regain the Digital Dreamscaper. Well, thanks to young Melvin, Lorraine, and not forgetting Vince here, Terrence has indeed been apprehended, and I'll wager there's a Digital Dreamscaper in that shoulder holster."

Mr Good summoned a ball of string from somewhere and placed it in Keith's hand.

Mugwump produced a teak dining chair and placed it between the sofa and one of the armchairs. After a gentle persuasive push, Terrence was sitting on it before he could do anything at all about it.

Certain words that were being said were troubling Terrence at this point – words like 'apprehended' and 'plan' and 'exact likeness.' Was the bearded figure in the calf-length brown tunic really Mr Good? Surely not. He looked too pathetic to be a dream ambassador. Terrence was also beginning to have an inkling that Vile maybe wasn't Vile at all but rather some old guy, with a false moustache and just a passing resemblance, called Arthur. But why? Terrence was at a loss to understand why someone would pretend to be Vile.

From Terrence's shoulder holster Mr Good quickly removed the Digital Dreamscaper.

"What are you doing?" screamed Terrence. "Give me that back!"

Mr Good was relieved to see the Digital Dreamscaper was undamaged. It was a little low on power but almost certainly still in good working order.

Mugwump grabbed Terrence's wrists and pulled them round to the back of the chair.

"Vile will never let you get away with this," he shouted.

Nervously, Keith began to bind Terrence's wrists together.

"I'm like a son to him, you know." Terrence struggled. "So, I'm warning you."

Keith wrapped the string round and round the chair and round and round Terrence's middle until he reached the end of the ball.

"However, I can't deny that this news is a blow," continued Mr Good when there was no more string left. "Vile is aware of Arthur's existence. Therefore, we cannot continue with the second part of my plan."

Lorraine sighed. "We're so sorry, Mr Good."

"Fortunately," Mr Good said with a smile, "I have a Plan B. It's an astutely cunning and cunningly astute plan, and we must proceed with it without a moment's delay."

The medicine, a reduced dosage this time, had begun to work wonders for Arthur already. He managed to sit up, allowing Melvin and Lorraine to take a seat either side of him on the sofa. Keith stood behind the seated Terrence, and Vince sat in the armchair opposite.

Mr Good stood in the middle of the room, where he was able to observe everyone apart from Mugwump, who sat astride a chair at the teak dining table. "You, Melvin, and you, Lorraine, are very good at finding things," he announced.

There was silence.

"Are we?" said Melvin and Lorraine suddenly and together.

"It's in your files."

Melvin remembered Mr Good telling them about a filing cabinet back at the palace that had details on absolutely everyone. He still couldn't begin to imagine how enormous that filing cabinet was and how heavy the drawers must be.

"I kept a dossier on all my clientele," explained Mr Good. "It specifically says in your notes that you are both excellent at finding the mean average of ten or more numbers."

Melvin and Lorraine leaned forward and looked at each other. They were both surprised and clearly unaware that they were particularly gifted at finding mean averages, especially of ten or more numbers. "We are?" they asked.

Mr Good nodded. "It's one of the many reasons why you were chosen."

Keith rolled his eyes. It seemed everything revolved around those two. He frowned. So they were good at finding things. Big deal. He shrugged.

He was more interested in this Plan B. He wanted to know if it involved the use of a water pistol. He raised a hand slowly, but before he could attract Mr Good's attention, Lorraine spoke.

"So, what is it you want us to find, Mr Good?" she asked.

With his elevated hand Keith quickly adjusted his red and blue diagonal neckerchief instead.

"It's not what I want you to find. It's who I want you to find," replied Mr Good mysteriously.

Nobody spoke.

"I want you to find ..." He paused enigmatically.

Nobody moved, or perhaps they did. Maybe they all subconsciously leaned a little closer and waited for Mr Good to elucidate.

"I want you to go and find ..."

Nobody took their eyes off the Dream Ambassador for Tranquil Dreams for one second.

"I want you to go and find Lord Riddle," said Mr Good finally.

There was silence.

"Lord Riddle?" It was Terrence who shattered the silence with a sudden, noisy expulsion of air from his lungs. "Lord Riddle?"

"Yes, Terrence." Mr Good smiled calmly. "Lord Riddle."

"Who is Lord Riddle?" asked Melvin.

"The third dream ambassador," replied Mr Good.

"Possibly," suggested Mugwump.

"Probably." Mr Good smiled. "They have an image of a penguin rolling downhill. It nestles snugly in their subconscious. Someone must have put it there, old chum."

Lorraine was puzzled. "We thought there were only two dream ambassadors. Nobody mentioned a third one."

"We are surrounded by unbelievers." Mr Good glanced at Mugwump and smiled. "Most dream folk, when they reach a certain age, stop believing in Lord Riddle, just as the existence of Santa Claus, the Tooth Fairy, and the Easter Bunny are denied by grown-ups in your world."

"This is ridiculous." Terrence turned to the others. "You're all ridiculous. Is this the great plan to regain the Palace of Somnium? To seek the help of a fictional character from a children's fable?" He scoffed.

"What kind of dreams does this Lord Riddle do?" wondered Lorraine out loud.

It was Mugwump who answered Lorraine's question as he stood up and joined Mr Good in the middle of the room. "If Lord Riddle exists, and Mr Good seems to be quietly confident that he does, then he would represent those peculiar, strange, inexplicable dreams that make no salmon – I mean sense."

"And you," Terrence said, nodding in the direction of Arthur, "look nothing like Vile." He scoffed again. "Only a fool would think so."

Arthur's cheeks flushed an unhealthy purple colour.

"The time has come to ask for the assistance of Lord Riddle," said Mr Good. "He has left an image in their minds, and we need to find out why."

Mugwump was doubtful. "No one, as far as I know, as ever met Lord Riddle."

"Now there's a surprise," laughed Terrence.

"But we do have a vague idea where he might live, don't we, old chum?" said Mr Good.

"According to the myth, he lives up the wooden hill to Bedfordshire, way beyond the Uncharted Borders, in a place called the Land of Nod." Mugwump sighed. "But in those tales, everyone who enters the Uncharted Salmons – correct me if I'm wrong – never returns."

Melvin's jaw dropped. It was closely followed by Lorraine's.

"That is a part of the story highlighted by parents to frighten their children, to stop them wandering off towards the edge of Limbo," said Mr Good to Mugwump. "And the reason no one has ever returned is simply because, as far as I'm aware, no one has ever actually been."

"Possibly," agreed Mugwump reluctantly.

"I feel we must try, old chum. Lord Riddle's mind capacity is so huge, I feel sure he will know what to do. He is the only being in existence who can comprehend fully the vastness of each of the eleven universes."

Mugwump shrugged. "So the story goes."

"I am sure he is horrified by Vile's recent antics." Mr Good turned his attention to Vince. "Vince?" he gently called out.

Vince was asleep, but this didn't deter Mr Good.

"Vince, I would very much like you to accompany Melvin and Lorraine on a long journey across the Uncharted Borders to the Land of Nod."

"This is ludicrous," Terrence scoffed for a third time.

Mr Good waited a moment until he was sure his words had penetrated Vince's subconscious. "We need Lord Riddle on our side if we are ever to remove Vile from the Palace of Somnium."

"For such a journey Vince will require a new keyword," Mugwump reminded him.

"I hadn't forgotten." Mr Good nodded kindly. "These are troubled times. Vince, the keyword 'Elvis' that has served you so well for the last epoch or so is now obsolete. Therefore, you will need to borrow one."

"He could use the keyword 'rolling,'" suggested Mugwump. "He likes that rocking and rolling music, after all. So he should be able to salmon it. I mean, remember it."

"Good idea, old chum." Mr Good smiled. "Arthur doesn't need it for the time being."

Keith couldn't wait a moment longer. He had to know. "Mr Good," he began in determined fashion. "When you say Plan B, does it or does it not involve –" He faltered. "The gun?" he mouthed silently.

Mr Good saw Keith standing there in a determined fashion, yet so clearly nervous and apprehensive, and his smile wavered just a touch. "Unfortunately, Keith …"

Keith stared. Mr Good didn't have to say another word. Keith knew. Somewhere in the distance, Mr Good was telling him he was sorry and there was no need to worry, because Plan B was simply brilliant and brilliantly simple. But Keith didn't hear any of it. He just stared. He could feel the red, plastic water pistol weighing heavily in the pocket of his navy blue activity trousers.

Keith's thoughts were interrupted by an angry Terrence. "I demand you release me immediately!" he yelled. "Vile will be here with all the muscular guards to rescue me before you know it."

He writhed and squirmed in the chair. "And he won't be very pleased to see me like this," he added.

Mr Good turned his attention to Keith and smiled. "I believe you have something in your pocket, young Keith, that may keep Terrence quiet while I am talking."

Keith's hand was already in his pocket. He was holding it, and it was cold. Slowly and nervously, he removed it.

Terrence immediately stopped wriggling and trying to free his arms. He blinked at it. It was vivid red. "What's that gun-shaped thing?" he asked with a puzzled expression on his face.

"It's a gun." Keith trembled. "And don't think it's just a water pistol, because it most certainly isn't. For your information it's a real gun. And don't you doubt for a minute that I will use it." He moved just a touch closer and studied Terrence's face. "Are you doubting the fact that this is a real gun?"

Terrence managed to shrug even though his arms were pinned tightly to his sides. "No. Why? Should I?"

"I just wondered, that's all. Because this definitely isn't a water pistol."

Mugwump coughed gently. "Keith." He smiled. "We do have an important plan to be getting on with here. Just point the gun in his general salmon and don't say a word."

"Sorry, Mr Salmon," replied Keith. "That's the trouble. I always talk a lot when I'm nervous. Gosh and double gosh! I've got butterflies in my stomach. Even my butterflies have got butterflies."

Mr Good waited a moment until he was sure that Keith had stopped whining. "Mugwump will point you in the right direction," explained Mr Good to Melvin, Lorraine, and the sleeping Vince. "Unfortunately, he will not be able to accompany you on the journey."

"Oh? Why?" asked Lorraine, alarmed.

"Prior engagement." Mugwump smiled weakly. "A wizard's convention, you see. For black-robed wizards like myself. They are held every eleventh dream span, and attendance is mandatory. The fact that Mr Good has been kicked out of the Palace and Vile is now ruling Dream Land is of no consequence. Wizards are not concerned with such salmons."

"So, how do we get there on our own?" asked Melvin. "Do you have a map?"

"A map? Well." From a pocket Mr Good produced a sheet of paper and handed it to Melvin.

Melvin looked at it, turned it over, and looked at the reverse side. "It's blank," he said.

"Exactly," said Mr Good. "Uncharted Borders, you see. We were hoping that during your journey you could make notes as you go along."

"You want us to chart the Uncharted Borders?" asked Lorraine.

Mr Good nodded. "It would be most useful. Meanwhile, if you presume that the edge of Limbo is at the bottom left-hand corner of that sheet of paper, then we believe the ocean is probably towards the top right-hand side."

"Ocean?" queried Melvin. "What ocean?"

"You will need to sail across this ocean to reach the Land of Nod, I'm afraid," explained Mr Good.

"Sail across an ocean?" exclaimed Melvin. "But, how are we going to …"

Melvin was disturbed by Keith waving the water pistol around in the air. "I'll have you know I'm a crack shot."

Terrence laughed. "A crack shot? But you're just a kid." He turned his head to look at Melvin and Lorraine. "Just like those pesky ones that Vile doesn't like. Except you're fat."

"I'm not fat," Keith retorted. "I'm thickset."

"You're fat."

Meanwhile, Vince yawned and stretched and opened one eye and then another. "What we waitin' for?" he asked as he looked around the room. "We have a long journey across the Uncharted Borders to the Land of Nod ahead of us."

"Shut up, Elvis," sneered Terrence. "The place doesn't exist, you fool."

"I'm stocky, actually," suggested Keith.

"You're fat."

"Now, everyone," announced Mr Good. "The time has come to begin Plan B. We must regain the Palace of Somnium and …"

"May I remind you who has the gun here?" Keith pointed it at the side of Terrence's head. "If you upset me I'll shoot you, and then what will you do?"

Terrence shrugged. "Find a towel?"

Mr Good sighed and turned to Mugwump. "Will you gag him, please, old chum?"

With his left hand Mugwump took a silk scarf from the right-hand sleeve of his black robe. "Who do I gag?" he asked as he folded the scarf carefully along its length. "Terrence or Keith?"

Chapter 43

A girl with her blonde hair in pigtails walked off into the distance down a long amber corridor. On another monitor, at the same time, the same girl wearing a lime-green circular skirt with pink polka dots was captured on screen approaching a T-junction. She hesitated, looked both ways, hesitated again, glanced up, and waved before slowly moving on and eventually out of shot.

There was no one watching. The black leather swivel chair was empty.

#

Vile was moving smoothly and stealthily through the magenta maze on his way to the white room. He had a determined look in his eye and a mad, contorted smile.

Bleep.

It was the hand-held Dream Navigation Device with built-in Portal Locater that went bleep. Vile halted immediately and squinted at the small rectangular touchscreen with interest. He saw a flashing arrow; each flicker of the large, red directional symbol was accompanied by another short, high-pitched tone. The arrow, he realised, was pointing towards the solid-looking wall to his right. Tentatively, Vile reached out an unsure hand towards it. But instead of the hard, strong, conglomerate construction material he was expecting, he discovered the wall was actually soft and spongy. His fist disappeared inside it as if it were a large magenta marshmallow. Encouraged by this, Vile raised a shiny two-tone shoe and stepped inside the wall.

Vile didn't know what to expect as he stepped inside. He didn't know much about portals. In fact, he knew next to nothing. However, what he didn't expect was a complete and utter absence of light and sound. He thought, at the very least, there would be candlelight and possibly bland, instrumental piped music playing somewhere in the background.

He stood in the total darkness and silence of the portal and waited for a long moment. At the end of that long moment there was another moment, a shorter moment, that ended with a click followed by a clunk, a thud, the scrape of metal on metal, and a moving floor. Under his feet the floor was moving forward slowly and taking him gently along with it. But as it gradually accelerated, he was forced to position one foot in front of the other and stretch out his arms perpendicular to his body in an effort to maintain his balance, very much like an acrobat on a tightrope. In no time at all the floor was travelling at an incredible speed and making very sudden changes of direction. Just as Vile was about to congratulate himself on somehow managing to keep his feet, the floor, without warning and without the slightest suggestion or hint that it was about to do so, stopped abruptly. Unfortunately, Vile didn't. Instead, he was catapulted forward into the gloom, through the air, and deposited unceremoniously on the seat of his cuffed trousers on the hard surface of a bright new corridor. He skidded a short way, hit the back of his head on the far wall, banged a knee, and scraped an elbow.

Somewhere inside his head, something, or possibly someone, laughed. The device bleeped.

Vile cursed.

Chapter 44

"I want to stand here a while and give it a good think," said Midrib. He was very tall and wore a cream, chunky knitted cardigan zipped up at the front.

Midrib was a dream philosopher, and so therefore he did a lot of thinking. Ever since the beginning of time, dream philosophers like Midrib have offered views and theories on many profound questions, although for the first few hundred eras there was really only one question on their minds. Well, it was two questions really, but they were linked. Where does Limbo end? And if it does end, what is on the other side?

They considered the question carefully and at length. They kicked it around. They mulled over it, mused over it, brooded over it, and reflected upon it. As the eras passed they found they were no nearer to coming up with the answer than they had been when they first started to contemplate the mysteries of Dream Land all that time ago.

Then one dream span someone out walking discovered, on a long sweeping curve of a green labyrinth, a door. It was a steel fire exit door with a push bar to open and four heavy-duty stainless hinges. On the other side of the door was something that could only be described as 'outside'. As far as the eye could see there were fields, rolling hills, and deep valleys, all bathed in an unusual bright shine from a tangerine sun. At first it was thought that this was just another abandoned Dreamspace. But on closer examination it was decided that this place wasn't created by a Digital Dreamscaper at all, as there were no other entrances to be seen. This really was the other side of Limbo, they realised.

They called it the Uncharted Borders.

The dream philosophers were furious. What were they going to think about now? They had nothing to ponder, nothing to ruminate on, and nothing to chew over. For the several epochs that followed, they really were at a loose end. Then, gradually, one or two dream philosophers turned their thoughts to the eve of the Big Bang and the legendary dream ancestors. It is widely accepted that the Ancient Tea Set of Firmamentum was on display on a welsh dresser in the Palace of Somnium, but what about the other items of historical interest? Those one or two dream philosophers began to wonder about what had happened to the picnic blanket. And indeed, whatever became of the half-eaten buttered scone? The rest of the dream philosophers were delighted. At last they had something of deep meaning and great significance to ponder. They had an aged picnic blanket to ruminate on and a half-eaten buttered scone to chew over. And what was absolutely brilliant about it was that it was extremely unlikely they would ever know the answers. That suited the dream philosophers admirably.

"Why?" replied Mugwump. "Why do you want to stand here a while and contemplate the whereabouts of a half-eaten buttered salmon? What's the point?"

Wizards were not interested in profound questions. They were rarely concerned with such matters. Wizards preferred to do wizardy things, like magic and spells.

Mugwump's negative comment irked Midrib. "You wizards are all the same. All you ever seem to do is wave your brightly coloured wands around a bit." He smiled in an offensively self-satisfied manner. "What's the point in that?"

Mugwump had met Midrib in the Prussian blue maze and disliked him immediately.

"Magic has a very important role to play in Dream Land, actually," responded the wizard. "An impressive piece of magic can spruce up the dullest of dreams."

Moments earlier Mugwump had sent Melvin, Lorraine, and Vince through a portal situated at the end of one of the many blind alleys in this region. It was a very long portal across the vast expanse of Limbo to the edge of the lime maze. He had given them directions from there to the green corridors and told them they needed to look out for a door.

"Pulling a rabbit out of a hat is not my idea of entertainment," said Midrib with a smirk.

Mugwump reacted indignantly. He didn't pull rabbits out of hats. A black-robed wizard was more sophisticated than that. Anyway, he decided to bite his tongue and not argue the point. He was running late. He looked at his watch but then realised he didn't have one. Well, he didn't need one. Time was different here. It didn't exist here in a seconds, minutes, or hours kind of way.

"My dear fellow," said Mugwump with a bow, "I would love to stop and chat." His rosy red cheeks got a touch redder, as they tended to do when he told an untruth. "But I need to be somewhere else."

Even though time didn't exist here in a seconds, minutes, or hours kind of way, there was no getting away from the fact that he was running late, and there is nothing worse than arriving at a wizards' convention after it has already begun.

Midrib didn't appear to be listening now. Mugwump hadn't noticed him put it on, but Midrib was now wearing a brimless head covering, with a visor, turned round the wrong way, and he was sort of meditating.

Mugwump shrugged. Their conversation was clearly over. He moved away slowly at first before lengthening his stride and walking briskly past a trick corner, leaving Midrib standing all alone with his thinking cap on.

#

"Got to be rushin' ... Need to be dashin'." Vince was striding purposefully along the lime corridor and chanting monotonously under his breath. "Got to be rushin' ... Need to be dashin'."

"I'm worried, Melvin."

It was Lorraine who spoke as she struggled to keep up with the pace Vince was setting.

"Worried?" Melvin too was finding it difficult to stay in contact. "What are you worrying about, Loz?"

"The Uncharted Borders, of course," she replied breathlessly. "Do you remember what Mugwump said? He said that no one who has ever entered the Uncharted Borders has ever returned."

Melvin was concerned about this too, but his voice remained calm. "Yes, but do you also remember Mr Good's reply? The reason no one has ever returned is because no one has ever actually been."

"I think Mr Good was just saying that to make us feel better."

Melvin had already considered this and felt there was probably some truth in it, but he was determined to remain cheery. "Maybe it's so nice there, so wonderful, that folk choose not to return," he suggested.

"Do you really think that's likely?"

Melvin shrugged. "It's fresh air. It's outside. That's got to be better than all these endless corridors."

Lorraine sighed. Vince strode purposefully.

"Anyway," continued Lorraine, "I don't care how nice it is there, Melvin. I want to go home. I miss my mum."

Melvin nodded sadly. He thought about his own parents and what they must be going through.

Vince slowed down ever so slightly. He suddenly realised he missed his mother too, although, strangely, he realised he couldn't quite remember if he ever had one. He turned as he reached the end of a long corridor. "I came back," he said.

Lorraine slammed into and bounced off his rather large frame.

Melvin came to a halt too and looked up at him curiously. "You came back from where, Vince?"

He reached inside his blue-draped jacket and fumbled for his comb. "From y'actual Uncharted Borders."

"You've been there?" gasped Lorraine, rubbing the part of her shoulder that had made contact with him. "Really?"

Vince nodded. "So don't get worrying yourself." He ran the toothed strip of plastic through his thick, black, wavy hair before setting off again, at speed, down another corridor to the left. "Got to be rushin' … Need to be dashin'."

"See, Loz, everything is going to be just fine. Vince came back. We will too, and we'll have Lord Riddle with us. You'll see." Melvin took her hand, and they both ran. "Wait for us, Vince."

It must have been two hours before they eventually caught up with him.

"Sorry, Melvin." Lorraine squeezed his hand when they had slowed down sufficiently for her to explain. "I'm a worrier," she began, breathless from running. "I worry a lot. I can't help it."

Melvin wondered if this information was in her notes in that filing cabinet back at the palace.

"I'm a typical Virgo," continued Lorraine, interrupting Melvin's thoughts.

Melvin stared at her for a long moment. "Is that what Virgos do, Loz? Worry a lot?"

"Most of us, yes. Obviously there are exceptions, but taken as a whole people born under a particular star sign do have similar attitudes."

"I see."

It was approximately three-quarters of a mile further along the lime corridor before Lorraine spoke again. "When is your birthday, Melvin?" she asked.

"I was born on All Hallows' Eve." Melvin smiled.

"Scorpio." Lorraine nodded. "I should have known. Scorpios are deep thinkers and always trying to improve themselves."

"Well, it does sound like me," admitted Melvin.

Lorraine laughed. "What about you, Vince?"

Vince was concentrating on walking fast.

"What star sign are you?"

Putting one suede shoe in front of the other in quick succession isn't easy when you're looking to find your way out of a maze and trying to answer difficult questions too, all at the same time. "I don't have one," he said finally and hoped that would be the end of it.

"Everyone has an astrological sign, Vince," persisted Lorraine. "When is your birthday?"

Vince sighed. "Don't rightly remember." He shrugged. "When you haven't had one for almost an epoch you kind of forget."

They continued along the lime corridor in companionable silence for several minutes.

"Well, I would say you're a Capricorn, Vince," Lorraine decided finally. "You're satisfied with life, not looking for changes but just basically content with things as they are. I think that sums you up."

Vince didn't comment. Instead, he took another left turn and then almost immediately a right turn down a corridor with a gradual incline. "Got to be rushin' ... Need to be dashin'."

Melvin was fascinated. "So you can guess a person's star sign just by knowing a little of their character?"

Lorraine nodded. "More or less."

"That's seriously weird." Melvin laughed. "So, take Mr Good for example. What sign would you say he is?"

"Mr Good?" Lorraine pondered briefly. "Leo. They are fair-minded, caring, and tolerant. Yes, Leo, definitely."

"Interesting. I wonder if you're right. Mugwump?"

"Pisces," she replied without hesitation.

"Of course, I should have guessed." Melvin smiled. "The wizard who says 'salmon' a lot could really only be the sign of the fish."

They both laughed. The downward slope of the corridor was becoming more pronounced now. Vince knew they were nearing the end of the lime maze at last. Very soon they would be entering the green labyrinth. The Uncharted Borders were close. "I know y'actual Elvis's birthday," he suddenly announced.

Melvin and Lorraine looked up at Vince in surprise.

Vince slowed his purposeful stride just a touch and half turned. "January 8. A Tuesday in 1935. About teatime."

Lorraine smiled. "Well, that makes Elvis –" she moved alongside Vince and looked up at his face so she could see his reaction – "a Capricorn."

At first Vince's expression didn't alter. But somewhere inside his head a coin was spinning on the edge of something. "Capricorn?" he whispered.

"Just like you, Vince." Lorraine grinned.

The penny finally dropped. "Just like me?" He stopped still. "Elvis?"

Lorraine nodded.

Vince was dazed. This news had stunned him like a blow on the head. He remained motionless for a long time.

Melvin moved ahead of Vince for the first time. "What are we waiting for, Vince?" He turned and stood with his hands on his hips. "Got to be rushing, remember?"

"Need to be dashing," added Lorraine.

"Vince?"

"Vince?"

Vince stared at Melvin and Lorraine with glassy eyes. "Y'actual Elvis is just like me." He beamed.

Chapter 45

Not many dream folk are aware that the white room has a secret rear door. It's well hidden down a blind alley. Vile would never have found it without the help of the hand-held Dream Navigation Device with built-in Portal Locater.

There is only one way to gain access through it: You have to be Mr Good. Failing that, the only other choice you have is to forcibly kick the door open.

Vile chose that option. With the door and jamb shattered he swiftly made his way up the back stairs despite his sore knee and poorly elbow.

#

"I'm Zygote," declared the giant in the green woollen tunic. "And I always tell the truth."

"Poppycock," countered the giant with the red pointy shoes. "I'm Zygote."

"We can't both be called Zygote," said the taller giant.

"We're not," replied the giant wearing the crimson padded turban. "One of us is called Flagellum, and that's you."

"You just said 'poppycock'," said the giant in the leggings fastened with cross-gartered leather strips. "Flagellum always says 'poppycock'. I'm Zygote, and I always say 'balderdash', as well you know."

Soft, feathery clouds, carried along by currents of air, ambled across the white room.

"Balderdash," said Flagellum.

Zygote frowned.

"Who are you?"

The disagreement had gone full circle and was about to start again, for the umpteenth time, it seemed. "I'm Zygote," sighed the giant wearing the open-toed sandals. "And I always say 'balderdash'."

"Not you. I wasn't talking to you this time." The giant in the deep, purplish-red gown was pointing the longest of his six fingers across the white room. "I was talking to him!"

Zygote turned. Standing to the right of the white floating door was a man with very long whiskers. His black and gold pinstriped jacket was somewhat dishevelled, his wide white kipper tie was hanging loose, one of his red braces was unattached, and his cuffed trousers had a slight tear just below the right knee.

"What is your business here in the room with two doors?" growled Flagellum as he took a giant step closer.

The newcomer looked at the floating door to his right. Then, with a confused expression, he looked to his left and turned to see what was behind him.

"It's okay." Zygote smiled. "There is only one door."

"Two doors."

"Forgive my fellow tall person." Zygote quickly moved alongside Flagellum and rested a hand on his shoulder. "It's been a very long shift for us, you see. We are long overdue a coffee break. Two other giants should be taking over very soon, actually."

The stranger sneered.

"You haven't seen a couple of giants, looking a bit lost, on your travels at all?" asked Zygote hopefully.

The stranger sneered a bit more.

Flagellum was becoming impatient now. "What do you want?" he asked brusquely. "We've got better things to do than stand here all dream span looking at your sneering face, you know."

"Who are you?" asked Zygote calmly.

"Me?" He replaced the sneer with a smirk. "You want to know who I am?"

He moved closer to the giants and looked up at them with contempt. "My name is Vi…" He faltered. He had decided not to reveal his identity at this stage. He needed to test the water first. He took a deep breath. "I'm a friend of Mr Good." He cringed.

Flagellum was unimpressed and frowned. "Mr Good, eh? He's in our bad books at the moment."

Vile's eyes lit up. This was encouraging. "Really?"

"He's upset us," continued Flagellum. "He said we were untidy."

"Untidy?" That was not the worst insult Vile had ever heard, by any means. "How awful for you," he added smirkingly.

"No he didn't, Flagellum," recalled Zygote. "According to the Boy Scout it was untrustworthy. Remember? 'Untrustworthy' was the word he used, not 'untidy'."

"Either way." Flagellum shrugged. "We're not his friends anymore."

Vile was delighted. He decided it was time to show his hand. After completing an anticlockwise lap of the two giants, he stood in front of them and below them, looking up at them. "Giants, this could be your lucky dream span." He grinned. "Now, when I said I was a friend of his –"

Zygote interrupted him. "I've been thinking, Flagellum. Knowing Mr Good, he probably meant 'untrustworthy' as a compliment in some way."

Vile scoffed. "Come off it. How can 'untrustworthy' be a compliment? Mr Good was bang out of order."

Zygote paused and regarded the stranger closely. "I thought you said you were a friend of his?"

That's right. You said you were a friend of his. Let's see you get out of this one.

"What?" Not the bird inside his head again, tickling the inside of his mind with its bristly feathers. Not here. Not now. "I am. I am a friend of his."

Vile was suddenly flustered. "It's just that –" He needed to regain control, and quickly. "It's just that ..."

It's just what?

"There's been a bit of a mix-up," Vile suddenly revealed.

"A mix-up?" Zygote was intrigued.

Vile couldn't understand why he had said there was a bit of a mix-up. "Mr Good never said you were untrustworthy," he added. He didn't know why he added that either. It wasn't helping. He was painting himself into a corner.

Flagellum nudged Zygote. "See, I told you it was untidy."

"What he actually said was ... un ... un ..."

Un? Un? The bird was enjoying this.

Vile was thinking on his feet. He wasn't Dream Ambassador for Nightmares for no reason. He was Dream Ambassador for Nightmares because he could always be relied upon to think on his feet and come up with wicked and nasty ideas, quickly and under extreme pressure. "What he actually said was –" He paused. "Unnecessary."

"Unnecessary?" Zygote was taken aback.

Vile nodded. "That's right, and I am here to apologise on his behalf."

"I've never heard such nonsense." With his beady eyes Flagellum gave Vile a piercing stare. "Why couldn't he come himself?"

Good question. Why couldn't he come himself?

"Too busy." Vile returned Flagellum's piercing stare with a fiercer, angrier one. "He's got his hands full at the moment trying to cope with that tricky and wily Vile fellow, who is proving to be a lot more cunning and crafty than anyone ever gave him credit for."

Cunning and crafty? Don't you mean clueless and crazy?

Vile frowned.

"What did Mr Good mean by 'unnecessary'?" wondered Zygote.

"Standing here, of course." Vile removed his fierce and angry stare from the slightly smaller giant to the one in the green woollen tunic. "And this place." He assumed a derisive facial expression as he turned and gave the white room a cursory glance. "It's all so unnecessary."

"Balderdash!"

"Poppycock!"

Vile grinned. "But you'll be pleased to learn that Mr Good thinks you have both earned a spot of promotion."

The two giants looked at each other with surprised faces.

"Promotion?"

"Promotion?"

Promotion?

"Promotion," confirmed Vile smiling broadly, baring a full set of yellow teeth.

Zygote was baffled. He quickly glanced at Flagellum, who didn't appear baffled at all but rather more bewildered. "Do you mean a new job?" he asked finally.

"Exactly," replied Vile. He was pleased with how his wicked and nasty idea was shaping up now. See, he was cunning and crafty after all.

Flagellum leaned forward, positioned his giant head above Vile, and looked down on him. "What sort of job?" he queried.

Vile took a sideways step, turned his back on the giants, and walked slowly across the room. "Well, you know." He shrugged. "Guarding. That sort of thing."

"Guarding?" Flagellum stood up straight again, placed his hands on his hips, and glared after him. "But that's what we do now."

"Excellent. Previous experience is an essential criterion," Vile mumbled as he weaved in and out and in between the four beds. At the foot of one of the beds were three teddy bears. He chose a fluffy, grey, beany one, tightened the burgundy scarf around its neck, and grinned sadistically.

"But we've been guardians of the white room since time immemorial," said Zygote.

Flagellum nodded. "Custodians of the room with two doors since the year dot."

Vile squeezed the cute teddy bear's throat more tightly. "Well, it's about time you had a change then, isn't it?" he snapped.

"We can't just leave here," reasoned Zygote. "What would happen if, after we'd left, a visitor arrived?"

Vile dropped the throttled teddy bear on its head and kicked it under the tubular frame of the student sleeper bunk bed. "Are you turning down this once-in-a-lifetime opportunity?" He spoke slowly and menacingly as he approached the giants.

"It's a tempting offer," admitted Zygote, "but I am more than satisfied with my current role. Thank you very much."

Vile stared at Zygote and seethed with anger. After a long moment he turned his attention to Flagellum. "What about you?"

Flagellum took a quick, sly sideways glance at Zygote before revealing his enormous, crooked teeth in a mischievous grin. "The new job sounds fine," he replied. "When do I start?"

Zygote frowned and decided to change tack. "Let me put it this way," he said as he watched Vile make his way to the floating door, turn, and wait for Flagellum to follow him. "I would be delighted if you could thank Mr Good for his kind offer and inform him that we'll only be too glad to accept." Zygote barred Flagellum's path to the door. "Won't we, Flagellum?"

Flagellum stopped to consider Zygote's words. "No," he answered bluntly. "I'm not budging an inch. And stop calling me Flagellum."

Vile stared at the taller, more annoying giant and considered a number of simple relaxation techniques. He decided it might be wise to count to ten before continuing. After all, his blood was boiling, and he needed to calm down these angry feelings he was currently experiencing.

He reached six before he started to scream and shout. "I've just had about enough of you," he roared.

Temper.

"Don't you know who I am?" he yelled.

The teddy bear strangler?

"I'm …" He paused. "Never mind who I am for the moment. Suffice to say nobody, just nobody, crosses me!"

He pulled open the floating door and turned. "I'm warning you. You haven't seen the last of me. I'll be back, and are you going to regret that!"

He wanted to slam the door shut to show how angry he was and underline how annoyed he was. He yanked at the door with all his might, but it didn't slam. It closed slowly like a raft floating gently down a stream.

Flagellum and Zygote stood in stunned silence for quite a long while.

"What a dubious character he was," said Flagellum finally.

"Decidedly questionable," agreed Zygote.

On the ground near their feet lay a copy of the *Dream Times*, neatly folded and open at page thirteen as a long trail of visible white moisture drifted by.

Chapter 46

Somehow Arthur had worked out that if he were back home he would be having his afternoon nap about now. Carefully he lifted up his legs and rested his head gently on the arm of the chocolate-brown sofa. In no time at all he was in that transition state between sleep and wakefulness. Moments later his eyes began to roll slightly, and he started snoring noisily and forcefully through his nostrils like a horse. He was asleep. He found himself at the entrance to a dark cave.

#

Terrence was less comfortable sitting on the teak dining chair. The string had fretted a groove in his wrists, and his ankles were beginning to chafe.

"What are big, red, and eat rocks?" he cried.

Riddles were starting to backlog in his mind faster than he could process them. He desperately needed to discharge them orally, but that wasn't easy with a silk scarf stuffed in his mouth.

"What are big, red, and eat rocks?" he repeated in a sort of muffled grunt.

#

Arthur found himself on a beach in a small recess in the coastline surrounded on three sides by huge cliffs. He could taste the salt in the wind, and close by he could hear the slosh of waves against the shore. He sensed the tide was moving in rapidly. Very soon, he knew, the ocean would cut off his only hope of escape. Up above the harsh wailing of the gulls was deafening. Their squawking calls seemed, in some way, to be warning him not to enter that dark cave.

The dark cave was scary, and he knew for certain that something vile lurked within. Yet, against his better judgement, his mobility scooter edged forward slowly into the gloom.

#

Mr Good was standing tall with his bare feet approximately two shoulder widths apart in front of the teak sideboard. Keith looked at him. Keith didn't want to be here. He wanted to be somewhere else, anywhere else. Anywhere that didn't involve guarding Terrence with a water pistol. "What are you doing now, Mr Good?" asked Keith wearily.

Mr Good turned to the right and lifted his right leg until his thigh was parallel with the ground and his lower leg was vertical. "Some hip and thigh stretches, old chum," he replied.

Keith sighed. "And you're doing hip and thigh stretches because …?"

Mr Good gradually lowered his body, keeping his back straight and using his arms to balance. He could feel the stretch along the front of his left thigh and along the hamstrings of his right leg. "Because, young Keith, exercising makes me feel … it makes me feel three hundred years younger."

"Three hundred years younger?" Keith gulped. "So, how old are you?"

Mr Good stood tall once more. "That's a difficult one to answer." He moved from behind the sofa, slipped his feet into his flip-flops, and sat in the armchair opposite. "Unfortunately, age is not something we have around here."

Keith was perplexed. "That's ridiculous. Everyone has an age."

Mr Good smiled. "You see, unlike you, we have nothing to measure the passing of time by. We have no sun or moon or stars. 'I feel three hundred years younger' is just an expression we have in these parts for when one is feeling particularly good."

"Well." Keith contracted his brow in displeasure. "I don't mind telling you, Mr Good, that I feel three hundred years older guarding Terrence with this water pistol."

He flashed Terrence a quick look. "I mean, this real gun." He waved it around in the air menacingly, but Terrence didn't seem to notice. He was mumbling something incoherent to himself.

"Not to worry, old chum," said Mr Good reassuringly. "All is well."

"Is it?" Keith was unconvinced. "I'm not so sure."

"At least it will be when we have Lord Riddle on our side."

Keith's eyes narrowed. "Who is Lord Riddle, anyway? Exactly."

"Lord Riddle is the Dream Ambassador for those peculiar, strange, inexplicable dreams that make no sense." Mr Good leaned forward. "Probably."

"Probably?"

Mr Good nodded. He didn't want to be overheard. He certainly didn't want Terrence to mock him. "Well, seeing as no one I know as ever met him," he whispered, "we can only suppose."

Keith stared at Mr Good open-mouthed. "Gosh and double gosh! Do you mean you're not even sure he exists?

"Of course he exists, young Keith. There's plenty of evidence to suggest he does. For example, in the pump room in the basement in the Palace of Somnium there are three thick, black iron pipes that send dream waves along their length. Obviously, one pipe supplies power to the palace, and one leads to Torment Towers in the Nether Regions. But where does the other one go?"

Keith shook his head dumbly.

"That's a whole band of dream frequency that must go somewhere, young Keith. I like to think that that thick, black iron pipe travels underground in the direction of the Uncharted Borders and eventually connects to a very large dream tank in an enormous airing cupboard somewhere on the Land of Nod." Mr Good stood up and resumed his hip and thigh stretches. "So, if the Land of Nod exists, then it follows there must be a third Dream Ambassador. Add that supposition to the various tales of an odd sort of a fellow wearing a funny hat seen occasionally in Limbo and in Dreamspaces down the eras, and the legend of Lord Riddle is born."

"Legend?" Keith shook his head in disbelief. "So you're saying that the very nub of your plan hinges on a mythical character in some travellers' tale?"

Mr Good shrugged as he lifted his left leg until his thigh was parallel with the ground. "Basically, old chum, yes."

Keith sighed. "I want to go home."

#

"A big, red rock eater," uttered Terrence incomprehensibly.

When he said it, he felt a release. It was like a sneeze. He felt better, but he knew there would be another one along very soon.

"Get it?" he asked. "What are big, red, and eat rocks? A big, red rock eater?" He grunted in the direction of the Boy Scout, who for some reason was looking a little dejected in the cream armchair opposite. "Get it?"

Keith didn't get it. Keith didn't catch a single word of it. Actually, Keith wasn't even listening. Then the old man who looked like Vile woke up.

#

"Go away," screamed Arthur, shielding his eyes as if he'd arrived here suddenly from a dark place. "Leave me alone. Stay away from me, you rotter."

"Grandpa?" Keith stood up. "What's the matter? Are you all right?"

Arthur sat up gingerly. He had pins and needles: a burning, prickling, and tingling sensation in his arms and legs. "Where is he?" He looked around the room anxiously. "Is he here?"

"Is who here, Grandpa?" Keith put his arm around him. "What happened?"

Arthur took a few long, wheezy breaths and eventually appeared to calm down. "I had a dream."

Mr Good paused in mid-stretch. "What sort of dream, old chum?" he asked, suddenly interested.

Arthur looked up. "A sort of nightmare it was."

Mr Good's feet located the flip-flops once more. He sat on the arm of the sofa next to Arthur. "Elucidate."

"Pardon?"

"Explain the dream to us, young Arthur, if you can."

Arthur took a few more deep, wheezy breaths. "Well, I was in a dark cave," he began. "There were spiders, and I could hear rats or mice scampering all around me. But it wasn't that that concerned me. I knew there was something evil in the cave with me. Then I heard a movement. I looked up, and Vile was standing there."

Keith could feel his grandpa was shaking with fear.

"Go on," said Mr Good calmly.

"At first I thought it was me. I thought I was looking in a mirror." He managed a half smile and pulled nervously on his whiskers. "Until he spoke. Then I knew it wasn't me."

"What did he say, Grandpa?"

"'What's the square root of forty-seven?' That's what he said. Of course, I didn't know. I've never been very good at arithmetic, have I, Keith?"

Keith swung his head slowly from side to side.

Arthur looked up at Mr Good. "Then he asked me to pass on a message to you."

Mr Good was fascinated. A dream within Dream Land. How was it possible? How was Vile able to manage this? Clearly Vile had a better understanding of the technology available to him at the palace than he ever had.

"What was it, Grandpa?" asked Keith. "What was the message?"

"The message? Let me think. He said, 'You can tell that goody-goody Mr Good and that salmon features person that I am on to their little scheme. They will never recapture the Palace of Somnium because I've secured the services of a couple of giants to guard the front door.' Oh, and then he said that evil is a far stronger force than good."

Mr Good smiled. "Is that all?"

"No. Then he asked what the capital of Norway was. Well, this I knew. I said Oslo, and he gave me a red plum. I said thank you, thinking he wasn't that bad after all. But when I looked at the plum again, it was a gooseberry. And I don't like gooseberries. Do I, Keith? He started to laugh. It was a horrible, evil laugh, and he was coming towards me. I slammed my mobility scooter into reverse, but the back wheels were spinning round and round, and I couldn't get away. He had a collection of pins in his right hand and a cluster of needles in his left. He started poking me in my arms and legs with them. Then I woke up."

Keith hugged his Grandpa. "What does all this mean, Mr Good?"

Mr Good stood up and pondered his reply for a long moment. "I think it's safe to say that Vile is getting worried, young Keith."

Chapter 47

The Dream Ambassador for Tranquil Dreams didn't have a nasty bone in his body. Vile, however, had 206 of them, and his encounter with Arthur in the dark cave just now had really tickled the funny one that ran from the shoulder down to the elbow. The big white button with the large black capital letter I on it was such fun.

Three muscular guards were lined up on the far side of the room by the door. "Now then, you imbeciles." He turned to face them.

"I don't know how much you know or understand," he said in an offensively condescending tone. "But things are happening out there in Limbo."

He quickly scanned the corridors and passageways, with their numerous different colours, on the closed-circuit television monitors as if looking for something that was happening just to prove his point. He didn't see anything. He rubbed his ample chin thoughtfully.

"It took me many eras to get this place off Mr Good, and I don't intend to surrender it now." He returned to the walnut desk and sat on its edge. "We don't want to go back to the old place, do we? We like it here, don't we?"

The three guards stood tall and silent without a spark of intelligence between them.

"Mr Good has a plan," he informed the guards. "So, we need to be careful. We must always remember that Mr Good may be righteous, Mr Good may be virtuous, and Mr Good may be gracious, but that doesn't mean he's completely stupid. In some respects he's almost half as cunning and crafty as I am." Vile stood. "Okay, so I'm exaggerating a little." He grinned as he approached the guards. "But we still need to be careful." He halted in front of the first guard. "What do we need to be?"

"Ugh!" the first guard grunted.

"Exactly." He moved along the line to the second guard. "What do we need to be?"

"Ugh!" the second guard grunted.

"And you." He looked up at the third guard. "What do we need to ...?"

He faltered and sniffed. Vile drew air in through his nose and traced the source of the smell to the guard's tunic and cloak. "Are you one of the guards who didn't lock the cell door earlier, allowing those pesky kids to escape?"

The third guard's head nodded, ever so slightly, inside his iron helmet.

"Tell me." Vile grinned. "The porridge. Was it cold?"

The guard's expression remained expressionless.

"With lumps in?" His grin widened. "And too much salt?"

He looked into the guard's eyes and tried to determine if the guard was in full possession of all his faculties. He decided it was most unlikely. "Nobody enjoys being dipped in cold, lumpy, salty porridge, do they? It's a particularly nasty substance to be dipped in. That's why I use it." He continued on to the fourth guard.

There wasn't a fourth guard.

Vile was flummoxed. "I am sure I have more than three of these so-called guards."

On a spot monitor over Vile's right shoulder the three so-called guards noticed several pink polka dots move across the screen. It was Peggy Sue. Her lime-green circular skirt blended in exactly with the surrounding environment. She looked left and then right before continuing on her way.

"Where are the other guards?" he demanded.

Right on cue the door opened, and a dozen or more guards bounced in. They struck one another or collided one against the other in a desperate attempt to find some space and settled on a carpet tile each. Eventually they all stood to attention and waited.

Vile made them wait a little longer as he walked slowly round to his black leather swivel chair, leaned back a little, and put his hands behind his head. "Better late than never, I suppose," he snarled. "On second thoughts, you guards are such an incompetent bunch of losers, better never than late might be more apt."

He sat forward and rested his elbows on the desk. "I know you don't possess the faculty of reasoning and understanding, but I am going to tell you the situation anyway. Things are slowly but surely reaching something of a climax hereabouts. We are nearing very much the crisis point situation, as it were."

He paused for dramatic effect, but it was wasted on the guards.

"In just two dream spans," he informed the collection of brawn and very little brain, "my most fearful, gruesome, hideously horrid nightmare yet will be taking place. But this fearful, gruesome, hideous, and horrid nightmare will not happen unless we are careful."

Vile leaned forward. "Very soon we will be leaving this place and setting off on a journey. We are going to set about two giants forcibly and violently in an unprovoked and frenzied attack."

In front of him were approximately seventeen bored muscular guards.

"Now, I know what you're all thinking." Actually, Vile didn't know what they were all thinking. He wasn't even sure if they could think. So he corrected himself. "If you lot were capable of any mental activity, you might be considering, at this point, the security aspect. Who will be guarding the palace if we all leave here to set about two giants forcibly and violently in an unprovoked and frenzied attack? What would stop that Mr Good from just strolling over and walking in?"

The approximately seventeen bored muscular guards were all staring blankly. None of them were considering the security aspect. None of them knew what that meant.

"Security is going to be tightened," Vile announced as he stood up. "I have a simple yet clever idea, but I'm not going to waste my breath explaining it because you're all stupid." He pushed his way through their massed muscular ranks towards the door. "Follow me, you simpletons." In the doorway he turned. "So, what are you waiting for?"

Meanwhile on one of the monitors, a monitor divided into sixteen different images, a teddy boy, a young lad with tightly curled ginger hair, and a girl wearing blue jeans and sensible shoes walked determinedly across the lime-coloured screen.

#

Vile entered the drawing room through one of the mirrored panels along the wall. He was closely followed by what Larry later estimated to be more than twenty muscular guards. Barry had a more conservative judgement; when they compared notes afterwards, he thought there were somewhere between fourteen and eighteen of them. Harry, on the other hand, didn't care how many there were. One muscular guard on his own would be bad enough, but so many of them all together at the same time in the same place was going to give him a headache for sure.

"Now then, you useless assortment of Normans." On the balcony overlooking the grand entrance hall, Vile turned and faced the large gathering of dream actors and dream actresses sitting at occasional tables.

"There are going to be a few changes around here," he informed them. "Security is going to be tightened."

He allowed his gaze to roam their scary faces and noticed a general lack of interest in the room. He saw impassiveness and indifference, and it annoyed him. "You!"

Because Larry was very tall and ungracefully thin, he tended to be the one who got picked on. Indeed, it was in his direction that Vile's long, bony index finger was pointing.

"What is security going to be?"

Larry gulped. "Tightened, sir."

"Exactly." Vile pushed his way through the gaps between the caned seats and circled the ghosts' table. One of them wasn't paying attention. One of them was holding his head in his hands. "You!"

Harry sat bolt upright in his chair. The dull thump in his temple was suddenly replaced by what felt like the pounding of an orchestral bass drum inside his head.

Vile leaned closer. "So," he hissed. "Tell me. How are we going to do it?"

Harry's jaw dropped, and his eyes bulged. "I ... I ..." he stammered. "I ... don't ... know."

"Excellent." Vile grinned. "Of course you don't know. How could you possibly know? How can you hope to be on the same wavelength as the most evil dude in Scarydream Land? It just isn't feasible, is it?"

"Yes, sir. I mean –"Harry shook his aching head urgently. "No, sir."

Vile stepped out onto the balcony once more. "Now listen, you Normans, to my simple yet clever idea." He looked down on the grand entrance hall below and pointed. "Henceforth, that door to Limbo will be locked at all times."

"Good idea, sir," shouted a demon somewhere at the back of the room. Vile nodded a satisfied nod. "Yes, but wait until you hear the clever bit."

"Wasn't that the clever bit?" asked a devil sitting at the same table.

Were they being sarcastic at the back? Surely not. He scanned the tables at the far end of the room, trying without success to locate the owner of the voice. "That was the simple bit," said Vile slowly and dangerously. "The clever bit is this."

He paused. Now they were interested. Now the Normans were listening. "Entry to the Palace of Somnium will only be gained by the use of a ... secret password." He grinned. "Ingenious, eh?"

"Well call me a taxi!" gushed Larry.

"That's astounding!" admitted a vampire.

"Remarkable!" agreed a zombie.

"However did you think of it?" asked Barry.

Vile waved a hand dismissively. "I'm Vile. Everything I do is astounding and remarkable – and quite often wicked and nasty too at the same time."

"Extraordinary!" commented a lunatic brandishing a half-moon sod cutter.

"Enough!" Vile slapped the balustrade with the flat of his hand. "There isn't time. I'm in a hurry. I have important business to attend to. All I want you Normans to do is lock the door after me. I won't be gone long, but when I do return I'll knock the door and give the secret password. Any questions?" He didn't anticipate any, and so with a nod he signalled the guards to follow him. He lifted his right foot, fully intending to place it on the first step down the freestanding graceful staircase.

I have a question.

Vile paused, his right leg hanging in mid-air. He grabbed hold of the solid oak rail for support and looked round at a sea of faces. "Who said that?" he demanded as he picked his way through the muscular guards queuing up behind him at the top of the staircase. He looked around the room, threateningly, from table to table.

I did. It's me, the annoying bird inside your head.

Vile's face creased into a frown. "Oh, it's you."

Have you forgotten something?

His brows remained wrinkled as he attempted to grasp its meaning. "For – gott – en some – thing?" He said it slowly and one syllable at a time in the hope that by doing so the question might make sense. He was Vile, the most evil dude in Scarydream Land. So of course it didn't make any sense.

"Obviously, if I have forgotten something, then obviously that something is obviously not worth remembering," he replied with a confident smirk.

The secret password. You haven't said what it is.

Vile's confident smirk wavered just a smidgen. He was suddenly aware that the dream actors were watching him, nudging each other and whispering. How dare they entertain the idea that he may be displaying the first signs of madness? He glared. It was a carefully chosen glare, a glare that exuded confidence and authority, a glare designed to put an end to the possibility, once and for all, that he was going a little bit doolally.

"I've sent you all the secret password," he said as his piercing eyes darted around the room. "Don't you Normans ever read your dream-mails?"

Across the spacious drawing room there were a few heads shaking, some shrugs, and a lot of blank faces.

"Look." Vile sighed. "I haven't got time for all this. Opening night of my new nightmare is fast approaching. I can't hang around here for the rest of this current dream span waiting for you all to log on, so I will tell you." He took a deep breath. "The secret password is …"

Even though he hadn't got time for all this and opening night was fast approaching, he felt a long pause was appropriate here to heighten the tension.

"Egg and chips."

The bird inside his head laughed.

Vile ignored the laugh. As secret passwords went, he thought 'egg and chips' was a smart choice. It certainly wasn't in any way amusing. For reassurance he searched the faces of the dream actors at nearby tables, looking for smirks. He spotted a table of grotesque classical mythological characters and singled out a bearded dream actor holding a hammer and tongs. "Do you think it's funny?"

Hephaestus, the Greek god of fire, shook his head frantically. "No, sir."

Vile eyed Hephaestus suspiciously for a long, uncomfortable moment.

"So 'egg and chips' it is." He grinned triumphantly. "When I do return, if I don't say 'egg and chips', then you must not under any circumstances let me in, even if I rant and rave and scream and threaten to use your guts for garters. Is that understood?"

Across the spacious drawing room there were a few heads nodding.

"What if we look through the keyhole?"

It was a female voice. Vile's eyes narrowed.

"And when we do look through the keyhole," continued the evil stepmother, "and we see that it's you standing there, it will be okay to open the door, I suppose?"

"No!" A look of alarm spread quickly across his face, and his whiskers twitched nervously. "You couldn't make a worse move. It might not be me. It might be someone who looks like me."

Someone who looks like you? Oh, I see. Of course. It could be Arthur.

"It could be an impersonator," continued Vile. "Look, it's quite simple. If I don't say 'egg and chips', then it isn't me."

You have the look of a worried man, Vile. I saw your whiskers twitch nervously back there.

Vile ignored the voice in his head. This was his new tactic. If he ignored it completely it might lose interest, go away, and climb inside another head.

"Any questions?" he asked again. Hopefully he was asking it for the final time.

"What shall we do if you say 'fish and chips'?" asked another dream actress.

"What?" Vile gave the Wicked Witch an incredulous stare. "I won't be saying fish and chips, will I?"

"But, what if you do?" persisted the withered old crone.

Vile sighed wearily. "Look, if I say 'fish and chips', 'kebab and chips', or even 'steak and kidney pie and chips with mushy peas', keep that door locked! Get it?"

"Got it," said Barry.

"It's 'egg and chips' or nothing!"

"'Egg and chips' or nothing," agreed Larry.

"At last." Vile took a couple of backward steps in the direction of the freestanding staircase. "Now, before I go I need to leave someone in charge. The problem is, the muscular guards are leaving with me, Terrence is missing, Peggy Sue isn't here, and I can't find the cat anywhere. So, unfortunately, it will have to be one of you Normans."

Across the spacious drawing room there were a few heads bowed in the hope that this would prevent them from being seen or chosen. Vile's eyes were drawn again to the table of grotesque classical mythological characters. It wasn't Hephaestus this time who caught his attention. It was his neighbour. "You!" he pointed.

It was Cyclops.

"While I am away I want you to keep your –" Vile grinned a yellow-toothed grin – "eye on things."

Vile had always known he had the ability to perceive and express things in an ingeniously humorous manner. But 'Cyclops, keep your eye on things' was, he decided, just too droll even for the Dream Ambassador for Nightmares. Vile took the opportunity to congratulate himself on his spontaneous wit as he passed the landing where the stairs divided into two just below the monumental stained-glass window. 'It's all the more astounding and remarkable that I can be so comical when you consider the pressure I am under with opening night so close, a certain Mr Good to contend with, and an annoying bird inside my head to ignore, not to mention the stress of the missing cat,' Vile mused to himself as he reached the grand entrance hall below.

"Now lock the door after us," he shouted at Cyclops. "And keep the key about your person."

Vile was followed by between a dozen and a score of muscular guards marching across the pink and white marble flooring through the hand-crafted, solid arched door and out into Limbo to begin their journey to the white room.

Chapter 48

Melvin, Lorraine, and Vince rushed and dashed along the continuously bending curve of the green labyrinth for what seemed, to Lorraine at least, like about a week to ten days. Yet, in reality, the time that elapsed from leaving the lime maze to reaching the door was probably no more than a day or two. At last they reached a steel fire exit door with a push bar to open and four heavy-duty stainless hinges. It was the entrance to the Uncharted Borders.

Separating them from the steel fire exit door with a push bar to open and four heavy-duty stainless hinges, however, was a turnstile.

Vince was the first to reach it. He grabbed hold of one of the three bars that blocked the way. "What is it?" he asked.

Melvin examined it closely. "If I'm not mistaken," he said, tapping it with his knuckles, "it's a turnstile."

Vince tried to push and then pull one of the bars, but it wouldn't budge. "We will have to climb over it," he decided.

"I wouldn't do that," said a slow, robotic voice, "if I were you."

Melvin jumped back.

Lorraine looked along the green corridor ahead. "Who said that?" she called.

"I have a beam that would detect anyone who contravened the system," said the monotone voice.

"Where the dickens are you?" asked Melvin, spinning round. "We can't see you."

"I am the turnstile," it replied with an evenness and flatness. "Similar to the type you find in banks and financial institutions."

Vince looked down at the shiny silver mechanical contraption in awe. "You can talk?"

"I offer security in areas where restrictions are required to prevent unauthorised access," it explained, "whilst still maintaining an open-plan feel."

"That's all very interesting." Lorraine frowned. "But —"

"I am made completely of polished stainless steel apart from my housing, which is clad in timber," it informed them.

"I see," said Melvin, admiring the timber the turnstile's housing was clad in.

"I find it gives me a warmer, furniture-style appearance."

Lorraine shrugged. "Well, I suppose it does, but —"

"My name is Tripod," continued the shiny silver mechanical contraption. "So called because of my three steel arms."

To demonstrate, the three steel bars that blocked their way clicked and rotated full circle.

"Good name," admitted Lorraine. "Tripod. Three arms. Very apt." She looked past the turnstile towards the steel fire exit door. "But —"

"But," said Melvin, taking over, "we were wondering if —"

"If you could enter the Uncharted Borders?" asked Tripod slowly in a single tone without harmony or variation in pitch.

"Yes." Melvin grinned. "That's exactly what we were wondering."

Tripod didn't utter a word for a long moment.

Vince shifted uneasily from one blue suede shoe to the other during the silence. He was just about to open his mouth and suggest they clamber over the turnstile and continue on their way when Tripod spoke.

"How many of you are there?"

Melvin looked at Lorraine, and Lorraine looked at Melvin. Then they both looked at Vince.

"Three," said Lorraine.

"There are three of us," confirmed Melvin.

Vince measured the height of the turnstile against himself. The top of it reached just short of his waist. He felt he could leap over it with no problem and was seriously considering doing so when he remembered the beam. What harm could a beam do anyway? he wondered.

"Unfortunately, to enter the Uncharted Borders you will need three keywords," said Tripod in an unvaried tone. "Sorry you had a wasted journey."

"But we do have keywords," said Lorraine excitedly. "We all have."

"I wouldn't get too excited if I were you," said the turnstile. "Ninety-nine point nine per cent of all keywords are now obsolete," it informed them in its monotonous, low drone.

"The probability of you having valid keywords is at best –" It paused briefly to consider the likelihood. "Unlikely," it decided. "I hope you haven't travelled far."

A look of disappointment crossed Lorraine's face, a feeling of helplessness washed over Melvin, and Vince combed his hair. He put away his comb and turned to them. "We will have to climb over it."

"No," said Lorraine. "We can't. It has a beam."

Vince shrugged. "A beam? A ray of light?" He looked down at the turnstile. "That's really scary," he mocked as he lifted his right blue suede shoe and rested it on the first steel bar.

"And an alarm will sound," Tripod warned him. "So loud you will have a ringing or a buzzing in one or both of your ears for the rest of your dream spans."

"Look, Vince," said Melvin. "Let's just try our keywords, shall we?"

"Melvin's right, Vince," said Lorraine. "There's no harm in trying."

Vince sighed, reluctantly lowered his leg, took a step back, folded his arms, and sulked.

"When you are ready, place the palm of your right hand on my housing and tell me your name and reveal your keyword clearly."

Lorraine stepped forward first. The polished stainless steel surface felt cold to the touch. "My name is Lorraine and my keyword is Penguin." She said it loud and clear.

"Never mind," said Tripod. "But I did say there was only zero point one per cent chance of –" Its voice faltered. "What did you say?"

"Penguin," she repeated.

"Well I'll be a monkey's uncle," it said as the three steel bars clicked and dropped down, allowing Lorraine plenty of space to squeeze past. "Access granted," it announced.

Melvin strode forward confidently. "Melvin. Downhill." He said it loud and clear too and with a grin.

Tripod fell silent for a moment or so as the three steel bars clicked and dropped begrudgingly. Melvin pushed past and punched the air in triumph, and as he joined Lorraine on the other side he gave her a congratulatory hug.

"Access granted."

"Your turn, Vince," Lorraine called out.

Vince, who had been standing with his arms folded in a sullen manner only a moment ago, was now encouraged by Melvin and Lorraine's successful passage through the turnstile. He was hopeful of being able to reach the steel fire exit door in the correct manner without having to resort to climbing over a large heap of polished steel. He realised that might have been a bit tricky in his tight drainpipe trousers. He placed the palm of his right hand on its housing. "I'm Vince," he said as he gave Melvin and Lorraine a little wink.

"Now reveal your keyword clearly," said Tripod. "And no conferring."

Vince opened his mouth to speak but then said nothing.

"Come on, Vince." Melvin grinned. "Got to be rushing, need to be dashing. Remember?"

"I am going to have to hurry you," uttered the turnstile impatiently.

"Vince!" shouted Lorraine.

"Access will be denied," continued the turnstile in its usual single tone of voice. "In ten, nine, eight ..."

"Quickly, Vince," pleaded Lorraine. "You don't want to be stuck in Limbo!"

"Seven, six, five."

"Your keyword," shouted Melvin anxiously. "Vince, we can't enter the Uncharted Borders without you!"

"Four, three, two."

Vince moved his jaw. The two bones that formed the framework of his mouth swung and swayed loosely, but no words came forth.

"One," said Tripod.

#

"Vince?"

It was a female voice that spoke. A beautiful girl with a small button nose and high cheekbones was standing just a few strides away. She was wearing a lime green circular skirt with pink polka dots, matching scarf, and a white short-sleeved top.

"How you rocking, Vince?" added the girl with the large, round eyes and long, dark lashes.

Vince blinked several times. In his eyes there was recognition, a memory, an awareness. It was a voice he knew. It was a voice he had longed to hear again.

He turned, and their eyes met.

The first thing Vince noticed was her dazzling white smile. His reply was a whisper, his vocal cords hardly vibrating at all. "I'm rollin'," he gasped.

"Access granted," said Tripod.

Chapter 49

Mr Good stood tall with one leg in front of the other, his hands flat and at shoulder height against the brown, orange, tan, and yellow wallpaper. Keith looked up from his notebook and sighed. "How long have they been gone now?" he asked.

"What was that, old chum?" Mr Good eased his back leg further away from the wall.

"Melvin, Lorraine, and Vince. How long have they been gone now?"

With his leg straight Mr Good pressed his heel firmly into the floor. "Well, young Keith, that's a difficult question to answer."

"I know I asked you this earlier, and you said that time here moves mostly crabwise. But to me that doesn't make any sense at all. So, I've been giving it some thought," said Keith, referring to his personal notes. "According to my calculations, I reckon they've been gone –" He paused, looked at Mr Good, and chewed the end of his pencil. "Three days?"

Mr Good made no comment. He faced the wall with his rear leg and spine in a straight line.

"But without any windows to look through it's quite difficult to judge," continued Keith. "It would help if I knew whether it was night or day outside."

When Mr Good felt the stretch in the calf of his rear leg he turned and faced the boy scout. "Outside?" He smiled. "Day or night?"

He shook his head, moved closer, and stood behind the chocolate-brown sofa. "Time is different here, old chum. It doesn't quite work like that."

Keith shrugged. "So how does it work? How long do you think they've been gone?" he asked.

Mr Good considered the question for a long moment and then took a deep breath. "Well, let me put it this way, young Keith. Imagine an epoch is a length of wood. Now imagine you divided that length of wood into a million pieces and you took one of those pieces and broke a little bit off the end." He sat on the arm of the sofa and rested his hands on his knees. "And you took that little bit off the end and placed it between the jaws of a vice. Then from your tool box you took a chisel and a mallet, and you sliced away a small, thin, sharp piece from the top left-hand corner."

Keith was intrigued. He stared at Mr Good, open mouthed, and nodded.

"Well." Mr Good stood up and slowly made his way back to the area of wall near the invisible doorway. "I think that small, thin, sharp piece, that little splinter of time, best represents the duration that has elapsed, old chum."

Mr Good resumed his calf stretching exercises. Although not entirely happy with Mr Good's explanation and his strange way of reckoning the passage of time, Keith wrote it all down in his diary anyway.

Suddenly Arthur sat up quickly – too quickly when you consider the inflammation in his joints. "Cockroaches!" he announced.

Keith looked up.

"And really big, hairy spiders."

"Are you all right, Grandpa?"

"The cave." Arthur flinched with the pain and the stiffness and the memory of that dark place. "There were giant red ants in there too." He shook.

"It's over now," said Keith, leaning forward and resting his hand reassuringly on his grandpa's knee. "You're safe here."

"Safe?" Arthur was unconvinced. "At my time of life and with my ailments, I shouldn't be traipsing around strange worlds." He adjusted his position on the sofa in search of a more comfortable one. He screwed up his face tightly with the effort of it. "Traipsing around strange worlds is a young man's game."

"Old chum." Mr Good paused in mid-stretch. "Are you in pain?"

Arthur grimaced and nodded. "It's my arthritis. It's starting to play me up again."

Keith was surprised. "But – the medicine?"

"Clearly hasn't worked." Mr Good ran his fingers through his tangled silvery beard, something he always did when he was in deep thought or concerned about something or other, and sat down on the sofa next to Arthur. He looked at the old man closely. He was a dead ringer for Vile, that was for sure. When Lord Riddle arrives he would surely want to utilise that fact. But would there be any point? If there was one thing you could say about Vile, it was that he was sprightly. Vile was quite nimble and agile, and you never, ever heard him complain of arthritis, tendinitis, or recurring pain in his lumbar region. Suspicions would surely be aroused if he were seen to be taking a breather every twenty strides or so.

"Hasn't worked?" asked Keith, alarmed. "Begging your pardon, Mr Good, I thought that medicine cured ninety-nine per cent of all known ailments."

Mr Good sighed. "It does, young Keith, it does. But ..."

"But what?"

"But only temporarily," explained Mr Good. "It is effective for a time only. I was just hoping that time would last longer than —"

"Longer than a small, thin, sharp piece sliced away from the top left-hand corner of a little bit off the end of a millionth part of a wooden epoch?" asked Keith.

"Exactly." Mr Good nodded.

Keith frowned. Arthur winced.

Something rustled. The row of colourful beads fluttered and swished as if a current of air had burst into the room from somewhere. This was unusual because currents of air rarely occurred in the royal blue labyrinth, especially at its centre. The centre of the royal blue labyrinth was generally draught-free. Looking up they were surprised to see, framed in the invisible doorway, a wizard wearing a designer ankle-length black robe with gold stars.

"Mugwump!" beamed Mr Good. "You're back."

"My dear fellows." The wizard performed an elaborate bow. "Indeed I am."

"How terrifically pleasing and pleasingly terrific to see you return, old chum." Mr Good stood up and offered him his space on the sofa. "The wizards' convention went well, I trust?"

"Most constructive," replied Mugwump, "and I also had a very pleasant journey home in the company of my good friend, the wizard who frequently mentions mackerel."

He turned his back to the sofa and was just about to descend to a sitting position when he caught sight of Arthur's stockinged feet. Arthur had kicked off his shiny two-tone shoes, revealing a pair of sore ankles that were so swollen and puffed out they looked like a couple of red balloons. "I see that the tiny capillaries that supply blood and lymph fluid to your feet, Arthur, are leaking again."

"The medicine hasn't worked," Keith said with a sigh.

"Well, not for anywhere near long enough," added Mr Good.

Mugwump finally fell back into the sofa and idly played with the rope tie around his waist as he considered this. "Two salmons," he announced at last.

Mr Good and Keith looked at each other blankly.

"No. Not two salmons. Two spoonfuls," he corrected himself. "Magic is mostly trial and error, you see." He stood up smartly, moved to the teak sideboard, and opened the two cupboard doors. "If you remember, the first time I administered medicine to Arthur I gave him three spoonfuls, which made him hyperactive and forgetful. Last time I only gave him one spoonful of my mysterious elixir. And that, unfortunately, has resulted in the premature return of his various medical conditions." He looked from Mr Good to Keith to Arthur. "Two spoonfuls will solve the problem," he assured them.

Mr Good breathed a huge sigh of relief. "I'm so pleased."

"Did you hear that, Grandpa?" Keith enunciated each word loudly and clearly. "Mr Salmon is going to take the pain away for you."

Arthur nodded uncomfortably. There was nothing wrong with his hearing.

From the single adjustable shelf Mugwump chose a glass bottle a third full of the special thick yellow liquid. "So," he asked, "has anything happened while I have been away? With his back to them and holding the stopper, he shook the bottle firmly. "Have I missed anything?"

"Well," Keith said with a shrug, "Grandpa had a dream."

Mugwump turned his head quickly. His jaw had already dropped. "Really?"

"A dream within Dream Land," said Mr Good. "I didn't even know it was possible."

The wizard sat on the arm of the sofa, next to Arthur, and poured out a level spoonful of the medicine. Arthur swallowed it eagerly, and it was followed swiftly by a second one. They all watched as Arthur twitched and then wiggled and wriggled before he writhed and thrashed and flailed about for a bit. Mugwump waited. He waited until Arthur lay still. He waited until he was sure the old man's features were calm and peaceful. "A dream, you say?"

Arthur, pain free at last, leaned closer to Mugwump. "A sort of nightmare it was," he whispered.

"Fascinating," said Mugwump as he returned the clear stopper into the mouth of the glass bottle. "Please explicate."

"Pardon?"

"My dear salmon," he said with a smile, "tell me what happened."

Arthur took a deep breath. "Well, I was in a dark cave," he began. He then proceeded to give the wizard a detailed resume of events. It was the same story he had told Mr Good and Keith earlier, except in this version there were far more creepy-crawlies to contend with.

Mugwump listened with growing astonishment.

"Then I woke up," Arthur said finally.

The wizard remained silent for a long moment.

"What do you think it means, young Mugwump?" asked Mr Good when the long moment had passed.

"I think –" A smile spread across the wizard's round, jolly face. "I think Vile is getting worried."

Mr Good smiled broadly. "That's what I said."

"You will be back in the Palace of Somnium, where you belong, before you know it, Mr Good," said Mugwump confidently as he stood up, returned the glass bottle inside the teak sideboard, and closed the cupboard doors.

Mr Good's broad smile turned into a sad one. "I hope so, old chum. I really miss the old place. I miss my exercise bike particularly."

Terrence began to move about restlessly and impatiently on the teak dining chair and pull frantically on the string that bound his wrists and ankles. He tried to speak, but his words were muffled behind the silk scarf that filled his mouth.

Mr Good sighed with a touch of melancholy. "And I miss my porcelain tea set, of course."

"Look," said Keith suddenly. "Terrence is moving about restlessly and impatiently."

Mugwump had noticed too. "And he's pulling frantically on the string that binds his wrists and ankles, I notice."

"He is also trying to speak, but his words are muffled behind the silk scarf that fills his mouth," observed Keith.

The wizard moved closer to Terrence to get a better look.

"I wonder what he's trying to say," wondered Keith.

Curiously, Mugwump removed the gag.

"Not to mention my beautiful little writing desk," added Mr Good wistfully.

Terrence laughed. Instinctively, Keith's fingers slipped into the left-hand pocket of his navy blue activity trousers and quietly wrapped themselves around the hilt of the water pistol.

"Vile hates all dainty, elegant furniture," said Terrence between chuckles. "Your beautiful little writing desk? He's burned it."

"Be quiet!" demanded Keith.

"For firewood."

"You barbarian!"

"I helped to chop it up."

Keith pulled out the red, plastic water pistol and held it aloft. "I've a good mind to hit you over the head with this gun. This real gun," he quickly added.

"Calm down, old chum," said Mr Good. "There's no need for us to resort to Vile's level."

"But, Mr Good, he chopped up your beautiful little writing desk!"

Mr Good smiled weakly. "Not to worry, young Keith. It's unfortunate, but what is done is done."

"Yes, but …"

Terrence sneered. "It had woodworm anyway."

Mr Good leaned forward and looked Terrence in the eye. "What news of the Ancient Tea Set of Firmamentum?" he asked with more than a little trepidation.

Terrence stared blankly.

"My porcelain tea set."

"Oh." Terrence grinned. "That crockery on the Welsh dresser?"

Mr Good nodded. "On two illuminated display shelves."

"Smashed."

Mr Good's expression didn't change. Or perhaps the kindness and sparkle in his deep blue eyes dimmed a little.

"Vile threw them." Terrence was enjoying this. "Mostly in my direction, actually, and the ones that didn't hit me on the head all smashed against the wall."

He was enjoying seeing the shock and horror on everyone's face. He quickly tried to think of something else to upset them with. But then he felt another riddle coming along the conveyor belt in his mind. He frowned. He didn't know where all these riddles came from or why, but he knew he had to spit them out.

"When is a timid girl like a stone?" he spat.

Everyone was too shocked and horrified to care.

"When is a timid girl like a stone?" he repeated.

"We're not interested," snapped Mugwump.

"Not interested?" Terrence looked at the wizard and then at Mr Good and smirked. "So, shall I tell you what Vile has done to your exercise bike instead?"

"Mugwump!" said Mr Good firmly.

Mugwump nodded. He knew what had to be done. Quickly, he replaced the silk scarf securely between Terrence's teeth.

Chapter 50

"Then I had it painted a sickly green colour," he said with a grin. "And the saddle and the pedals have come in useful for something hideous I'm making in that little room under the stairs."

Vile knew he was talking to himself even though he had between twelve and twenty muscular guards gathered around him. He tried the door and was surprised to find it locked. The men in dark blue overalls and tool belts had obviously made a temporary repair, since his last visit, by replacing the striker plates and securing them with drywall screws. It wasn't a problem, though, for a strong size-fourteen leather sandal on a muscular guard's foot.

On the other side of the door it was dark, chilly, and damp, like being inside an enormous water well. A flight of slippery stone steps, barely two strides across, spiralled upwards and followed the curve of the dank wall. Vile led the way, and the guards followed in single file. They kept to the right-hand side of the steps, as close to the wall as possible, because to their left was a vast chasm of blackness: a deep, shadowy, immeasurable space that reached down to a subterranean lake far below.

And there was no hand rail.

#

"He does exist."

"He doesn't."

"He does!"

"This is laughable," laughed Flagellum.

"Lord Riddle exists, I tell you," insisted Zygote.

"You'll be telling me next you believe in Santa Claus and the Tooth Fairy."

"I only believe what my eyes tell me, Flagellum."

"Really." The slightly shorter giant's lips formed a smirk. "So you've seen this Lord Riddle, have you?"

"As a matter of fact I have," replied Zygote.

Flagellum guffawed. "I've never heard such nonsense."

"It was many eras ago now. I was out walking with my brother when ..."

"Your brother? I didn't know you had a brother. I suppose that's a lie is it?"

"No, it's not a lie. I do have a brother. He's called Midrib, and he always tells the truth."

Flagellum raised an eyebrow. "So, you're the black sheep of the family?"

"I always tell the truth too!"

"Poppycock!"

"Midrib and I were out walking aimlessly," recalled Zygote. "We were in the remote outer confines of Limbo along the redder mazes and labyrinths when ..."

"You're making this up."

"I'm not. This is where we saw him."

"Lord Riddle?"

Zygote nodded. "Lurking, he was, and only a few long strides away from us. He was an odd sort of a fellow, and he wore a funny hat. But no sooner did he appear than he disappeared."

"Disappeared?" Flagellum scoffed. "So, he didn't actually introduce himself, then?"

"Of course he didn't."

"Yet somehow you knew it was him?"

"Midrib and I were convinced. We sensed it."

"You saw an odd sort of a fellow doing a spot of lurking, and you automatically assumed it was Lord Riddle? I've seen hundreds of queer folk snooping round Limbo in my time. I once saw an elf carrying a bag of magical sand. I suppose that was The Sandman, was it?"

Zygote frowned. "The Sandman is fiction, as well you know, Flagellum. Lord Riddle is fact."

"Poppycock!"

"Tell me, Flagellum, who do you think it is that transmits all those peculiar dreams?" asked Zygote, exasperated.

"What peculiar dreams?"

"All those strange, singular, unusual, and downright extraordinary dreams?"

"What strange, singular, unusual, and downright –" But before Flagellum could complete the sentence, the two giants were suddenly shrouded in a large lump of passing white cloud.

"What's going on?" shrieked Zygote.

"I can't see a thing!" bellowed Flagellum.

"Get off me!" shouted Zygote.

"Let go of me!" screamed Flagellum.

As the big chunk of whiteness slowly moved on they were horrified to see that approximately seventeen large men wearing iron helmets were setting about them forcibly and violently in an unprovoked and frenzied attack.

"What's going on?"

"Stop hurting me!"

The giants were taller, but the muscular guards were stronger, and they were hopelessly outnumbered. They struggled for a bit, but it was pointless. They were securely held by at least five guards each.

When he was sure the guards were in total control of the situation, Vile emerged through the floating door and smirked.

"You again!" groaned Zygote.

"Did you really think you'd seen the last of me?" Vile swapped the smirk for a grin. "Did I not say I'd be back?"

One of the guards had his arm around Flagellum's neck, but somehow the giant managed to pull his head back and away from the large bicep. "Just who are you, anyway?" he spluttered.

"Isn't it obvious?" Vile's grin widened. "Who could be so despicably depraved? Who so wicked?"

"You mean?"

"You're?"

He decided on a third and final clue. "Who could be so nasty?"

Flagellum and Zygote gasped in unison. "Vile!"

The Dream Ambassador for Nightmares laughed. It was a despicably depraved, wicked, and nasty laugh.

Chapter 51

At all four corners of the horizon stood four impossibly large yellow wheels. Melvin and Lorraine stood on top of a small, rounded hill and stared. They had an unobstructed view of the Uncharted Borders in all directions.

"Seriously weird," said Melvin.

The sky was blue, and all four sides were of equal length. The blue, perfectly square sky appeared to be resting on top of the yellow wheels somehow.

"Breathtaking," said Lorraine.

Vince was staring too. "Beautiful," he uttered.

His utterance, however, was not directed at the panoramic view before him but at Peggy Sue.

A tangerine convex polygon floated somewhere in the heavens. It was a sun, and it bathed them all in a reddish-orange shine.

Peggy Sue smiled as she made her way up the semi-circular knoll. It was that captivating smile she used. "Thank you, Vince," she said. "Have you missed me?"

Vince grinned foolishly and started to nod, but then Melvin spoiled the moment.

"What the dickens are you doing here?" he shouted.

"You can't come with us," added Lorraine.

Peggy Sue was taken aback. "But, guys," she pleaded. "I've been searching everywhere for you."

Vince reached out a hand, and Peggy Sue took it. As he helped her up to the summit they almost, but not quite, embraced.

"And I've been searching for you all my life, Vince," she whispered.

As far as the eye could see there were fields, rolling hills, and deep valleys. The landscape was littered with trees. Many of them were orange trees, several of them were hazelnut trees, and some of them were caramel trees, but they were all, without exception, triangular trees. Most were isosceles, but there were a few equilateral ones too, way off in the distance.

Lorraine frowned. "Don't deny it. We know that Vile has sent you."

Peggy Sue nodded. "He did, you're right," she admitted. "He wants me to spy on you, find out all your secrets, and report back."

Vince's sharply drawn breath almost choked him.

"But, I promise you guys, I'm not. I'm not going to do any of that." Her large, round eyes dilated, and her long, dark lashes fluttered rapidly and repeatedly.

Melvin was unconvinced. "You tricked Vince into revealing Mr Good's plan."

She sighed. "I know, and I'm sorry." She looked at Vince and squeezed his hand. "But I was desperate."

"Desperate?"

"Terry and I are supposed to be getting married."

Another sharply drawn breath almost choked Vince for a second time.

"I don't want to marry him at all," she added quickly. "No way. But if I found out what your plan was my uncle said he would consider putting a stop to the wedding."

Melvin threw his hands in the air. "Hold it right there," he said. "Vile is your uncle?"

It wasn't a secret. She thought they knew. She thought everyone knew. She nodded.

Lorraine laughed. "And you wonder why we don't trust you!"

Peggy Sue shrugged. "You can't choose your relatives." She smiled sadly. "But, guys, I am not a bad person. Until recently I was wild, sometimes boisterous, I admit. I played rough games and enjoyed boyish things like wrestling, sword fighting, and climbing trees in abandoned Dreamspaces."

"Until recently, you say? What changed?" asked Melvin suspiciously.

"Now I find I love singing and I love dancing," she continued. "And I have an interest in embroidery, and I want to arrange flowers."

"That's quite a turnaround," remarked Lorraine.

Peggy Sue nodded in agreement. "Something happened to me on the journey from Torment Towers to the palace with my uncle, Terry, and the guards." She paused thoughtfully. "Something happened. Yet for the life of me, I can't remember what it was."

A warm, upslope hexagonal breeze passed along the hilltop.

"There's a gap in my memory," she added.

Melvin didn't understand any of this, and there was something else he didn't understand: "How did you get past the turnstile without a valid keyword?" he asked.

"Do you mean Tripod?" Peggy Sue smiled. "He let me pass. Tripod and I go back a long way."

A butterfly-type creature with broad, kite-shaped purple wings landed momentarily on the velour trim around the lapel of Vince's three-quarter-length drape jacket before continuing on its aimless way in the sunshine.

"Tripod was stationed at the front door of Torment Towers for more epochs than I care to remember," she explained. "I was devastated when my uncle left him behind. Tripod was my childhood friend."

"That's all very interesting," said Lorraine. "But it doesn't explain what you are doing here. Why are you following us?"

"When I met you, Vince," she said, smiling up at him, "something inside me stirred. Something emotionally moved me. I was strongly affected."

Vince reddened.

She turned back to Lorraine. "I had to escape. I knew I had to find you guys."

"So, presumably, you couldn't believe your luck when Vile told you to leave the Palace and find us?" said Melvin.

"I was so excited and thrilled." Peggy Sue smiled. "Now I'm never going back."

Melvin and Lorraine looked at each other. They wanted to believe her story. But could they? She was Vile's niece after all. It could so easily be a trick. Yet she did have the most captivating smile.

"Look," said Melvin. "You can walk with us. But we're not going to tell you any secrets, just yet."

"Not until we are sure we can trust you," added Lorraine.

"That's wonderful." Peggy Sue laughed and gave Vince a big hug.

Vince grinned and looked down at Peggy Sue as her arms were clasped tightly around his waist. "I trust you, Peggy Sue," he told her and rested his hands on her shoulders.

"Come on, Vince," said Melvin. "Let's go. We have an important journey ahead. Which way is it?"

Peggy Sue separated herself from Vince but held on to his arm as he made his way down the slope. Melvin and Lorraine fell in behind. At the bottom of the slope was a path. The path was made of tiny little rocks that crunched as they walked on them. They began to walk between two rows of larger rocks that formed a border and ran perfectly parallel, extending a short distance towards, and disappearing into, a thicket of small, orange, three-cornered trees.

"So, where are we heading?" asked Peggy Sue. "You don't have to tell me," she quickly added.

"We won't," Melvin answered. "If it's all the same to you."

Vince reached the edge of the copse. "We're searchin' for y'actual Lord Riddle," he whispered privately.

Melvin heard. "Vince!"

Lorraine heard too. "For pity's sake, Vince," she screeched.

Peggy Sue smiled. "You are funny, Vince." Then she looked at Lorraine's serious face and then at Melvin's. She noticed Vince wasn't smiling either.

"But Lord Riddle isn't real," she informed them. "They are tales Nana Vile used to read to me. 'The Adventures of Lord Riddle and the Cassowaries', 'Lord Riddle and the Kiwi Birds', 'Lord Riddle and the Penguins', and my favourite, 'Lord Riddle and the Kakapo Parrot'. I've read all those stories. But, that's all they are: stories. It's all make believe." Then a note of doubt crept into her voice. "Isn't it?"

Melvin and Lorraine shrugged. They weren't sure themselves. They walked on through the trees in silence until suddenly Vince stopped still. Several really large rocks were scattered or discarded at the side of the path. Many of them appeared to have large chunks missing, like giant, half-eaten bread rolls. He looked around nervously.

"Is something wrong, Vince?" asked Melvin.

Vince took hold of Peggy Sue's hand and set off again along the path. His pace noticeably increased. "Got to be rushin' ... Need to be dashin'."

Melvin and Lorraine followed. As they emerged from the grove of trilateral trees they found themselves on a grassed area with a level surface considerably raised above adjoining land on both sides. The plateau afforded them a wonderful view of the Uncharted Borders. Vince, however, didn't stop to admire the scenery. Still holding Peggy Sue's hand, he continued quickly down the gradual slope of a valley along the unerringly straight rocky path.

Lorraine stopped. Her attention focused on the yellow wheels at the four corners of the horizon. They were huge, with thick yellow rods radiating from hub to rim. The wheels rested on the ground but reached all the way up to the square, blue sky. She took three strides, stopped, and then took three more. "Have you noticed, Melvin, that when we walk the yellow wheels rotate, but when we stop, they stop?"

Melvin tried it. She was right.

"And have you noticed, Loz, that everything is an exact geometrical shape?" Melvin looked across the land for examples. "Those yellow wheels are circles, of course. The sky is square, and the trees are triangular. The sun, the hills, the butterfly's wings —" He stooped to pick up a couple of rocks from the side of the path. "Even these rocks are perfect dodecagons."

Melvin was interrupted by a loud roar from somewhere in amongst the trees. This was followed by another even louder roar.

The Uncharted Borders shook. The roar sounded like it might be a really angry lion, but a lot scarier, more dangerous, probably bigger, and very close by.

Vince had stopped by a large fruit tree. Its flowering branches hung in a swooping arch. He turned and stood protectively in front of Peggy Sue. He looked scared too. "You shouldn't have touched the rocks," he said when Melvin and Lorraine reached him.

They looked back up the slope. There, standing on the plateau, were three extremely large monsters, standing and watching them.

Melvin gulped. "They're big."

"And red," observed Lorraine.

"And ..." Peggy Sue hesitated. "And ... what are they doing, Vince? Are they eating rocks?"

They all turned to Vince.

"What the dickens are those creatures, Vince?" asked Melvin.

Vince didn't take his eyes off the beasts for a single moment. "Y'actual big, red rock eaters," he replied slowly.

The big, red rock eaters stood, watched, and chewed.

Melvin, Lorraine, Vince, and Peggy Sue stared, unable to move.

"Are they dangerous?" whispered Melvin.

Vince nodded. "What's that thing when you think everyone's plottin', plannin', and schemin' behind your back?"

Melvin looked to Lorraine for help.

"Paranoia?" she ventured.

Vince's head continued to nod. "They think everyone's after their rocks."

"But that's ridiculous," exclaimed Lorraine, and she took a step forward. "We are not interested in your rocks," she called out. She turned to Melvin for support. She looked at his hands.

Melvin looked at his hands too, and he held them up. The big, red rock eaters glared. Their eyes gleamed with malice.

Melvin's hands held something tightly in their grasp. Slowly, he unwrapped his fingers. He couldn't believe he was still holding them, but resting on both palms was a pair of twelve-sided rocks.

The big, red rock eaters weren't best pleased. One of them growled, and the other two, baring their fangs, let loose a loud, deep cry and took a couple of menacing steps closer.

Melvin let the rocks fall to the ground. He wanted to run, but his legs wouldn't respond. The impending danger had immobilised both of Lorraine's lower limbs, too.

The big, red rock eaters knew this as they moved closer still. Vince knew that this was the end of their journey unless something quite remarkable happened to save them.

Quite remarkably, from behind the fruit tree stepped a ghostlike figure holding a square box gift wrapped in an attractive floral paper decorated with white roses.

Lorraine was astonished. She recognised the ghostly form immediately.

Chapter 52

"Show them no mercy," said Vile with a grin.

The two giants were being pushed and shoved expertly through the magenta maze. No sooner would they recover from a vigorous push than along would come an almighty shove in the back.

"Hurt them," he demanded.

The muscular guards were able to exert, with each push and shove, tremendous bodily power. It was enough bodily power to satisfy Vile's request.

"You're evil," yelped Flagellum. "That's what you are."

"Compliments will get you nowhere," said Vile as he walked behind the guards observing each push and shove with delight. "So there's no point trying to get on my good side, because I don't have one."

"It wasn't a compliment," groaned Flagellum after surviving a particularly robust shove.

"I do have a slightly less offensive side," Vile conceded. "But it's rarely used. And to prove it, when we reach the palace, I shall most probably submerge you in a vat full of a cold, sticky, gummy sort of liquid." He smirked. "Which I haven't thought up yet."

"I just hope you know what you're doing, that's all," moaned Zygote.

"Know what I'm doing? Of course I know what I'm doing," responded Vile with just a touch of irritation. "Inventing cold, sticky, gummy liquids is my speciality."

For his troubles Zygote received a powerful push that sent him spinning along the corridor.

"I can always be relied upon to come up with something exceedingly tacky," Vile added.

When Zygote came to a stop he found himself on all fours with his knees resting on a pink and white marble surface. "I'm not talking about gummy liquids." He winced as he struggled to his feet. "I'm talking about your decision to leave the white room unattended."

The muscular guards turned and marched down the narrow passageway, propelling the two giants along with them helplessly, like two pieces of balsa wood in a tidal wave.

"I am holding my sides lest they should split," said Vile sarcastically as he reached the end of the magenta maze, the spot where it met the cyan and yellow corridors. "Having two giants permanently guarding a room that no one is the slightest bit interested in is like putting a padlock on a broom cupboard. It's pointless!"

"It's a very important role, actually," replied Zygote from somewhere in amongst all the muscular guards who were now milling around in front of a reddish-brown wooden door.

"Important role?" Vile sneered. "It's ludicrous!"

He walked along the marble flooring. "Move! Get out the way! Shift!" he barked as he squeezed and pushed past them all and made his way to the door.

The door was locked. Vile frowned.

He tried the door again and then banged on it with his fists. "Let me in," he shouted.

He waited.

"Let me in, I say." Vile tried to look through the keyhole, but there was something obscuring his view.

"There's something obscuring my view," he groaned.

It was an eye.

"It's an eye," he decided.

A big eye.

Vile sighed wearily. "Cyclops? Is that you?"

Silence.

"Open the door," Vile hollered impatiently.

Some more silence.

"But you told us not to let you in," said a nervous voice from within. "Unless you said 'egg and chips'."

Vile glowered.

"I mean ... unless you said the secret password. Sorry."

Vile kicked the door in anger. "Cyclops, open up. Now!" he demanded.

On the other side of the door, a key made several failed attempts to locate the hole. Eventually it did, and it rattled as it turned in the lock. The door opened slowly, too slowly. Two muscular guards leapt forth and shoulder-charged it open a bit wider. Well, a lot wider – so wide, in fact, that it took Cyclops along with it. He struck the back wall with an ear-splitting wallop.

Vile entered the grand entrance hall first. The guards pushed and shoved the giants inside too, and one of them closed the door.

A stunned dream actor with a single round eye in the middle of his forehead slid gently down the wall onto his bottom. A rare painting, disturbed by all the commotion, teetered for a moment, slipped off its hook, fell, and hit him on the back of the head.

"This is your new workplace," said Vile as he reached the middle of the large hall and turned to face the two giants. "Much better working conditions than your previous employment, I am sure you will agree."

With a motion of the hands he picked out some of its finer points. "There are some appalling old tapestries on the walls, an unnecessary and ugly row of marble columns here, and some absurd carvings in the stone above those arches over there."

He paused to gauge their reaction. Flagellum was clearly unimpressed.

"All a bit kitsch, I know, but so much better than that white place you were so reluctant to leave."

Zygote clearly disagreed.

"And, not forgetting," said Vile as he strode across the pink and white marble flooring, "the door."

The muscular guards parted to let him through, and he had to step over a comatose Cyclops to reach it. "This is the door you will be guarding." He tapped on it with his knuckles.

The two giants regarded the door with interest.

It's solid. That was Flagellum's first impression.

Hand crafted, noted Zygote.

Mahogany, thought Flagellum.

And arched, observed Zygote.

Vile allowed himself a triumphant grin. With these two oversized goons guarding the door, the Palace of Somnium would be near enough impregnable.

"Im – preg – na – ble." He repeated it out loud with a short pause between each of its four syllables. 'Impregnable' was an excellent word, he decided. 'Unconquerable.' Now, there was another fine word, possibly a better word because it had five syllables.

"So, security has been tightened," said Vile as he took his place back in the middle of the hall. "The Palace of Somnium is now officially impossible to be broken into or taken by force."

Flagellum had his own announcement to make. "We want to return to the room with two doors," he said as he reached one of his six fingers under his crimson padded turban and scratched the top of his head.

"He means the white room, and I agree with him for a change," said Zygote. "We don't like it here. Do we, Flagellum?"

"Flagellum?" asked Flagellum. "You're Flagellum. I'm Zygote."

"That's balderdash." Zygote sighed. "I'm Zygote, as well you know, Flagellum!"

"I'm Zygote," persisted Flagellum.

"Shut up!" shouted Vile. He waited a moment to be sure their bickering had ceased. "You will take up your new positions immediately," he informed them.

"No, we won't," protested Zygote.

"Here are your job descriptions," said Vile, ignoring the protest of the giant in the green woollen tunic. From the back pocket of his cuffed trousers he took out a sheet of paper.

Zygote moved closer, took it, and quickly read the seven words that were printed there. He read it again but this time out loud. "Don't let anybody in or anybody out." He checked the reverse side. "Is that it?"

Vile nodded. "Even you brainless beanpoles should be able to manage that."

"Yes, we could, but we are not interested," insisted Zygote.

Flagellum clicked the heels of his red pointy shoes and took a step forward too. "Let's not be too hasty." He took the sheet of paper from Zygote and studied it with his beady eyes.

"I've changed my mind," he decided. "This task is much easier."

"Much easier?" Zygote stared at the slightly shorter giant in disbelief. "How is it easier?"

"Only one door," replied Flagellum. "Fifty per cent less doorage."

"He's right," agreed Vile with a smirk. "You just can't argue with mathematics."

Zygote sighed and changed tack. "Flagellum, do you recall your astrological prediction for this dream span?"

"It's not twaddle," snapped Flagellum.

"I know," said Zygote calmly. "If you remember, your stars told you to beware of a dubious or questionable character." He willed Flagellum to follow his eyes as he flicked his head in the direction of Vile.

"Who may attempt to lure you away –" He reached in and prodded at the seven words written on the sheet of paper. "And involve you in evil goings-on."

"Astrology," scoffed Vile. "It's all mumbo jumbo."

"Horoscopes are quite often astonishingly uncanny, actually. Is that not right, Flagellum?" asked Zygote. This change of tack was going well.

Flagellum looked at the job description once more and then up at Vile. "Yes." He slowly nodded his head. "You're right, for once."

Encouraged, Zygote pressed on. "And we won't be taking up this offer of new employment, will we?"

Without taking his eyes off Vile, Flagellum crushed the sheet of paper into a ball and dropped it on the marble floor. "We've got better things to do than stand here all dream span involving ourselves in evil goings-on, you know."

Vile was furious. His face turned a shade of livid pink. "I've just had about enough of you two," he roared. "Especially you!"

Zygote shrugged.

"Guards!" he shouted. He always shouted at the guards. He figured the louder you shouted at them, the better they understand. "Prepare the vat of …" He paused while he considered his options. They deserved to be dunked in something sticky and gummy and positively gooey. "Prepare the vat of …" He hesitated. Then he had an idea which made him grin an evil grin. "Prepare the vat of … custard!"

Custard? A concerned look passed between the guards. They thought the punishment was a little harsh, particularly for a first offence. For a first offence they were expecting something bearable, like mashed potato. But who were they to question the most evil dude in Scarydream Land? They did as they were told, for a quiet life.

"Take them away!" Vile bellowed.

The guards pushed and shoved the giants towards and up the first few steps of the graceful staircase.

"Put plenty of cornflour in," he bawled. "I want it thick."

They all nodded as one and continued their ascent.

"And guards," he yelled. "Make sure it's cold."

With one more push and shove they reached the landing where the stairs divide into two.

"Oh and guards," his voice boomed across the hall. "With a skin on top."

In no time at all they were climbing the last few steps before the drawing room.

"And up to their necks!" he called out.

Through the balusters on the balcony Vile watched the last of the muscular guards disappear from view. He was alone in the grand entrance hall. Well, apart from Cyclops.

"It's all over. I have won. I am the winner," he declared.

All over?

Vile spun round. He looked at the one-eyed dream actor, but Cyclops was still slumped up against the wall and unconscious.

You have won?

It was the bird inside his head again. "I'm not talking to you. It's my new tactic. I'm ignoring you."

You are the winner?

Vile frowned and sighed at the same time. "Yes I am," he replied defiantly. "I am victorious."

What brings you to that conclusion?

"I've employed a couple of giants to guard the door. The palace is now unconquerable."

Unconquerable, you say? Good word. Five syllables. That's impressive. But, correct me if I'm wrong – didn't the giants just turn you down?

"Believe me, after a short space of time dipped in custard they will be begging me to guard the door."

If you say so.

"Yes, I do say so," snarled Vile. "I told you I'm not talking to you. I know that Mr Good put you in my head. Or rather, that pet wizard of his has cast a spell or something. But I'm not going to be intimidated. Now go away and climb inside another head."

Go away? Do you mean like Peggy Sue went away?

"Peggy Sue? What's that stupid niece of mine got to do with it?"

She has become part of the plan to oust you. She has teamed up and made friends with the other side, Mr Good's side.

"Well, that's just where you're wrong, see. It's a clever trick of mine. I told her to infiltrate enemy lines and spy on them all. Very soon she will report back."

She's not coming back.

"Don't be ridiculous!"

And Terrence. He's missing too, I understand.

"That dimwit. He's no loss."

Tell me. I believe you have a new nightmare coming soon.

"In just one dream span." Vile nodded proudly. "I shall be unleashing my most fearful, gruesome, hideously horrid nightmare yet."

And you can do this without a Digital Dreamscaper, can you?

"What? No. Obviously not." Vile's complexion paled. "But …"

You don't have it, do you? Terrence does.

The bird had pushed him into a state of agitated confusion. "I know that," he said, trying desperately to compose himself. "I know Terrence has the Digital Dreamscaper. But he will be back soon."

I doubt it. He's been captured.

"Captured?" Vile gulped.

As we speak Terrence is securely tied to a teak dining chair.

"How dare they tie Terrence to a teak dining chair?" Vile seethed. "He might be a dimwit, but he's my dimwit."

Mr Good has confiscated the Digital Dreamscaper.

"He's done what?" he yelled with a sudden outburst of ill temper.

It's all over. Mr Good has won. Mr Good is the winner.

"Never!" exclaimed Vile. It was an exclamation of either contempt or annoyance – or possibly both. "We'll see about that," he added aggressively. "Guards!"

He stood at the foot of the freestanding staircase, holding the solid oak balustrade with one hand. "Guards! Come back! Come back here now!" he shouted. "We are going to rescue Terrence."

You will never reach the centre of the royal blue labyrinth and come back in just one dream span. You're a beaten man, Vile.

"Beaten man?" He turned as if the bird were behind him and not inside his head. "I am not the Dream Ambassador for Nightmares for no reason. I am Dream Ambassador for Nightmares because I am so wicked and nasty, and also because when the chips are down I can always be relied upon to have something clever up my sleeve."

From up the sleeve of his black and gold pinstriped jacket he produced, with a flourish, a small box with a rectangular touchscreen. It went bleep.

Vile's thin lips arched slowly into a wicked and nasty grin. "The centre of the royal blue labyrinth, you say?"

Chapter 53

"Can I just say something at this point?"

The big, red rock eaters hesitated as the apparition stood a few strides ahead of them down the rocky path.

The ghost, its arms fully extended, offered them the square box.

Big, red rock eaters are inquisitive creatures by nature. Invariably, if someone offers them a box, especially a gift-wrapped one, they have to know what's inside it.

"I thought this might be of interest to you," said the ghost.

They eyed the spooky visitor and his unusual box suspiciously for a moment. It was only a brief moment before the nearest one grabbed it and shook it. Almost immediately the next one snatched it and ripped off its attractive floral paper before the third one wrestled it away from both of them. The third one, instead of separating it from its removable cover, slashed a large hole in the box with its sharp claws.

The three big, red rock eaters peered curiously into the opening. Inside the cardboard receptacle they were amazed to see twenty-four small, spherical rocks presented in individual paper fluted cups.

Small, spherical rocks are a delicacy. They are extremely rare and considered by big, red rock eaters to be exceptionally pleasing to the taste buds.

"I have injected the rocks with a selection of succulent fillings," explained the ghost, "such as hazelnut and caramel."

The big, red rock eaters salivated. This was all too much for them. A horrible, sticky, watery fluid oozed from between the folds of flesh that hung from their jaws.

"And orange creams," added the ghost.

The three big, red rock eaters attempted to grab a handful each. However, they had very large, hairy hands and there just weren't enough small, spherical rocks for three large, hairy handfuls apiece.

"Be careful," the ghost called out. "Some of them may contain traces of nut and soya."

They bickered. A squabble ensued. Chisel-edged teeth were bared, and the nearest one and the next one squared up to each other, hissing and growling aggressively. The third one took advantage and ran off with the box. The beast was across the plateau before the other two were even halfway up the slope. As they disappeared into the grove of trilateral trees, the enormous yellow wheels at the four corners of the horizon started to follow, rolling in the same direction. As the yellow wheels revolved, they slowly took the square, blue sky away too.

"Garry," whispered Lorraine when the big, red rock eaters were finally out of sight.

"Garry," repeated Melvin in a hushed tone and not quite believing it. "What the dickens are you doing here?"

The rocky path had gone. So too had the plateau and the triangular trees. The Uncharted Borders had shifted a few notches to the left. Suddenly it was overcast and breezy, and there was a little drizzle in the air. They found themselves high up on a flat shelf of rock protruding from a vertical cliff face. Above them a dome-shaped, uninterrupted grey sky stretched upwards from the far edge of the ocean.

"The ocean!" gasped Melvin as he peered through the mist. From the inside pocket of his maroon school blazer he took out a sheet of paper. "We must be here," he declared excitedly as he pointed to the top right-hand side of the blank sheet.

Vince stood so close to the edge it frightened Peggy Sue. She held on to his hand and tried to pull him back as he leaned over and listened. Very faintly, but unmistakably, he heard the sound of a harmonium being played far below. As the beautiful melody, carried in the wind through the dimness and light rain, reached him, he turned and smiled.

"Let's go," he said. "I have friends I would like you all to meet."

Melvin and Lorraine looked at each other with puzzled shrugs.

Cut into the mass of white stone were hundreds of uneven steps that made their way, in a zigzag fashion, all the way down to sea level. Still holding Peggy Sue's hand and keeping her on the cliff side, Vince took the first step off the ledge into a strong breeze. The others followed him in single file.

"That's twice you've saved our bacon, Garry," said Lorraine with a smile.

"Can I just say something at this point?" asked Garry as he stopped to undo the zip at the front of his ghost costume to reveal a short-sleeved black polo shirt, khaki multi-pocket combat shorts, and grey knee-length socks.

"First you distracted Vile with that get-well-soon card," recalled Melvin.

"And now here you are again, miraculously, rescuing us from –" Lorraine looked back up the steps nervously. "Those scary, large, red rock munchers."

Garry knelt down to tie up his black, lace-up walking boots with their comfortable textile lining and non-slip soles. "Can I just say something at this point?" he repeated.

Melvin and Lorraine took a step or two further before they stopped and turned.

"Of course," said Melvin.

"What is it?" asked Lorraine.

Garry stood up, small and mouselike, on the top step. "Where are we going?" he asked timidly.

A little way ahead Vince and Peggy Sue reached the first sharp turn. They waited for Melvin, Lorraine, and Garry to catch up before continuing their descent.

\#

"So, after *King Creole* you never saw another Elvis movie?" Peggy Sue had to raise her voice to be heard over the rattle of the wind.

With his free hand Vince tried to keep his thick, black, wavy hair under control. "I seen *Jailhouse Rock* and y'actual *Love Me Tender*, but ..."

"But none of the others?" she asked. "Elvis made many more wonderful films, Vince."

How he would have loved to have seen all those many more wonderful films. Vince sighed and shook his head. "I came here," he told her.

Peggy Sue looked up at him and waited.

Vince took a few silent steps down into the mist that was pinning itself to the side of the cliff before he explained. "My mates and me had a big party to celebrate y'actual Elvis comin' out the army." He paused as he recalled that time more than an epoch ago now. "Afterwards, I kipped on the floor, and when I woke up I was in this white place with a couple of giant geezers telling me I had to decide which door to go through."

"That's awful, Vince," said Peggy Sue after a moment. "You must have been really confused."

Vince nodded. "I was." He looked down at her and shrugged. "Because there was only one door."

#

"You wouldn't believe us if we told you," said Lorraine happily as Garry walked alongside her.

"Nobody else does," said Melvin at the rear.

"Try me," said Garry.

Lorraine took a deep breath. "Well, we're searching for a dream ambassador, actually."

"Yes, I know." Garry nodded. "You're searching for Mr Good. He hasn't been feeling too well, I remember."

"No, not Mr Good," said Lorraine. "We found Mr Good. He's fine."

Garry was puzzled. "So, if you're not searching for Mr Good, then ..."

He suddenly realised and shook his head. "Surely not? I don't think searching for Vile is ever a particularly good idea."

"Not Vile either," said Lorraine.

"We're searching for a third one," said Melvin. "Believe it or not."

Garry looked round at Melvin in surprise. "A third one? A third dream ambassador?"

Melvin nodded.

"I did say you wouldn't believe us," said Lorraine.

Garry was shocked. He really wanted to say something at this point. But he couldn't.

"But there's only one problem," continued Lorraine.

"He may not really exist," added Melvin.

"It's quite possible that Lord Riddle is just a myth," sighed Lorraine.

They walked on down several steps before they realised Garry wasn't with them. They turned to see Garry had stopped and was staring at them with his mouth open.

#

"When all this trouble is over," said Peggy Sue, looking up at Vince with her large round eyes, "maybe Mr Good will help you to get back home."

Home? Go back? It had been so long since Vince even considered the possibility. "I –" He faltered. "I'm not sure I want to go back now." He blushed.

Peggy Sue smiled, and her flawless skin reddened just a touch.

#

"Lord Riddle?"

Lorraine shrugged and waited for the inevitable sarcasm. "Yes, I know. You think it's just a fairy tale. But Mr Good believes it, and ..."

"So do I," said Garry, interrupting her. "I believe too."

Lorraine took a moment to process this information. "You do?" she said.

"I can assure you that Lord Riddle does exist," Garry told Melvin. "And he most certainly isn't a myth," he said to Lorraine as he passed her and made his way downwards.

Melvin was the first to follow. "How can you be so sure?" he asked.

"I read it in a book," said Garry as he skipped down the steps. "A very, very old book."

Melvin wondered how reading about something in a book proved that it was true. Especially if it was a very, very old book of fairy tales, as Melvin suspected it was. But he didn't say anything.

Garry quickly caught up with Vince. "The Land of Nod?" asked Garry excitedly. "Is it close? Is it this way?"

Vince didn't reply. Instead he listened. They all stopped and listened. The haunting melody of the harmonium had resumed and was much louder now. Its continuous background note and rhythmical succession of single tones reached up to them through the gloom. They listened in silence for a long moment.

That's awesome," said Lorraine, filled with awe.

Melvin nodded in agreement. "It's beautiful," he said.

"Wonderful," said Peggy Sue.

"Are we near the Land of Nod?" asked Garry.

They all turned to look at Garry as if he were some sort of philistine for not appreciating the awesome, beautiful, wonderful music.

"What?" asked Garry when he saw their faces. "What have I said?"

Vince sighed. With the spell broken, he took Peggy Sue's hand, and they walked on. Before too long they reached the last of the steps, but their journey continued down a steady slope that twisted first to one side and then to the other. The scent of the ocean air, the salt mixed with the aroma of paint and white spirit, suddenly hit them. Gradually, as they descended out of the mist, they were able to make out shapes below. They saw outlines of large, square objects, cylindrical wooden containers with bulging sides, and, most amazingly, on a slipway, silhouetted against the grey sky, a magnificent two-masted sailing ship.

As the path finally levelled out they found themselves in what looked like a small ship repair yard.

Garry was disappointed. He didn't recall any mention of a ship repair yard in the very, very old book. "This isn't the Land of Nod," he whispered to Melvin.

Vince took a couple of steps forward and cleared his throat. "Hello!" he shouted. The music continued from somewhere beyond the large shipping crates and barrels that were everywhere.

"Hello," he shouted again, more loudly this time. After a few beats the music stopped. There was silence.

The silence lasted only a moment before a young child began to cry. Then they heard muffled voices. A few seconds later a head peeked round the side of a large blue, metal container. It was the face of a man, probably in his late thirties, with dark brown, receding hair and a full beard. His expression was one of apprehension at first. This was quickly followed by puzzlement, surprise, and finally delight.

Wearing a long black frock coat, the man stepped out into full view. "Vincent!" He grinned as he strode forward, carefully stepping over ropes and cables on the ground. "How splendid."

Vince walked forward to meet him halfway. "Benjamin," he cried.

"Is it really you?" said the man as they embraced. "Because it sure seems to be."

He laughed as they slapped each other on the back like long-lost friends. "To what do we owe this pleasure?" Benjamin asked. "Something important, I shouldn't wonder. Nobody risks the wrath of the big, red rock eaters otherwise."

He laughed again. Over Vince's shoulder the man noticed, for the first time, Peggy Sue, a confused Melvin, a puzzled Lorraine, and a disappointed Garry standing at the end of the cliff path. "Vincent, you have brought along friends, it seems," he said with a smile.

Vince nodded and turned to them. He placed his hand on the man's shoulder. "May I introduce –" He paused. "Y'actual Captain Benjamin Spooner Briggs."

Chapter 54

Three dream actors were sitting at an occasional table near the top of a freestanding graceful staircase in a spacious drawing room that was carpeted, curtained, panelled, and finished in mauve.

"You've heard something, haven't you, Harry?" said Barry. "Tell us all about it."

"I wasn't eavesdropping, honestly." Harry shifted his short and stocky frame uneasily on the caned seat and tapestried cushion. "I just sort of overheard, by accident."

"A rumour, is it?" Larry frowned. He had a low opinion of rumours. There was something about stories that were passed around verbally, without confirmation or certainty of the facts, that Larry didn't like.

"So, what rumour did you overhear?" asked Barry.

"Accidentally," added Larry.

"It's more than a rumour," replied Harry.

Barry's eyes widened. "You mean you heard it on the grapevine?"

"No, I heard it through the balusters." Harry pointed towards the balcony and the closely spaced supports for the solid oak balustrade. Larry shot Barry a puzzled glance.

"I wasn't brought up to pry, you understand," continued Harry. "My mother used to say if I listened at the top of the stairs to conversations that didn't concern me or looked through keyholes or did anything naughty, I'd be sent to the Land of Nod."

"Up the wooden hill to Bedfordshire." Larry nodded.

"And into the clutches of the very strange Lord Riddle."

They all laughed. There was a very brief pause as their thoughts turned to a lost friend and his futile search for the fictional dream ambassador.

"Where do you think he is?" wondered Barry.

Larry shrugged. "Lost somewhere in the vast expanse of Limbo, I imagine."

"Our Garry." Harry sighed.

"I miss him."

"So do I."

"Me too."

They all smiled sadly.

"So," said Barry a moment later, "getting back to the matter in hand. Are you going to tell us what you overheard through the balusters?"

Harry looked around to make sure no one was listening at nearby tables. There were no other dream actors in close proximity, but he lowered his voice anyway. "Well, I just happened to be walking past the top of the graceful staircase when I heard, accidently of course, Vile talking in the grand entrance hall below."

"Talking?" asked Barry. "Talking to who?"

Harry shrugged. "To himself."

Larry leaned his gaunt frame and prominent bones closer. "To himself?"

Harry nodded.

"What was it he was saying?" Larry asked.

"Well, his tone was one of anger," continued Harry. "But from what I can make out, it seems he sent his niece, Peggy Sue, out into Limbo a couple of dream spans ago, and she hasn't come back. What's worse, apparently, is she's gone to the other side."

Larry stared at Harry for a long moment, hoping he would carry on or explain. But he did neither. "The other side of what?" he asked.

"I don't know," admitted Harry. "But Vile was not happy about it. And there's more. I haven't told you the most amazing bit yet."

"Tell us," said Barry. "Tell us the most amazing bit yet."

Harry moved his caned seat closer to the white table. "Terrence has been captured by Mr Good," he whispered.

"Well call me a taxi!" declared Larry.

"Mr Good is holding him prisoner, and he's confiscated the Digital Dreamscaper."

Three tables away, two dream actors, one holding a half-moon sod cutter and the other a machete, looked up at Harry's mention of the Digital

Dreamscaper. The lunatic and the one with the antisocial personality disorder stared at them for a while before turning away and resuming their deep and meaningful discussion.

"But those two visitors from the physical world told us Mr Good wasn't feeling too well," said Barry.

"Yes, that's right," said Larry, rounding on Harry. "Those two children said he was depressed."

"Well, those two teenagers," Harry corrected him. "Maybe they found him and cheered him up. I don't know. All I know is that Vile is very angry, and he's gone."

"Gone?"

"Gone to rescue Terrence?"

"No." Harry shook his head. "The Digital Dreamscaper."

Barry contemplated this for a moment. "Of course. With opening night of Vile's new nightmare only one dream span away, he would need the Digital Dreamscaper desperately."

"He's taken most of the guards too," added Harry.

Barry was pleased that Mr Good's spirits had been lifted, but now he was concerned that Vile and most of the muscular guards were on their way to snatch the Digital Dreamscaper off him. This could set him back several dream spans. They would almost certainly hurt him too while they were at it. "Most of them?" he asked.

"Well, all of them, actually," replied Harry. "Apart from one."

"Apart from one? That's strange," said Barry, looking around anxiously in case the one remaining muscular guard was in the vicinity.

Larry sat back in his chair against the interlaced strips of cane. "I already know this."

"You do?"

Larry nodded. "I have news to impart too," he told them as he leaned forward. "I had almost forgotten about it after hearing your tasty titbit, Harry."

Harry was surprised that Larry considered what he had told them to be just a tasty titbit. He reckoned it was more of a choice morsel, actually, but he didn't like to say.

"What news?" asked Barry.

"A most reliable source has informed me that a guard, obviously the one remaining guard of which you speak, is at this very moment guarding two giants."

"Two giants?" asked Barry. "I too have heard something about a couple of giants. On the grapevine, of course. Let me think."

"The grapevine?" Larry frowned. He didn't trust the grapevine. The spreading of gossip from person to person like Chinese whispers, where the truth gets distorted along the way, was most unreliable.

"Oh yes, I remember now," remembered Barry. "The grapevine was buzzing with it recently." He leaned in closer. "Apparently Vile is hoping to recruit two giants to guard the front door down there." He bobbed his head in that direction.

"Well, it seems they have declined the opportunity," said Larry. "Hence the reason they are now up to their necks in a vat of what my reliable source describes as cold custard."

Harry winced. "Cold custard?"

"That's harsh." Barry shuddered.

Larry sat bolt upright. He felt a sudden sharp twinge inside his head. A little bird with coarse, bristly, hair-like feathers was scratching the walls of his cranium with its razor-sharp claws. It was like a scene from that children's tale. What was it called? Oh yes, 'Lord Riddle and the Kiwi Birds'. The bird had a message for him: a crazy idea that involved escaping, a most preposterous idea that they go and find Mr Good, a totally nonsensical idea of maybe helping him somehow. Larry shook his head and tried to dismiss the thought from his mind. He jumped up in an effort to rid himself of the discomfort.

"Larry?"

"Are you okay?"

"You have a strange, cross-eyed expression on your face."

The kiwi bird was now kicking him relentlessly. "Yes. I mean, no. I mean ..." He held his head in his hands. "We've got to escape!" he screamed.

Barry looked up at him. "What?"

"Escape?" said Harry.

"Have you taken complete leave of your senses?"

The little bird ceased kicking him, but it had its sharp, three-toed foot poised threateningly. Larry, breathing hard, took a moment to compose himself before continuing. "We need to find Mr Good and help him somehow."

Barry gulped. He wanted to help Mr Good. Of course he did, but he was sure he wasn't brave enough.

"What's to stop us? said Larry as he sat back down. "Vile isn't here, Terrence's missing, virtually all the guards have gone, and the key's in the door. We'll never get another opportunity like this."

Harry could feel the beginning of a headache forming at the base of his skull.

"But we can't go," sighed Larry. "We can't go and leave those two giants on their own in the custard."

"Can't we?"

Larry shook his head slowly. "We should help them escape too."

It was Harry's turn to gulp.

Barry's expression was one of bewilderment with a touch of terror. "I don't see the point of looking for trouble, Larry. If we've got to escape, let's just do it."

"He's right, Larry," said Harry. "It's not as if we know these two giants."

"We don't even know their names."

"Yes we do," said Larry. "They are Flageolet and Zygon."

"What?"

"Their names are Flageolet and Zygon."

"Are you sure?"

"Positive." Larry nodded positively.

"They're pretty odd names, aren't they?" said Barry. "A flageolet is a small wind instrument."

"And a zygon is a H-shaped fissure," added Harry.

Larry frowned. "Look, it doesn't matter what their names are. What matters is they are on Mr Good's side. They could come in useful. After all, they are big."

"Are they?" asked Harry.

"They're giants," Barry reminded him.

"But you're forgetting something," said Harry. "There is the problem of the one remaining guard's prominence of muscle tissue."

Larry didn't reply. Instead, with half-shut eyes he gazed off into space – or rather, it seemed, at the chandelier above the graceful staircase. The kiwi bird was sitting in his frontal lobe. It had another message: a crazy idea concerning the problem of the one remaining guard's prominence of muscle tissue; a most preposterous idea that, due to the guard's lack of brain, they could trick him; a totally nonsensical idea that maybe three dream actors and two giants could save Dream Land somehow.

Barry placed a hand on Larry's shoulder and shook him gently. "What's happening, Larry?"

"We can do this?" he replied.

"Can we?"

"How can you be so sure?"

Larry turned to look at them with unseeing eyes and shrugged. "A little bird told me," he whispered.

Chapter 55

"Land ahoy!"

The shout came from somewhere above, possibly Volkert, a German seaman high up amongst the square-rigged masts. Melvin was exhausted and damp as he gazed across the ocean's endless succession of long and unbroken waves towards the boundary between sea and sky in the distance.

They had been at sea for three long days and nights. He knew this because the sun had set and risen three times since their voyage began. At dusk at the end of the first day, it disappeared beyond the edge of this world to the east. And after a long, dark, moonless, starless night, it emerged the following morning in the north. The second night it fell away to the south and appeared at dawn, yet again in the south. Last evening it descended slowly to the west, and eventually, this very morning, it peeped its tangerine head above the horizon in the east. It had been three days since he had met Captain Briggs.

#

"Captain Benjamin Spooner Briggs?"

Melvin had been flabbergasted, to say the least, when Vince had introduced him. He recognised him, of course, from old photographs. Captain Benjamin Spooner Briggs was a master mariner and captain of the ill-fated merchant ship *Mary Celeste*. He had done a project on it in year eight, and the story of how the brigantine was discovered unmanned and drifting in the Atlantic Ocean near the Straits of Gibraltar had fascinated him ever since.

"Is it really you?" asked Melvin tentatively as they walked in the shadow of a large sailing vessel with two masts, only the forward of which was square-rigged. It was a brigantine, and it rested on a firm, sloping track of railroad sleepers that ran down into the water.

The crew laughed, and Captain Briggs found this amusing, too. "So it seems." He smiled as he pulled at the sharply peaked collar of his double-breasted coat as they all made their way across the small ship repair yard.

"This is seriously weird," Melvin said to himself. He couldn't believe he was walking side by side with Captain Briggs – and it wasn't an actor playing the part in a movie, either. It was the real Captain Briggs, although he looked about forty and not getting on for two hundred years old like he should be. As they entered the paint shop he saw the captain's wife, Sarah, on the far side of the room sitting at her harmonium, a keyboard-like instrument with small metal reeds and a pair of bellows below which she operated with her feet. As everyone sat on benches around the large wooden hut, she began to play a slow, haunting tune as her young daughter Sophie Matilda stood at her side, shyly pulling at her skirts.

Melvin knew them all, of course. They were like old friends. Sitting next to Lorraine was the first mate, Albert, a thin American man with a neat moustache. On either side of Vince and Peggy Sue sat Edward, the steward who was also American, and Andrew, a Dane, the second mate. Garry sat impatiently in the middle of four German seamen. Melvin was keen to find out what happened to them all on that December morning in 1872.

#

"Land ahoy!"

Lorraine stood on Melvin's right-hand side. They were both exhausted, quiet, and reflective.

They had been at sea for three long days and nights. It had been an eventful voyage, particularly on the second day, the day of the storm.

They had left the small ship repair yard excited and in good spirits, bound for the Land of Nod. They stood on deck and waved to Sarah and young Sophie Matilda and watched as they got smaller and smaller until they were too small to see. The ocean was calm that first day. That evening, as the tangerine sun set in the east, they all sat on deck singing songs in the lamplight. Vince and Peggy Sue taught Albert and Edward Elvis songs and other rocking and rolling classics. They laughed so much at one point, when the second mate, Andrew, became the Danish Bill Hayley with the four German seaman his unlikely Comets, singing 'Rock around the Clock' a capella. Vince and Peggy Sue jived through the night, and even Captain Briggs and Garry had a go. Lorraine couldn't help thinking how bizarre it all was to see these nineteenth-century sailors singing and dancing to 1950s chart hits. They all had so much fun.

Just before dawn, however, the wind started to pick up noticeably. The mood changed, and Captain Briggs and his crew became suddenly serious.

"It seems we have a storm approaching," said Captain Briggs. "It might be best if you confined yourselves to my quarters for the duration."

But Vince refused to move. "I want to help," he insisted. Captain Briggs knew his friend was very strong across the shoulders and could be useful if things got rough.

"Very well," said the captain. "But do as I, or my crew, tell you at all times."

Vince nodded and hurriedly slipped away into the dark with Albert and Andrew to set about some task or other.

Peggy Sue didn't want to leave Vince, but Edward gently yet firmly led her, Melvin, Lorraine, and Garry below deck and into a room that spanned the width of the stern with large windows and a sea view. Through the large window they watched the daylight slowly emerge in the north. They saw dark and scary clouds and lightning followed by a low rumble of thunder in the distance.

Melvin counted the number of seconds between the flashes and the thunderclap.

"What are you doing?" asked Peggy Sue.

"We can work out how far away the storm is," he told her. "The sound of the thunder will take about two seconds to travel one kilometre."

Meanwhile, the winds were getting stronger and the waves a lot higher.

"The storm is getting closer," Melvin announced. Moments later, the thunder was no longer a low rumble in the distance but more of a loud crack less than half a mile away. The ship rolled from side to side and pitched up and down like a see-saw. They tried desperately to hold on as waves as big as giants crashed into the starboard side. With each roll they were flung across the room, slamming into the wood-panelled wall on the opposite side of the cabin.

"Can I just say something at this point?" asked Garry as the ship pitched and tossed them all headfirst towards the door.

Torrential rain lashed against the windows. "What? What is it?" shouted Lorraine above the fierce winds.

Garry looked into her eyes. "I think we're going to sink," he said. For longer than he could remember he had yearned to meet Lord Riddle. Almost an obsession, it was. He had read everything there was to read about him. And now, ironically, the brigantine he was sailing on to reach the Land of Nod and to finally meet him was, almost certainly, not going to make it through the storm.

Lorraine didn't reply. She looked away, but she was sure he was right.

Another roll sent them hurtling back to where they started. Melvin hurt his wrist as he reached out a hand to stop his head smashing against the thick glass. "No, we're not going to sink," he said, wincing.

Up above them they could hear Captain Briggs or his first mate barking orders, running footfalls on the wooden quarterdeck, banging, ropes being pulled, and scraping as well as the thunder and the incessant whistle of the gale force winds.

"A ship floats because the volume of water that it displaces," gasped Melvin above all the noise, "is greater than its weight."

Garry frowned. "That's reassuring," he replied with just a hint of irony. He was holding tightly on to Lorraine and Peggy Sue as they braced themselves for the next big swell. But for a moment the storm seemed to lessen in intensity, as if it were taking a time out.

"It's all to do with the buoyancy," explained Melvin as he rotated his wrist and grimaced.

The ship settled for a while, but it was only a short while. Play resumed with an almighty clap of thunder directly above. The biggest wave yet hit the stern full on, and the ship deviated from horizontal to almost vertical in a split second. Their legs slipped from beneath them, and they slid on their bottoms the full length of the cabin.

They all lay, dazed and in a heap, on the floor.

"You still think we won't sink?" screamed Peggy Sue. "You still believe in this buoyancy of yours?"

Melvin smiled bravely. Of course he did. "It's the Archimedes Principle," he cried.

Garry and Peggy Sue looked at him blankly, but before Melvin could explain the ship lurched again. From being at the bottom of the cabin they were suddenly at the top and falling headfirst on their backs in the opposite direction.

Melvin realised, as he fell headfirst on his back in the opposite direction, that Garry and Peggy Sue, living in Dream Land as they did, would never have heard of the Archimedes Principle. This worried him. It worried him because he wasn't sure if this storm, this ocean, or indeed this ship were aware of it either. He just hoped so.

#

"We were out at sea in calm conditions one moment."

"And the next thing we knew —"

"We were here."

"Well, not here, as such."

"No, not here." Albert shook his head, looked around, and laughed. "Not here in the paint shop."

"We found ourselves in a strange room in a strange world," said Captain Briggs.

"And that's when we met Mr Good."

Melvin was shocked. "Are you saying that Mr Good summoned you all too?"

"It was a mistake."

"It wasn't us he wanted."

"It was the tea set he was interested in."

Melvin was having trouble getting his head round this. "The tea set?"

Captain Briggs nodded. "A matching collection of cups and saucers."

"And side plates," added Andrew.

"And a cake plate," recalled Edward.

"If I remember rightly there was a milk jug too," said Albert. "And a sugar bowl."

"Don't forget the teapot," Andrew said with a smile.

"The tea set was a wedding present to Sarah and me from my mother," explained Captain Briggs. "So it was a surprise to see it there too, neatly stacked on Mr Good's walnut desk."

"I think I've seen it," said Peggy Sue. "It's on the Welsh dresser in my uncle's office now. Mind you, most of it has been smashed. Last time I looked the spout was missing off the teapot."

Captain Briggs sighed. That's a shame," he said.

"My uncle likes to throw crockery at folk. Usually at Terry. But sometimes me." She forced a smile, and Vince gave her a hug.

Melvin tried to make some sort of sense of all this. "But why was Mr Good so interested in your tea set?" he asked.

Captain Briggs shook his head slowly. "It was of historical significance, it seems."

Melvin's expression moved from bemused to befuddled.

"When was all this?" asked Lorraine.

Albert shrugged and looked at Edward and Andrew for confirmation. "Back in the seventies?"

"The 1870s," Melvin clarified immediately.

Lorraine blanched. "The 1870s!"

"December 4, 1872, to be exact, Loz," added Melvin.

Lorraine looked at Captain Briggs and Albert and then the other crew members. "And you are all still here?"

Captain Briggs smiled sadly. His wife, Sarah looked up from her harmonium, caught his eye, and smiled too. "Mr Good did try to return us," he began. "But by this time the *Mary Celeste* would have been drifting aimlessly in open seas."

Albert nodded. "Just the slightest of errors in his latitude and longitude coordinates and we would have found ourselves stranded in the Atlantic Ocean without lifebelts."

"Too dangerous," said Captain Briggs. "We had our daughter to think about."

Sarah rested her hand on the small of Sophie Matilda's back, pulled her close, and hugged her tightly.

"So, what happened? asked Melvin. "How did you end up here?"

"Mr Good apologised profusely, and he did his best to help us, of course," explained Captain Briggs. "He found us a place with an ocean and harbour with strange-looking boats without sails."

"A Dreamspace," whispered Peggy Sue.

Captain Briggs sighed and proceeded to tell them about their life in the harbour. "Nothing was real," he told them. "For example, there were no seagulls, just the sound of their incessant screeching through a two-channel audio system."

"Even the ocean was a synthetic material moulded into a hard, long-lasting ocean shape," said Albert. "It didn't look right, feel right, or smell right."

"We found it all so tedious, perplexing, and tiresome, and we were all terribly homesick," recalled Captain Briggs. "Then one day, not long after we arrived – a few decades, maybe – we met two strangers."

"They were just passing," explained Albert.

"Two passing strangers," agreed Captain Briggs, and he continued. "The one was an odd sort of a fellow, and he wore a funny hat. The other was a large, flightless bird, and she told us of a place. It was a place with an ocean that had tides and waves, a place where you could taste the salt in the wind and feel the sea spray on your face. It sounded splendid, and we couldn't wait to see it for ourselves. Everything thereafter happened in a whirl. By some enchantment, it seems, the two strangers whisked us away. And, well, to cut a long story short, that's how we ended up here," he concluded. "It's not exactly Massachusetts, but now we've got fairly settled to it."

Garry stood up suddenly. "Can I just say something at this point?" he said as he stood and faced Captain Briggs.

All eyes turned to the normally quiet and timid dream actor, and the music stopped.

"Did I hear you correctly?" he asked excitedly. He could feel himself trembling as he spoke. "Did you just say 'an odd sort of a fellow, and he wore a funny hat'?"

\#

"Land ahoy!"

Land of Nod ahoy, thought Garry, and he smiled. He stood on Melvin's left-hand side and watched with growing anticipation as the brigantine sailed closer to the island. He had known immediately. As soon as Captain Briggs had said 'an odd sort of a fellow, and he wore a funny hat', he knew. "Lord Riddle," he whispered. He knew it without a doubt. There had been numerous sightings of Lord Riddle in Limbo and in Dreamspaces down the eras, but this was the first time he had met someone who had actually spoken with him. Garry had never been so excited.

Then in the paint shop Vince had stood up, placed a hand on the captain's shoulder, and revealed that Mr Good had sent them there to find Lord Riddle. Melvin and Lorraine hurriedly told him why. They told him that Vile had taken over the Palace of Somnium, they told him about opening night, and they told him how very soon everyone, everywhere, every night, would be having nightmares. They also told him that the consequences for the physical world would be catastrophic unless they found Lord Riddle very soon. Captain Briggs and his crew were horrified to hear that Mr Good was in such a predicament and agreed to set sail for the Land of Nod immediately.

They had been at sea for three long days and nights, and at one point, early on the second day, Garry was quite sure they weren't going to make it. But somehow they managed to ride out the storm. Now, as the brigantine rounded the verdant isle and the tangerine sun rose high in the sky, he suddenly realised that the moment he had spent his life wishing for, and waited so much for, was about to happen. He dearly wanted to say something at this point, but he couldn't find the words.

Captain Briggs, Albert, and the crew had become good friends during the voyage, and so it was with mixed feelings that they said their good-byes. The brigantine was anchored off the western edge of the island, and a boat was lowered into the greenish-blue sea. The German seamen joined Melvin, Lorraine, Vince, Peggy Sue, and Garry in the boat, and the four of them rowed the quarter of a mile to a small wooden landing stage.

Chapter 56

Off to the left-hand side of one of the magnificent rooms halfway between the library and the great central hall were two white, hollow panelled doors. They opened out into a cream room of medium size with a spineless yucca evergreen indoor houseplant placed in each corner. In the centre of the room, chiselled out of a single piece of rich marble, was an enormous, black, broad, round, open vat.

Contained within the vat was a sauce of sweetened milk, thickened with cornflour —and two heads.

"I've never been so humiliated in all my life," said the first head.

Flagellum frowned. "You've never been so humiliated? You know how I hate custard! You always liked it."

"Eating it," replied Zygote, "poured lovingly over a rich, sticky toffee pudding. Not being placed up to my neck in it!"

"Well, even so, it's worse for me," decided Flagellum.

"No, it isn't!"

"Yes, it is!"

"It isn't!"

"It is!"

Larry stood facing the two white, hollow panelled doors. He took a moment to pluck up some courage from somewhere before grabbing and pulling at both doorknobs. Nothing happened. He thought they were locked, but then he pushed, and the doors swung open. He took a step into the medium-sized room. He saw the spineless yucca evergreen indoor houseplants first, and then he saw the enormous, rich marble vat. Then he saw the muscular guard.

The muscular guard appeared from behind the door and stood menacingly. "Ugh!" he grunted with his upper lip raised and his teeth bared.

Larry was ready. On the way over he had planned what he was about to say. But now that the moment had arrived, he thought his nerve might fail him. Could he make it sound convincing? He wondered. *But I'm an actor*, he told himself. *Of course I can.*

"Guard!" he shouted. "Guard! All the dream actors have escaped!"

"Ugh!" grunted the guard in a 'pull the other one; it's got bells on' kind of way.

"It's true," insisted Larry. "All of them just upped and left."

"Ugh!" responded the guard. His loose-fitting iron helmet rattled as he shook his head in disbelief. He wasn't buying it.

"Through the mahogany arched door and out into Limbo they went," Larry persisted. "The cheek of it! They've all gone to find Mr Good."

"Ugh!" went the grunt. Maybe there was just a hint of doubt in its tone.

Larry was encouraged. "Vile will be ever so angry with you when he gets back."

The guard's eyes widened. "Ugh!" There was definitely concern there.

"I wouldn't be surprised if he plunges you headfirst into that vat over there."

The guard turned and regarded the vat with a worried expression. "Ugh!"

"Full to the brim with rice pudding, I would imagine," said Larry with a grin. "Or possibly tapioca."

The guard was still staring at the vat, but when he turned his head Larry saw his bottom lip was trembling and his eyes were moist. "Ugh?"

"Or maybe golden syrup or something equally as sweet and cloying," he continued. "Either way," Larry said, moving in for the kill, "you'll never get out."

The guard gulped back a sob and then panicked. He suddenly began to run around in circles like a dog chasing its own tail, and after several such rotations he bolted out through the open door.

Harry and Barry commented later that the muscular guard streaked across the spacious drawing room and down the graceful staircase with a look of absolute terror on his face. He wasn't seen again for quite a while.

#

Larry sniffed the air and listened. He could smell something baked and sweet, and he could hear two voices engaged in a petty squabble.

Being a gangly beanpole, Larry was just about tall enough to be able to peer over the rim of the vat. As he did so, he saw a yellow mixture of eggs and milk, and he saw two heads that appeared to be floating in it.

The heads stopped bickering immediately and looked up at Larry's long, thin face.

"Who are you?" said the head with the crimson padded turban upon it.

Larry noticed that the custard was really thick and cold, with an unpleasant skin on top. "I'm Larry," he replied finally.

"What do you want?" asked Flagellum abruptly.

Larry couldn't believe the giants were sitting there so calmly up to their necks in such a stodgy dessert. "I've come to rescue you," he told them.

"Rescue? We don't need rescuing," Flagellum scoffed. "I was just about to get up and go anyway."

"Balderdash!" laughed Zygote.

"I was!" insisted Flagellum. "I was cooking up a plan."

Larry cut in. "It's just that myself and a couple of the chaps were thinking about leaving the palace and setting off to find Mr Good, and we thought …"

"Find Mr Good?" Flagellum rolled his beady eyes.

"We thought, or rather I thought, you would want to come along with us."

Flagellum sneered. "Why would you think that?"

"Because Mr Good needs all the help he can get if he's going to put a stop to Vile's new nightmare. And correct me if I'm wrong, but a reliable source has told me that you two are giants."

He paused for confirmation. He received none, so he continued. "If you are, your size and strength will come in useful. I just had to come and free you. I couldn't leave you both here in custody." He smiled. "Get it? Custardy?"

Flagellum frowned.

"Vile could return at any moment, though," continued Larry. "We have to hurry."

"Don't let us stop you," said Flagellum curtly.

Larry was suddenly alarmed. "But you will be joining us? Surely?"

"No." Flagellum shook his head.

Zygote's head turned to Flagellum's head. "Let's not be too hasty here, Flagellum." Then he looked up at Larry's alarmed face. "Now, if you wouldn't mind just pulling open the sliding panel, we can discuss this standing up and not sitting here in this horrible yellow substance."

"Of course," said Larry as he rushed around the vat to look for the opening. He found a silver handle and pulled it. The panel opened out on its hinges a few centimetres, and then Larry was able to slide it fully across. The custard didn't flow out, as you might expect. It lay there stubbornly, like a huge glob of yellow cement.

The two giants forced their way through the mixture, wading through it on their knees. Flagellum was the first to climb out. "There's nothing to discuss," he said as he stood up tall.

Zygote followed him out and stood up taller. "But Mr Good needs help," he reasoned.

"Not our problem," replied Flagellum. His deep, purplish-red gown of fine woollen cloth was decorated now with large clumps of yellow custard. "We will be returning to the room with two doors immediately," he announced.

Zygote sighed. He wanted so much to help Mr Good, but he conceded that his fellow giant had a point. They were the guardians of the white room, after all. They had a duty. "You're right, I suppose," he agreed reluctantly.

Larry was disappointed too. "Mr Good will not be pleased," he told them. "But if that's your decision …"

"It is," said Flagellum. He grinned with his enormous, crooked teeth on full show. "Bye!" he waved dismissively and turned his back on Larry.

The dream actor smiled sadly, sighed, and walked out the room. He closed the two white, hollow panelled doors behind him and made his way back to the drawing room. On the way he met several dream actors travelling in the opposite direction. They were on their way to the Dream Theatre for their final dress rehearsal.

Larry, Harry, and Barry were not attending the final dress rehearsal. Instead, they left the Palace of Somnium and went out into the corridors of Limbo to begin their quest to find Mr Good.

Chapter 57

"There it is!" gasped Garry. He stood and stared across the narrow stretch of low land between the hills.

Melvin and Lorraine were on their knees at the edge of a small stream that ran along the bottom of the valley. They reached out for a heavy length of wood with a paperboard sign that had become entangled with a marine plant with sharp, pointy, spiky leaves.

"It's a placard of some description," said Melvin as he pulled it from the shallow water.

"There are words written on it," said Lorraine, turning it over. She read them slowly. "Labyrinth ... blue ... centre ... royal ... choose."

Melvin read it too, and as he said it he looked at Lorraine. "I've seen and read these words somewhere before, Loz."

"Me too." Lorraine nodded and ran the palm of her hand across the words. She tried to grasp at the memory of a flightless, aquatic sea bird by the name of Auk waddling along this actual narrow stretch of lowland. Against his white underside, held tightly by his flipper-like wings, he carried the wooden placard. Along the way he stopped several times to switch the heavy length of wood from one flipper to the other, and yet each time he somehow managed to hold the sign a little higher. He was determined that nothing was going to stop him from conveying this message to those who were watching. With a swaying gait and with short, weary steps, Auk travelled to the very spot where they now stood. Lorraine remembered now how he rested here by the small stream in the tangerine sunshine and waited for Tula.

"There it is!" uttered Garry noisily.

The memory suddenly faded, and then it was gone. As she looked up she saw that Garry was still standing and staring off into the distance.

#

From the moment the five of them had stood on the headland above the rocky beach, looked out to sea, and watched the brigantine turn and set sail for the horizon, their journey across the Land of Nod had been a long one, a tiring one. Garry had found a faint trail through the trees that proved to be quite difficult to follow. They found the curling pathway blocked many times by fallen branches, bushes, ferns, and small trees growing beneath larger trees. Sometimes the obstacles were so dense they couldn't fight their way through. Any detour they took was always slow going, and they were often stabbed, pricked, prodded, and scratched by plants with leaves the shape of daggers before they managed to find their way again. The tangerine sun, which had been directly above them when they set off, was now quite low in the northern sky as they entered the valley.

Vince had helped Peggy Sue by holding her hand, steadying her, and encouraging her along the way. It meant, though, they were lagging a little way behind the others. "What's y'actual favourite Elvis song, Peg?" asked Vince as they finally reached the stream.

Peggy Sue looked up at him and smiled. *That's easy,* she thought. "I want you, I need you, I love you," she said.

Vince blushed. "Me too." He smiled awkwardly.

"I mean, that's one of my favourites too," he added quickly.

"With all my heart," sang Peggy Sue, because that was the next line of the song.

"There it is!" Garry cried for a third time, and this time he set off towards it.

Melvin and Lorraine stood up and watched Garry stride away from the path they were taking. "Where you going?" they shouted.

"What's happening, guys?" said Peggy Sue as she joined them.

Melvin's shoulders went up half an inch and then dropped.

Vince stared across the lowland, and his eyes widened. "There it is!" he gasped.

"What?" said Lorraine impatiently. "There's what?" She stared in the same direction as Vince, but she saw nothing of significance – just another hill.

Vince smiled. He knew their journey was nearly at an end. He had done exactly what Mr Good had asked of him. "It's y'actual wooden hill to Bedfordshire," he said.

#

They stood at the foot of the wooden hill to Bedfordshire and looked up.

"I would recognise it anywhere," said Garry.

It had a sharp incline. Its gradient, in places, approached the perpendicular.

"It is described extensively in that very, very old book I was telling you about," continued Garry. "It's unmistakable."

Lorraine looked up too. She had also seen this hill before, as she had seen the placard and the message on the paperboard sign before.

"It's like déjà vu," Lorraine whispered.

"Only seriously weirder," decided Melvin. He recognised the hill too, of course. But from where?

"A penguin," said Lorraine quietly, almost to herself.

Melvin nodded. "Rolling downhill," he said slowly.

"They're our keywords," said Lorraine. "Isn't that strange?"

Melvin didn't reply. Instead he stared up the hill towards its summit. The top was short and flat, just as he remembered. He recalled a penguin plunging down a steep, grassy slope. Down a hill that extended high above the surrounding terrain, they watched her roll. They followed her progress from the summit past the flame-coloured trees and the low shrubs until she came to an abrupt halt in the long grass at the foot of the hill, just a few yards from where they stood now.

"It was a dream," he concluded. But how and why were two questions he couldn't begin to answer yet.

With their heads directed skyward, they failed to notice something appear around the side of the hill and stand immediately behind them.

"It doesn't look like it's made of wood, does it?" said Peggy Sue.

Vince took a step forward and stamped on the ground at the beginning of the upward slope with one of his blue suede shoes. The ground was hard, and the sound it gave off was without doubt a hollow one.

307

"Of course it's made of wood," said a friendly voice.

They all very nearly jumped clean out of their skins. They turned as one to see an ostrich standing there.

"It's the wooden hill to Bedfordshire, after all," added the ostrich with a kind chuckle.

Instinctively, four of them backed away slowly and carefully and stood behind Vince.

Vince realised he was now the closest one to the large talking bird who had suddenly appeared from nowhere. He realised, too, that it was down to him to ask the obvious question. He took a long, nervous breath. "Who are you?" he asked.

"I'm Ostrich," she replied. She was nearly seven feet high. "But, of course, we've met already."

"We have?" asked Lorraine as she stepped forward. There was something about this bird. Maybe it was the friendly voice or the kind chuckle, but somehow Lorraine felt she posed no threat. "When? I don't recall."

"We were introduced," said Ostrich, "in a little while from now."

Lorraine scrunched up her face. "That doesn't make sense," she told her.

As the dusk gathered between the hills and over the valley, Ostrich motioned with an outstretched wing for them to follow her around the side of the hill. "Lord Riddle awaits," she announced.

"Lord Riddle!" exclaimed Garry. "Awaits? Did you hear that, everyone? Lord Riddle is awaiting!" His excitement levels reached new heights, and he was the first to follow the ostrich.

With their curiosity aroused, the rest of them followed the ostrich around the corner where they saw, turned upside down on the patchy grass, an enormous brown felt hat with a dome-shaped crown and a narrow, slightly curled brim.

"A flying hat!" Garry beamed as he climbed inside. "I've always wanted to ride in one of these."

"Me too," said Peggy Sue with a laugh. "It's just like the one in 'The Adventures of Lord Riddle and the Kakapo Parrot'," she said as she stepped in it and sat down.

Ostrich lifted her long, thin legs and stepped inside the hat too, closely followed by Melvin, Lorraine, and Vince. The stiff, hard sides of the hat supported them adequately. When they were all seated and Ostrich was satisfied the weight was distributed equally, the hat left the ground. For a moment or so it hovered a foot above the surface before moving off at a fairly sedate pace towards the back of the hill as the tangerine sun sank even lower in the heavens.

This is seriously weird, thought Melvin.

"Does Lord Riddle know we're here?" asked Lorraine.

Ostrich nodded.

"Does he know why?"

"You are here to ask for his assistance," said Ostrich. "Well, that's what you told him."

"We told him?"

"We told Lord Riddle?" asked Melvin. "That's impossible."

"When was this?" Lorraine was perplexed.

"In approximately fifteen minutes' time," said Ostrich.

The flying hat suddenly banked to the right, and they all held on tightly to its brim as they made their way around the back of the hill. The back of the hill was made of wood too, but unlike the front, it wasn't disguised to look like a grassy, natural elevation of the island's surface. It was bare timber, and it stood bolt upright.

"I think you are getting your tenses mixed up," said Melvin with a laugh. "You can say we will tell him in approximately fifteen minutes' time or we told him approximately fifteen minutes ago, but ..."

"But you can't say we told him in fifteen minutes' time," added Lorraine, shaking her head.

Ostrich listened, and then her eyes smiled. "You talk of the future as if it's something that hasn't happened yet."

Melvin and Lorraine exchanged a look.

"Time is different here," said Ostrich.

Ahead of them, a thick black iron pipe ran vertically upwards from out of the ground. It went parallel with the wooden structure for about thirty feet, and then an elbow allowed a ninety-degree change in its direction. The pipe disappeared inside the back of the hill.

"Mr Good did tell us that time was different here," said Melvin.

Ostrich considered this for a moment. "Yes, time is different in Limbo too," she admitted. "But here on the Land of Nod it's a lot differenter."

She chuckled kindly once more because she knew there probably wasn't such a word. "You see, unlike on the mainland, our clock doesn't always tick, and it doesn't necessarily tock in the present," she said as the flying hat began to steadily rise. In the partial darkness, it flew alongside the thick, black iron pipe, and thirty feet above the ground it found the same gap. "Time here is stretchy and springy," she explained.

It was warm inside the wooden hill to Bedfordshire.

"Time here can stretch into the future, but it can also spring back into the past," she added.

The flying hat continued to rise and follow the course of the black iron pipe. It was musty inside the wooden hill to Bedfordshire.

"What is this place? asked Peggy Sue as she leaned back and looked over the side of the hat into what seemed like a bottomless pit with slatted shelves. Vince held her by the shoulders and gently eased her back into a safer, upright position.

"This place?" said Ostrich. "This place I can only describe as an enormous airing cupboard. Look," she said, pointing upwards. "You will see a very large dream tank."

It was murky inside the wooden hill to Bedfordshire, but several slivers of light visible high above made it just about possible to make out shapes through the thick layer of murk that surrounded them.

"A dream tank?" Through the gaps between the slats, Melvin could see a very large box or cube. And as they got closer, he saw the thick, black iron pipe connect to it on its underside. "What is it for?" he asked.

The flying hat continued to rise, and eventually it flew over the top of the dream tank and hovered there. The top was open, enabling all of them to look inside.

"This tank should be full of the liquid gas that Lord Riddle uses to transmit his dreams. But as you can see, it's almost empty now," said Ostrich sadly. "Someone, somewhere, has isolated the flow of dream power."

Peggy Sue frowned. "My uncle."

Ostrich nodded. "Yes, you said."

"Did I? When?" Then Peggy Sue remembered that time here stretched like an elastic band. She must have mentioned it in the future sometime.

"There's maybe enough juice left for one more dream span, but after that ..." Ostrich faltered.

The flying hat moved on and upward towards the light.

"Lord Riddle must be very worried," said Garry.

"He is." Ostrich took a deep breath, hesitated a moment longer, and then nodded. "That's why he's summoned you all."

Chapter 58

Flagellum took off one of his shoes and started to hit a vase with it. A large blob of custard fell out. "Nobody puts me in custard and gets away with it," he grumbled as he slipped his foot back inside his red, pointy shoe.

"They have and they did," said Zygote. "Get over it!"

They walked on and entered a lounge finished in a cool shade of blue.

"Why couldn't those guards pick on someone their own size?" Flagellum continued to moan.

Zygote turned and looked at him. "Someone their own size? Are you serious? You're a giant. You're twice the height of their tallest one."

"Well, there must have been about thirty of them. It wasn't fair."

Zygote sighed. "Flagellum, in a situation that causes powerful emotions to be expressed there can be no firm rules of behaviour."

Flagellum frowned.

"I'll tell you what isn't fair, though," said Zygote as they made their way across the magnificent room thronged with choice pieces of furniture and an abundance of spineless yucca evergreen indoor houseplants.

Flagellum waited for his fellow giant to continue.

"The imbalance of power," continued Zygote. "Vile has all the guards with the big biceps, but Mr Good just has the wizard who says 'salmon' a lot.

The next doorway they passed through led into a library crammed full of books and manuscripts.

"A confirmed pacifist," added Zygote.

"Is he?" Flagellum sneered. "Has he seen a doctor?"

Zygote shook his head wearily. "He doesn't need to see a doctor, Flagellum. A pacifist is someone opposed to war, someone who would rather placate using friendly overtures, someone who would prefer to settle a dispute by arbitration."

"Arbitration?" Flagellum scoffed. "He's living in cloud cuckoo land if he thinks this particular conflict can be sorted out with a cosy chat around the dining room table."

"Now there's the rub." Zygote sighed. "How can a pair of peace mongers possibly win a war?"

Flagellum shrugged. He didn't care.

"I am sure Mr Good is well aware of it, and so I have been thinking."

Flagellum came to a halt at the access to an enclosed antechamber. "This sounds ominous," he said.

Zygote stopped just short of the great curtain and turned. "I think we should go and help them."

Flagellum gulped. "Them? Help them? Mr Good and the wizard who says 'salmon' a lot?"

"It's the least we can do."

"No chance," said Flagellum. "We need to return to the room with two doors immediately."

"Mr Good has been very kind to us over the eras, Flagellum."

"I've never met him."

"You have!"

"I haven't!"

"Shut up," snapped Zygote. "Shut up and tell me what our horoscopes say for this current dream span."

The brows above Flagellum's beady eyes arched. "What? Our horoscopes? I thought you didn't believe in astrology. I thought you said it was twaddle."

"It is twaddle," responded Zygote. "I'm just curious."

Zygote pulled the curtain across its heavy-duty curved track and stepped into the spacious drawing room as Flagellum fished out the latest edition of the *Dream Times* from a pocket somewhere in his deep, purplish-red gown. It was sodden.

"Shall I read out your astrological prediction?" Flagellum smirked. "Or shall I tell you what is says for Sagittarius?"

Zygote frowned. "I am Sagittarius, as well you know."

Flagellum carefully peeled the pages apart, found page thirteen, folded it in half, and followed Zygote through the curtain. "Sagittarius," he read. "November 22 to December 21. Emphasis is on property matters, and this current dream span is a good time for making travel plans. Meanwhile, someone who you haven't seen for a while needs your help urgently. So, don't delay. Procrastination is the thief of time." He looked up and shrugged. "Whatever that's supposed to mean."

"It means do what needs to be done and do it quickly," Zygote told him as they made their way past the deserted tables and chairs towards the balcony.

"Now, what's your star sign?" asked Flagellum. The smile on his face was a wry one.

Zygote sighed a heavy sigh. "Just read yours, Flagellum. You're a Taurus, remember?"

Flagellum ran his finger down the page until he found it. "Taurus. April 21 to May 21 …"

Without breaking stride, Zygote took the graceful staircase three steps at a time. Flagellum's descent was a little slower as he held the newspaper in his left hand and the solid oak balustrade in the other.

"Emphasis is on property matters, and this current dream span is a good time for making travel plans. Meanwhile, someone who you haven't seen for a while needs your help urgently. So, don't delay. Procrastination is the thief of time." Flagellum paused on the landing where the stairs divided into two and adopted a puzzled expression. He read the astrological prediction for Taurus again but in his head this time. "It's the same," he said.

Zygote stood at the foot of the staircase looking up. "I told you it was twaddle."

Flagellum passed Zygote without saying a word. He made his way across the grand entrance hall in full stride and in deep thought. Zygote followed on, and they both exited the Palace of Somnium through the mahogany arched door they had been brought there by Vile to guard. It was wide open.

Halfway along the narrow passageway, Flagellum stopped and turned. "If it's in the stars then it must be true," he said without making eye contact with his fellow giant.

Zygote shrugged.

"I think," Flagellum continued, looking down at the pink and white marble flooring, "we should go –" he hesitated – "and find him."

Zygote smiled, although he tried to suppress it. ""Find him? Do you mean find and help Mr Good?"

Flagellum looked up slowly. "It's the least we can do."

"For once I agree with you, Flagellum," said Zygote. Together they started walking. "We will make our way to Mr Good immediately."

"Sounds like a plan," agreed Flagellum.

Ten paces further along they reached the junction where a cyan, a magenta, and a yellow corridor come together. "Only one problem with that plan," said Zygote as he considered the options. "Which way do we go?"

Chapter 59

In normal circumstances it is recommended one attends several counselling sessions before a meeting with Lord Riddle takes place. Even more care should be given after meeting him, so the trauma can be addressed through a course of hypnotherapy. But there wasn't time for all that. Their first meeting with Lord Riddle was less than thirty seconds away.

"Welcome to Bedfordshire." Peggy Sue read the words emblazoned on a large banner that was billowing in the breeze as the flying hat emerged from an opening in the warm, musty, murky, and enormous airing cupboard at the top of the hill just beyond its short, flat top.

They had all been stunned by Ostrich's revelation, particularly Melvin and Lorraine.

"Summoned us?"

"Lord Riddle?"

"But that's not possible."

Night had been falling when they entered the inside of the hill no more than ten minutes ago. Now the tangerine sun was blazing high up in the noon sky.

"It was Mr Good that sent for us," Melvin insisted.

"He told us so," Lorraine affirmed. "It was his plan."

Ostrich smiled. Or rather, Ostrich would have smiled if it were possible for an ostrich to form its beak into a smile shape. She smiled on the inside. She smiled because she knew it wasn't Mr Good's plan at all. It never was his plan.

The flying hat flew quickly through the two poles that held the large banner aloft and on through a long, narrow avenue of ancient oak and mature pine trees clipped or trimmed into shapes not dissimilar to bedside lamps.

"Mr Good certainly believes he summoned you," said Ostrich. "But I can assure you he didn't. That's what Lord Riddle wanted him to believe. Lord Riddle put a thought in his head."

They were all flabbergasted, especially Melvin and Lorraine.

"When you say he put a thought in his head," said Peggy Sue, "do you mean he put a kiwi bird in his head?"

"Have you read 'Lord Riddle and the Kiwi Birds'?" asked Ostrich.

Peggy Sue nodded. "Nana Vile used to read that one to me many times. It was her favourite."

"Then you will know that Lord Riddle uses these remarkable birds to pass on thoughts and messages," said Ostrich. "They have the ability to make themselves as small as a button, travel great distances, and climb unnoticed inside people's minds."

"So, it's all true?" gasped Peggy Sue. "Lord Riddle really does exist?"

Ostrich waited a moment before continuing. "I understand there are many who think Lord Riddle is just make-believe, a fictional character in a fairy tale, perhaps." She chuckled kindly. "Let me assure you here and now that Lord Riddle truly exists, and you will be meeting him in approximately twenty seconds."

Garry's eyes widened. At the end of the topiarian bedside-lamp-lined avenue, the ground fell away sharply to reveal a valley: an extraordinarily large bedspread landscape far below with quilted patches of dark greens, light greens, yellows, and browns, like a vast expanse of rural scenery that reached towards and beyond the horizon. Or rather, it reached where the horizon would be if there had been one. This peculiar land didn't feel the need for such a thing. In the far distance just off to the right, resting on the mattress of a gigantic divan bed, was a city. It was a magnificent city with incredibly tall buildings that appeared to be jostling for position and reaching up and rubbing against the sky.

The hat banked sharply to the right and joined the main road, a thoroughfare floating in the air above the square and oblong patchwork landscape. Other hats were flying in the same direction along the invisible thoroughfare, and several were travelling the other way too. Ostrich waved as they passed by, and the passengers waved their feathers, their wings, their flippers, or whatever was to hand.

As they approached the gigantic divan bed they saw that the incredibly tall buildings were in fact incredibly tall wardrobes and other examples of bedroom furniture. At the outskirts of the city, the first constructions they encountered were just plain and simple storage solutions, canvas boxes and shelves dotted here and there alongside wide dirt tracks. But the roadways got narrower as they travelled deeper into the deserted city, and the wardrobes grew taller. Each bureau and chest of drawers was wider, every bedside table bigger, and all of them grander and more stylish as they moved closer to the centre of this unusual city. Every now and then they caught a glimpse of the sky as they made their way along the dark, claustrophobic, narrow lanes between the large, imposing cherry and mahogany edifices.

Eventually, the flying hat entered a large square space. It was maybe a hundred yards square and flanked on all four sides by enormous cushioned footstools.

The city square was very busy. It seemed that every inhabitant of this strange city was gathered there. The square was alive with many penguins, countless cassowaries, no end of emus, and umpteen kiwi birds. The flying hat flew above the heads of the multitude of flightless birds that were crowded close together and made its way quickly to the centre of the open space.

Then they saw themselves approaching from the opposite direction. Of course, they weren't approaching from the opposite direction at all; it was their reflection in a full-length mirror. The full-length mirror towered above them, and the flying hat showed no intention of stopping or even slowing down. If anything it seemed to accelerate as it neared the glass. They braced themselves.

#

As they braced, Ostrich took the opportunity to prepare them. She leaned forward. "You are about to meet Lord Riddle," she began, "the dream ambassador for those peculiar, strange, inexplicable dreams that make no sense. He is an odd sort of a fellow who wears a funny hat and a direct descendent of one of the three legendary dream ancestors."

She paused. "Probably the one who poured the tea from the pot." She looked at Garry for confirmation. Garry nodded.

The flying hat hit the reflecting surface. The impact wasn't the smash or the shattering experience they were expecting. It was more of a splash that sent ripples scurrying outwards in a circular motion as they entered the gloomy interior of an antique, long-case clock. They found themselves inside an oak dome decorated and cross-banded in mahogany. The hat flew down from the darkness of the rafters and hovered just above the ground for a moment before landing gently.

Then they saw him. There he was, sitting cross-legged on the carved oak flooring, blowing soap bubbles. Lord Riddle. There was no doubting it. He had a sort of aura about him.

Ostrich stood and stepped out of the hat as a large pendulum swung by. Tick.

"He operates on a higher astral plane, and his mind exists on many wavelengths," Ostrich continued to explain. "To survive as a dream ambassador he has to think and act on a different level of sanity. If you can recall those peculiar, strange, and inexplicable dreams you have all had, you will realise that to actually create and perform those dreams one must have a consciousness and imagination superior to Mr Good and a deceptiveness and cunningness far greater than Vile. I will warn you now, his manner may seem odd, erratic, and changeable at times. But in his own way, Lord Riddle understands everything, absolutely everything. His mind capacity is so huge, he is the only being in existence that can comprehend fully the vastness of each of the eleven universes."

The large pendulum swung back the other way. Tock.

"The world is full of yellow things," said Lord Riddle suddenly. He was suddenly on his feet too. One moment he had been sitting cross-legged and blowing soap bubbles, seemingly in a world of his own. Then in an instant he was standing up and moonwalking across the hard, durable flooring."

"Do not pass go, do not collect stamps," added Lord Riddle, and he grinned foolishly. Tick.

Ostrich sighed. "Unfortunately, you will not understand much that Lord Riddle says. The language he speaks is Daftness," she told them. "Daftness is the most complex language imaginable, a cryptic dialect built and mixed with reality and unreality and a very confusing alteration of syntax. I have been Lord Riddle's companion since the very first Tuesday, and even now, after all this time, after all those Tuesdays, I only know the basics."

The large pendulum swung past once more. Tock.

One by one they stood up out of the hat and stared at Lord Riddle in awe. His facial features were sharp. He was slender and moved gracefully despite his Wellington boots being a size or two too big. He wore a long, striped gown of many different, clashing colours. He was certainly very odd, and he wore a hat. Lorraine noted that it wasn't really a funny hat, as legend would have it. It was a high, flat crowned felt hat with a wide, uncocked brim and a silver buckle on a ribbon band. It certainly didn't match the rest of his outfit, but it wasn't particularly funny either. Finally, Vince took Peggy Sue's hand and helped her out of the flying hat too.

As the large pendulum swung by again, Lorraine looked up and noticed it was attached to several stretched elastic bands and a rotating horizontal bar shaped like an anchor that released a tooth from an escapement gear. Tick.

But before the gear could spin past the first tooth, the pendulum swung back, and the anchor caught the next tooth. Tock.

Lord Riddle approached Melvin. He made a fist and held it out to him. Nervously, Melvin did the same, and their clenched hands met briefly. "Communist leader," said Lord Riddle with a slight bow.

Melvin was confused.

Lorraine smiled. "Communist: red. Leader: head. Redhead. He is referring to the colour of your hair."

Before Melvin could even think about that, Lord Riddle reached out, caught the large pendulum, and stopped it. There was silence.

Then two seriously weird things happened.

Chapter 60

The first seriously weird thing to happen was that Garry spoke Daftness to Lord Riddle. "In air of special need. A quest for aid," he said.

It so happened that Garry spoke fluent Daftness. He learned it from that very, very old book he mentioned earlier. It was one of the reasons why he was chosen.

Lord Riddle hopped on one leg, stopped in front of Garry, and looked him directly in the ear. "Another speaker of the five-dimensional tongue." He beamed. "Not alone I in higher sanity. Gosh a lot."

"The question rises and fades I feel," replied the dream actor.

"An orange piece of string," responded Lord Riddle.

Garry laughed loudly and turned to everyone. "Lord Riddle is as wonderful and witty as I always imagined him to be."

Everyone gaped. "You can speak Daftness?" said everyone in harmony.

The second seriously weird thing to happen was that they entered a rip in the bedsheet of space and time.

Using both hands, Lord Riddle grasped two pieces of thin air and pulled them apart as if he were opening a pair of heavy curtains. They all followed him through a gap they didn't think was there previously into a long, narrow room with an orange glow that definitely wasn't. When they were all inside the long, narrow room, red and blue lights along its four walls began to flash, followed by green and yellow ones. The stretched elastic bands, still visible above their heads, slackened as the escapement gears shifted into reverse.

"What's happening?" asked Lorraine.

"We are springing back into the past," Ostrich informed her.

The large-toothed wheels turned anticlockwise and gradually increased speed. In no time at all they were spinning at an incredible rate, and yet the intermittent illumination gave the illusion that everything was happening in slow motion.

"We are travelling from the Land of Nod, present dream span, to the Land of Nod six dream spans earlier," Ostrich added.

As they travelled back in time Lord Riddle reclined, suspended in a sitting position and defying gravity, as if he were relaxing in his favourite armchair. "Stormy performance reveals treachery," he said.

Garry agreed. "Foul play indeed. A candle is bad."

Lord Riddle stretched out his legs. "Chicken paste!" he announced.

Garry arched an eyebrow. He turned to the others again. "Opening night of Vile's new nightmare is almost upon us," he told them. "But fear not, Lord Riddle has told me he has a plot to thwart the bad and horrid one, to send him back to Torment Towers where he belongs, to return Mr Good to the Palace of Somnium, and to find and open the valve that is currently isolating the flow of dream power to the Land of Nod. The plot involves all of us here and four flightless birds."

Melvin stared at Garry for a long moment. "Lord Riddle told you all that?"

Garry nodded.

"But he only said 'chicken paste'!"

Garry shrugged. Then the strobe lighting stopped, and Lord Riddle was gone.

They found him talking to two penguins halfway along the narrow room, where it widened a little into a kind of waiting area with a few chairs lined up along one wall and a coffee table with a collection of newspapers and magazines on top.

The conversation that took place between them, though, was not what you might call normal. For one thing, no words were uttered. It was a communication of minds as Lord Riddle conversed in Daftness telepathically and the penguins exchanged thoughts, opinions, and feelings in a sort of unspoken way.

Roughly translated, however, the dialogue took the following course.

"Tumble down a sharp incline?" gasped the first penguin, somewhat alarmed.

Lord Riddle nodded. "It has to be an image those tuned into a frequency just below the level of conscious perception will never forget."

"But I'm an aquatic, flightless sea bird," insisted Tula speechlessly. "Rolling down a hill doesn't exactly come naturally."

"I fully appreciate that, but it needs to be memorable," said Lord Riddle. "It must be something that will nestle snugly in their subconscious," he added as Ostrich handed the second penguin a wooden placard.

"What's this?" wondered Auk silently.

"It's a paperboard sign," replied Lord Riddle. "Written upon it is a message. It gives instructions for those who will be watching."

Auk looked the heavy length of wood up and down. "What do you want me to do with it?"

"I want you to carry it," said Lord Riddle.

"Carry it? How am I supposed to grip it?" Auk asked wordlessly. "In case you haven't noticed, I don't have fingers or thumbs – or arms, for that matter."

Lord Riddle wrapped two hands around the large post and felt its weight. "I was thinking you could grip it securely against your torso with your flipper-like wings."

Auk stared at Lord Riddle open beaked.

"If you could hold it as high as possible," Lord Riddle continued, "and make your way along the narrow stretch of lowland between the hills, that would be perfect."

"But our feet are short and are not made for walking," Tula argued soundlessly.

"That's why we waddle," explained Auk.

"You will only have to waddle to the small stream that runs along the bottom of the valley. It's not far." Lord Riddle smiled. "Ostrich will show you the way," he added.

Their conversation was cut short by a roller shutter door.

It lifted noisily at the opposite end of the long room to the one they entered. Tula, with her weight tilting from one foot to the other, made her way nervously towards it. The thought that those tuned into a frequency just below the level of conscious perception would soon be watching her roll down a hill was enough to bring her out in a cold sweat, despite her thick layer of insulating feathers. Auk held the wooden post against his white underside and walked heavily and clumsily with a pronounced sway towards the slanted tangerine sunlight that was streaming in through the exit.

After Ostrich and the plump silhouettes of the two penguins had disappeared into the glare, the roller shutter door lowered, and the rip in the bedsheet of space and time set off again. It did not move back in time on this occasion. Instead, it remained six dream spans earlier and moved sideways through space to a corridor in Limbo just over halfway between the Nether Regions and the Palace of Somnium.

"Where are we? asked Peggy Sue as the roller shutter door lifted once more.

Vince's expression was one of astonishment as he looked out into the corridor. "In a reddish-blue maze," he replied. "It's y'actual Limbo."

"Yes." Garry nodded. "But not now. We are visiting Limbo in a previous dream span."

Melvin frowned. "Sometime in the past?" he asked. He was struggling to get his head round all this. Basically, it was seriously weird.

Lorraine cocked her head to one side and listened. "What's that noise?" she asked.

A deep, booming sound, like the beating of a drum, resounded along the corridor, causing the walls to vibrate. It was the sound an army of twenty-five muscular guards might make when their fifty leather sandals slapped against a hard floor.

Garry saw the muscular guards turn a corner up ahead and advance in step towards them. The first one Melvin spotted was Vile, striding out in front of the procession, splendiferous in his black and gold pinstriped jacket. It was Terrence, walking a few paces behind, that Lorraine noticed first in his tight-fitting, black, moth-eaten blazer.

The first person Peggy Sue saw was herself. She gasped.

Vince, of course, noticed her immediately. "Peggy Sue?"

She was chewing gum and acting all wild and boisterous, like a tomboy. She had on denim dungarees and looked like she'd been climbing trees in an abandoned Dreamspace or something similar, and she was holding hands with Terrence. Vince turned to the Peggy Sue standing next to him in the lime-green circular skirt with pink polka dots and a white, short-sleeved top. What was happening? He wanted to know. What was going on? He wanted to ask. Unfortunately, he didn't have the words in his vocabulary to attempt it.

Peggy Sue was still gasping.

Suddenly, Lord Riddle stepped out through the exit and stood in the middle of the violet maze wearing a sombrero. He held up his arms, and the loose-fitting sleeves of his striped gown slipped down past his bony elbows. "And now I see with eye serene the very pulse of the machine," he chanted. "A being breathing thoughtful breath, a traveller between life and death."

Melvin wrinkled his freckled nose. "Hold on." He turned to Lorraine and whispered. "That wasn't Daftness. That was ... William Wordsworth!"

Garry, standing next to Melvin on his other side, leaned over. "Yes, but do you know what it means?"

Melvin shrugged. "Well, not exactly, no."

"Then it's Daftness," he concluded.

As Lord Riddle slowly lowered his arms, Vile and his entourage gradually came to a halt. They stood motionless like life-size figures reproduced in wax, staring with unseeing eyes, not noticing or perceiving anything at all.

Melvin was aware that a lot of seriously weird things had happened since they had been here, but what happened next was the seriously weirdest. Two kiwi birds appeared from nowhere. One of them rested on Lord Riddle's shoulders. It then immediately shrank to the size of a small button, jumped onto Terrence's blazer, and bounced into his left superior frontal gyrus. The kiwi bird, once inside Terrence's brain, quickly placed several thousand riddles on a conveyor belt. Terrence would have no choice but to utter all of them.

An instant later the bird left Terrence and was inside Peggy Sue's mind. It positioned a small device somewhere near her temporal poles. The small device would pick up every riddle that Terrence uttered. Terrence couldn't possibly know it, but with each uttered riddle, bit by bit, Peggy Sue's fondness for him would diminish. With each unfunny joke, little by little, she would care for him less and less. She would eventually dislike him intensely. At the same time Peggy Sue would metamorphose, inch by inch, into a polite young lady with an interest in embroidery, flower arranging, and rock and roll.

It was a clever little device.

"Trooper without identification feels persecuted," sang Lord Riddle to the strange-looking bird with nostrils at the end of its long beak. It bounced clear of Peggy Sue, entered Vile's head, sat down, and made itself comfortable.

"What's happening?" whispered Lorraine.

"Trooper without identification feels persecuted? What the dickens does that mean?" asked Melvin.

Garry considered this for a moment. "Paranoid. Something to do with paranoia." He turned to Lorraine. "But I don't know what's happening," he admitted. "Maybe Lord Riddle wants Vile to have paranoid thoughts."

"Paranoid thoughts?" said Lorraine. "Let me see if I understand this. 'Trooper' can have a prefix 'para'. Yes? Without identification would be ... no I.D. Right? Put them all together and you have paranoid! I get it!" She beamed.

Garry smiled too and nodded. "You learn fast."

No one saw the other kiwi bird leave. It had a long journey to undertake and the interior of several heads to visit, including some dream actors, a giant, and of course Mr Good, who at this very moment in time was unaware that he was about to be kicked out of the Palace of Somnium.

Lord Riddle spread his arms wide. Vile, Terrence, Peggy Sue, and all the muscular guards suddenly came to life and continued on their way, albeit with a short gap in their memories.

The roller shutter door was lowered, and they were on the move again. The long, narrow room transformed into a discotheque once more as they left Limbo six dream spans earlier and stretched back to the future towards Limbo in the present dream span.

On arrival Lord Riddle took one step out through the roller shutter door and then another step through a row of hanging, coloured beads. Nobody spoke until they had all passed through the invisible doorway.

"Where are we?" asked Peggy Sue.

"This ..."

"Is ..."

"Mugwump's ..."

"Residence!"

Melvin and Lorraine shared the words of that sentence. They were surprised to find themselves back at the centre of the royal blue labyrinth and shocked to find it deserted.

"Are we still in the past?" Peggy Sue wondered as she looked around the room and noticed the retro furniture: the teak sideboard, the three-piece suite, and the lava lamps.

Garry shook his head slowly. "A gift, for now," he replied in Daftness. "The present," he quickly translated.

"But this décor!" She stared at the brown, orange, tan, and yellow wallpaper. "It's so dated, so old-fashioned. It's like we're in a 1970s time warp!"

Vince was surprised to hear Peggy Sue describe the room as old-fashioned. "It's so futuristic," he argued.

Peggy Sue smiled and squeezed his hand.

"Mr Good!" Melvin called out and circled the room.

"Keith! Arthur!" Lorraine shouted. "When we were last here Arthur was sitting on that sofa."

Melvin pointed. "And Terrence was tied to that chair." The teak dining chair was tipped over, and the string that bound him was on the bright orange carpet.

The place had been ransacked.

"Something bad has happened here," Peggy Sue surmised.

Slowly, a dimpled face appeared from behind the chocolate-brown sofa, followed by a red and blue diagonal neckerchief. A Boy Scout stood up nervously, holding a bright red water pistol in one hand and a pencil in the other.

Chapter 61

The door opened and Terrence entered the control room without knocking. He was excited because he knew something that Vile didn't know, and that didn't happen very often. He couldn't wait to tell him that three dream actors had escaped while they had been away.

Vile was sitting on his black leather swivel chair busily writing his opening speech on a scrap of paper. "Escaped?" He reacted angrily by throwing his pencil across the spacious walnut desk.

"Yes, your grumpiness."

"How dare they!" he bawled. "There's far too much of this escaping lark going on around here just lately, and I don't like it."

"Shall I take a few muscular guards and go after them, your not-very-pleasantness?"

"No!" Vile banged his fist down hard on the desktop. "Don't be so stupid!" Vile glared at him. "The last couple of times I've sent you out into Limbo to find folk, you've made a complete and utter mess of things, haven't you?"

"Yes, your scruffyness, I have. Sorry, I forgot."

"Besides, I don't give a tinker's cuss about a few missing Normans. Dream actors are ten a penny. It's just the principle of the thing. There are too many liberties being taken, Terrence."

"Yes, your gruesomeness, too many liberties."

"I want you to pin a note up on the notice board: the next person who escapes will be placed up to their Adam's apple in a vat full of flour and water."

"Nice one."

"Not so nice if you happen to be up to your neck in it, though." Vile grinned.

"Of course not, your ..." Terrence hesitated. A few small creases appeared on his brow.

Vile had never seen this expression on Terrence's face before. "Is that your thinking face, Terrence?"

Terrence nodded. "I was just thinking. How will you be able to put them in the flour and water if they've already escaped?"

Vile frowned. "It's called a deterrent, you lame brain. Are you questioning my wisdom?"

"No, your unsightlyness. I was just wondering, that's all."

"Well, don't wonder about it. Just do it!"

Terrence turned to go.

"But first –" Vile stopped him in his tracks. From under his black and gold pinstriped jacket he removed a gun-shaped thing from a shoulder holster.

"But first," he repeated. "Opening night of my new nightmare is just moments away. The coordinates have been set. Now get yourself into Limbo and select a suitable corridor for a haunted house Dreamspace." He handed Terrence the Digital Dreamscaper. "Off you go."

After a second or two he realised that Terrence hadn't gone. He was still standing there and pulling his thinking face again. "Now!" demanded Vile.

"Now? Oh yes. Now. I'm on my way." He turned to go once more, but then he stopped. "It's just that ..."

Vile's eyes narrowed dangerously. "What?"

"My fiancé. My betrothed. My other half. The love of my life. Where is she? I'd just like to let her know that I'm back." He took a step forward. "Where's Peg?"

"Where's Peggy Sue? That's what I'd like to know." Vile glanced up at the closed-circuit television monitors lined up along the wall. "I sent her out into Limbo ages ago to find out what's going on." He quickly hit a couple of black keys across the middle of the keypad. "And I haven't clapped eyes on her since."

Terrence was shocked. "You sent Peg out into Limbo?" He took another step forward. "On her own?"

Vile shrugged. "Yes. Have you got a problem with that, Terrence?"

Terrence did, and he really wanted to say so, but in the end he thought better of it. Instead, he shook his head. "No, your scepticness," he said. "I'm just disappointed she may miss your glorious new nightmare, that's all."

"We will *all* miss my glorious new nightmare if you don't get a move on, Terrence. Now go!"

"Yes, your cheerlessness. Sorry, your riff-raffness. I'm on my way."

Terrence turned, and this time he made it halfway back to the door.

"Oh, and Terrence, pop in and see how that Zygo-thingamajig and that Flage-what's-his-name are getting on in the custard." He grinned. "They should be more than ready to accept my job offer by now."

Terrence grinned too. "Yes, your grotesqueness."

"And Terrence."

Terrence had almost reached the door. Again he turned.

"One more thing." Vile was leaning back in his black leather swivel chair with his hands clasped together behind his head and his feet resting on the walnut desk. "Send in the prisoners."

#

Only a matter of moments later the prisoners were pushed through the door and shoved across the room by three muscular guards. Mr Good, Mugwump, and Arthur stood crestfallen a few feet away from the soles of Vile's shiny two-tone shoes.

Vile sat forward, swung his legs off the desk, and stood up. "You look like a beaten man, Good." He smirked as he approached his fellow dream ambassador.

Mr Good didn't reply. Instead, he looked around his old office. He was perturbed to see his exercise bike was missing and distressed because there was no sign of his beautiful little writing desk. To complete his disquiet, his priceless porcelain tea set was lacking a milk jug, a sugar bowl, several cups, saucers, side plates, and a teapot.

"Don't you believe it," replied Mugwump defiantly. "There's plenty more fight left in us."

Vile sighed. "Oh dear, and I thought you would accept defeat gracefully, like gentlemen. Perhaps I was expecting too much."

"We are far from defeated," added Mugwump.

Vile ignored the wizard and spoke to Mr Good. "Your plan to repossess this place has been the laughing stock of Scarydream Land. Do you know that?"

Mr Good wasn't listening. "My Welsh dresser," he said.

Puzzled, Vile turned his head to look at it. "What of it?"

"Look at the dust on those illuminated display shelves."

Vile stared at the Welsh dresser for a moment and then longer at Mr Good, trying to ascertain if he was serious or not. "Well, it's ..."

"It's a disgrace," said Mr Good. "That's what it is."

"Yes, but ..."

"And those monitor screens could do with a wipe over with a damp cloth," said Mugwump, joining in.

"These carpet tiles," said Mr Good, looking down. "When was the last time you ran the hoover over them?"

Vile's forehead was lined with a deep furrow. He had sent for the prisoners in order to taunt them, to deride them with mockery and sarcasm, and to make jeering remarks. But, instead they were teasing him. They were gaining the upper hand, and he had to put his foot down.

So he did. He stamped it down hard on Mugwump's topaz slippers.

"Salmon!" shrieked the wizard.

Vile grinned. "Now, where was I?" Oh yes," he remembered. "Laughing stock." He was back in a position of control.

"This plan of yours has got everyone giggling behind your back. Do you realise that, Good?" He sneered and gave his silver beard a sharp pull. "Summoning pesky kids from the physical world? What were you thinking of?" he taunted.

"A teddy boy and a Boy Scout too," he jeered. "And you put a bird inside my head?"

Mr Good and Mugwump looked at each other with puzzled expressions.

"Don't look at each other with puzzled expressions," shouted Vile. "I know you put that bird in my head. Or rather, your pet wizard here did."

He turned his attention to Mugwump. "So, the idiot who says 'salmon' annoyingly often." It was very close attention. "I'm not interested in how you did it. The questions are why, and what were you hoping to achieve by it?"

"My dear fellow," replied Mugwump. His round, normally jolly face was now round and somewhat baffled. "I haven't a clue what you're talking about."

Vile scoffed and prodded Mugwump's chest with his index finger. "Don't give me this 'I haven't a clue what you're talking about' stupidity! You're a wizard! Not a very good one, I grant you, but nevertheless you used some sort of magic! Somehow you put a bird between my ears! A small, flightless bird, I believe. Shouting its mouth off, it was – or rather its beak – about how good the plan is and how smart the pesky kids are and how I might as well give up, pack my bags, and go home!"

He stopped prodding and waited for a reaction. There wasn't one, so he continued. "Interestingly, I haven't heard from it for a while. I wonder why that is? Is it because I have won and you're a pathetic loser? Do you think?"

He slowly walked back towards his desk "There's something else." He circled the desk and made his way back towards them. "I heard a whisper that you have a guy who looks like me. Is this true?"

Mr Good and Mugwump, as one, turned their heads in the direction of Arthur.

Vile looked at Arthur for the first time. "Him!" he laughed. "Him? But he looks nothing like me!"

"You must admit there is a bit of a salmon."

"A resemblance," Mr Good clarified.

"Where?" Vile smirked. He took a closer look. He situated his considerable nose and ample chin inches from Arthur's considerable nose and ample chin.

Arthur was having difficulty breathing. He could feel a constriction in his chest. He was certain his blood pressure was rising and knew his ankles were slowly swelling. He was in desperate need of more medicine.

"There's a kindness in his face," decided Vile. "He's the sort of guy who loves his family, who buys his wife flowers when it isn't even her birthday, and who helps old ladies across the street!"

"Well, yes," Arthur wheezed. "I have been known to."

Vile moved even closer to Arthur's large, red, bulbous nose to intimidate him further. "I haven't!" he whispered menacingly.

Arthur gulped.

"There's an evil streak in me," Vile informed him. "See the look of depravity about the eyes? The touch of corruption around the mouth? I'm a nasty piece of work. And you –" With two fingers of each hand he drew some inverted commas in the air. "Are a nice guy."

"Thank you." Arthur exhaled forcibly through his nose.

"It wasn't a compliment," snapped Vile. He continued to stare at Arthur for a long moment before turning away and making his way back to his desk and the black leather swivel chair.

"Nobody," he continued, "nobody with any sense would mistake you for me."

"Terrence did," said Mr Good.

"I rest my case." Vile grinned. "Now, where are the pesky kids?"

Mr Good was momentarily flustered. "I don't know. I'm not sure." He wasn't expecting this question. He turned to Mugwump for assistance.

"They're lost," assisted Mugwump.

Mr Good nodded. "Yes, they're lost."

Vile was amused, and he did a little swivel in the chair. Terrence had already told him that Mr Good had sent the pesky kids out into Limbo. Out into Limbo to find Lord Riddle! It was no wonder they were lost, if they were roaming around Limbo searching in vain for a fictional character from a children's fairy tale.

"I'll tell you what I'll do," he told them. "To prove I have some compassion, I'll send a few muscular guards out to find them. I can't promise they won't hurt them, but at least they won't be lost anymore."

Mr Good paled. "Look, Vile, there's no need to bring the children into this."

Vile leaned forward and rested his elbows. "It was *you* who bought the children into this."

Mr Good squirmed.

"I could sit here and watch you squirm for the remainder of this dream span, Good. But I have the small matter of a fearful, gruesome, hideously horrid nightmare to attend to." Vile stood.

"What's to become of us?" asked Mugwump with just a little apprehension.

Vile shrugged. "Prepare to spend the rest of your dream spans in a cell that you might find a bit on the small side and quite damp."

The kindness and sparkle in Mr Good's deep blue eyes wavered not a whit.

Arthur experienced a tingling in his arms, a numbness in his legs, and a sudden urge to sit down. Mugwump frowned.

Vile noticed the wizard's brow contract. "You look displeased, fish face." He grinned. "Still suffering terribly with claustrophobia, are we?"

Mugwump nodded.

"You'll forgive me, I'm sure, if I decide not to believe a word of it," said Vile as he passed his hands quickly over the wizard's clothing and through his pockets until, from under his black robe, he found a large brass key.

"As I suspected. Now, I'll look after this." He grinned. "There'll be no escaping this time. But to make doubly sure, I'll put those three muscular guards in the cell with you."

There was a knock at the door, and it slowly opened.

Vile placed the large brass key in the inside pocket of his black and gold pinstriped jacket and looked round towards the door. "That will be Terrence now to tell me that the haunted house Dreamspace is set, all the dream actors are in place, and it's time for me to make my opening speech."

Indeed it was Terrence. But he didn't say any of those things. Instead, he was the bearer of bad news.

"Bad news?" growled Vile.

Terrence stood to the side of the three muscular guards. "It's those two tall ones with the funny names who you had put in the custard earlier, your unsavouryness."

Vile's eyes narrowed. "What about them?"

"They've —" Terrence hesitated. "They've taken a liberty, your terribleness."

Chapter 62

Flagellum stopped walking and looked up and down the long stretch of the cobalt blue corridor. "We're lost," he decided. This wasn't a sudden decision he had arrived at by any means. A strange feeling of having no clue as to his whereabouts had grown progressively stronger since they had left the cyan maze earlier.

"We're not lost," responded Zygote. "We just don't know where we are, that's all."

Flagellum gave Zygote a quizzical look. "Is there a difference?"

"Of course." Zygote nodded. "'Lost' suggests we're confused. 'Lost' implies we're helpless, and 'lost' insinuates we're a little bewildered."

Flagellum considered this for a moment. "And we're not?" he asked.

"Not at all," Zygote assured him. "We're heading in the right direction, I'm sure of it. If we keep walking we'll eventually reach the royal blue labyrinth."

"So what?" Flagellum shrugged. "Yet another labyrinth. This place is full of them."

"Yes," agreed Zygote. "But at the centre of that particular labyrinth is the home of the wizard who says 'salmon' a lot," he informed him as he resumed his determined walk.

Flagellum yawned and reluctantly followed.

"Do you know I once saw him?" recalled Zygote after a short pause.

Flagellum sighed. "I suppose that's another one of your little lies, is it?"

"It was several eras ago now," continued Zygote. "We were out walking when, lo and behold, there he was. He suddenly appeared through a row of colourful beads hanging in an invisible doorway."

"He was hanging in an invisible doorway?"

"Not him! The colourful beads were doing the hanging."

"I've never heard such nonsense!"

"He was wearing an ankle-length black robe with gold stars and a pointed hat."

"Poppycock!"

"It's true," insisted Zygote. "I was walking with my brother, Midrib, at the time."

Flagellum scoffed. "Oh no! Not the imaginary brother tale again? You know very well you're an only child!"

"I'm not!"

"You are!"

"I'm not!"

"You are!"

They bickered.

And as they continued to bicker they turned the final corner of the cobalt-blue maze and strode purposefully along a short passageway that linked it to the beginning of the cerulean blue labyrinth.

#

"It's them," whispered Larry.

The lanky dream actor was peeping around the opening turn of the cerulean blue labyrinth.

"Who?"

"It's them," repeated Larry. "Flagon and Zedonk."

"Are you sure?"

"Positive." Larry nodded positively.

"They're pretty odd names, aren't they?" said Barry. "A flagon is a container for holding liquids."

"And a zedonk is the offspring of a zebra and a donkey," added Harry.

Larry frowned. "Look, it doesn't matter what their names are. What matters is they're striding purposefully along the small passageway towards us."

#

"I'm not!"

"You are!"

"I'm definitely not!"

"I'm sure you are!"

Larry stepped out from the concealed turn and stood at the threshold of the new labyrinth. "Forgive me for interrupting your bickering," he uttered apologetically.

The two giants were surprised to see the tall and thin dream actor standing there before them. They halted and saw two further Dream Actors shuffle nervously into view too.

"I think you're right," said Barry. "Well, they certainly look like they could be giants."

"What a relief," said Harry. "I was sure it was going to be Vile and the muscular guards." He looked nervously back along the small passageway. "They are sure to be searching for us."

Larry smiled. "So, you've changed your mind, then?"

"What?" snapped Flagellum, grinding his enormous, crooked teeth.

"About helping Mr Good. You've changed your mind?"

"No." Flagellum shook his head.

"Yes," said Zygote. "Yes we have changed our minds."

He cast a sideways glance at his fellow giant, "Remember, Flagellum?"

"Poppycock!" said his fellow giant.

Zygote frowned. "So, your astrological prediction for this current dream span is poppycock, is it?"

Flagellum hesitated. "I didn't say that. It was you!"

"Me?"

"We're searching for a wizard who says 'salmon' a lot, you said. Someone who lives at the centre of some labyrinth or other, you said. We're not looking for Mr Good anymore, you said."

Zygote groaned. It was a prolonged, stressed groan. "I never said we weren't looking for Mr Good anymore!"

"You did!"

"I didn't! As well you know, Flagellum."

"You did!"

"Balderdash!" Zygote turned his back on Flagellum and calmly addressed Larry and the two other dream actors instead. "Yes," he told them. "We are on our way to help Mr Good, and when we reach the centre of the royal blue labyrinth we are sure to find him. After all, the wizard who says 'salmon' a lot is his old chum."

Barry gave Larry a little shove. "Go on!"

"Ask them," said Harry.

"I'm going to!" Larry took a step forward and cleared his throat. "You see," he began, "it's like this. We've been walking along these bluish corridors for ages now, and, well ..."

"We're confused," said Barry.

"And helpless," said Harry.

Larry nodded. "Yes, we're confused and helpless."

"Also a little bewildered," added Barry.

"That's true," agreed Larry. "A little bewildered too."

"And I've got a headache," said Harry.

Larry took a deep breath. "So, I was wondering."

Harry and Barry moved either side of him. He glanced at both of them in turn. "We were wondering ... if you would mind, too much, if we ..."

"Walk with you?" asked Barry.

"Some of the way?" Larry quickly added.

"Most of the way?" Harry put this forward for consideration.

"All of the way?" Barry suggested hopefully.

The three dream actors stood and waited for a response. A response was soon forthcoming.

"No chance!" responded Flagellum. "Never! There's no mention of you lot in my astrological prediction for this current dream span. So it's not going to happen! Ever! It's bad enough walking along these bluish corridors with him!" He gave Zygote a look. "But, you lot! You lot would slow us down terribly. Especially you!" he pointed the longest of his six fingers on his left hand towards Harry. "Those stumpy legs would never be able to keep up! I'm just not having it! No way!" he thundered. "No way." And just in case there was any doubt as to his feelings on the matter, he said it again. "No way!"

#

"Thank you ever so much for allowing us to walk with you," said Harry. They had more or less circumnavigated the cerulean blue labyrinth and were now very near the monestial blue corridors.

"Yes, we appreciate it," said Barry.

"Think nothing of it." Zygote smiled. "Many hands make light work."

Flagellum was sulking. "Too many cooks spoil the broth," he grumbled under his breath.

Everyone ignored him.

"We would never have found the centre of the royal blue labyrinth without you," admitted Larry. "Our sense of smell is not that good."

Zygote gave Larry a puzzled look. "Sense of smell?"

Larry nodded. "Yes, they say there's a strong whiff of fish there."

"Really? I never knew that," said Zygote.

"It comes from a very reliable source," Larry informed him.

"Which one? Tartar?" Flagellum chuckled to himself. "That's a reliable sauce. Especially with fish."

Everyone ignored him.

"Rumour has it, there's the odour of mackerel about the place," said Harry.

"I heard on the grapevine that it's more haddocky," said Barry.

"No, it's definitely mackerel."

"Haddock," insisted Barry.

Flagellum had heard enough. "I've never heard such nonsense!" he shouted from the rear.

"Actually," said Zygote. "If the centre of the royal blue labyrinth smells of fish at all ..."

"Which I very much doubt," Flagellum interjected.

"Then, surely, it must be salmon," Zygote reasoned. "Why else would he say it a lot? It makes sense."

The three dream actors considered this possibility as they all continued to walk around the gentle curve of the labyrinth.

"It does make sense," admitted Barry.

They all nodded.

"I'm surprised we haven't made the connection before," said Harry.

Larry knew why. "It's because we don't call him the wizard who says 'salmon' a lot, do we? That's why we haven't made the salmon connection. We know him by his given name."

"Given name?" asked Zygote. "Which is?"

"Mugwort."

Harry and Barry looked at each other and then at Larry in a bemused fashion.

"Larry, I don't think you've got that quite right," said Barry. "Mugwort is a perennial herbaceous plant."

"With aromatic leaves," added Harry.

It was Larry's turn to have a bemused demeanour. "Is it?"

"The wizard who resides at the centre of the royal blue labyrinth goes by the name of Mugwump," Barry told him.

"That's it," said Larry, remembering now. "Mugwump." He turned to Zygote. "That's what we call him."

"Poppycock!" That's what Flagellum thought of Larry's explanation. "Poppycock!" And he told him so to his face.

Larry frowned. Then suddenly he came to a halt. Immediately, his expression altered. His brows slowly lifted, the ridge over his eyes smoothed out, and the frown was replaced by a strange, cross-eyed countenance.

Everyone else stopped walking too and looked at Larry's strange, cross-eyed countenance.

"What's the matter?" asked Barry concerned. "Are you ill?"

"Can you smell mackerel?" queried Harry hopefully. "Is that it?"

"Salmon?" wondered Zygote.

"Parsley sauce?" Flagellum grinned.

Larry shook his head. It was none of the above. "A message," he rasped. The little bird with the razor-sharp claws was back and sitting comfortably in his frontal lobe. "A message," he murmured again.

Everyone looked at each other and shrugged.

"We are heading in the wrong direction," Larry announced. "We must turn around at once," he added with a croak, as if he had a frog in his throat instead of a kiwi bird in his head.

Zygote put his hand on Larry's shoulder. "This doesn't make sense," he told him. "We can't turn around now."

He faltered. His giant face suddenly twisted, his eyes and nose turning in the opposite direction to his mouth and chin. A bird with no tail, tiny two-inch wings, and a long, slender bill was standing in the left hemisphere of his cerebrum, giving out instructions. "We must locate a Dreamspace without delay," Zygote whispered hoarsely.

Next, in a small area somewhere in Harry's forebrain, the kiwi bird stamped its sharp, three-toed feet on the hard surface of the surrounding grey matter, causing his head to ache. "There's a purple, heather-clad moorland with a deep wooded gorge. We must go there immediately." He winced.

Flagellum sniggered. "Am I the only sane one here?"

"A Dreamspace featuring a haunted house on a hill," said Barry quietly. A bird with rough, greyish-brown feathers told him so. "Straight away," he added.

"At once." Larry nodded.

"Without delay," Zygote agreed.

"Immediately," Harry concurred.

Flagellum couldn't believe his beady eyes. His big, hairy ears were having difficulty comprehending it, too. He watched them dance from one foot to the other with their facial features awry and contorted, as if they had all drunk a tankard of a sour-tasting liquid. He listened to what they were saying. It was some hogwash about a bird inside their tiny minds, a little bird with no tail, tiny wings, rough, greyish-brown feathers, and razor-sharp claws. Apparently, the bird was telling them to find a particular Dreamspace.

"I've never heard such nonsense!" Flagellum scoffed. But as he scoffed he noticed Zygote, Larry, Harry, and Barry were already making their way back, hurriedly, along the cerulean blue corridor. "You're not really going, are you?" he called after them.

"Come back," he shouted. He stood with his hands on his hips and watched them disappear round the gentle curve of the labyrinth.

"This is poppycock!" He stood alone and in silence for a long moment. "So, why haven't I had a bird inside my head?"

Chapter 63

"Keith!" everyone exclaimed.

Well, everyone who knew who he was, that is.

"Who are you?" exclaimed Garry.

Keith gripped the back of the chocolate-brown sofa. "Gosh and double gosh!" he gasped.

Peggy Sue nudged Vince. "Who is it?" she asked.

Vince looked from the thickset lad with the wavy brown hair and dimples to Peggy Sue and back again. "It's Keith," he told her. "He's a Boy Scout," he added.

Peggy Sue had worked that bit out for herself.

Melvin strode from near the Welsh dresser to the middle of the centre of the royal blue labyrinth. "Where's Mr Good?" he demanded to know.

Vince moved forward and stood next to Melvin. "And the old-timer?"

Lorraine joined them. "What happened here, Keith?" she asked calmly.

Keith took a long, deep breath and held up his left hand. "I dropped my pencil," he began nervously.

"It was all quiet. Mr Good was exercising," he recalled. "Some upper-back stretches, I believe. Grandpa was dozing, Mr Salmon was polishing his golden wand, and Terrence was tied and gagged. We were just waiting. I was writing in my diary, deep in thought, and twirling my pencil like a drumstick." He raised his left hand and gave a quick demonstration. "Then one time I rotated it a little too rapidly, and I dropped it on the floor. I leaned over to pick it up, but I couldn't see it. It wasn't there. So I rested my notebook on the shiny chrome highlight strip on one arm of the chair, placed my water pistol on the other, and stood up. I looked under the chair at the front and down the side, but there was no sign of the pencil. On my hands and knees I crawled behind the chair in search of it. It was while I was scrambling around on the floor behind the chair that I heard the commotion. I said to myself: myself, you don't handle commotion or disturbances too well, so it might be for the best if you keep your head down. So I did, and I listened. I heard the heavy tread of many feet, lots of grunting, a vile-sounding voice shouting orders, and bangs and thuds like the sound of furniture being tipped over or thrown around. Then as suddenly as it had all started, the uproar was over. There was silence. I didn't move for a long while. I don't know how long I sat there. Time is different here, you see. I'm not sure how many revolutions of the Dream/Time Continuum I waited before I dared to look. But when I did look, I saw I was all alone. My grandpa was gone." He sighed. "Mr Good and Mr Salmon were gone too. Even Terrence, who had been tied to one of those teak dining chairs, wasn't there anymore. I didn't know what to do. I felt sure they were going to come back for me. So it was no surprise when some time later I heard footsteps approaching. I was terrified. I grabbed the water pistol, and I hid behind the sofa this time."

His audience listened to his story with rapt attention.

"But then I heard Melvin's voice and Lorraine's too, and I knew it was safe to reveal myself."

No one spoke for a long moment. Then Vince took a step forward. "Did you find the pencil?" he asked.

Melvin frowned. "We have more important things to worry about than a pencil, Vince."

Lorraine nodded. "Mr Good has been kidnapped, if you hadn't noticed!"

"What now?" wondered Peggy Sue with a sigh.

They all turned to Lord Riddle. Gone was the sombrero. In its place he wore a small, round, sporty hat with a low crown and a small, upturned brim. He sat cross-legged on the bright orange carpet playing Ludo with an imaginary friend.

"Perfect but inconclusive thought?" Garry asked him.

Lord Riddle didn't take his eyes off the invisible game. He was in a winning position. Three of his blue pieces had already circumnavigated the board. Two of them were safely back in the triangle, and the third was

343

halfway along the home column. He threw a six, smiled, and looked up. "Scheme for part of garden," he replied.

Garry nodded and turned to the others. "Fear not, Lord Riddle has a plot," he assured them. "A sort of plan."

They all breathed a sigh of relief. But before they could ask any further questions, Lord Riddle was upright. Their eyes never left him, yet not one of them saw him climb to his feet as he moved from sitting to standing instantaneously. Then with his feet held tightly together and his knees bent, he advanced towards the chocolate-brown sofa with a series of little jumps. "A rectangular piece of luggage causes it," he said directly to Keith.

The Boy Scout was taken aback. He didn't understand what the odd sort of a fellow wearing the funny hat was saying.

"Causes what?" wondered Melvin.

"Causes it," said Garry. "Is an anagram, of course."

Melvin shrugged and rolled his eyes. "Of course!"

Garry moved alongside Lord Riddle facing Keith. "The suitcase?" he asked him. "Lord Riddle wants to know if you have it."

"The suitcase? Lord Riddle?" Keith gasped, and suddenly he realised. "Gosh and double gosh! It was you!"

He reached down, and with the push of a button he released the locking trolley mechanism. "It was you who summoned me!"

He stared in awe at the dream ambassador for those peculiar, strange, inexplicable dreams that make no sense as he wheeled the plum and grey suitcase out into the open. "It was, wasn't it?"

Lord Riddle grinned.

#

"I shouldn't be here," grumbled Arthur. "I'm weakened by old age. I'm feeble and infirm. I'm a decrepit man who can hardly walk," he griped as he sat on the wooden bench below the barred window.

Mr Good sat next to him. He ran his fingers through his tangled silvery beard several times as he contemplated the contents of the cardboard box resting on his lap. "The porcelain cups, saucers, and side plates are all broken into little pieces," he lamented. He picked up what was left of the teapot. "The spout is missing," he whined.

Mugwump was standing amongst the three muscular guards.

"The majority of my internal organs are not functioning properly," Arthur moaned.

"Vile has destroyed the Ancient Tea Set of Firmamentum!" Mr Good declared. "The man is totally lacking in aesthetic refinement."

He shook his head and sighed. "This beautiful tea set was also a part of his heritage. It belonged to his ancestors too."

"And large portions of my body are either hurting or aching," continued Arthur. "Or both," he added.

"Ugh!" said Mugwump.

"Ugh!" replied one of the guards.

"Ugh! Ugh!" grunted the wizard.

"Ugh!" responded another guard.

Mr Good looked up from the box and watched Mugwump and the guards for a long moment. "If I didn't know better, old chum, I would say you were having a conversation with those muscular guards just then."

Mugwump turned and smiled. "Yes, I am."

"I didn't know you could speak their language, young Mugwump. In fact, come to think of it, I didn't know they had a language at all."

Mugwump nodded. "This type of speech is more sophisticated than you might think."

Mr Good was puzzled by this. "But all they say is –" He grunted. "Ugh!"

"It's a vernacular that relies heavily on patterns of stress and intonation. It's the emphasis you put on the *Ugh!* that makes the difference."

"Surely there can't be that many different ways you can emphasise an *Ugh!*" Arthur joined in with a grunt.

"Mark my salmons, you could explain the entire history of the mysterious and fascinating world of dreams from the Big Bang to the present dream span inclusive in Guardspeak if you so desired."

"How interesting," said Mr Good as he put the teapot back and placed the box on the floor under the wooden bench.

"Ugh?" asked Mugwump, turning back to the guards.

"Ugh! Ugh!" answered the guard standing closest to the pump and storage tank.

"Ugh! Salmon! Ugh?"

"Ugh!" said the guard nearest to the large metal door, nodding.

Mr Good was intrigued. "What are you talking about now?" he asked.

Mugwump took a step away from the guards and one closer to Mr Good. "We're having a most interesting discussion on astrology, actually."

"Fascinating," said Arthur, trying to sound fascinated.

"Did you know that astrology played quite a large part in medicine up to the late medieval times?"

Mr Good shook his head slowly.

"Neither did I." Mugwump laughed.

"Ugh?" asked a guard.

"Ugh!" Mugwump shrugged. "I'll ask him. What star sign are you, Mr Good?"

"Me? Star sign? Leo. Why?"

"Ugh!"

"Ugh!" The three muscular guards all nodded and smiled at the same time. "Ugh! Ugh!"

The bright metallic yellow brooch at Mugwump's waist glistened with little gleams of purplish-red light that shone through the bars of the window. "They say they could've guessed you were a Leo – fair-minded, caring, and tolerant. A typical Leo, evidently."

Mr Good smiled sadly. "Well, thank them very much for the compliment. But I'm locked up in a cold and damp room, an abominable new nightmare is about to première to an unsuspecting worldwide audience, and to top it all my priceless tea set has been smashed to smithereens. So forgive me if I'm not feeling particularly caring or tolerant at the moment."

Mugwump sighed. "Something will turn up, Mr Good," he replied tactfully.

Mr Good stood, kicked off his flip-flops, hitched up the hem of his calf-length brown tunic, and climbed onto the wooden bench to look out into Limbo. "Maybe it already has," he said after a short while had elapsed. "Your knowledge of Guard Language may come in jolly useful, old chum."

"Are you concocting a plan, Mr Good?" It was Melvin who asked the question.

"Possibly," said Mr Good without looking round or realising who had spoken.

"Plan C, is it?" Lorraine speculated curiously.

Mr Good pushed his face against the bars and looked along the magenta corridor as far as he could see. "What was that?" he asked distractedly.

"This plan that you are possibly concocting," continued Melvin, "will be called Plan C, I assume?"

Straining upward on his tiptoes, Mr Good looked down the corridor the other way. "Plan C?" With the slightest of nods and the merest of shrugs he agreed. "Yes, young Melvin, Plan C. I rather think it ..." He faltered.

When he turned he saw Melvin grinning up at him. Lorraine was too.

"Melvin, but? What is? How did?" Mr Good was so surprised he was struggling to form sentences.

Vince was next to step out from the interior of the rip in the bedsheet of space and time. "We're back," he announced. He turned to Peggy Sue who was holding his hand. "Mr Good, this is the very beautiful Peggy Sue. She is y'actual Vile's uncle."

Peggy Sue laughed and gave Vince a playful slap on his upper arm. "You are silly, Vince."

She stepped forward and addressed Mr Good. "Very pleased to meet you, your Excellence." She curtsied. "Vince has got that slightly wrong, by the way. Actually, Vile is my uncle, unfortunately."

Before Mr Good could comment on that incredible revelation, Garry and Keith materialised out of thin air too.

"Grandpa!" called out Keith, pulling his suitcase behind him.

"Keith!" beamed Arthur. They hugged and sat together on the wooden bench.

Mr Good recognised the small, mouselike character in the short-sleeved black polo shirt and khaki multi-pocket combat shorts as one of his dream actors. With the aid of Melvin's hand, he stepped carefully down from the wooden bench just as an odd sort of a fellow wearing a funny hat appeared.

Lorraine cleared her throat. "Mr Good, may I introduce ..."

"Lord Riddle!" gasped Mr Good.

Part 4

What Is Black and White and Black and White and Black and White?

Chapter 64

Vile entered the haunted house through a side door. He closed it, leaned back against it, and paused to savour the moment, his moment of victory. At the conclusion of the moment he punched the air and allowed himself a triumphant grin before making his way quickly along a couple of narrow passageways, past the kitchen and the heat of the furnace and ovens, the buttery, the pantry, the top of the cellar steps, and finally through an archway into the long medieval hall where everyone was waiting.

The dream actors were seated at a very long table with trestles, and the muscular guards stood at intervals around the perimeter of the hall. Vile made his way to the dais at the far end. It was a part of the floor raised a step above the rest of the hall. He opened his mouth to speak, but he stopped himself when, from his vantage point, he saw Terrence applying a light lubricant to the hinges of the panelled front door.

"What are you doing?" he bellowed.

It was an impressive front door, set into an arch and partially glazed with a diamond-shaped pattern.

Terrence looked up from his task. "Bit of a creak on this door, your loathsomeness. Thought I'd sort it out before we get started."

Vile frowned. "Bit of a creak?" he shouted. "Look, when the dream person knocks on that door and I slowly open it, I think a bit of a creak at that point would be quite atmospheric." He paused as the large fire crackled and the light from the candles stuck into metal lanterns flickered. "There's nothing like a good creak to put the willies up someone!" he grinned.

Terrence backed away from the door. "Sorry, your uncleanness. I didn't think."

Vile nodded. "Nothing new there," he muttered under his breath.

"Now." His voice boomed down the middle of the long line of dream actors sitting both sides of the table before him. "I am sure you Normans are keen to get started with the acting, but first I have an opening speech." From the back pocket of his cuffed trousers he removed several scraps of paper. He arranged the notes into some sort of order, and when he was satisfied with that he looked up and addressed his audience. "We are gathered here this dream span," he began. But before he could say another word, he saw something that disturbed him. The front door was still open. But it wasn't that that troubled him. "Terrence!" he yelled.

Terrence was sitting at the far end of the table next to a lunatic holding a half-moon sod cutter. He stood up.

Vile spoke slowly. "Is it —" He couldn't believe he was asking this question. "Sunny outside?"

Terrence nodded. "Yes, your ruthlessness, it's a beautiful day for it."

Vile glared. "A beautiful day for it?" His stare was a fierce and angry one.

"A beautiful day for it?" he repeated it an octave higher this time. "This is a nightmare, you meathead! A fearful, gruesome, hideously horrid nightmare! It's not a picnic by the river!"

The dream actors shifted uneasily in their seats.

"I need thunder." He stamped his foot. "The loud and explosive kind. I want lightning, and I want it in jagged streaks across the night sky." He stamped his other foot. "And I must have torrential rain," he demanded and stamped both feet at the same time. All that stamping of feet was making Terrence anxious. "Sort it out, Terrence," said Vile sternly but a touch calmer. "Now!"

"Yes, your rotten-to-the-coreness. I will. I'm on my way." He started to walk, and then he hesitated.

"How?" he asked nervously. "How do I do that?"

Vile exhaled heavily. "There'll be a distribution board, probably down in the cellar. You'll find a switch has been turned off or a fuse will have tripped out. It shouldn't be too difficult to figure out, even for you." He grinned.

Terrence nodded. "Leave it to me, your despicableness," he said and made his way towards the archway in a determined fashion.

"If you're scared of the dark," Vile said, still grinning, "take a muscular guard down there with you." He watched Terrence disappear from view and then turned his attention back to his notes. With his expression serious again, he looked up, paused, and waited for the murmuring and mumbling amongst the Dream Actors to subside. "We," he began, "are gathered here this dream span ..."

#

Amidst the hullabaloo that ensued in the moments that followed the first-ever meeting between the two dream ambassadors, two incidents worthy of note occurred.

The three muscular guards sprang forward instinctively, as they were well trained to do in times of disorder, disturbance, or conflict. In the middle of so many in so small a space, they could have wreaked a lot of havoc. But before any havoc could be wreaked, they stopped, looked at themselves, looked at each other, and suddenly decided they'd had enough of pushing and shoving and being mean to folk. They explained all this to Mugwump. With a sequence of grunts they told him that when next they met up with the other muscular guards, they would persuade all of them to this new way of thinking too.

Also, and perhaps most notably, the pump room moved. It disengaged itself from the rest of the Palace of Somnium and floated away.

"What's happening?" asked Arthur, feeling his delicate stomach lurch.

Vince held on tightly to Peggy Sue.

Lord Riddle was sitting on the wooden bench holding, with both hands, an imaginary steering wheel with his right wellington boot pressed down heavily on a non-existent accelerator.

Lorraine planted her feet firmly. "I'm sure it's a part of Lord Riddle's plan," she said.

"More of a plot, actually," Garry corrected her.

"Plot, plan – either way he's going to return Mr Good to the Palace of Somnium," said Lorraine, "where he belongs."

Mr Good smiled sadly. "It's too late for that, I'm afraid, old chum."

Twelve pairs of eyes turned to look at Mr Good as Lord Riddle changed gear with his left hand and the pump room hastened forward smoothly.

"The nightmare has already begun." Mr Good sighed. "At this very moment Vile will be making his opening speech."

"Opening speech?" said Melvin. "If he's only making his opening speech, does that mean ..."

"The nightmare hasn't actually started?" wondered Peggy Sue.

Mr Good shrugged. "Strictly speaking, yes," he agreed. "But ..."

"The nightmare doesn't start until the first Dream Person falls asleep," Mugwump informed them.

"So there's still time?" asked Keith hopefully.

"Unlikely," said Mr Good.

Then the pump room stopped with a click.

#

Holding a lantern with a metal frame and sides made of thin, transparent horns, Terrence made his way carefully down the steps. He counted them as he went slowly down into the gloom. He counted three, four, and five and then took a turn to the right, where he had to bend under a low beam. Eventually he counted thirteen steps before he reached the dirt floor of the cellar.

It was a large, empty space, very dark and very spooky. He wished now he had brought a muscular guard or two with him. He wanted to, but he knew Vile would have ridiculed him for the rest of his dream spans. It wasn't worth it. He held up the lantern, hoping the light from the candle would permeate the room. It didn't.

He heard something, a sort of click. He listened again. There was no sound at all apart from his own heavy breathing. Cautiously, he made his way forward into the darkness towards where he thought the sound had emanated from. He walked on, looking around and about him nervously all the time, until he reached the far end of the cellar. He found nothing, only a large metal door. It had a keyhole but no handle. He pulled at it with his free hand, but it was locked. If the distribution board was behind this door, then he was stumped. He bent down to look through the keyhole but stopped himself. He suddenly had a funny feeling he was being watched. Except it wasn't funny at all. Actually, it gave him the heebie jeebies. He decided to move away from the metal door quickly, follow the wall round, and make his way back towards the cellar steps.

#

Lord Riddle applied the hand brake with a sharp pull. He stood up and glided across the pump room as if his wellington boots were on casters. They all stood aside and allowed him through, each of them wondering what was about to happen next. What happened next was interesting. Lord Riddle stood on one of the three thick, black iron pipes and pushed his head through the wall. He looked out into what was once a view of the undercroft and a small, narrow stairway, panelled in oak, that led up to the great central hall. That was back at the Palace of Somnium. What scene Lord Riddle was looking out on now, none of them could begin to guess.

When he pulled his head back into the room he was wearing a different hat. It was a hat shaped like a truncated cone and trimmed with a tassel. He observed them all, gathered there bathed in the lemony yellow light that shone through the barred window above the wooden bench. "It's safe to promote unspoilt beach," he said as his sharp facial features softened into a wry smile.

All eyes turned to Garry for a translation.

"The coast is clear," came the reply.

But it wasn't Garry who said it. It was Mugwump.

If Lord Riddle was surprised, he didn't show it. He wafted down from the black pipe and landed gracefully on the floor by the storage tank.

Mr Good narrowed his eyes. "Don't tell me you can speak Daftness too, old chum?" he asked.

The wizard shrugged. "I've got a smattering."

"A smattering?"

"A superficial knowledge," he admitted. "But don't ask me to conjugate any irregular verbs or I will be well and truly salmoned." He grinned.

Then Lord Riddle revealed the final phase of his plot.

Chapter 65

Three-quarters of the way back along the right-hand wall of the cellar, Terrence found a double wooden door, one side of which was slightly ajar. He pulled it open wider. It wasn't a room but a wiring closet. He pushed the lantern inside and saw the small area was a mess of wires, cables, and conduit. He released the vertical bolt on the inside of the second door. Inside he found meters with dials and what he hoped was the distribution board with circuit breakers arranged in two columns.

He looked back along the pitch-dark cellar in the direction of the large metal door. Whoever or whatever had been watching him there had scared him a lot. Right now he wanted nothing more than to run away, up the cellar steps and into the light of the medieval hall. But he knew he couldn't. He had to find the fuse that had tripped or the switch that was turned off.

He held the lantern closer and strained his eyes to see, but nothing was marked up. He flipped a few breakers back and forth at random and listened for thunder. He didn't hear thunder. He didn't hear a torrential downpour either, and he didn't hear someone or something approaching him across the dirt floor.

"Ahem!" said the someone or something.

Terrence wheeled round, fully expecting to see a ghostly apparition standing there holding his arms out and advancing towards him. But it wasn't a ghostly apparition. It was something far more terrifying. It was Vile.

Terrence dropped the lantern and slumped back against the wooden door, his breathing fast and deep and his face a deathly shade of ashen. "You startled me, your atrociousness."

Arthur picked up the lantern and waited patiently for him to recover. "I didn't mean to frighten you," he said kindly.

Terrence took some more long breaths. "I wasn't expecting you, your badness."

"Of course not." Arthur nodded sympathetically. "How could you?"

Before Terrence could comprehend Vile's tolerant disposition he noticed an orange glow in the distance.

Arthur pointed at it and nodded. "She's back." He smiled.

"She?" whispered Terrence. "She?"

He looked and fancied he saw a figure standing within the glow. The figure had a figure he knew well. "Peg?" he gasped.

Arthur held out the lantern, and Terrence took it and stumbled through the lightlessness of the cellar towards her. She was smiling and holding her arms out to him. He was holding his arms out to her too. But with each step he took, Peggy Sue took a step backwards away from him and deeper into the orange shaft of light, deeper into the rip in the bedsheet of space and time.

Terrence hesitated. He looked round for encouragement from Vile, but Vile wasn't there.

"Peg!" Terrence cried out as he reached the entrance. The glow had an entrance? He didn't dwell on the strangeness of that. His only concern now was reaching Peggy Sue and holding her in his arms once more. She was beckoning him, enticing him with her finger at the other end of the passage. "I'm coming, Peg," he told her as he lifted his feet and moved closer with clumsy steps. Ahead of him he saw a roller shutter door lift noisily. Peggy Sue exited through it hurriedly only to be replaced by four others. He recognised the first three immediately. It was the pesky kids and Mr Good. He didn't know how that was possible, but there they were. The other was an odd sort of a fellow wearing a funny hat. "Where's Peg?" he demanded, stepping forward towards the door. But before he could get there, it quickly lowered and closed.

"She doesn't want to see you," Lorraine told him.

"She didn't even want to be in the same room as you," added Melvin.

Terrence turned. "That's madness! Peg and I are getting married. She's my fiancée. Now, where is she?" he snapped. As he snapped, he glanced to his left and saw a line of chairs with muscular guards occupying three of them. "Guards!" He grinned. "Excellent!"

Two of the guards were sitting with their feet up on the coffee table, and the other was engrossed in a magazine. Terrence was concerned about their general disinterest.

"Are you dopes just going to sit there and let these pesky kids take the mickey?" he shouted. "Do something! Start hurting people!"

The guards grunted quietly to each other.

"A defection by the overly muscled, true it is," said Lord Riddle.

Terrence looked at the guy in the long, striped gown with disdain. "Who are you, exactly?"

The roller shutter door lifted again.

Terrence's heart skipped. "Peg?" he called out hopefully. But it wasn't Peggy Sue. It was Garry. A dream actor? Terrence frowned. This was getting confusing. He turned back to the guards. "You lot! Run amuck! Do some punching!"

"Not this time, old chum," said Mr Good. "The guards are on our side now."

"On your side? You'll never persuade them to go over to your side because … because … well, because they've always been on our side. They've always been with Vile, that's why!"

Lord Riddle hopped forward. "Detailed soundings have revealed it is well developed at sea level," he announced.

"What did he say?" asked Terrence with a heavy sigh laced with a touch of annoyance.

"It is time to continue with Lord Riddle's plot," said Garry.

"Lord Riddle!" Terrence shook his head in despair. "Has Scarydream Land gone completely crazy?"

"A mutual transfer, a vice versa of minds for the characters extreme," continued Lord Riddle, tapping Mr Good on the shoulder. "How card players show affection."

"Hold hands," said Garry to Mr Good. "He wants you to hold hands with Terrence." Garry stood between Melvin and Lorraine and watched events unfold. "What happens next is going to be most unusual," he told them.

"Do what?" Terrence was horrified. "I'm not holding his hand!"

He reversed slowly away as Mr Good approached, and as he did so he launched a final appeal to the guards. "Protect me!" he demanded. "I order you to push and shove them. That's all you're good for, after all."

Mr Good took Terrence's hand.

Garry was right. What happened next was most unusual.

"Vanilla essence. A blending of digits into one," cried Lord Riddle.

A low, vibrating, humming sound filled the waiting area within the rip in the bedsheet of space and time. Terrence and Mr Good, with their hands clasped together, writhed around as if electricity were coursing through the bulging veins of their hands, arms, and neck. After a few seconds the buzzing ceased, and they separated.

Melvin broke the silence. "Are you …"

"All right?" Lorraine asked.

Mr Good and Terrence stared at each other, dazed and confused. Their minds and personalities had been exchanged.

"How extraordinarily strange and strangely extraordinary," said Terrence.

"You'll never get away with this," said Mr Good.

#

With the opening speech completed, Vile was standing on the dais and barking out orders to the assembled dream actors sitting around the very long table. "Now, you Normans, to your starting points," he bawled. "Firstly, I want the demons and the devils in the ballroom." He waited for them to stand and begin to amble away. "Hurry it along," he shouted after them. "Next, the vampires," he decided. "I want you in the conservatory. Zombies, make your way to the library."

He paused as the vampires and zombies stood, scraping their chairs along the floor as they did so. He watched them make their way out of the medieval hall, through the arch, before continuing.

"Werewolves." He looked for them and spotted them sitting together halfway along on his left-hand side. "Dining room," he ordered, and then he grinned. "Grotesque classical mythological characters, will you stand?" There was something about these grotesque classical mythological characters that made him want to taunt them. "To the billiard room now!" He bellowed. As they stood he picked out Cyclops again. "Cyclops, that's quite a shiner you got there. What happened? Walk into a door?" he smirked.

Cyclops thought it might be for the best if he didn't make eye contact with Vile. Instead, the single round, black eye in the middle of his forehead stared straight ahead as he scurried away and out of sight.

"Now, evil stepmothers and wicked witches, go and wait in the lounge."

Amidst the confusion of many dream actors moving in many different directions, three muscular guards slipped into the hall unseen. They mingled with the other guards and began the task of persuading them to the new way of thinking.

"Finally, the rest of you." Vile looked along the length of the table and saw Dracula, Frankenstein, a few ghouls, a lunatic holding a half-moon sod cutter, and a dream character with an antisocial personality disorder still sitting and awaiting instructions. "Upstairs." He pointed to the oak staircase that opened at the back of the hall through an arch and ascended two storeys round a square well. "Find a bedroom each," he told them and waved them away dismissively.

Mr Good entered the hall and stood before the raised platform looking up at Vile.

"Where the heck is Terrence?" Vile groaned. He should be back by now. It was only a simple task: Find the fuse that had tripped or the switch that had been turned off. What could be easier? "Where is he?" He grumbled impatiently. He was just about to consider the possibility of maybe going to find the nitwit when he saw him standing before the raised platform looking up at him. "Terrence! There you are! What took you?"

"I came as quick as I could," replied Mr Good.

Vile moved quickly to a deep, recessed bay window at the end of the dais and pulled back the heavy lined curtain. "It's still daylight," he said. "The sun is still shining."

The only sign of thunder was the look on Vile's face as he turned to Terrence. "It's still a beautiful day for it," he said sarcastically. "Why is that?"

Mr Good pulled nervously at the tight sleeves of his black moth-eaten blazer. "Bit of a problem, old chum," he said.

Vile looked down on him with a furious scowl. "I don't want problems, Terrence, I want solutions," he growled. "And don't call me 'old chum'!"

"Sorry, old ch – I mean, sorry."

"I'm not your chum. You'll do well to remember that."

Instinctively, Mr Good reached for his tangled silvery beard, but he didn't find it there. Instead he ran his fingers through the uncombed, drab, pale brown hair. "If you'd just let me explain," he pleaded.

Vile shouted. "I don't want to hear your explanations, Terrence!"

"It's the pesky kids."

"I'm not interested in your pathetic excuses. I don't care about …" He faltered, stopped pacing up and down the length of the dais, and stared at Terrence. "What? What did you say?"

"The pesky kids," said Mr Good. "They're here."

"Where?" He looked around the medieval hall. Surprisingly, the look was an anxious one. He had a feeling about these pesky kids that began the very first moment he saw them.

"In the cellar."

Vile's eyes narrowed. "What they doing down there?"

"Plotting. They are endeavouring to put a stop to your new nightmare."

"It's a bit late for that." Vile laughed unconvincingly. "Any moment now the first dream person will be knocking on that door.

Mr Good shook his head.

Vile looked at him. "Why are you shaking your head, Terrence?"

"They said that nobody is going to be knocking on that door. Ever."

"Ever!" He slackened his wide white kipper tie so he could breathe a little more easily. "I don't think I've ever heard such rot." Vile stepped down from the raised platform a worried man. "What else did they say?"

"Apparently they've opened a hotel out there on the moors, a small bed and breakfast establishment."

Vile just stared. His mind boggled.

"So when the Dream Person walks across the heather and the open wasteland seeking sanctuary," continued Mr Good, "they simply book in there overnight as opposed to the scary haunted house up on the hill."

Vile grimaced.

Smart.

Vile frowned.

I told you earlier those schoolchildren were smart. Did I not?

The bird inside his head was back. Vile had thought he was rid of it for good. His mood dipped considerably.

No, you haven't got rid of me. I've been here all along. I've just been sitting back and watching you make a fool of yourself.

"I think you've been defeated," said Mr Good finally.

The end is nigh, Vile.

"Defeated?" he roared. "Defeated? I don't know the meaning of the word 'defeat'!"

To overcome in a contest or battle. To thwart or frustrate.

"We'll see about that." Vile pushed Mr Good forward forcibly. "Lead on, Terrence. I'll soon put an end to their little game. Nobody thwarts or frustrates me."

But as they reached the arch Vile hesitated. "The cellar?" he asked. "Is it dark down there?"

Mr Good nodded.

"And spooky?"

Again Mr Good nodded.

"Maybe we should take a few of the guards with us."

#

"What's bright orange and sounds like a parrot?"

"A carrot."

The conveyor belt of riddles inside Terrence's mind had been inactive for a while, but suddenly, without warning, it started rolling again.

"Why did the banana go to the doctor?" he asked. He was sitting on a chair in the orange glow of the waiting area.

Lorraine had to keep reminding herself that the person sitting next to her, wearing the calf-length brown tunic, wasn't really Mr Good. The deep blue eyes were the same, but they lacked the sparkle and kindness now. It was his body, but it was Terrence's mind and personality. "Because it wasn't peeling very well?"

Melvin looked up from his magazine and smiled at that one. Garry, sitting next to him with his arms folded, had to smile too.

"What's black and white and read all over?" Terrence was going to have fun with this one.

"When you say read, do you mean red? The colour?" Lorraine was going to enjoy spoiling this joke for him. She picked up the latest edition of the *Dream Times* from the table and waved it at Terrence. "It's a newspaper." She sighed because that was the oldest and corniest joke ever.

"No." Terrence shook his head.

"A sunburned badger?"

"No." Terrence grinned. The grin got lost somewhere in the bird's nest of his silver beard.

"A skunk wearing too much lipstick?" she suggested.

Terrence frowned, undid the belt of white cord around his waist, and then tied it again angrily. "What's black and white and eats like a horse?" he asked.

"A zebra."

Terrence took a deep breath. "What is black and white and black and white and black and white?"

Lorraine opened her mouth to answer, and then she hesitated and closed it. Terrence was delighted because obviously Lorraine didn't know.

Melvin skimmed his magazine across the top of the coffee table. "I know that one." He smiled and leaned forward.

"You do?" Lorraine was surprised because Melvin didn't do jokes.

"It's a ..."

Before Melvin could hit Lorraine with the punch line, he was interrupted by a noisy disturbance at the entrance. They both looked round to see the dream ambassador for nightmares advancing through the orange glow a stride or two ahead of someone he clearly thought was Terrence.

Vile saw the pesky kids first, and he quickly assumed a facial expression that was most probably contempt. Then he saw Mr Good, and his countenance changed from a contemptuous one to a shocked, surprised, and angry one. "What are you doing here?" he snarled.

Terrence stood up and slipped his feet into his flip-flops. "I'm not Mr Good, your lousiness. I'm Terrence."

"I gave clear instructions that you should be locked up in the cell!" He turned. "Terrence! Why isn't he locked up in the cell?"

Mr Good shrugged. "I'm not Terrence, old chum. I'm Mr Good."

Terrence stepped forward, and Mr Good reached out his hand. Terrence took it without objection. They did the writhing, the electric coursing, and the veins bulging thing for a few seconds until the low, vibrating, humming sound ended.

Vile had seen enough. "Enough!" he shouted and turned to the guards behind him. "Guards! Round them all up and ... and." He wavered, unsure what to do with them all. "And ... just guard them for a bit. I've got a fearful, gruesome, hideously horrid nightmare to be seeing to."

"Ugh!" said one or two of the guards.

"Ugh! Ugh!" grunted some others.

"Hurry up!" Vile demanded. He stared at them, waiting for at least one to spring into action.

They didn't move.

"Now!" he yelled.

Then an odd sort of a fellow wearing a funny hat appeared and stood amongst the guards.

"Who the heck are you?" roared Vile.

Lord Riddle addressed the guards closest to him. "Hug! Hug!" he grunted cryptically. It was an anagram. Immediately two of the guards, the two best at crosswords, rushed forward and proceeded to push and shove Vile and Terrence forward.

"Stop it!" shrieked Terrence.

"What do you think you're doing?" Vile staggered forward. Then he managed, for a moment, to stand his ground and look back along the passage to the line of muscular guards standing at the entrance.

"I command you to do something!" he commanded. "I'm ordering you to badly injure all these people. What are all those muscles for if not for a bit of physical violence?" He sneered.

The guards placed their thumbs on their noses and waved four fingers at him. The roller shutter door lifted, and Vile and Terrence were sent flying through it. At the same time a sling was strung up around them as Vince, Mugwump, and Keith pulled on a rope and lifted them up, their weight supported from the beams above.

"Terrence, do something. I'm dangling several feet in the air!" Vile was frantic.

"So I see, your hideousness," replied Terrence. "But, unfortunately, so am I."

"Get me down!" demanded Vile. As he swung round he saw there wasn't anyone there. There wasn't anyone to get him down. He was in an empty room. He suddenly realised he was dangling in a cell – and not just any old cell but the cell in the basement of the Palace of Somnium.

How did that happen?

"Terrence!" he growled. "This is your fault!"

Chapter 66

With the curtains open the medieval hall was not so gloomy now. The large windows, made up of a multitude of small rectangular panes separated by thin mullions, invited in the sunshine.

Mr Good was sitting on the floor with tall posture. "What Vile has done to the Ancient Tea Set of Firmamentum is unforgivable," he commented as he eased his feet up and placed his soles together, which allowed his knees to come up and out to the side.

"Not to mention what he has done to your exercise bike and your beautiful little writing salmon," said Mugwump, sitting at the nearest chair.

Mr Good sighed. He rested his hands on his ankles and lowered both knees slowly towards the ground. Immediately he felt the stretch along the inside of his thighs.

Keith pushed the suitcase underneath the long trestle table and sat next to the wizard. Several dream actors entered cautiously through the archway and sat alongside and opposite them. Others descended the oak staircase at the back of the long medieval hall and pushed past Melvin and Lorraine, who were sitting on the bottom step.

"You never did tell me," said Lorraine.

"Tell you what?" asked Melvin.

"What's black and white and black and white and black and white."

"You're right," Melvin smiled. "I didn't, did I?"

Vince and Peggy Sue were sitting, whispering, giggling, and holding hands slightly away from the others when Lord Riddle suddenly appeared behind them and placed a hand on their shoulders. "I sense bedazzled vibes from you both," he told them. "Inamorata, a question to pop," he added.

Garry was at Lord Riddle's side. "He says he hopes you'll be very happy together," the dream actor explained.

Peggy Sue smiled and gave Vince's hand a squeeze. Vince blushed.

"Mr Good." Melvin thought the moment was right to broach the subject.

"Yes, young Melvin?" smiled Mr Good as he climbed nimbly to his feet.

"It's not that I want to, you understand. Well, not straight away necessarily, but ..."

"What Melvin is trying to say, Mr Good," said Lorraine as she stood up too, "is can we go back now? Home, that is."

"Our parents must be worried silly, and ..."

Mr Good laughed. "Of course, old chums, of course. Arthur, you'll notice, has already gone."

They quickly scanned the long medieval hall searching for the old man. "Gone?"

"Returned," explained Mr Good. "I'm afraid all the excitement was proving a little too much for him. The pressure of pretending to be Vile was taking its toll, so Lord Riddle and I, as dream ambassadors, decided it might be best to arrange an appointment with his general practitioner. Right now, at this very moment, Arthur will be sitting in the doctor's waiting room." Mr Good made his way down the side of the long trestle table towards the dais. "But not to worry, young Melvin and young Lorraine. You shall be returned to your homes very shortly. But first I have a few loose ends to tie up."

Lorraine was excited. "Are we really going home? She whispered and sat down on the bottom step again.

"Very shortly he said," nodded Melvin. "I can't quite believe it, Loz. It's almost over."

They sat in silence for a moment.

"Melvin?"

"Yes, Loz?"

"I've been thinking."

Melvin didn't look up, and he didn't reply. Instead he waited for her to continue.

"Why were we summoned?" she continued. "We haven't really been much help, have we?"

Melvin shrugged. "Well, we did find Lord Riddle."

"Did we?" Lorraine sighed. "Did we really? Vince knew the way, and it was Vince who found him, with a little help along the way from Garry. Mr Good went to all that trouble to find us because we are sensible, because we remember things, because we are excellent at finding the mean average of ten or more numbers, and because our favourite colour is blue. But in reality, he could have chosen anyone, and they would have still found Lord Riddle."

"You have logical, sequential, and analytical minds too," said a kind voice they hadn't heard for a while.

They looked round. There sitting halfway up the stairs was Ostrich.

"Ostrich!" they shrieked. "What are you doing here?"

They were so pleased to see her. They hadn't realised just how much they had missed the large bird.

Ostrich crossed and then uncrossed her long legs. "Your time has yet to come," she told them.

Lorraine looked at Ostrich. "Our time has yet to come?" she asked, a little puzzled. "But, we're going home shortly."

"Yes, we are," agreed Melvin. "Very shortly. It's almost over. Vile is locked up in the cell and dangling several feet in the air."

Ostrich nodded. "I know. But, unfortunately, in a little while Vile is going to escape."

"Escape!"

#

"My fault?" Terrence dangled in gloomy silence for a while before Vile's words finally permeated his consciousness. "My fault?"

Vile nodded. "If you didn't go around pretending to be Mr Good I wouldn't be in this mess."

What? Are you serious? It was Mr Good pretending to be me, you fool! Can't you see that? Anyway, if you didn't look so much like that Arthur person, I wouldn't be in this mess either. And another thing, your idiotness. If you had set the coordinates for the Digital Dreamscaper properly and factored in the essential elements, such as the correct weather conditions and preferred humidity levels, as you should have done, then your nightmare would be underway by now and we wouldn't be here hanging several feet off the ground. So, don't you dare apportion blame at my door!

Of course, Terrence didn't say any of those things out loud.

"Yes, your disagreeableness. Sorry, it was my fault," he agreed.

"Yes, it was." Vile looked at Terrence angrily. "And you'll pay for it. When we escape from here I'm going to harm you," he added threateningly.

Terrence brooded on that for a moment. Towards the end of the moment his brooding gave way to puzzlement as it gradually dawned on him what Vile had said.

"Escape?" he asked. He looked around the room. They were suspended and tied to a beam. Even if they hadn't been suspended and tied to a beam, they were still in a cell with a large, locked metal door. "How we going to do that, your nauseatingness?"

Vile's irritation caused him to sway a little in mid-air. "Something will turn up," he replied.

They hung there in sullen silence for a lengthy period of time until eventually something, actually, did turn up.

It was Terrence who spotted the something. And it was outside through the window where it turned up. From his vantage point he could see out into the lemony yellow corridor, and he was sure he saw something or someone pass by. He managed with a great effort to swing towards the window, grab hold of the bars, and look out into Limbo. "It's a guard!" he exclaimed.

"What?" Vile looked up. "A guard? Out there?" With a sharp pull and a series of little thrusts, twists, and swings to and fro, he managed to manoeuvre himself along the oak beam parallel to the one Terrence was dangling from. At the window he gripped a bar, nudged Terrence out the way, and looked out. He couldn't believe it.

"You're right. It is a guard – a muscular one, too." He turned to Terrence. "Why is there a guard out there in Limbo?" he asked.

Terrence gave it some thought. "It's the guard who was watching over those two giants in the vat of cold custard earlier," he decided. "It must be. He went missing, if you remember, your awfulness."

Vile nodded without taking his eyes off the guard. "Guard! Guard! Come here! This is Vile speaking!"

Shouting.

Vile was annoyed at being interrupted again. "What?"

You're shouting, not speaking.

Vile frowned. You had to shout at the guards. The louder you shouted at them the better they understood. He considered himself an expert on such matters. "Come here at once," he demanded.

The guard was scared and a little confused and puzzled as he approached the window warily.

"How wonderful to see you," Vile told him.

This puzzled the guard even more. He had thought Vile would be angry. He expected to be plunged headfirst into a vat full of rice pudding, tapioca, or maybe golden syrup. Well, he did run away from the palace without permission, after all.

"Tell me," continued Vile. "You wouldn't happen to have your pen knife handy, would you?"

"Ugh?" the guard grunted.

"Your pocket knife, then? Where is it? In your pocket, by any chance?" Vile tried to explain with a few slashing and stabbing movements with his hands, but this only seemed to confuse the guard more. Then with the side of his right hand he made a sawing motion on the rope that held him aloft.

A lightbulb seemed to come on in the guard's head under his iron helmet. "Ugh!" he grunted, and from a pocket somewhere in his leather-plated kilt he produced a knife.

"Excellent." Vile grinned. "Now guard, listen to me and listen well. I want you to pass that pocketknife through this window and hand it to the idiot we call Terrence. Understand?"

"Ugh!" nodded the guard.

The angle that Terrence was dangling from allowed him to push his arm out further through the bars. He did so, grabbed the knife with one hand, released his hold on the bar with the other, and swung down.

Vile swung down too and took it from Terrence. Holding it by its soft comfort grip, he opened the knife out to its full size.

"If you thought Vile was defeated, then think again," said Vile to himself. Or maybe he said it to whatever it was listening inside his head. "Nobody thwarts or frustrates me."

His grin was incessant.

#

Soon afterwards, with their ropes cut, Vile and Terrence stood on the floor of the cell.

"This is all very well," said Terrence. "But we are still locked in a cell with no hope of escape."

Vile grinned. "I think you underestimate me, Terrence." From the inside pocket of his black and gold pinstriped jacket he removed a large brass key. "The key to the door, I believe."

Terrence was amazed.

Vile guided the key into the lock and turned it. The large metal door opened out a touch.

"Do you have a plan, your abhorrentness?" asked Terrence excitedly.

Vile nodded. "I do. When I open this door we'll quickly run up the narrow stairway and into the great central hall," he began.

Terrence was impressed so far.

"There we will round up all the muscular guards," he continued. "We'll threaten them a bit and tell them that they're back on my side again, and then we'll take it from there."

Take it from there?

"Take it from there?"

Is that your plan?

"Is that your plan?" If so, Terrence was disappointed with it.

Vile opened the door a little further and poked his head out into the gloom. "Wait! This isn't the undercroft!" he perceived.

Terrence joined him at the door. "You're right, your beastlyness, it isn't. This is the cellar. We are still in the haunted house." He groaned.

Vile did a double take. He looked back into the cell and then out into the murk again. "How can that be?" he wondered.

Oh dear. Does this mean your quite complex and very complicated plan will have to be abandoned?

Vile recognised sarcasm when he heard it and was determined not to rise to the bait.

"What are we going to do?" asked Terrence.

"I already have another plan," Vile lied.

Really? So quick?

371

Terrence was impressed. "Really? So quick?"

"I am not dream ambassador for nightmares for no reason, Terrence." With Vile leading and Terrence following in the dark, they made their way cautiously across the dirt floor towards the steps. "I am dream ambassador for nightmares because I can come up with alternate plans, and I can come up with them quickly," he boasted. Up they climbed, and after six steps they stooped under the low beam. "And I can come up with them even when I'm in the dark," he added. They turned left, and five steps later they reached the top. They listened. They could hear voices and laughter coming from the direction of the medieval hall. "They're celebrating!" he scowled.

"How dare they?" said Terrence. "Little do they know you have another plan, your detestableness.

Vile was disconcerted. He didn't really have another plan. He stood there a little ill at ease, maybe even a little embarrassed.

"A plan that's going to wipe the smiles off their faces," said Terrence loudly, taking a step closer to the medieval hall. "Forever!" he shouted.

Vile grabbed Terrence by the collar and pulled him back. "Shut up, you dimwit! Do you want them to hear us? They mustn't know we've escaped."

"Mustn't they? Oh, sorry, your fearfulness. I didn't realise."

Vile frowned. "Follow me!" he ordered, and he set off hurriedly to the right. As they walked by the pantry he thought about what Terrence had said. *Wipe the smiles off their faces forever.* As they passed the buttery and the kitchen a thought was starting to form. Slowly, from somewhere, it was formulating. It was a plan. *I don't always come up with alternate plans quickly,* he admitted to himself. *But I usually come up with alternate plans eventually. Wipe the smiles off their faces forever.* He recited those words over and over as they walked along a couple of narrow passageways.

"That's it!" he announced as they reached the side door of the haunted house.

"That's what?"

"The Digital Dreamscaper?" said Vile urgently. "Do you still have it?"

Terrence pulled open his blazer. There it was in his shoulder holster.

"Excellent!" Vile grinned. He opened the door and looked out on a purple, heather-clad moorland.

Terrence stepped outside too and surveyed the wide-open landscape. A path led away from the door down the hill until it disappeared into a deep, wooded gorge below. On the other side of the deep, wooded gorge were the entrances: each one a different colour, in every colour you could possibly imagine and every shade of every colour too.

"When we reach those entrances," said Vile, pointing, "I am going to pull the trigger."

Terrence was dumfounded. "You mean?"

Vile nodded. "I'm going to pop this Dreamspace like a balloon." He grinned.

Terrence knew it was just a simple case of reversing the settings on the control panel. "But –" he gasped.

"Trapping everyone inside." Vile grinned. "Just think, Terrence. No more Mr Good, no more wizards, and no more pesky kids. The smiles will be wiped off their faces forever."

"But Peg!" Terrence gasped again. "She's in there too, I think. I saw her."

Vile shrugged. "That wasn't Peggy Sue. It was just a three-dimensional image of her made by holography. A trick by that wizard, no doubt."

Terrence wasn't so sure.

"Quickly!" shouted Vile. "We must seal the entrance and give this story the happy ending it deserves."

Together they ran down the path as fast as they could go. Sometime later, as the path was about to enter the deep, wooded gorge, Vile had to stop for a breather. He looked back up the hill one last time. The baroque gables of the haunted house towered above in gothic splendour.

"But my fiancée!" cried Terrence. "She'll be lost to me forever."

"Shut up, Terrence!" shouted Vile.

Hurriedly, they entered the deep, wooded gorge. The sunlight faded, the temperature dropped, and the pathway immediately split into three. An old wooden signpost gave them three options: the quickest, the shortest, and the scenic route. Vile chose the quickest path and followed the arrow in the direction it was pointing. They took no more than a dozen strides along this path before they met someone coming the other way. The stranger was very tall, and he wore a cream, chunky knitted cardigan zipped up at the front.

"Who are you?" snarled Vile.

"Do any of us know who we really are?" replied Midrib.

Vile considered that to be a ludicrous answer. "What you doing here?" he asked instead.

"What are any of us doing here?" responded the dream philosopher.

Vile took a step forward along the path. As he took a second step, his hip and knee collided with something hard and shiny.

"Watch where you're going," said the hard and shiny thing.

Terrence moved alongside Vile and glanced around. "Who said that?" he asked.

Vile looked down and examined the object that was blocking his way. "It's a heap of old iron," he decided after a moment's careful attention.

"I am made of polished stainless steel, actually," said the voice slowly and deliberately. "Highly resistant to rust or tarnish," it added without inflection.

"I think I've seen a similar pile of scrap metal to this somewhere before," said Terrence as he knelt down to get a closer look.

"Of course you've seen me somewhere before," it replied. "I was the solution for pedestrian access control at Torment Towers for more epochs than I care to remember."

Terrence stood up and pondered. He had a vague recollection now. There had been a mechanical barrier with three metal arms back at Torment Towers. It was always blocking the door and getting in the way a lot, he recalled. But surely this couldn't be the same one.

"My name is Tripod," it said in a monotonous, low, dull voice. "I'm a turnstile."

"Unfortunately," said Midrib, "we can't let you past."

Vile assessed the situation. "Terrence, we'll try another path!" he decided. They turned and quickly ran back up the slope. Back at the signpost, Vile considered the choices and swiftly made his selection from the two remaining options. They set off down the path that the weathered signpost suggested was the shortest way. But again, no more than a dozen strides along this path they were stopped in their tracks once more. As the way ahead took a sharp right turn, through the trees, three dream actors appeared around its corner.

"Normans?" gasped Vile.

Larry, Harry, and Barry stood three abreast across the path.

"It's the three Dream Actors who escaped earlier, your grimness," said Terrence.

Vile's eyes narrowed. "Escaped? Did you tell me about this?"

"Yes I did, your grisliness. You said you didn't give a tinker's cuss about a few missing Normans. Dream actors are ten a penny, you said."

Vile contemplated this as he approached the dream actors. "You are indeed very insignificant. Now, move out of my way," he demanded. "Before I push you into those stinging nettle bushes over there."

The dream actors didn't move out of the way at all. They stood, defiantly, with their arms linked.

"Unfortunately," Larry began.

"We can't," Harry continued.

"Let you past," Barry completed the sentence.

Vile was taken aback, but he couldn't help a little smile as he turned to Terrence who, in turn, rolled his eyes.

"And who, just out of interest, is going to stop me?" asked Vile.

"I am!" said Zygote.

Vile looked up and was dismayed to see two giants standing at the sharp right turn.

"Me too!" said Flagellum.

Vile frowned. The giants were big and strong and tall – very tall. They were taller even than many of the trees in the deep wooded gorge hereabouts. Without the muscular guards he was no match for them, and Terrence was no use either. Vile tried to come up with an alternate plan quickly. But he couldn't.

"Scenic route?" suggested Terrence.

Chapter 67

"Congratulations, young Keith," Mr Good was standing on the dais and shaking the Boy Scout's hand with enthusiasm. "You've completed the challenge of a lifetime, and you are fully deserving your award."

His words were greeted with a half-hearted ripple of applause from the dream actors sitting on both sides of the long table. Mugwump stood alongside Mr Good holding a large belt with a special buckle.

"Gosh and double gosh!" gasped Keith as he straightened his red and blue diagonal neckerchief. "Am I really going to get my explorer belt now?"

The answer to that question was unfortunately no. Because at that moment Lord Riddle stepped up on the raised platform and interrupted the ceremony.

"Begging your pardon," said Keith, a touch annoyed with the interference at such an important juncture. "But I'm just about to receive my explorer belt I've worked so hard for. Can this wait?"

Lord Riddle shook his head. "Heavy sledge carrying bags," he said.

"It's time to open the suitcase," said Garry.

#

"Your brother?" Flagellum had never heard such nonsense.

A giant in a green woollen tunic and a dream philosopher in a cream, chunky knitted cardigan met where three pathways merged into one by an old wooden signpost. Zygote held Midrib at arm's length and studied his features closely. "It's been many eras since we last met." He grinned. "And you don't look a dream span older."

"And you're looking well too, bro," said Midrib as they hugged like long-lost brothers do and slapped each other on the back several times.

"The figment-of-your-imagination brother?" queried Flagellum.

Zygote turned to his fellow giant. "Flagellum, meet my brother, Midrib."

"The made-up one?" asked Flagellum, seeking clarification.

Zygote frowned. "Does he look made-up to you?"

"Any friend of Zygote's is a friend of mine," said Midrib, stepping forward. "I'm very pleased to meet you," he added, holding out his hand to the slightly smaller giant.

Flagellum ignored it and walked off up the hill towards the haunted house.

"I felt so sorry for you, Midrib, when I heard the news. When I heard that someone had found the end of Limbo and discovered what was on the other side," said Zygote sympathetically as they followed Flagellum up the path. "You must have been so disappointed."

Midrib nodded sadly. "I was furious, bro."

"My brother is a dream philosopher," said Zygote just on the off chance that Flagellum might be interested. He wasn't.

"What are you thinking about now?" asked Zygote.

Midrib brightened. "I have turned my thoughts to the eve of the Big Bang and the legendary dream ancestors and what took place there," he replied. "What happened to the picnic blanket? And indeed, whatever became of the half-eaten buttered scone? That's the sort of thing I'm pondering at the moment, bro."

"It's extremely unlikely you will ever know the answers to those questions." Zygote smiled.

"That's the absolutely brilliant thing about it." Midrib grinned as they approached the large glass porch at the front of the haunted house.

#

"It's going to be splendid," decided Larry. "No more nightmares."

Harry nodded. "Just nice, pleasant, happy dreams."

"With beautiful colours and pretty flowers," added Barry.

"And the four of us back together," said Larry with a smile.

"Awesome," said Harry.

"Tremendous," agreed Barry.

Garry held up a hand and stopped his friends in full flow. It had been wonderful to see his closest friends again after such a long time. It was such a surprise to see them enter the medieval hall earlier and great to catch up on all the gossip. "Can I just say something at this point?" he asked them.

Larry, Harry, and Barry paused for breath and waited with puzzled expressions for Garry to say something.

At this point Lord Riddle turned and gave Garry an impatient look. On his head he wore a cap with visors at the front and back and earflaps outside and tied on top.

Garry hesitated. He wasn't sure how he was going to break this news to them. "Well, it's like this," he began. "I'm not going back."

"Not going back?" asked Barry.

"What do you mean?" asked Harry.

"I'm not returning to the Palace of Somnium," said Garry. "I'm going to the Land of Nod. Lord Riddle has asked me to be his new right-hand second man in command."

"Lord Riddle?" They all looked at the odd sort of a fellow wearing a funny hat standing nearby.

"Well call me a taxi!" declared Larry.

"One must understand terms of foreign exchange," said Lord Riddle urgently.

Garry nodded. "Sorry, I have to go," he said. "Lord Riddle wants me to do a bit of translating."

The three dream actors stood on the raised platform in stunned silence for a long moment.

#

Its secure corner housing made for easy manoeuvrability, and with the help of Mugwump the suitcase was lifted up onto the long trestle table. Keith found the zip, paused, and waited for a signal. Lord Riddle nodded.

Keith pulled the sliding tab around three sides of the suitcase before coming to a stop. Slowly, he lifted up the lightweight polyester flap.

Everyone tried to peer in. The dream actors at the back moved closer to try and get a better look at what the contents of the suitcase might be.

The contents of the suitcase were held secure by two useful internal straps.

"Domestic service on the estate," declared Lord Riddle.

"It's a tea set," translated Garry.

"Company meant to move heaven," added Lord Riddle.

Garry gasped and then paused before revealing what Lord Riddle had said. "It's the Ancient Tea Set of Firmamentum!" he revealed.

All eyes turned to Mr Good to see his reaction.

The shock had rendered Mr Good temporarily paralysed. "It can't be," he somehow managed to say. His mouth had dropped open, and he was struggling for breath. "The Ancient Tea Set of Firmamentum is on my Welsh dresser. Or rather it was," he corrected himself. "Before Vile destroyed it." He shivered.

Amongst the matching collection of cups and saucers, side plates, a cake plate, a milk jug, and a sugar bowl, Lord Riddle picked out the teapot. "It never rains but it pours." He smiled and handed it to Mr Good.

Mr Good took it and cradled it gently. "I can't believe it," he whispered. "It has a spout." He smiled. "Thank you so much, Lord Riddle."

From the suitcase Garry took out a woollen rug backed with a waterproof fabric. "The picnic blanket of yore, I presume," he said as he passed it to Lord Riddle. "Are all yesterday's tomorrows back to front?" he asked.

Lord Riddle took and held it close. "Hope abandoned rounding cape for a time," he replied. Then he lifted it up, buried his face in it, and smelled the lingering aroma of bygone times and dream spans of old. He listened too, and, with respect tinged with awe, he fancied he heard their voices in its fibres: the voices of dream ancestors echoing down through the eras as they made their important decisions, sitting on this tartan material spread out on a large chunk of matter and energy on the eve of the Big Bang so very long ago.

"There's something else in here," said Larry, reaching inside the suitcase. Between his thumb and forefinger he picked up a small, plain, doughy sort of bread. He pulled a face and held it at arm's length.

"It's been split down the middle," observed Harry.

"And buttered," noticed Barry.

"And," said Larry, taking a closer look, "someone has taken a bite out of it."

From somewhere a prolonged, mournful cry was uttered. First the Ancient Tea Set of Firmamentum, then the picnic blanket of yore, and now this. "I don't believe it!" cried Midrib. The dream philosopher stormed out through the impressive front door in tears.

Zygote followed him. Flagellum smirked.

"A cork tree," said Lord Riddle as he took the small, stale bread and knocked on it with his knuckles.

Garry smiled. "Lord Riddle said that the small, stale bread is so hard even a big, red rock eater would have trouble chewing it."

Everyone laughed.

When he saw Peggy Sue was laughing, Vince knew the moment was right. He went down on one knee of his slim-fitting drainpipe trousers, took Peggy Sue's hand, and looked up into her large round eyes.

Everyone cheered before he could even ask the question.

"Remit you," said Lord Riddle, amidst all the cheering and congratulating, as he handed the half-eaten buttered scone to Melvin and Lorraine.

"Chaos me," he added. At the same time he pointed towards an enormous brown felt hat with a dome-shaped crown and a narrow, slightly curled brim at the rear of the dais.

"Your time has come," said Ostrich.

"A pantomime dame has this," suggested Lord Riddle. They were the last words he said to them as the hat slowly lifted and moved away from the raised step.

Chapter 68

The scenic route proved to be a tortuous pathway that wended its way down the hill with repeated turns and bends. The views were splendid, though. In addition to the purple, heather-clad moorland that stretched off into the distance, there were the beautiful lake-like reservoirs, the dark forests, the green valleys, and the tumbling, rocky rivers, too. But Vile and Terrence were not interested in the scenery. They were more concerned about reaching the entrances before anyone had realised they had escaped.

After walking along the twisting path for what seemed like a quarter of a dream span, or possibly a third of one, they finally stepped out from the deep, wooded gorge and into bright sunlight again. Vile shielded his eyes and grinned. He liked what he saw. The path they were on descended gradually a little way and then levelled out as it reached an old stone bridge that spanned a wide, flowing river. There, just beyond the bridge, were the entrances: each one a different colour, in every colour you could possibly imagine and every shade of every colour too. They were so close.

They scurried down the incline, hit the level ground, and approached the bridge. Nothing could stop them now. This was going to be a memorable and magnificent victory for evil, a major success for wicked and nasty, and a triumph for all things downright unpleasant. Vile rested a moment by the keystone at the top of the arch and looked back up the slope. There was no sign of anyone. He rubbed his hands with glee. This was too easy. Very soon Mr Good and all his pathetic cronies would be trapped inside this Dreamspace forever.

"Which particular entrance are we looking for, Terrence?" he asked as they took half a dozen more steps up the gentle slope on the other side of the bridge and closed in on the vast array of openings.

Terrence shrugged. "A reddish one, I think, your unkindness."

"You think?" Vile glared. "You think? You need to know, Terrence. A Dreamspace has to be sealed in the very same corridor it was created. It says so on page one of the instruction manual."

Terrence gave it some thought. "I remember now," he remembered. "It was crimson. I mean ruby. Or was it raspberry? No, it was definitely crimson."

Vile frowned. Are you sure?"

Terrence nodded. "Positive. It's this one." He pointed at the nearest corridor.

"This is magenta," sighed Vile.

"Yes, that's the one," said Terrence. "I'm certain."

Vile hoped so. He pointed at Terrence's blazer. "Pass me the Digital Dreamscaper," he demanded.

Terrence removed it from his shoulder holster and quickly and skilfully inverted the coordinates before handing it to him.

Vile took a step forward and stood at the threshold of the magenta maze. He held the Digital Dreamscaper aloft, slipped his middle finger through the loop, rested it gently on the trigger, and took aim.

#

In the next instant a ball of fire shot out of the magenta corridor and knocked the Digital Dreamscaper clean out of Vile's hand. A beast with the sharpest, pointiest teeth ever poked its snorting nostrils out through the entrance. The dragon's bulging eyes surveyed the Dreamspace.

"Derek!" Lorraine squealed with delight. She rushed up the gentle slope and gave his long neck a huge hug.

"You came!" cried Melvin, patting the side of Derek's handsome, elongated head.

"You called," replied the dragon.

"It's been a long time," said Lorraine as she hugged him tighter.

"A frightfully long time," agreed the dragon.

How long had it been? A year? Two? They couldn't be sure.

Lorraine tried to explain everything that had happened to them quickly. She described how they had found Mr Good, but before that they had been captured by Vile. Then they escaped, and eventually, after a very long journey, they met Lord Riddle.

"At the Land of Nod," added Melvin.

"Lord Riddle?" Derek smiled. "Does he really exist?"

Lorraine nodded excitedly. "And his last words to us are the reason you are here."

"It was his idea to call you," said Melvin.

"That's right. 'A pantomime dame has this,'" said Lorraine. "They were the last words he said to us. That was the message."

"More of a suggestion," suggested Melvin.

"'A pantomime dame has this'?" Derek considered the words for a moment. "It would require a logical, sequential, and analytical mind to be able to understand that."

"Drag on." Lorraine smiled. "Dragon."

"We only know one dragon. And you did say if we ever got into any trouble or needed any help, we could call you and you would be there immediately."

"It was meant to be," said Lorraine. "We just knew we were doing the right thing in calling you."

"Pesky kids!" groaned Vile as he shook his hand and examined his singed fingertips. "What are you doing here?" he demanded to know.

Derek somehow squeezed out of the magenta entrance, and with Melvin and Lorraine on either side of him he walked forward towards Vile and Terrence.

"We have a gift for you," said Melvin as he held out a small, plain, doughy sort of bread made of oatmeal.

Vile looked at it suspiciously as he slowly backed away. "What is it?"

"Something from the past," said Lorraine.

"It belonged to your ancestors," said Melvin

Vile grimaced. "Ancestors? I don't want anything off that bunch of losers."

Derek, Melvin, and Lorraine followed them down the gentle slope until they reached the river's edge and Vile and Terrence could retreat no further.

Melvin took a final step forward. "Take it and go," he said as he handed him the scone.

Vile took it, felt it, sniffed it, and was clearly unimpressed with it. "What am I supposed to do with this?" he asked.

"Go back to Torment Towers with it," suggested Lorraine.

"After all, that's where you belong," said Derek.

"That's not going to happen," said Vile as he stood his ground on the riverbank.

"Do something, your repugnantness," screamed Terrence. "You are the dream ambassador for nightmares, after all, and these pesky kids should be no match for you."

Vile had a feeling about these pesky kids that began the very first moment he saw them. But he looked at Terrence and nodded. "You're right. I am not dream ambassador for nightmares for no reason," he reasoned. "I am dream ambassador for nightmares because I can always get out of sticky situations."

"Correct," agreed Terrence.

"Because I'm a powerful problem solver, and because I'm a critical thinker with excellent decision making skills."

"Correct again, your repellentness." He grinned.

Don't make me laugh.

Vile frowned. Not here. Not now.

It's all over.

Not the bird inside his head again.

Mr Good has won.

But the bird wasn't in his head. It had jumped to the ground and stretched itself up to its full height. It stood resolutely alongside Melvin, Lorraine, and Derek.

"Run," said Lorraine, and she pointed towards the vast array of openings.

"Run away," said Melvin.

"Run away and don't come back," added Derek.

"Never!" Vile shouted defiantly.

You're a beaten man, Vile.

The dragon coughed and threw his head back. Vile and Terrence saw at the back of his wide mouth an enormous, spherical burning mass spinning on his red, raw tongue, almost ready to be released.

They ran.

#

Vile's face was almost purple. It almost matched the colour of the corridor they were running along. "It's all over, Terrence, and it's all your fault," he raged. "Because of you Mr Good has won, and thanks to you I'm a beaten man!"

There was steam coming out of his ears. He looked at the scone. He looked at Terrence. He looked at the scone again, and then he threw it at him. It hit him smack on the forehead, causing him to stagger forward a couple of paces against the crimson wall.

Holding his head, Terrence fell to his knees in a daze. Vile stood over him and watched as a globule of butter trickled down through the gap between Terrence's eyebrows and down the bone of his nose until it hung down off the end like an edible, fatty, yellow stalactite.

Terrence opened one eye. "Good shot, your deplorableness."

#

It had the feel of a summer's day, like they were relaxing in the late afternoon sunshine. The kiwi bird sat alone nearby in the shade, and Derek lay full length on the grassy bank.

"We're going home shortly," said Lorraine. "Mr Good told us so."

"Very shortly is what he actually said," said Melvin.

Derek's wide mouth spread even wider into a definite grin. "I'm so pleased for you," he said. "You must be frightfully excited."

Melvin and Lorraine smiled and sat in silence watching the river wander aimlessly away towards the distant hills.

"You should keep in touch with each other," suggested Derek after a while. "Text messages, social network, email addresses – that sort of thing. I've heard that's how you young people keep in touch these days in the physical world."

Melvin and Lorraine thought it was a really good idea. Melvin immediately took out some paper and a couple of pencils from the inside pocket of his maroon school blazer, and they quickly set about writing down their contact details.

When Lorraine had finished she looked up at Melvin. "So, what is it that's black and white and black and white and black and white?" she asked.

Melvin didn't reply. Instead he folded up his sheet of paper and handed it to her.

Then she fell.

Head over heels she fell into nothingness.

When she landed it wasn't with a bump, nor was it in a heap on the floor. It was a comfortable landing on a mattress in her bedroom.

The first thing she noticed was the time: 07:33. Next to the clock was a mug with wisps of steam rising from it.

"Mum?" She swivelled her head on the pillow and rolled over onto one elbow.

Her mother was pulling open the bedroom curtains, moving with extreme care and quietness across the room towards the door. She stopped and turned. "Sorry, dear. You looked so peaceful there I thought I'd give you a few extra minutes before I woke you."

"Mum," whispered Lorraine. "I'm back."

Her mother gave her a puzzled smile. "Back?"

Tears welled up in her eyes. "I've missed you, Mum."

Leaning over, her mother picked up the mug from the bedside table. "Here, I've made you a coffee. Drink it. It will wake you up."

"Mum, I've met giants, a friendly dragon, and a wizard who says 'salmon' a lot." Lorraine stared at the mug in her mother's hands and the steam as it silently swirled up towards the ceiling.

"I've been thrown in a cold and damp cell and escaped twice. I've been chased by big, red monsters who eat rocks. I've sailed across the ocean to the Land of Nod in an old wooden boat, and I've travelled in a flying hat with a talking ostrich," she added breathlessly and buried her face in her mother's arms. "But now I'm back, Mum, for good."

Her mother held her and gently stroked her ponytail. Her hands followed the braids from her neck up to the crown. "Now, that was an exciting dream, dear."

"A dream?" Lorraine pulled away from her embrace. "No, Mum, it wasn't a dream. I haven't even slept, not for ages. This really happened."

"Of course it did, dear," her mother replied. She stood up and returned the mug of coffee to the bedside table. "And after all that excitement you should rest. Meeting giants, dragons, and wizards can be very tiring, I've heard." She smiled. "I'll see you downstairs for breakfast."

After her mother had left the room Lorraine sat in silence for quite some time. A dream? No. It couldn't be. It was so real, for pity's sake. Gradually, she became aware of something in her hand. She was holding something tightly. Slowly, she released her fingers from around it. There resting on the palm of her hand was a folded sheet of paper.

She recognised it immediately. Melvin had given it to her.

She unfolded it halfway and looked at what was written there. She read his mobile number, his email address, and something else. Melvin had written something else at the bottom just above the crease.

"What is black and white and black and white and black and white?" she whispered.

She opened the sheet of paper fully and spread it out on her lap. She sat perfectly still. Only her lips moved as she read the words that Melvin had left for her. Finally, she shook her head and a smile slowly spread across her face. She chided herself for not working it out sooner. After all, they were the keywords.

Three pairs of eyes were watching her. Three teddy bears sat at the foot of her bed were leaning forward, ever so slightly, as if they too were waiting for the answer.

She looked up and met their gaze.

"A penguin rolling down a hill," she whispered.

THE END

About the Author

Kevin Tranter is in his fifties, and this is his first novel, although he's had several short stories published. He was born in Wolverhampton, UK, and from an early age he went to school until he was told he could leave. There then followed several jobs, some marriages, and a few children. In his late forties he sat down in his favourite armchair and wrote this fantasy adventure. It took him five years to complete. He hopes you like it.

Kevin lives in Staffordshire with his wife and no pets.

Lightning Source UK Ltd.
Milton Keynes UK
UKOW03f2223270117

293055UK00002B/129/P